fOCUS

fOCUS

The (almost 100%) True Tale of an Intrepid
News Photographer

A Novel by Rodger Howard

Briton Publishing, LLC

1237 Glenwood TRL
Batavia, OH 45103
www.britonpublishing.com

ISBN
978-1-7353834-9-1 (Hardcover)
978-1-7353834-8-4 (Paperback)

Copyright © 2021

Published by Briton Publishing
Distribution by Ingram Content Group

PREFACE

The writing of this book began many years ago in my head. I'd been "shooting news" in Los Angeles for decades and had begun to realize just how unbelievable the experiences of a photojournalist can sound to the average person. Of course, I've always been an average person, so many of the things I witnessed left me in awe as well. For that reason I kept a journal, a daily record of every story I ever shot. I found it immensely helpful in writing this book.

I quickly learned that when I was with a group of people just getting to know one another, the obligatory question, "What is it that you do?" was sure to be asked. I had to make a conscious effort to tone down my answer, pull it back a bit, lest I become the center of every conversation, regaling the throng with story after story about some celebrity I'd just been hanging out with or some gory scene I'd witnessed.

People generally have no idea what a News Photographer does on a daily basis, nor did I when I chose this profession.

I always knew I had 'an eye'. I was the guy at the zoo with his camera mounted on a tripod, testing his family's patience while waiting interminably for that "perfect" shot of the baby giraffe. I would see something curious or amusing while driving, perhaps an interesting sign or a person with an intriguing look, anything unusual, and I'd invariably take the time to circle the block, find a place to park, and try to capture a photo of it. I was the guy climbing halfway up the mountain just to frame a snapshot the way I wanted it. So, I knew I had the knack and the determination for on-the-spot photography.

Not everyone is cut out for the life of a photog. Trust me, you'll be a different person after doing the job for a few short years. You'll see things and learn things that can't be taught in school. You'll undergo changes, both physical and mental. You'll question your values, your priorities, and the things you hold dear. You'll pray that you'll still be a sane, healthy human being when you finally put the camera down. I hope this story explains that evolution accurately.

The subtitle of this book is "An ALMOST 100% True Tale of an Intrepid News Photographer." I've been asked which parts are untrue. There aren't many.

This is technically a novel. All of the names have been changed, and the main character, Ron Sharp, is not me, really. He's a hybrid of all the photogs I've gotten to know and respect, guys from whom I've learned so much over the years, talented photojournalists like the late Steve Chacon, Larry Greene, Artie Williams, Andy Weintraub and so many others. The stories and events described are true to life, with a few dramatizations. The dates, times and locations are in some cases fictional, but are based upon entirely real occurrences. Things that happened months or years apart may occur here, using license within days of each other, but only for dramatic effect.

My advice to those trying to figure out which parts of this book are true and which come from my imagination: When you read something and say to yourself, "That could never happen, not in a million years." – that part's true. Almost 100%.

PROLOGUE

Ron Sharp had been taught well.

George Sharp, his late father, had always said, "Try to learn something new every single day". Working the streets of Los Angeles as a news cameraman made that a fairly easy task. Even on seemingly routine days, something would invariably occur that made his job interesting and memorable. Often, a news photographer's assignments would take them places that the majority of people simply could not go. A journalist's credential, or Press Pass, would open the door to a panoply of exciting and unique happenings, the opportunity to work with fascinating, famous, often infamous people. And those were just the routine days.

Then there were the extraordinary days. They'd start off mundane like the others, but then, without warning, all hell would break loose.

In Los Angeles, a journalist needs to be prepared for any eventuality. Invariably, someone, somewhere will go nuts, ruining your plans for a quiet evening.

Covering horrendous, unthinkable stories, of course, takes its toll on a person's psyche. And someone like Ron, whose profession requires an artistically trained eye behind a video camera, inevitably finds that over time, exposure to real heartbreak and tragedy can be life changing.

But there are other issues as well. Ron's relationships at home and at work proved to be a reflection of his relationship with himself. He resisted the changes he was feeling, making a conscious effort to remain unjaded when confronted with life's cold realities. The ability to stay focused on an ugly, brutal, news story, without losing touch with his humanity, turned out to be a much bigger challenge than he had expected.

Then there was the news business itself. Changes were coming at him fast and furious. Budget cuts and new technologies placed demands upon everyone who chose television news as their profession. Ron was at that in-between stage in his career, not wishing to learn another vocation, but anxious about the demands of the future. A new hire would be expected to not only do a photographer's job, but also to write, edit, and report news stories on-air, all as a self-contained, one-person unit called a Multi-Media Journalist.

Ron and his colleagues saw the potential for numerous problems with this plan, not the least of which being safety and security in the field. So many stories took place in high-crime areas of the city. Knowing that news managers would be willing to send a young, inexperienced reporter into the worst parts of town without a burly cameraman as a partner made them resentful. They also viewed it as an insult to their talent. The quality of the videographer's work was being placed on the back burner, the reporter's on-air appearance being the top priority.

But Ron Sharp's dedication and love of the business kept him out there, giving his all every day, despite the frustrations and the scars, fighting hard against the changes to his life, his relationships and the world around him.

CONTENTS

Chapter One:

A FLY ON THE WALL

Wednesday, February 12th

The first thing the Cameraman noticed was her left ankle, as it swung up into the front of the Channel 6 News van. Ron Sharp had just driven the oversized, top-heavy vehicle from the maintenance garage around to the front entrance of KSIX, and stopped on the gray paving-stone driveway, just past the security gate.

Day after day, hundreds of times over the last thirteen years, always following the same routine, Ron entered the underground parking garage through the security gate on Sunset. He'd park his mustang convertible somewhere on level P-2 and take the elevator up to the Lobby level. There he'd greet Louis, the morning security guard, who was normally seated behind the large desk in the station's spacious lobby, surrounded by the monitors displaying the live pictures from the various surveillance cameras, which were placed in virtually every corner of the facility. Then, using his "Prox-card", Ron would pass through the heavy set of fireproof security doors, and into the station's remote garage, where the new vans were parked and maintained.

After inspecting the truck and camera equipment, Ron loaded up Microvan 21, the specially equipped Ford van with the giant painted KSIX NEWS on the side. He tossed in his own personal gear, which he'd retrieved from his locker; extra clothes, jackets, hiking boots and even a bullet-proof vest which the station provided to all the cameramen, just in case it would all hit the fan that day.

On this particular morning, Ron said hello to Chuck, the station's maintenance chief, who was in the midst of servicing Microvan 18, one of the older news vans, which had over 200,000 miles on the odometer, and seemingly always had some sort of breakdown. This time it was the microwave dish motor gears that had stripped and needed to be replaced.

"We all fall apart sometime," said Ron.

"Ain't that the truth?" Chuck answered as he spit a small, broken cotter pin into a yellow trashcan on the concrete floor to his right.

Ron's steps echoed as he walked across the garage and picked up the phone to check in with the assignment desk. Next, he unplugged the long, spring-loaded power cord that was used to charge the batteries overnight from the side of the van and let it retract into the coiled receptacle mounted on the ceiling. Each day, he took all of the allotted fifteen minutes to thoroughly gear-up and make certain that all of his camera equipment was functioning properly before carefully backing the van out of the cramped garage and pulling it around front to pick up a producer or reporter, and to head out on assignment. All of this was the routine part of the job. Once the van left the lot, and entered the world of TV newsgathering, not much was routine at all.

The new reporter stepped up from the steel running board, grasping the thick plastic handle to the right of the white van's windshield, and pulled herself up stiffly into the passenger's seat. Ron could tell, from first glance at that ankle, and the speckled white pump attached to it, that this was going to be an interesting day.

"Hi," said the perfectly made-up young blonde, with a smile, while shuffling her behind into the seat and straightening out her tight beige Chanel pencil skirt, which perfectly complimented her semi-sheer red/orange silk blouse.

"My name's Shelby. You must be Ron," she said, holding out a well-manicured hand. "The pleasure's mine," he replied, shaking her hand and quickly looking over his passenger, as he put the van in drive.

Shelby instantly reminded him of Cheryl, one of his recent missteps. Then, just as quickly, he forced the memory from his brain, lest the day start off with guilt and regret. The perfect body and amazing sex didn't come close to making the short relationship worthwhile, what with the demands, the control, the neediness. Move on, Ronnie.

Clunking down the driveway and out onto Sunset Boulevard, Ron reached for the microphone attached by cable to the station's two-way radio, mounted below the dash, right next to one of the van's two police scanners.

"Microvan 21 is on the road," Ron said after keying the mike. After a few seconds, a voice came back through the speaker, just a bit too loud, causing Shelby to jump in her seat- **"Ten-four, Micro 21. Your passenger has your assignment."**

Ron made a quick left turn and pulled the news van into the parking lot of the Starbucks on Sunset, across from Home Depot, where more than the usual number of day laborers loitered outside, looking for work cleaning yards, building fences, or painting walls. Two of them strolled leisurely through the crosswalk, back toward the Home Depot, prompting Ron to mutter, jokingly, "Dudes, you don't want to get between me and coffee." He waited for traffic, then made the turn. Spotting no available parking spots, he pulled up next to the brick building, stopping on the yellow painted "No Parking" stripes on the asphalt.

"Can I get you anything?" he asked as he jumped out to run inside the store for his usual Grande Latte, no foam, with one packet of Sugar in the Raw added.

"No thanks, I'm alright," replied Shelby. "Are you sure you can park here?"

"Umm, we'll be fine," he said with a devilish smile. "I'll be right back. Gotta have by coffee. You don't want me surly."

While standing in line, waiting for the barista to take his order, Ron peered out through the row of full-sized picture windows, which lined the entire eastern wall of the crowded coffee shop. He could see Shelby in the van, smacking her polished lips together and checking her makeup and hair in the small passenger's side visor mirror.

Ron had become a fairly good judge of people. His first impression was that she was trying just a bit too hard to be camera-friendly, too interested in being on TV.

Nice wardrobe, great body, but basically another bottle-blonde, who didn't know when to say when at the mascara counter, trying to cover up a slightly rough complexion with just a bit too much makeup. Probably attractive to some guys, but not really my type at all. Not anymore.

The line was moving slower than usual, held up by a young woman in a black sweatshirt and army boots carrying a khaki green backpack, who seemed to be ordering drinks for an entire regiment of millennial revolutionaries. On the back of her right arm was a sample of her body art, a flower tattoo with the words LOVE NATURE, though Ron was pretty sure that the color of her hair was not found in nature anywhere.

Every seat was full, students and budding writers hard at work on their laptops, so he waited at the counter looking over the notices on the bulletin board which were not really any different than last week.

Finally, he picked up his drink and exited through the back door.

"So, where are we headed?" asked Ron, as he hopped back into the van with his coffee. He started the engine and pulled out again onto Sunset and headed west, toward the Hollywood Freeway,

"Oh, let me see," answered Shelby, digging through her oversized handbag for the "situationer", which Maggie Ostertag, the long-time morning Assignment Editor had printed for her. It contained the address and instructions for their first shoot together.

"OK, here it is. There's an 11a.m. news conference at the Sheriff's Station in Lost Hills. They're going to be offering a reward for information regarding a woman who's been missing since last week. Do you need the address?"

"Nope," said Ron, taking a sip of his latte as he turned left from Wilton Place onto Hollywood Boulevard, then on to the northbound 101 freeway, "Been there a few hundred times."

The hour-long drive through morning traffic gave the two a bit of time to get to know each other. But Ron observed a number of things about Shelby Falconer right away. First, that she was very, very young, possibly barely old enough to drink, legally anyway. She was, admittedly, moderately attractive, more suited to be a Price is Right model than a street reporter, but her lack of maturity and life experience detracted from the appeal of the 'whole package'. And he could also tell that she had absolutely no idea what this job entailed, nor was she in any way prepared for it. *What's with those shoes?* He wondered to himself. *What if we get sent to a fire, or a cliff-rescue? Can't wait to see that.*

"So, what's your story?" asked Ron.

"My story?" Shelby answered with a slight chuckle. "Well, I just came out here from Pittsburgh, where I was in school. Finished my junior year and decided that I'd had enough of the college life, so I thought I'd try working for a change. You know, *make* a little money instead of giving it all to the school."

"Really," said Ron, somewhat intrigued. "You have family in L.A.?"

"No, they're all in Delaware. I thought I'd give it a try on my own, and see what happens."

"So, you've never been here before?"

"Once, when I was a kid, we came out, saw the beach, Universal, Disneyland, you know, the usual 'touristy' places. I really liked it, especially the weather. Made up my mind to work here one day."

"So, how much experience do you have working in news?" he asked, fearing the answer.

"Well, I interned at the Pittsburgh affiliate last summer. It was interesting. And in college we learned to do it all, you know, shoot, edit, write, produce a show, the whole nine yards, but as an intern, they don't really let you do too much."

"So, no real experience in the field?"

"Well, no." she said, somewhat defensively. "But I'm hoping to get that here. My Dad went to school with Larry Garner, and after seeing my resume, Larry was nice enough to give me a tryout."

"Well, OK, then," said Ron. As they made the transition on the 101 West into the San Fernando Valley, Ron wondered to himself why Garner, the assistant news director, had not told her how to prepare for a day doing news on the street. Then he realized Garner had always been in management. He probably hadn't given it much thought.

"I talked to other stations, but Larry called me first," continued Shelby, unsolicited. "I mean, I give him props for that. A lot of people think that I'm dumb, just because I'm pretty. Well, I'M NOT DUMB."

I don't think you're that PRETTY, either, thought Ron, biting his tongue, raising one eyebrow and hoping that this day with Princess would prove uneventful.

"What about you," asked Shelby. "What's YOUR story?"

"Well," replied Ron. "I've been here for almost fourteen years, worked in Phoenix for a couple years before that. Couldn't stand the heat and I've got no family, so I started sending resumes around once I'd been there long enough to know what I was doing." he said, with just a slight hint of sarcasm. She never got his meaning.

"Where were you born?" she asked.

"Oh, I grew up in Racine and went to school at Wisconsin. Never even really left that part of the country until I graduated. I started working at a small station there, but then my Dad died, and I had no reason to stay."

"Oh, I'm so sorry, what about your Mom?"

"That's OK," said Ron. "She passed away when I was a kid. I kinda had to stick around there for Dad's sake, you know?"

"Wow, I can't imagine losing a parent. That's just so sad." said the Princess.

"So, your folks are still alive?"

"Oh, heavens yes." replied Shelby. "My dad is President of Oxford Bank back in Delaware, and Mom was Miss Florida back in the 80's. I forget which year. I can't imagine anyone I know dying. I've never even SEEN a dead body. That's just so gross!"

Oh, boy, Ron thought with a sigh. *This could be really entertaining.*

"Check that out." Ron smiled and motioned with his head toward the driver of the faded yellow Corolla in the lane just to their right. "That guy is playing a flute while sitting in morning traffic on the freeway."

"Wow," said Shelby, looking up from her smartphone. "How did you notice that?"

"I'm a trained observer," he answered, half-joking. "You need to be one, too. Besides, from up this high, you can see just about everything. I always see drivers doing weird shit on the road; shaving, putting on makeup, brushing their teeth, reading the paper, but that's one I've never seen before. Yikes!"

Shelby tried to get a photo on her phone, but the man spotted her and put the flute down on the passenger's seat.

"You've also got to try to be a little more 'stealth'," said Ron with a wink.

"What's the most interesting story you've covered?" asked Shelby.

"Well, that's really hard to say, there have been so many. One of the great things about this business is that you never know what to expect, especially here in L.A. I mean, one day you're interviewing a movie star, and the next you're hiding behind a SWAT officer while he's shooting it out with some guy. I've been to the Oscars, Super Bowls, World Series games, NBA Championships. Over the years I've met famous athletes, actors, musicians,

Senators, Presidents, you name it. Sometimes, when I find out that someone I'd like to meet is going to be on our morning show, I'll stick around the studio and hang with them in the green room for a few minutes before they go on the set, maybe get a photo taken with them. I've got dozens of them."

"Wow!" Shelby said. "Isn't that embarrassing, I mean asking for a photo like that?"

"Well, sometimes, if it doesn't feel right, I'll just say hello. But, most of the time I'll try to get a picture. It's usually worth a few seconds of embarrassment."

"The most famous person I've ever met was Bill Cosby," said Shelby. "We ran into him at a restaurant back in Philadelphia when he was visiting his family a few years ago."

"That's pretty impressive. I'll bet he loved meeting you, too. Did you get a photo?" asked Ron, with a slight smile. "Because without evidence it didn't happen."

"Nope. No picture unfortunately." She giggled. "You'll just have to take my word for it."

Traffic was moving slowly on the westbound 101 through the Valley, and Shelby glanced at her Raymond Weil wristwatch and wondered aloud if they'd be late to the news conference. "This is about par for the course on a weekday morning," said Ron. "Actually, a little lighter than usual. It should free up in a few minutes, once we get past the 405. We'll be OK."

"I don't know how they do it out here. This traffic would drive me out of my mind," Shelby said, wondering to herself if she really could ever get used to living in L.A.

"So, where do you see yourself in ten years, Ron?"

"Wow, I've never really thought about that," he answered, adjusting his sunglasses and changing lanes in anticipation of the exit ramp coming up in a few miles. "Never really wanted to do anything but what I'm doing. I don't know how to do much else. See, being out in the field, you learn how the world works, with no filters. You see people at their best and their worst. Stuff the average guy will never ever see. What I mean is, I've learned a little bit about a million different things. I'm just not sure that I know a lot about any one of them. So I'll probably be sitting on my ass in a news van in ten years, watching the world go by. What about you, Shelby? Where do you see yourself in ten years?"

"Well, I'm sure I'll be an anchor by then. I don't really want to be in the field. I'd really rather just write stories and read them on the air. Have the newsmakers come in and sit down with me for an interview in studio. Except, you know, the really big stories, where they pack up the whole show and take it on the road. I'm much more comfortable at a desk looking into a camera than out here in a noisy, smelly truck. No offense. You know, like Katie Couric. Or Diane Sawyer. They're my heroes."

Ron bit his upper lip and hoped she didn't notice his wide eye-roll. "No offense taken."

The KSIX News van exited the freeway at Lost Hills Road, in the far-west end of Los Angeles County, a beautiful, mountainous, upper middle-class area, with relatively little crime. The biggest problem the Sheriff's department usually faced there were the gang-bangers from nearby Ventura County- areas like Oxnard and Santa Paula, 'low-lifes' who liked to make the short drive into towns like Calabasas and Agoura to burglarize the residents who'd gotten a bit too complacent, leaving their valuables unguarded in their homes, or in an unlocked car. The proximity to the freeway made it incredibly tempting for scumbags to swoop in, commit petty crimes, and split town. It was fairly unusual for the media to be called out here for a story unless it involved a brush fire, or some crazy celebrity caught driving drunk, or somehow misbehaving in their hillside mansion on Mulholland or Malibu Canyon.

Ron turned left off of the ramp, crossed over the freeway, made a right at the corner and then a quick left into the Sheriff's Station parking lot. It was about 10:40 a.m., giving him plenty of time to get his tripod set up in a decent spot for the news conference. There were already two other news vans in the small parking lot, and Ron pulled into one of the remaining available spaces. The Sheriff's Media Relations people were already at work, setting up the podium and testing the sound system at the base of the concrete stairs near the front door of the tan brick station-house.

One by one, crews and reporters from all the Los Angeles TV and radio stations arrived for the presser, and Ron introduced Shelby to some of his friends as they walked up. First she met Russ Nixon from Channel 3, a tall, thin African-American cameraman with an engaging smile who loved jazz and always had an amusing story. Then, Phil Loudin, a sixty-ish, balding, heavy set videographer from Channel 8, and several other crews from foreign language stations. Each station had also sent a reporter to work this story, some riding with their cameramen, plus one or two who preferred to drive their own cars.

Ron was among the youngest photogs of the group. In his thirties, but still boyishly handsome, with steel-blue eyes, and a full head of slightly disheveled brown hair, slightly graying at the temples. He stood just over six feet tall and somewhere near 200 lbs. His tan, somewhat leathery complexion came from years of working outside, only occasionally remembering to slather on the SPF 40. Somehow, Ron always had what appeared to be a two-day growth of whiskers. Years of carrying heavy camera gear kept him in fairly good shape, and he had not yet developed the paunch that besets many photojournalists after a while on the job, thanks to all the driving and terrible eating habits.

All the cameramen seemed to dress similarly, in blue jeans, lightweight hiking boots, and polo shirts, or long sleeves worn as a second layer over a dark t-shirt, emblazoned with either a Hawaiian pattern, a picture of a rock band, a Fire Department emblem, or the logo from some company that had given them away as a freebie to get the media to show up for some event. The sign of a successful shoot, it's been said, is food or a free t-shirt.

It was still early in the year, and the morning had been much too chilly for shorts. If it warmed up later, as all the weather casters had predicted, the outer shirts could be ditched, just as the sweatshirts and jackets had been by the early morning crews hours earlier. The good news for this outdoor news conference is that there was no rain.

Shelby made an attempt to fit in with the other journalists she was meeting for the first time. She introduced herself to the reporters and tried hard to remember all of their names. She must have answered the same questions at least a dozen times; Where are you from? Where did you work last? Where did you go to school? Phil told Shelby that she reminded him of his daughter, who was attending San Diego State.

Soon, a number of the Sheriff's Deputies, who've never been known for their shyness, also began to form a circle around Shelby. Her ego had never been so well fed, but at the same time, she found herself a bit overwhelmed by all the attention. One deputy in particular, a tall two-striper with dark, wavy hair and military-looking tattoos on his oversized biceps began a conversation in a low but powerful voice.

"I'm Deputy Lyons, but you can call me Mike. Are you new in town?"

Just then, at precisely 11 o'clock, Sergeant Ted Hairston, the Public Information Officer, stepped to the podium and asked if everyone was ready. He offered a mike check and held up a press-release which explained the purpose for the news conference. Turning it over to offer for a moment as a white balance to the cameras, he then introduced the Lieutenant, who would be making the remarks to the press.

"Good morning, ladies and gentlemen, and thank you all for coming. I'm Lieutenant Mark Walters and I'll be making the announcements here today, and afterwards, I'll be glad to take any questions. On Friday, February 7, at approximately 8:45 pm, deputies received a call of a missing woman in the city of Calabasas. We took a report from her husband and hoped that she would return home after a short time. It is now nearly a week later, and we have had no contact with her, and neither her credit cards nor her cell phone have been used. The phone is off and not transmitting a GPS signal, and we've been unable to contact her, so we are asking the public's help.

"Our missing woman's name is Jennifer Nealey, and we've made a photo of her available to the media. She's 28 years old, about 5 foot seven inches tall with long blonde hair and weighing about 125 lbs. She was driving a 2015 Chevrolet Impala, red in color, California license number 4 William Tom Mary 962. Her husband, Peter, is completely distraught. He, along with their two young sons will be handing out flyers with the missing woman's picture at the Target store on Mulholland Highway this afternoon. You are invited to get video of the family while they hand out the flyers, as well as to follow the deputies, while they continue their search on foot, and on horseback, through the canyons surrounding the area. We've also had our helicopter assisting with the search, in some of the less accessible areas."

"The Los Angeles County Board of Supervisors has voted to offer a reward in the amount of $10,000 for information leading to the location of Jennifer Nealey. We are hopeful, that with the help of the media, and the public, she will return home to her family soon. If anyone has any information about Ms. Nealey's whereabouts, or if you see her vehicle, we ask that you contact the Los Angeles County Sheriff's Department at the number provided. Now, if there are any questions..."

Reporter Bill Torme of Channel 3 News raised his hand and shouted out the first question for the Lieutenant. "Is there anything to indicate trouble between Mrs. Nealey and her husband?"

"At this point," the Lieutenant replied, glancing at his notes, "we have no reason to suspect that the husband was in any way involved in her disappearance. We're examining all possibilities, but at this time he is not under suspicion."

While the news conference was progressing, and Lieutenant Walters continued taking questions, Deputy Lyons had been involved in a whispered, but personal conversation with Shelby Falconer. He had given her his Sheriff's Department business card and taken her cell-phone number, and was seemingly ready to ask her on a date, when Hairston quietly stepped in, and with a tap on Lyons' shoulder, forced their attention back to the podium.

"Once again, her car is a red, 2015 Chevy Impala, with some minor damage to the front right fender from an earlier collision. The license number is 4WTM962. If anyone sees the car, we ask that they call the Lost Hills Sheriff's Station.

"Thank you all for coming, and if there are any additional questions, I'll be available after the news conference." With that, Walters stepped away from the mike and was quickly approached by the reporters and cameras from the Spanish language stations, to get some of his comments repeated for their viewers. Not being bi-lingual, he directed them to Sergeant Lenny Ortiz, a Spanish-speaking deputy who was there to handle that assignment.

Ron walked over to Shelby and handed her the copy of the Missing Person flyer that the Public Information Officer had handed out, along with a photo and all the vital information about the missing woman. He glanced at the yellow notepad in her hand and read what she had written with her red, fine-point pen: *Missing Woman News Conference- Lt. Walters*-----

Ron shot daggers at Deputy Lyons as he turned toward the truck with his equipment, shaking his head. He was obviously going to have to hold Shelby's hand and walk her through this story like the rookie she was.

As Ron hopped back behind the wheel, Shelby opened the passenger-side door and climbed inside, slightly embarrassed by her lack of understanding of the details of the woman's disappearance. "What now?" she asked.

"Well, we have an hour or so before the husband and sons start handing out flyers at the Target Store. Let's head over there," Ron said, as he pulled the van out of the parking lot. He dialed up the station on his cell and heard the ring on the Bluetooth connection.

"Channel Six Newsroom, How can I direct your call?" asked the young intern, assigned to answer the phones at the assignment desk.

"Let me speak to Maggie, please."

"And who should I say is calling?"

"Tell her it's Slappy White," said Ron, sarcastically.

"Hold please."

After a few seconds of listening to the Channel Six News theme music on hold, Maggie picked up the line with a laugh.

"Hey, Ronnie- was this thing any good?"

"Yeah, we've got a mother of two, missing for close to a week. No sign of her or her car. Her husband is distraught. He and the two boys are handing out flyers at the Target Store in about an hour. We're headed over to get some of that and maybe talk to the husband."

Hmm… talk to the husband. Great idea, Shelby thought silently.

"Good. See what you can get and we'll make some calls. I'll let you know if the deputies turn up anything."

"Thanks, Maggie." Said Ron.

"Anytime, Suh-lappy."

The Target parking lot was almost full, so the news vans lined up on the red curb in front of the Staples and the Best Buy, which were on opposite sides of the Target. With time to spare, Ron opened up his iPad and began showing Shelby a few of his Celebrity photos. He struck the same pose in each one, his video camera on his right shoulder and his arm around the celebrity standing to his left. There were literally dozens, and Shelby wanted to hear the story behind each one.

"Here's Daryl Hannah," said Ron, "I got this photo a few years ago after she came down from sitting in an old oak tree for about a week, protesting about developers wanting to cut it down, or something. She didn't smell real good, but she was still really cute. Oh, and this one is me with George Carlin. We interviewed him in his office a few months before he died. Smart, funny guy, and really nice."

Time passed quickly, and soon Ron spotted a man who was obviously Peter Nealey, in the van's side mirror, being tailed by several of the other camera crews. Nealey was just under six feet tall, with tousled, dark brown hair, a weakly attempted salt and pepper soul-patch and the mis-aligned, brown teeth of a chain-smoker. He was carrying a stack of flyers and walking purposefully with his two boys across the parking lot towards the front door of the Target. Ron shut down his iPad, and he and Shelby exited the van. They walked up and introduced themselves to Peter, who in turn introduced his two young sons, nine-year-old Brent and Luke, who was seven.

After meeting the other crews and reporters who had come to the store, Peter and the boys proceeded to hand out Missing Person flyers to all the customers as they left the store. Brent and Luke were crying and begging, barely audibly, "Help us find our Mom, Please help us find our Mom!" Most shoppers took honest pity on the boys, studied the photo of the missing woman, and kept the flyers, in hopes of solving the mystery that had befallen their idyllic little community. Some, however, never broke stride, refused eye contact, and kept walking to their cars.

This location was not chosen at random. It turns out, Mom had left the house, supposedly to come to this very Target store, to pick up a few things for Luke's birthday, which was last Saturday. She never returned home and according to detectives, neither she, nor her Chevy were seen at any point that day by Target's video surveillance cameras. If Shelby had been listening to the Lieutenant, she would have known that before Ron told her.

After about an hour, all the flyers were gone, and a few were taped up to the windows near the entrance of all the stores in the shopping center. In a small community such as Calabasas, the hope was that somebody saw something, anything that could lead to Jennifer's return.

Most of the reporters and photographers had left after getting some "b-roll", video of the flyers being distributed, off to another story, or perhaps to set up for an afternoon live-shot. But Ron and Shelby stayed until the Nealey and his sons were ready to leave. Shelby approached Peter and asked if he would be willing to talk to them on camera. His dark eyes scanned her fetching frame, and against his better judgment, agreed to meet them back at the house, away from the crowds, and after he'd had the chance to drop off the boys with their grandparents. He wrote down the address on the back of one of his flyers that he found crumbled atop an overflowing red trashcan in front of the store, and headed to his car with the boys. They had agreed to meet at the house in 45 minutes.

Ron parked Microvan 21 across the street from 2674 Calipatria Drive and shut off the engine. He always parked the van across the street from the assigned location, so as not to block a clean camera-shot of the house's exterior, should he need one- another tip for Shelby to pick up her first day on the job.

They stepped up over the curb, across the uneven sidewalk, past the mailbox, and up the narrow concrete walk that divided the drought-stricken front yard, which was full of dead grass, dying flower beds and dried out potted plants. It was only about a dozen steps to the porch of the modest yellow single-story house with white shutters, which were badly in need of a fresh coat of paint. Shelby walked a few paces ahead of Ron, since she was not weighed down with camera gear. She stood on the reddish-brown concrete stoop and pressed the small, round, painted-over button on the doorbell, and to both of their surprise, it actually worked. Peter Nealey answered almost immediately, as if he'd been standing just on the other side of the door, watching their approach through the opaque glass. Shelby once again shook his hand and, glancing over her shoulder at Ron, as if a bit spooked, entered the house.

Ron set up his tripod on the hardwood floor in the front room, a small family room that had ample space for them all due to the scarcity of furniture. A plastic cereal bowl still sat atop the small wooden table in the middle of the dining room, while three lightweight folding chairs provided the only seating within view. Ron could make use of the natural light that was coming in through the curtain-free windows. *This house looks like it's been packed up and ready to move out of,* he thought.

Ron was set up in no time, and surreptitiously began shooting "b-roll" of the only art in the house- the unframed, curled family photos, scotch taped on the grimy wall, and of Peter, walking room to room with Shelby. "Ready when you are, Shelby." This pleased her, since she was getting a really uncomfortable feeling, making small talk with this guy. He had led her on a short tour of the house, purposely walking a few paces behind her the whole time, scoping out her shapely derriere while showing her the photos of the boys as babies in the hallway, the inside of the bedroom he shared with his missing wife, and the closet filled with her clothes, undisturbed since she had left so unexpectedly.

"Let's do this," said Ron. Shelby led Peter back into the front room. Ron pinned a small, wireless microphone to Peter's wrinkled Hawaiian print shirt, stepped back behind the camera, focused and framed up his shot, and hit the Roll button.

"Tell us about your wife, Mr. Nealey."

"She was just so sweet and loving, and I don't know who would want to hurt her." Peter said, wiping his nose and choking back an invisible tear.

"Did you guys get along?" asked Shelby.

"Most of the time we did," replied Peter, staring off. "We had little spats like all couples, but nothing out of the ordinary."

"Is there anywhere you can think of that she might go for a few days? A friend's house, her parents…?"

"Not at all," Nealey said, looking her straight in the eyes, expressionless. "She would never leave the boys. She just loved them so much."

That answer struck Ron as a bit odd. *'She would never leave THE BOYS'? What about you, dude?*

Shelby persisted, nervously: "Do you have any other recent photos of your wife that we could take a picture of, besides the one on the flyer?"

"Actually, toward the end, she didn't like having her picture taken, so no I don't."

'Toward the end?' What the …?

Now Ron was creeped-out.

"Shelby, umm, I'm sorry, I'm out of battery power, but I think we're good."

Ron grabbed the lavaliere mike from the lapel of Nealey's shirt, and threw it back into his equipment bag, not taking time to properly dress the cable. They quickly thanked Peter for his time and headed out the front door, beating a hasty retreat toward the van.

"He DID it!" Ron said as soon as the microvan's doors were slammed shut. Then added, "He killed her, that creepy fucking bastard."

Ron accelerated around the corner and got away from the Nealey house as quickly as he could, then got the station on the phone.

"Channel Six Newsroom."

"Can I get Maggie, Please?"

"Who's calling, sir?"

"Tell her that Flip Wilson is on the phone and it's important."

"Yes sir, Mr. Wilson. Please hold."

"What have you got for me, Ronnie?"

"Nothing, except an interview with a guy who killed his wife."

"Excellent. And we know this how…?"

"He gave off this vibe that… I don't know, but some of the things he said. I'd put money on it."

"Alright, Ron. Find a location to get your video shipped in so we can cut it for teases, and then bring Shelby back to the station. We'll have her put something together for tonight."

"So, you don't want us to stay and shoot the Deputies searching on horseback, or…"

"No," interrupted Maggie. "We've got some aerials. And we'll hand the story off to the night side crew. That search will be going on for a while. "

"You got it," said Ron. "We'll find a place to ship and then be inbound."

"B'bye, Flip."

Ron and Shelby didn't know whether to feel proud of themselves, or scared shit-less.

"You realize that we may have been alone in a house with a killer, Shelby? How's that feel?"

"Well, I keep telling myself that the detectives don't think he had anything to do with his wife's disappearance," said Shelby. "But he was sure a creep."

"The cops always say that about someone they suspect," replied Ron. "That is, until they have enough evidence to bring them in. I'll bet they know that he killed her, too. You know that they've got to have lots more information than we have. They just never want to show their cards too soon. Remember, without evidence it didn't happen."

Ron parked the van in the lot of The Commons, an upscale shopping area near the 101 freeway. He started the truck's generator and powered up the rack of editing and transmission equipment inside. Then he hydraulically raised the van's mast to enable the microwave transmitter to have a line-of-sight connection with the station's repeater site atop Oat Mountain, in the northwest San Fernando Valley. Once he established the link with the station, he and Shelby watched the video of the news conference, the activity at the Target store and the interview with Peter Nealey as Ron shipped it back to the newsroom.

"TOWARD THE END?? What the fuck did THAT mean?" Ron asked, listening to Nealey's audio.

"I know, what's up with that?" said Shelby.

"And the house looked like he was getting ready to split town."

"What a creep," said Shelby. "You should have been a detective, Ronnie."

"What do you think is the motive?" she asked, carrying the investigative fantasy to the next level.

"I don't know, could be anything. Married couples fight about stuff, money, sex, you never know. Maybe he lost his job, or ..."

"Or, maybe he has a girlfriend," interrupted Shelby.

"Or, maybe SHE did!" They both laughed nervously, still a bit shaken.

"Oh, and those poor boys. They've lost their mom, and soon probably their dad, too." said Shelby, bringing the conversation back to reality.

"You know," said Ron. "I'm sure we're completely wrong about this whole thing, and the cops are probably right. She'll come walking in the front door any time now."

"Yeah, right..." said Shelby. "Do you really believe that?"

"Uhh… no."

"Microvan 21 is wrapped with the feed and inbound," said Ron over the two-way radio, as he cut the transmitter and lowered the mast.

"Thank you, Micro 21," replied Maggie. **"Nice job. We'll see you back at the barn."**

Both Ron and Shelby ran into the Corner Bakery to use the restroom and to grab a sandwich before heading back to Hollywood.

"Are you sure it's OK for us to take the time to eat?" asked Shelby, while they waited in line.

"I don't know about you," answered Ron, "But I can throw down a sandwich in a couple of minutes and be on my way. My motto is 'Eat when you can, because you never know when your next meal will be.'"

"Sounds like good advice."

Within fifteen minutes they were back on Highway 101 and feeling good about the story and their morning's work.

"So, right now we've got all the elements for a great story," said Ron, taking on the unfamiliar role of instructor. "We can put all the information out there about this family and see where it leads."

"And," said Shelby. "We can nail this guy to the wall."

"Easy there, Columbo. We can only report what we know; what we saw and what we heard. Let the viewers draw their own conclusions. We don't know anything about what happened to her at this point. But think long term. If and when they arrest this douche-bag, we've got some great stuff."

"You mean I can't use it tonight?"

"It depends," Ron answered. "You are strictly a fly on the wall. You can show him saying what it was that he said, but you can't try to spin or interpret any of it. That's not your job. And it wouldn't surprise me at all if the Sheriff's department called you tomorrow and asked to see the entire interview."

"You really think so?" asked Shelby.

"Who knows? Nealey may have said something that touches a nerve with the investigators."

"Beep- beep- beep- Task Force 88, Engine 73, Rescue 93, respond to the Traffic Collision, reported to be a truck versus multiple vehicles, with entrapment- Northbound 405 Freeway, Ventura Boulevard exit."

Ron generally kept the volume down low on his scanner radios when there was a passenger, but they were usually turned on nonetheless, just in case of a big emergency call. "We'll pass right by this accident on the way back to the station." he said, "We can check it out and see if it's anything."

He locked down the response frequency on the scanner, LAFD Channel 8, and waited for the first-in companies to arrive on scene. Since Fire Station 88 was just a stone's throw from the wreck, less than a half mile north on Sepulveda, it wouldn't take them long. Microvan 21 was still on the 101, approaching Reseda Boulevard from the west when a fire fighter radioed in from the scene of the wreck with a calm but steady voice:

"Control from Engine 88, on scene, the Ventura Boulevard off-ramp from the northbound 405. What we have is a large delivery truck, partially on its side, with entrapment and a vehicle underneath. The truck has broken through the divider, and collided with several vehicles at the bottom of the ramp. It's also forced a smaller vehicle through the wall of a restaurant. We have multiple injuries. Send me another task force for manpower, a Heavy Rescue, four additional rescue ambulances and an EMS Supervisor for a physical rescue. Notify DWP that there's a dislodged hydrant spraying water that we'll need to shut down."

"Wow, sounds good!" said Ron, his adrenalin addiction kicking in. "Let's go!"

"Oh my God!" cried Shelby. "I hope nobody's hurt. I can't stand the sight of blood!"

You, Lady, are in the wrong fucking business.

Ron reached for the two-way radio to inform the assignment desk what he'd just heard from the accident scene and that he and Shelby were going to check it out. Immediately, "Air Six", the station's helicopter, fired up its engine. Flown by Teddy Beamon, known to other TV chopper pilots as "Beamon the Demon", Air Six launched within minutes from Van Nuys Airport, just a few miles from the crash-site. As Beamon flew over the scene, his first report to the assignment desk was that this wreck looked to be very serious:

"The CHP has the off-ramp completely shut down," Beamon said, describing the video he was transmitting to the station. **"It looks like a large semi-truck tried to take the freeway exit too fast, or possibly had brake failure or some mechanical problem. It crashed through the barricades and the large sand-barrels at the bottom of the ramp and landed on several vehicles, pushing one completely through the side of this building I'm showing you, which appears to be a small café."**

"OK, Air Six, stay over the scene," Maggie answered. **"We're going to break into programming at the bottom of the hour. That's in three minutes."**

At 3:30 they were on the air with live aerials from over the scene.

"Emergency vehicles from the Los Angeles Fire Department are continuing to arrive on scene," Teddy reported, "with paramedics setting up a triage area in the middle of Sepulveda Boulevard. We're hearing from the Highway Patrol that there is at least one fatality on the scene, along with numerous other serious injuries. As you can see, water is shooting about fifty feet into the air from a broken hydrant, making this a spectacular sight, visible from the freeway, and making the rescuers' jobs much more difficult. This is going to be a major incident for several hours, affecting both the 405 and 101 freeways. Certainly not what we need heading into afternoon rush-hour."

Ron found himself in heavy afternoon traffic on the 101, as far back as Balboa Boulevard. He tried driving on the right shoulder to get around the congestion for as long as he could, but eventually cars entering the freeway blocked off that route as well. Traffic was at a standstill throughout most of the Valley so he hopped off the at Haskell Avenue, and then took Ventura Boulevard eastbound, hoping he could reach the scene while victims were still being treated. He had no idea, at that point, that the scene would be active for hours, not minutes.

The delivery truck was owned by McCabe Delivery, a fairly large grocery distributor in Southern California, but operated by a small trucking company out of the City of Commerce. It was loaded with about four tons of canned vegetables and other foods of various types. The driver, 43-year-old Freddie Garcia, was getting off the freeway to make delivery at several markets in the area, starting with the Whole Foods market which stood at the corner of Sepulveda and Greenbush, at the base of the freeway exit. The ramp had been the site of numerous collisions, simply because of its unorthodox design. It was long and unusually steep, also very difficult to maneuver, particularly hard for heavy vehicles. Drivers complained that it was steeper than most off-ramps, with a sharp right turn at the bottom, which caused a good number of vehicles to impact the steel rail on the left. The ramp was three lanes wide, and allowed for vehicles in the left lane to turn left, toward Ventura Boulevard. The center lane allowed traffic to either turn right onto Sepulveda, or to proceed straight onto Greenbush Street.

The truck's brakes had failed on the steep ramp, and while Freddie did everything he could, he could not control the rig. The cab had burst through the steel rail at full speed and across the on-ramp on the other side. There it made contact with a Honda Civic, a BMW, and a Dodge Durango, which became airborne, crashing through the wall of Cucina Bene, a small but popular Italian Restaurant on the corner. The Honda was forced off the road where it had snapped the hydrant off the sidewalk, shooting a powerful geyser of water into the air and down on the entire scene.

The intersection of Sepulveda and Greenbush instantly became a scene of utter pandemonium. As first responders continued to arrive on scene, Police and Firefighters set about to find victims of the crash and pull them out of the smoking wreckage. At the same time, they struggled to turn off the geyser, still gushing upward from the blown hydrant. A pair of Firefighters from Station 88 were able to locate the main valve under the street. While standing in the downpour, they used a large wrench and all of their strength to turn the valve, which was several feet below the asphalt, until the flow was stopped. By that time, however, the roadway was flooded and slick, which made the rescue operation that much more difficult. City Traffic Control Officers had begun to arrive, and quickly closed Sepulveda Boulevard to all non-emergency traffic at Ventura Boulevard on the north and Valley Vista on the south. The northbound 405 exit to Ventura Boulevard was also closed, which created a huge problem for afternoon commuters. Cal-Trans issued a Sig-alert for the area and broadcast warnings for drivers to try to avoid the vicinity of the 405 and 101 freeways for the foreseeable future.

A passenger in the Durango, a 36-year-old man from Arleta, had serious cuts, bruises, and a broken left leg, and was transported in fair condition to Valley Presbyterian Hospital. Both of the occupants of the Honda, the 44-year-old male driver, and his 16-year-old daughter were seated on the curb, being evaluated by paramedics. The driver of the Dodge and three patrons of the restaurant, were lying on the yellow plastic sheets that had been laid out in the middle of Sepulveda Boulevard as a triage. The Dodge's driver, 29-year-old Lupe Granato, was in critical condition. Her ear had been severed, she had deep lacerations to her skull, her left arm, and wrist. Her left ankle was shattered. She was unconscious and in cardiac arrest. It would take time, but Paramedics acted quickly in an effort to get her stabilized, bandaged, fitted with an IV, and readied for transport.

Tom and Louise Goodwin, a retired couple in their sixties from Encino, had been seated in their favorite spot, the corner table of the crowded Cucina Bene, where several times a month they enjoyed a late lunch and a lovely view of the quaint neighborhood through the side-by-side picture windows. They were still very much in love after 36 years of marriage, and made a date of their evenings out together, often seeing a movie down the street at the ArcLight afterward. Tom always moved one of the chairs at the table-for-two, so they could sit side by side, rather than on opposite sides. People often remarked about the "cute little old couple" seated in the corner, holding hands and whispering in each other's ears, unaware the Tom's hearing impairment made such an arrangement necessary. Luis, their usual waiter, had just delivered a glass of Chardonnay for Louise, and a Cabernet for Tom, and was standing to Louise's left ready to take their food orders, when their world changed. They had each heard the first collision, just outside the window, and Tom had just begun to turn in his seat. Louise had no more than an instant to see the Durango and to react, not nearly enough time to shout a warning to her husband, or to Luis. The out-of-control Durango crashed through the side of the building, half through the stucco wall, and half through the plate glass window, directly behind Tom's chair. The force of the impact took the couple's lives instantly, crushing them beneath the SUV's wheels, exploding and spraying shards of glass, wood and metal throughout the restaurant. Luis and at least a half dozen other patrons and employees were injured with cut, bruises, and broken bones, and in need of immediate help. Semi driver Freddie Garcia also lost his life, when the impact brought his cab to a violent, sudden stop, snapping his neck.

Rescuers made their way through the broken glass and debris of the restaurant and evaluated the injured, removing the patients to the triage area. The Battalion Chief called on his cell for a representative from the Department of Building and Safety to come and evaluate the soundness of the structure.

Lara Burns had been trapped behind the wheel of her new BMW for almost thirty minutes under the trailer filled with tons of fruits and vegetables. Fire Captain Joel Heller, along with Paramedic Ted Schweikart worked to keep Lara calm, and to prevent her from passing into a state of shock.

"What's your name?" asked Ted over the commotion of rescue workers shouting and firing up portable generators.

"Lara," she whispered through tears, unaware of the blood dripping down her blonde hair and onto the shoulder of her soft, pink sweater.

"I'm Ted," he said, as though they were meeting at a party, not a care in the world. All the while, the troops worked frantically to get her free. "And this is Joel. How's your day going?"

Lara chuckled through blood and tears, and replied, "I've had better."

"OK," said Ted, taking her hand. "Where does it hurt?"

"I can't feel my legs," replied Lara. "And my left shoulder feels broken."

"Well, we're going to get you home, and everything will be fine. Just relax and let us take care of everything. OK?"

"I'm- I'm pregnant. S- seven months." she said, trembling.

"OK, OK- just take a deep breath," Ted said, making brief eye contact with Joel. "We'll have you out of there in no time."

Micro 21 at last arrived on the chaotic scene, Ron parking on Sepulveda, about fifteen yards behind RA39, so to not interfere with the paramedics, as well as to be out of the way once the road was again opened up to traffic. He jumped out of the van, ran around to grab his video camera, and watched as Shelby, in her heels and tight skirt, carefully dismounted from the passenger's side of the van. She nearly fell on her face, taking her first step on the rough, wet asphalt, and Ron paused for a beat, shaking his head as if to ask, *"Are you coming?"*

They walked toward the scene together, crossing over behind the open rear doors of the rescue ambulance and onto Sepulveda, almost running head-on into the gurney carrying Lupe Granato, being wheeled furiously by firefighters toward the RA. Ron reflexively began shooting the transport. When Shelby spotted the woman, leg splinted, head bloody and battered, in the desperate care of five onrushing firefighters, one carrying an IV bag, she gasped and again, almost lost her footing on the rutted, oily pavement.

"My God!" she yelled, gasping for breath. "Did you see that woman? I, I can't believe what I just saw!" Ron was too busy shooting video of the gurney being loaded into the ambulance to pay any attention to the traumatized rookie reporter at his side.

Ron was set up at the corner and shooting video when Heavy Rescue 88, an oversized tow rig, began to stabilize the truck and lift it off of the BMW with its heavy-lift crane. At the same time, firefighters belonging to a specially equipped Urban Search and Rescue team used the pneumatic Jaws of Life to cut away the roof and snap the door off of the 328i.

Captain Heller called ahead to alert the hospital that their transport was a young, pregnant woman in serious condition with head trauma, severe injuries to her lower extremities, and possible broken bones.

Lara Burns was placed in a C-spine neck collar, and lifted gently from the crushed vehicle. Ted Schweikart started an IV drip into her right arm. Lara was placed on a gurney and tied down securely with what firefighters call a binder, resembling a shredded bedsheet, to prevent further injury. He assured her that he would stay with her the whole way to the hospital.

"Thank you, Ted," she whispered, crying and grasping his right hand.

Lara was wheeled to RA 88 to be transported to Sherman Oaks Hospital. One firefighter jogged alongside the gurney, carrying the IV bag in front of him, providing her with fluids in an effort to keep her and her baby alive until the trauma staff could take over at the Emergency Room. Schweikert made sure the gurney was loaded carefully into the rear of the RA, then climbed in and held Lara's hand throughout the duration of the transport.

The scene was still very active, with several patients still being evaluated in the triage area. The strong odors of oil, rubber and sulfur still hung over the scene. Meanwhile, up on the freeway, the CHP was diverting traffic around the closed exit ramp at the bottom of the Sepulveda Pass, one of the busiest freeway routes in the country. Surface roads throughout the area were also affected, as a number of neighborhood streets remained closed, with testy commuters trying to find the easiest possible alternative route home. Fire crews remained on scene, picking up their rescue gear, along with CHP officers trying to clear one or two lanes to allow for a bit of relief to the jammed early-evening traffic. MAIT (Major Accident Investigation Team) investigators took photographs and measurements, and Cal-Trans crews swept and picked up debris from the off-ramp. There were several heavy-duty tow trucks, belonging to independent operators, sitting along Sepulveda, waiting for the investigation to be completed, ready to up-right and off-load the delivery truck and remove the wrecked vehicles. The Coroner's Investigator had not yet been called for the dead at the Cucina Bene, or for Garcia, who was still sitting upright in the cab of his truck, covered with a white sheet. Ron kept shooting the wreckage, getting as close to the vegetable truck as permitted by the officers guarding the fatal scene. All at once, he spotted an old friend, CHP Officer Steve Baxter.

Steve and Ron first met about four years earlier, at a scene on the San Diego Freeway, in the Sepulveda Pass, not far away. On that occasion, the driver of a small Toyota coupe had apparently encountered some type of engine trouble and coasted to a stop in the fast lane on the downgrade between Mulholland Drive and the 101 interchange. It was before dawn on a pitch dark, moonless morning, with very light traffic, so the drivers speeding down the grade behind the Toyota had a difficult time seeing the stalled car ahead. Several reported that they had barely been able to swerve at the last second to avoid a collision, but the driver of a Chevy pickup, traveling at about 75 miles per hour plowed into the rear of the much smaller car, and the Toyota's fuel tank burst into flames. The driver of the Corolla was incinerated in the wreck, and the freeway was shut down for several hours. Ron showed up to shoot the accident for the early morning news on Channel 6, and was escorted around the scene by Officer Baxter. After he had shot enough video of the major Sig-alert in the Pass, Ron and Steve continued their conversation. They seemed to hit it off, soon discovering that they both possessed that morbidly dark sense of humor, forged by scenes just like the one that night. Baxter walked Ron right up to the door of the Toyota and showed him the driver, still behind the wheel, charred, black as coal and unidentifiable, not even enough there to determine a gender. That would require a DNA test at the Coroner's office. The driver's hands were adhered to the charred metal of the steering wheel, steam still rising from his or her arms, releasing the moisture remaining from the firefighters' efforts to douse the fatal inferno. Ron didn't bother shooting video of the burned body at close range, knowing that shots like that would never make it on the air, and would likely result in a complaint from the editors back at the station. But his curiosity would not let him look away from the driver, blackened and welded to the steel skeleton of the Corolla's seat by the tremendous, sudden heat of the exploding gas tank. Ron watched as the Coroner pried the driver's hands from the wheel, leaving narrow strips of red flesh attached as he pulled repeatedly to extricate the body, now stiff with the onset of rigor mortise. This scene would replay vividly in nightmare form in Ron's mind for weeks afterward, but served to inure him from other gruesome scenes he'd surely later witness in his line of work.

Steve and Ron became tight, and when possible, would get together for a beer or two after work, either at the Junction, a Cop-bar near Steve's home in the West Valley, or at the Dog and Pony, an industry hangout just over the hill from Channel 6, in Studio City. There, they and other media and law enforcement friends would swap stories of work and relationships, and often compete to see who could come up with the most gruesome tale, the winner getting a shot of Jager. Over the years, they and the others became like brothers, their horror stories of life and death in Los Angeles forging a bond and uniting them all in a culture that few others could fully understand.

The cameramen discovered that often it was they who had the more exciting tales to tell, covering big stories throughout greater Los Angeles much more often than anything memorable would occur in a cop's limited area of jurisdiction.

Ron walked over and gave Steve a big handshake and a bit of a man-hug, although man-hugs are largely discouraged among officers in uniform.

"Brother, how are you?" asked Steve.

"OK, Buddy," replied Ron, motioning toward Shelby. "They put me with a new reporter today. She's sweet, but she's kind of grossed out by this whole situation. Look." Ron pointed over toward one of the fire trucks where Shelby Falconer was leaning against the hood, forehead in hand, obviously traumatized from what she was witnessing. The two men shared a discreet laugh. Steve then leaned over to Ron and whispered a plan he had quickly concocted. Ron chuckled and, after a moment, agreed to go along with the prank.

Steve walked with Ron toward the corner, where Shelby was still holding herself upright against the truck. Ron introduced his friend and let Steve take over the conversation. "So, we've got to keep this area clear," he said. "We don't want to disturb any evidence. I'm going to need you guys to follow me over here so you'll be out of the way." Steve led them to a spot on the opposite corner, between the light pole and a bus bench, a vantage point from which the truck's cab and Garcia's body were readily visible. Shelby caught sight of the deceased driver, the white sheet having been removed by investigators, still belted into his seat behind the wheel. His head was tilted at an impossible angle to the left, mouth open, still wearing the green John Deere cap he'd put on when he kissed his wife and left for work that morning. Steve left them alone there and Ron shot some superfluous video just to appear busy.

A few minutes later, Steve returned straight–faced with a dilemma. "Miss Falconer, I wonder if you could do me a favor."

"I, I don't know, Officer," answered Shelby haltingly. "What do you need?"

"Well, we've got a deceased driver in that truck right there, I'm not sure if you knew that. But before we can open up this roadway, we've got to get him out and tow the truck away."

"Uh huh." said Shelby, swallowing and looking at Steve through a painful squint. Ron did his best to stifle a laugh while studying his shoes and avoiding eye contact with either of them.

"So anyway, he's kind of stuck in there." Steve continued, scratching his forehead. "Twisted debris, and all that. So, we've determined that the best way to get his body out of the cab is to remove his head. And, well, we were wondering if you could help us out and hold the basket."

Shelby turned colorless, and her eyes opened wide. She spun and tried to run back toward the news van, but slipped and fell, breaking the heel off of her right shoe. As she stumbled onto the asphalt scraping her knees, the young reporter vomited violently into the gutter.

Chapter Two:

VISIONS

Shelby had just 45 minutes to pull herself together sufficiently enough to attempt her first live shot. Ron had taken the time to smooth her feathers and offer an apology for the prank he and Steve had played. He retrieved a cold bottle of water from the truck for her and helped her prepare the story. The red and blue emergency lights continued to flash, reflecting off the wet asphalt and the windshield of Microvan 21 parked on Sepulveda. Shelby and Ron settled into their seats to prepare their story for the upcoming newscast. She was impressed with how Ron had worked the story – editing with smart but not-too-gruesome shots he had taken of the accident scene, sound bites with witnesses and investigators and a few short "black holes" which would be filled by an editor back at the station with aerials from the chopper above the scene. He helped her write and record her reporter track, although she told him that she had always hated the sound of her own voice. The finished piece was in-house with twenty minutes to spare.

"How do you handle it, Ron?" Shelby asked, standing in front of Ron's camera in the middle of Sepulveda Blvd. waiting for the cue to go on-air.

"Handle what?"

"Two minutes, Shelby." said the voice in her ear. She acknowledged by waving the microphone into the lens and nodding.

"The blood, the death…" she continued. "How do you not go insane?"

"You know," he said, looking away from the viewfinder. "You just can't let it get to you. I know, the victims are people and I know they have lives like you and me, families and all. I guess you just learn to tune it out and try to be thankful that it's happening to someone else and not somebody you know or care about. It gets easier over time."

"But how do you not care? Don't you ever just want to cry?"

"It's rough sometimes," he added. "You always hate to see an innocent person hurt in any way. Just keep telling yourself that you're doing your job. No more, no less."

"I hated even having to look at the video again," she said.

Ron was hoping for a clean live shot, one without the technical issues he'd been having so frequently of late. He knew that with live television, there were dozens of things that could easily go wrong. The 650-watt Lowell stand-light he'd put up could blow out, leaving Shelby looking flat and unimpressive in the waning sunlight of late afternoon. The truck's generator could unexpectedly shut down, the station could run the wrong video, the wireless IFB communication system tucked away in her ear could malfunction, causing her to miss her cue. Or one of the dozens of bystanders could, seeking a bit of fame, impulsively decide to interfere by shouting, flashing a bare body part, or by partaking in the latest craze, running right up in the middle of the reporter's report and yelling an obscenity into the mike before escaping into the wind. Ron, having experienced each of these and more, surveyed his surroundings one last time, picking out the sketchiest looking suspects. He stared down a trio of teenaged boys who had been huddled off to the side, whispering amongst themselves, and only occasionally glancing up at him. He'd keep an eye on them, hopeful that his glare had dissuaded them from trying anything stupid. Shelby's day had been tough enough. The last thing she needed was some immature douche bags pouring still more crap on her head.

"Stand by, Shelby. Charles will be throwing to you next…"

*****

"A horrible scene on a local freeway offramp tonight," announced Charles Hughes, longtime anchor at KSIX. "Our Shelby Falconer is at the scene."

"That's right, Charles. As you said, a major incident here in Sherman Oaks this afternoon has left three people dead, and ..."

Ron saw one of the young men he'd been watching creep around behind Shelby to her right, just out of camera range. Ron began slowly and smoothly zooming in the camera shot on his reporter's face tighter and tighter as the creep snuck in ever closer. Ron was ready to pounce and grab the guy in a few seconds as soon as Shelby threw to her package. But that would have been too late.

The creep took a quick step toward Shelby and tried to time his approach for the maximum shock and surprise.

"FUCK HER RIGHT IN THE PU..."

The creep's neck snapped painfully as he felt a muscular arm whip across his chest, forcing him to the ground like a wide receiver hit by a defensive back. He had been so focused on frightening the young reporter and getting his antics on live television, he failed to see Steve, who'd been standing next to the live truck, watching with interest as Ron and Shelby did their jobs.

Shelby jumped and gasped, and while none of the activity behind her was visible on camera, the crew back at the station had the presence of mind to cut away from the live shot and run her package. While it ran, Steve grabbed the creep, pulled him up by the collar and said, "Now get the fuck out of here before you go to jail." The kid took off like a bat out of hell, following his pals, who had already left him behind, laughing as they ran.

Shelby assured the director that things had settled down and they could come back to her on camera after the piece.

"...Authorities tell me that they hope to have the road repaired, the barricades back up and traffic moving normally by morning. Repairs to the ramp, however, could take weeks, if not longer. Live from Sherman Oaks, this is Shelby Falconer. Now, back to you in the studio."

*****

Once the live-shot was over, and the assignment desk cleared the crew from the scene, a barefoot Shelby Falconer climbed back into the microvan, shut the door, and heaved a huge sigh as she slumped into the seat.

"Rough day, huh?" asked Ron.

"Yeah, just a bit," she sighed, rubbing her forehead dejectedly.

Before it was all over, Shelby had given Steve a long hug in appreciation for his saving her from the creep. Ron took a long drink of water, and exhaled in relief, reasonably sure that the hazing of the rookie would forever remain their secret.

The scene would be clear hours later, after the two L.A. County Coroner's vans picked up the bodies of the deceased and left for downtown. Ron and Shelby had handed the story off to the nightside crew, who remained at the location to wait for the transport and prepare for their own live shot on the Late News. The Public Information Officer promised to give them a live interview with updates on the road closures.

Ron drove straight home from the station that night, too wrung out for anything else. He popped a frozen dinner into the microwave and grabbed a cold Stella and the remote, remembering that the Lakers were playing the Clippers, and the playoffs were still a possibility. The Dodgers season had not yet begun. Plus, there were still three unwatched episodes of True Detective waiting for him.

Friday, February 14ᵗʰ

Maggie spotted Ron walking across the newsroom. She pulled the situationer from the printer and returned to her seat behind the assignment desk.

"How much do you love me?" she asked as she held him the single sheet of paper over her head.

"I dunno, that depends," answered Ron. "What kind of prize-winning journalism have you got for me today?"

"Seriously Ronnie, you're gonna enjoy this one," she said, as he looked over the story plan. "It's a fashion piece, called *How to look like a Sweet Young Thing for your man*. It's at the photo studio for that magazine that has those beautiful models naked all the time. The chick who does the make-up is going to give tips to help average women look like models. They're shooting the 'SYT of the Month' today. It's in West Hollywood. Gretchen will meet you over there."

*****

Ron made his way west down Sunset, realizing that he had 45 minutes to make what was about a ten-minute drive. He pulled over to the curb, in front of the In-N-Out, just west of Hollywood High School, and reached for his iPad. He pulled up the "Sweet Young Thing Magazine" website just to see what to expect. There he found the feature "S.Y.T. of the Month", a series of photo layouts featuring some of the most stunning women he'd ever seen, in various stages of undress. Each shot was spectacular, beautifully shot and perfectly lit. No wonder, he thought, that so many women wanted to look like this for their boyfriends. Ron also wondered why it had taken him so long to become familiar with this magazine.

"This should be interesting." Ron muttered to himself, as he turned the vehicle back onto Sunset Boulevard.

The photo studio was on the border of Los Angeles and West Hollywood. The city of L.A. shunned pornography, even the soft-core type, ever since that battle over increased regulations in hard-core films a few years back. The industry fought back in a big way, moving many venues to areas like Santa Monica or West Hollywood, just to spite the bureaucrats who ran L.A. and deny them the business tax revenue.

Ron had to check the address twice. The non-descript, gray brick exterior with the frosted glass front door offered no clue that this was the location, except the small metal address numbers, 8995, above the door. Ron parked the van on the street and walked up to the building, carrying his video camera and tripod, and wearing his Porta-Brace equipment bag around his waist. He rang the buzzer and waited for a reply.

"Can I help you?" a woman's sultry voice responded from inside the small metal speaker box. Ron imagined, from her voice alone, that she would look like the women in the photos.

"Yes, I'm with Channel 6 News," he replied, into the intercom. "Am I in the right place?"

"Yes you are, I'll buzz you in."

The lock gave a loud click, and Ron pulled open the heavy glass door. He stepped inside to find an ultra-modern studio with perfectly clean white walls, and glass doors with stainless steel handles. The lobby had what appeared to be a brand new pair of black leather sling-chairs, and a black-and-white striped leather sofa. There were a few glass end tables and a larger table against the wall with a bouquet of three red roses. Adorning the walls were oversized photos of some of the previous models who had been photographed at the SYT Studio. Several ultra-modern pendant lights hung from the ceiling.

He heard a woman's footsteps approaching on the gray tile floor. Around the corner came a tall, striking brunette in a short pink skirt, a black satin top and strap heels.

"Good morning, I'm Renee, and you are…?"

"Oh, I'm Ron. I'm with Channel…"

"I know, Channel Six. Your reporter called and said she was running a few minutes late. Have a seat. Can I get you anything? Water, soda?"

"No thanks, I'm good," answered Ron, and she left him alone in the lobby.

Ron began leafing through the fashion, hair and make-up magazines on the table in front of him, then checking out the photos on the walls. Very tastefully done, he thought, not crass or pornographic at all, just great art, created using one of the most beautiful things on the planet, the female body.

The windows of the lobby were covered with light, opaque mini-blinds, which allowed a person to look out at the street, but not to see inside. He looked up as his reporter and former flame approached the door.

Gretchen Salvo had one of those faces everyone recognized, but not everyone was sure immediately how it was they knew her. Her camera-friendly features and disarming smile served her well, when it came to getting information. The kind of reporter Shelby could learn a lot from, Ron thought. She could compete with anyone out there, male or female, in the game of hard news. Unafraid to ask the tough questions, she'd gained a reputation as one of the most respected journalists in the Los Angeles television market. And it didn't hurt her career that she was beautiful, as well as intelligent, and blessed with hypnotic features.

For this assignment, however, it was strictly her feminine side that would be put on display, and her talents in that regard were without question.

This was to be a light feature story for the Morning News show's target audience, housewives who watch the news on KSIX after their men have left the house in the morning. And, hopefully, this piece would attract the men as well, with the subject matter- beautiful, scantily clad women- and a very sexy reporter. For that reason, this story was scheduled to re-air the following week on the Evening News, in the middle of "Sweeps", the period when stations pay closest attention to their ratings.

Gretchen rang the bell and was buzzed in. Renee came to meet her at the door and ushered her into the lobby. Ron stood up and together they were shown to the makeup room down the hallway, past more giant photos of previous "S.Y.T." models, which lined the walls on both sides.

In the makeup chair sat a young, frankly quite average looking young woman wearing a white terrycloth robe. She turned and smiled at the trio as they entered the room.

"This is Tami, our model," announced Renee, as the reporter and cameraman shook her hand. "And this is Kate Marks, our makeup and hairstyling magician."

Ron and Gretchen introduced themselves to Kate, a short, slightly heavy-set woman, around 40, wearing a stained gray hoodie and a pair of blue sweatpants. She had wild blonde hair and a round, sun-damaged face. She clearly cared much more about the appearance of her clients than her own.

"What we'd like to do," Gretchen explained, "is to put a wireless microphone on you and as you're working on Tami's hair and makeup, you can explain to us what you're doing and how women can do this for themselves at home."

"That's fine," said Kate. Ron handed her the mike, asked her to pass it up under her sweatshirt and out at the neck, so he could attach it. Then he showed her where to place the small transmitter on her waist.

Tami Morell had just turned twenty, six weeks earlier. She had moved to L.A. from Hood River, a small town about an hour east of Portland, the week of her birthday, determined to make it big as a model. She had the cute, but imperfect look of an everyday teenaged girl. Her nose was still coated with fading childhood freckles, while her chin fought off a few fresh blemishes, and a small scar on her right cheek, just below her eye, stood as a reminder of what was surely a childhood accident, or possibly a dog-bite, one that, while now forgotten, in her mother's mind must have come terrifyingly close to taking her young daughter's sight. Her wavy blonde hair was pulled back from her face in a blue band, but most of it failed to cooperate and fell uncontrollably over her neck and forehead. When she smiled, however, one was instantly struck by the near-translucent, unnatural whiteness of her perfect teeth.

Ron took some "Before" shots of Tami, to use as comparison with the finished product in the piece. Then, for the next 45 minutes, Kate worked to transform Tami into a world-class center-fold-worthy sex goddess, and explained what she was doing every step of the way. She began by washing Tami's hair, and placing it in oversized pink curlers. Then she got started on the makeup.

Kate demonstrated the proper way to use foundation, blush, eyeliner, powder, and shadow, applying each one slowly, for the benefit of the camera.

"Not too much," she said, testing small amounts on the back of her left hand. "And it's critical to use the correct shade for your skin type." Then came the false lashes, which framed and drew attention to Tami's nordic-blue eyes. Kate chose just the right shade of lipstick, and then framed Tami's lips with liner, creating a perfectly sexy shape for her mouth. Lip-gloss followed, giving her a stunning look, which even impressed Kate. "Wow! Nice," she uttered under her breath.

Tami's hair was blown dry, brushed, curled, and sprayed repeatedly, completing the metamorphosis, which would illustrate exactly what Gretchen wanted to demonstrate for the viewers with this piece.

Once the transformation was complete, and the "After" shots were taken in the make-up chair, Kate led the three of them into the photo studio where the layout would be shot. Kate introduced Ron and Gretchen to Duke Duvall, S.Y.T.'s longtime photographer. Duke was trim, about fifty, with short, wild salt and pepper hair and a leathery tan complexion that screamed Tennis Pro. The rolled-up sleeves of his light green linen shirt and his comfortably worn-in designer jeans conveyed his comfort with his talents, and his studio. He was in constant motion, thoughts seemingly two steps ahead of each situation. His concentration manifested itself with a toothpick, continuously hopping between sides of his mouth.

Ron removed the mike from Kate's shirt and handed it to Duke, then began rolling video as Duke gave them a quick tour of the studio.

"So, this is the set we built for Tami's layout," he explained. "We build a different backdrop for each shoot. It can take a week or more, depending on what kind of look we're going for. This is going to be the spread for mid-August, so there's a Baseball theme. Tami will be standing here, in front of this section of a team's locker room that we've constructed."

Ron's camera was rolling as Tami walked over to her mark and as Duke set his shot, to make sure that everything was in the proper place and the background looked perfect, so that no signs, poles, or other objects would appear to be protruding from her body in the photos.

Next, Duke adjusted the lights. For this, he had to have everything just as it would be in the actual photographs. He had Tami untie and remove her robe, and hand it to Kate, who was also double-checking her work on Tami's hair and makeup. Tami was now a living work of art. Duke explained that to be truly sensual, the model should never be entirely nude. His models always wore something, even if just a scarf, to tantalize the eye and draw it away from the body. For this shoot, Tami was rocking a pair of blue and white striped knee-high baseball socks and a smile. She playfully held a Louisville Slugger over her right shoulder. On the end of the bat hung a blue baseball cap.

Ron tried his best to stay cool and not stare at the near naked beauty in front of him. He found it interesting that to Duke, this was just another day at the office. He was relaxed and totally professional, working around this young woman as he adjusted the lights and checked the shot over and over.

Among the number of lights built into, and hung over the set, there were probably a dozen or more soft, diffused amber mini-portrait lights, just out of the frame, aimed at each part of Tami's body. The underside of her breasts, her shoulders, her thighs, were each given just the right shading and shadow to accentuate their natural form. Her long blonde hair was backlit with just enough intensity to create an angelic, golden halo. The "catch-lights", placed alongside the camera, reflected in her eyes. The set itself was lit with one main key light, placed inside an over-sized umbrella, simulating perhaps the warm light from a tunnel, open to a sun-lit field. The lockers behind Tami, in soft focus, displayed an array of uniforms, caps, and other accoutrements to give the "locker room" a look of authenticity. Much to Ron's surprise, these photos required no airbrushing or photoshopping, thanks to the meticulous lighting and makeup.

Once Duke had his shot set the way he wanted, he stepped behind his camera and shot a number of test shots. Ron was rolling, and being as careful as he could to show the photographer at work, while being discrete when it came to shots of Tami in her state of undress. He felt a bit uncomfortable making eye contact with the unclothed model, and quickly looked away when the model's eyes met his. This created a number of challenges for Ron, whose skills as a videographer were indeed being put to the test.

Ron enjoyed the occasional "fashion shoot", as opposed to a hard-news story, since they allow a photographer to duplicate shots, until he feels that he's got exactly what he's looking for. And once he's comfortable that he has all the necessary pictures to tell the story, he can begin to try more artistic images, to make the story more creative and interesting.

After getting all the basic wide and tight shots in the studio, Ron really went to work. He shot over Duke's shoulder, using the Macro setting on his camera to pull Tami into soft focus. He shot from behind her, looking at Duke with just the model's shoulder or hair in the foreground. He took tight shots of Duke's eye, his hand upon the shutter release, an image of Tami reflected in the glass of the lens, and the flashing studio lights.

Duke took what seemed to Ron to be at least a couple dozen shots of his model, and checked each one in the camera briefly, making slight adjustments in the lights or Tami's pose after each one. He worked to relax his model, talking with her like an older brother and taking plenty of time to guide her through her first shoot with him.

"Swing the bat a little." "Smile a bit more, tilt your head." "Stick out your tongue, it's ok to laugh just a bit", "A touch more mischievous. Have fun!" He had her put the ball cap on her head, turn it sideways, remove it again, toss a ball and catch it. Each shot more playful than the last. Ron shot Tami's face, her smile, plenty of artistic swish-pans, snap-zooms, every trick that came into his mind, knowing that if he should inadvertently capture video of a bare breast or worse, he could blur or crop the offending shot in editing, or just not use it at all.

The freedom Ron felt, knowing that he was working with a master studio photographer, was something that a grunt news-shooter rarely enjoyed, and he took his time and relished it.

After the photo shoot was finished, Ron asked Duke, with whom he'd become fast friends, how difficult it would be for him to jump in next to Tami and get a souvenir photo of himself with the soon-to-be celebrity for his collection. There was one condition, he was told. Tami would be allowed to put on a bikini, or what turned out to be more like a sheer bra and panties. Tami agreed, as did Ron, of course. She took a moment to slip on the lingerie, and Ron eagerly jumped into the frame, video camera on his shoulder, just like his other celebrity photos, but this one with much better lighting. Duke snapped a few quick shots of the pair. The smile on Ron's face spoke a thousand words.

Duke ejected the photo card from his Nikon and took it over to the Mac that sat atop the glass desk in the corner of the studio. He pulled up the shots on the monitor, and after he and Ron had decided on which one looked best, he sent it to the printer, and just like that, Ron had an 11 x 14 souvenir to display in his apartment. Tami signed it and he rolled it up in a rubber band before carefully putting it in his bag.

Ron and Gretchen packed up, and thanked Kate, Tami and Duke for the access they allowed and apologized for any disruption that their presence may have caused. They headed down the hall. Ron stuck his head in the front office to say goodbye to Renee, who got up from her chair to escort them out. She buzzed the door open, and they stepped out onto Sunset Boulevard and headed for their vehicles.

"Thanks," said Ron. "The piece should turn out great."

"Yeah, I think it'll be amazing!" replied Gretchen. "It's nice to do a fashion shoot once in a while. Kind of a relief from death and destruction, don't you think?"

"Absolutely," answered Ron, as he reached for the cell phone on his hip and hit the preset for "News Desk".

"Channel Six News."

"Hey, Maggie- we're wrapped here in West Hollywood."

"Yeah, how was it, Ron? Was it everything you dreamed it would be?" asked Maggie.

"And so much more," said Ron, playing along.

"Well good, I'm glad you enjoyed yourself with the naked chick. Now lemme see what we have for you next... I was going to send you to an interview with Henry Brooks, the Councilman who's running for Mayor next year, but he canceled on us again."

"Why don't you send Gretchen back to the station with your video, and take a lunch break. Then call me back and we'll see what else we can come up with for you."

"Sounds good, Mag. I'll talk to you later."

Ron handed Gretchen the video card from his camera and climbed into his news van. He watched as she got behind the wheel of her brand new red Jaguar and sped away. He shook his head, thinking about what might have been. At the same time, though, he knew the reality was that things were never going to work out with her. He learned that lesson in a most painful way, a lifetime ago, back at the University. Still, seeing how well they work together as a team now, so many years later, made it hard to process the stark fact of their utter incompatibility.

With the enticing aroma from a few hours earlier still fresh in his mind, Ron headed back to the In-N-Out Burger, just a bit east on Sunset, and pulled into the lot. Since the news van was too tall for the Drive-up window, he parked and walked inside to order.

The burger stand was located just west of Hollywood High School, and just a couple of blocks south of Grauman's Chinese Theatre and the Hollywood/Highland complex. Ron always found it entertaining to sit outside and wait to see what kind of characters would walk by. He'd parked along the red curb, just past the drive-thru exit and facing Sunset Boulevard. Directly across the street to the south, he could see the IHOP restaurant, made famous in 1975, when a group of terrorists from the Symbionese Liberation Army, including Sara Jane Olson, known at the time as Kathleen Ann Soliah, had placed a pipe bomb under an LAPD patrol car in the rear parking lot. It was just through pure luck, and the ineptitude of the bombers, that it didn't explode, killing the officers. But seeing that building always reminded Ron that working in a city like Los Angeles, momentous events could happen anywhere, and at any time.

He walked in and waited in line to order his usual Cheeseburger Combo #2 with no onions to go. The place was packed, as always, so the first ten minutes of his break were spent waiting for his food. He filled up his cup with Pink Lemonade and checked his phone for headlines and messages. Finally, his number was called, he grabbed his food and went back outside to eat lunch in the van.

Ron looked at his wristwatch, it was 1:22, and so it would be after 2:00 before he was available for another assignment, unless, of course, some kind of "breaker" caused the station to summon him off of his lunch break. He had learned long ago to eat quickly, since his phone could ring at any time, and the last thing you want is to wolf down a burger while doing 75 on the freeway, or worse yet, have to finish it cold at the end of your shift.

He opened the tandem doors on the passenger's side and climbed into the back of the van, where there was a padded seat that could swivel around to face either the door or the editing equipment in the rear. There was also a shelf in front of the computer screen that was often used as a dinner table, especially when crashing to get a piece edited in time for broadcast. Ron was well aware that a news van can be a giant "crazy-magnet", but nevertheless, he decided to do some people watching while eating his lunch.

This was among the most entertaining parking lots in the city, the clientele being about as diverse and interesting as you'll find anywhere. A young couple slowed as they passed, both sporting spiked jet-black Mohawk haircuts, numerous facial piercings, and tattoos. They whispered to each other and pointed at the van as if it were a UFO, just landed from another planet. A few minutes later, a small group of students from Hollywood High stopped by the van on their skateboards. One of them, a curly haired teenager in board shorts and a torn long-sleeved Anthrax t-shirt asked Ron what he was doing there, wondering if there was there a big story happening at the high school.

"Nope. Just stopping for lunch, that's all," Ron answered.

"My folks watch Channel Six all the time," said the skater, pointing to the station's logo on the side. "My dad's in love with that Gretchen chick."

"Very cool, I'll tell her." Ron said, biting his lip.

Soon after, a young family walked out of the restaurant and stopped by the truck en route to their car.

"...and with this truck, they can broadcast live from anywhere on the planet," Ron heard the father tell his son, who looked maybe ten, as he pointed out all the transmission gear and the telescopic mast atop the van's roof. "Isn't that right, sir?"

"Well, you're probably thinking of a Satellite Truck," Ron explained. "This one uses microwaves. So, in theory, that's possible, but there would have to be a receiving station set up near wherever it was that you wanted to go live. In reality, this truck can transmit live from pretty much anywhere in Southern California."

"So you can edit and basically be a mobile production studio on wheels," said the Dad, peering in to look over the rack of equipment inside the van.

Ron nodded, "That's right, but with all the new technology that's out there, we soon won't need a big, cumbersome rig like this. We can already pretty much do it all with a lap-top and a backpack."

"Wow, that's pretty cool!" said the boy.

The man apologized for disturbing Ron's lunch, and he and his wife and son headed off to their car.

"No sweat," said Ron. "Have a good one."

A few minutes later, Superman, Marilyn Monroe, and Chewbacca walked by the truck, on their way to lunch. Marilyn waved. Celebrity impersonators from Grauman's need to eat, too. Ron smiled and when they had passed out of sight, shook his head and rolled his eyes. *Welcome to Hollywood,* he thought to himself, as he went back to his burger.

"Are you Ron?" asked an attractive young woman who had approached the van's open side door with two friends. The three were all dressed in smart business attire, dark suits and skirts, white, lacy blouses and short heels.

He was startled, and had just taken a sizeable bite, so he swallowed quickly, and wiped the sauce from his mouth with a napkin as gracefully as possible. He turned toward the women and answered, "Yes, that's me. Do I know you?"

"You were at the news conference a few weeks ago at the Observatory, for the new electric vehicle, the Gen-Lex." she said. "I met you there. I'm the Public Relations rep, Sandra Thorne."

She offered her hand. "Oh, and these are my friends, Carol and Julie."

Sandra was young, probably about thirty, with shoulder-length honey blonde hair and a fetching smile. Once she removed her oversized sunglasses and placed them on her head, he immediately recognized her stunning green eyes. He recalled thinking at the time how he'd never before seen eyes that color. She reminded him of Katherine Heigl. Or maybe Keira Knightley. Or a young Meg Ryan. He couldn't decide.

"Oh, I remember now," he said, looking her over. "Nice to see you, how are you?"

"I'm good," replied Sandra. "I thought I recognized you. I remember you and the other cameramen up there at the Observatory were looking out at the Hollywood sign and talking about how some people walking their dog had found a human head near there the previous day."

"Yeah," Ron acknowledged. "That was pretty weird. Sorry if we grossed you out."

"Well," she said, smiling. "Some of the jokes were pretty tasteless, but they were funny.

"Anyway, I wanted to tell you that I watched your story about the new engine, and you did a terrific job. We've gotten lots of calls from people who saw it."

"That's great," said Ron. "It's always nice to know people are watching. And it was your interview that made the story."

"I was going to call you, you know, to thank you, but you never gave me your card," she said.

Ron reached over the passenger's seat and picked up his bag. He retrieved one of his business cards and handed it to Sandra.

She reached in her purse and removed one of her cards for him.

"Well," she said. "Got to get back to work. Nice seeing you."

"Likewise. Have a good day," replied Ron, as he watched Sandra and her friends walk over to Julie's silver Jetta. Sandra got in the passenger's seat and Carol climbed in the back. Julie started the car and drove slowly off the lot.

*****

SANDRA THORNE
Public Relations Representative
Holliday and Weber
6430 Sunset Blvd. Suite 420
Hollywood, CA 90028

"*The CNN Building,*" he thought to himself, as he put the card in a slot in his carry-all and turned his attention back to his lunch.

Ron still had had plenty of time left of his lunch hour, and started looking at the current Sports Illustrated Magazine he'd brought to work. He had just begun reading the story about the upcoming NFL Draft. Green Bay had the fifth selection this year and was looking at a star tight end from LSU as a possible first round selection. Suddenly, his downtime was interrupted by the sound of the scanner radio:

"Engine, Rescue and Squad 27, Light Force 52, Task Force 35 with an Air-bag, EMS and Battalion 5, respond to the Jumper, 5980 Sunset, cross of Vine. Sunset and Vine, a female on the roof of the bank building. This is a Channel 7 Dispatch- Your TAC Channel is 12."

Of course, there was no reason at all for Ron to respond to the emergency call, and plenty of reasons not to. He was still on a break, and people jumping off buildings were rarely newsworthy. But curiosity got the better of him, so he shut the doors, moved to the front seat and started the engine. Ron often treated emergency calls like this as a game, a challenge- aware that he was no more than a mile from the bank building, about the same distance as was Fire Station 27. He always liked to see if he could get to an emergency location before the first responders arrived on scene. He crumbled up his In-N-Out wrapper and tossed it in the plastic trashcan behind the driver's seat.

All of the tri-lights were in his favor on this one, and the light mid-day traffic through Hollywood helped him get to the corner of Sunset and Vine in about three and a half minutes. As he passed through the intersection, he looked in his side mirror and saw Engine 27 a couple of hundred yards behind him, lights and sirens on, followed by the station's Rescue Ambulance.

Ron passed the bank building, a 22-story structure, on his right, just east of the intersection. He proceeded down the block slowly, and made a quick u-turn at Argyle, then parked facing west on Sunset just in front of the Coffee Bean. He stepped out of the van, grabbed his camera and began walking slowly down the sidewalk back toward Vine Street, amongst the throng of pedestrians. A few were looking and pointing upward, but most were only now, with the sound of the sirens, becoming aware of the situation developing around them.

Ron kept his eye on the activity across the street, but was still too far away to get a good look at the person on the roof. Even though this story had most likely absolutely no news value, and he never raised the camera to his shoulder, Ron thought it would be interesting to watch how the fire crew set up and positioned the air bag that he'd heard dispatched. He'd only seen them used in movies, and knew that there had to be a bit more to it in real life when it came to rescuing people intent on throwing themselves from a skyscraper.

Traffic slowed, then stopped. Traffic officers had closed off Sunset in both directions. Hearing the excitement, people began spilling out into the street from The Coffee Bean and other businesses and offices near the bank building. Many had their cell-phone cameras ghoulishly trained upon the jumper, hoping to capture a video worthy of You-Tube.

As he neared the Emergency vehicles, now filling up a good portion of Sunset, he heard above the sound of the approaching sirens and the loud diesel engines, a Fire Captain on the radio, as he reported back to Dispatch:

"Control from Engine 27, on-scene of a 22-story high-rise, we have a female on the roof, we're standing by for Task Force 35. Have them stage to the north of the building on Sunset where we'll be deploying the air-bag. We'll need LAPD for crowd control."

"Roger, Engine 27. Task Force 35, stage on Sunset and prepare to deploy your Air-bag."

Ron looked up again and got a good look at the woman, tall and slim, with long, stringy black hair falling limply over her shoulders. She was wearing a flimsy cream-colored dress, almost a shawl, he thought, that was fluttering in the wind, and lightweight dark pants underneath. The woman appeared to be either Asian or Hispanic, and in her mid-twenties. She stood motionless, almost defiant, on the roof of the building, staring straight ahead toward the Hollywood Sign, on the hill a short distance away. She slowly scanned the streets below her, some of the most well-known avenues on the planet, from a perch few others would ever choose to occupy. Hearing the sirens, she glanced down incredulously at the flashing red and orange lights of the fire crews arriving on the scene.

Ron was sure that she had seen him too, for just an instant had locked eyes with him, and noticed him staring up at her. He was convinced that they had briefly made a connection, that she had somehow seen something in his eyes, something that softened her expression. He saw in her face a change, a sense of peace, and he felt her deep despair.

The siren of yet another responding rescue unit pierced the silence and the brief moment of peace was broken, their unspoken communication shattered. She stiffened her back. And her resolve.

The woman clearly did not want to be rescued, and just as L.A. Fire Department Truck 35 made the right turn from Vine onto Sunset, she chose to leave her perch.

*****

Ron had a vague memory of reading once in a college textbook about the human brain and what an amazing instrument it is, capable of untold and still undiscovered potential. Through its ability to suppress and manipulate feelings, as well as to manage senses, emotions, and memories, some experts say that the brain actually has the ability to control time, or at the very least, one's perception of time, perhaps even to predict the future. The sight of a human being plummeting 200 feet toward certain death, he discovered, has a bizarre effect upon one's ability to grasp and process reality.

*****

In a decade and a half on the streets as a photojournalist, Ron was sure that he'd seen it all. But he quickly discovered how different that is from seeing *everything*. Over the years, he'd become accustomed to witnessing the aftermath of vile and unspeakable crimes and accidents. He'd seen bodies in various stages of decomposition, people in demolished cars, or floating in rivers, or lying on pavement, bereft of life; corpses under vehicles, their organs and viscera spread across the roadway; the bodies of children, limp and lifeless, wrapped in bloody sheets, being carried from murder scenes. He'd become calloused and desensitized more than any normal, healthy person should be, to the loss of life. But this was different. She was still alive, and the concept of life as something precious, and death as something preventable and eternal, had not yet been entirely erased from his reality by this hideous business he worked in.

Ron stood motionless and stared. He couldn't *not* stare. The few seconds that it took for this poor soul to impact the street felt like minutes, during which time, his consciousness performed contortions such as he'd never experienced.

Witnessing her dénouement, his mouth agape, the first thoughts to cross his mind were completely irrational and illogical: *"I can catch her, I can save her, I can talk her out of this!" "Where are the fucking Firemen? Get the GODDAMN AIRBAG SET UP!"* Then, in the span of just moments, the synapses in his brain seemed to conduct a lengthy philosophical dialogue with themselves about life, death, grief, pain, and what could have and should have been done to prevent what he was witnessing right there before his eyes.

"This woman is living! Breathing! Someone can stop this! SHE CAN'T FUCKING DIE IN FRONT OF ME!" his mind screamed angrily and silently. Suddenly, with an audible thud, came the realization that nothing would, or could, come to this young woman's rescue. Ron stood frozen.

✳✳✳✳✳

"Control from Battalion Five, Cancel all assisting units. Subject has left the roof."

Ron must have been completely pale a minute later, as he slowly approached the Battalion Chief on the street in front of the bank, his camera still hanging by his side.

"Sir, I'm with, umm, Channel 6, and, uhh, I just saw what happened if you should need a witness."

"Thanks, but I think we've got this," replied the Chief matter-of-factly. "Did you want something on camera?"

"Oh, uh, no thanks. But do we know anything about the woman?"

"Well," the Chief answered, walking to the rear of his SUV, "She appears to be the same woman we talked down from this spot about two months ago." Ron watched as paramedics hurriedly covered the bloodied body with a yellow plastic sheet. "She had lost her child and her marriage had ended. We'd hoped that we could help her out, maybe get her some therapy, but it seems she was pretty determined."

"Thanks, sir." Ron muttered, as he returned to his van, never raising his eyes from the pavement in front of him. He walked in numbed silence through the muttering crowd, hearing nothing at all but the booming, silent throb of his own pulse in his ears. He hoped that no one noticed him wipe the moisture from his cheeks as he opened the van's door.

Ron drove the short distance back to the station and walked slowly up to the Assignment area. He couldn't escape the thought of what the jumper must have felt inside; to care for another person, and to feel their loss so inexorably that your own life becomes meaningless. How is that even possible?

Noticing his reddened eyes and somber demeanor, Maggie asked if he felt OK.

"Yeah, I guess so," he said, not wishing to explain, "I'll be fine."

*****

The scheduled interview with the City Councilman was still a no-go, so Ron's only other assignment was to shoot some web sites off the station library's computer for a story that Investigative Reporter Maria Lopez was working on involving Real Estate fraud. Afterwards he packed up and put his truck away for the night, his head still spinning from the developments of the day.

It had all started off so well, with an assignment that most men would kill for. How many of them, after all, climb in their cars day after day, and drive past the SYT photo studio, never realizing that their fantasies are just on the other side of the smoked glass doors? It wasn't lost on Ron that most of them would gladly trade places with him, to put aside their routines to work his job and experience his life just long enough for a morning of sensuous and provocative photographic images.

But those images, in Ron's mind, had suddenly been eclipsed by those of a live human being, floating in air for a few short seconds on her way to eternity.

Ron's emotions were raw and tapped out. He walked slowly through the garage quietly re-thinking his perspective on life. He sat quietly behind the wheel of his Mustang in the dark, secluded garage, assessing his priorities, the past, the future, and the things he had determined to be of value. *If only I could have met that woman before today, what could I have said to her? Could I have helped her? Could she have helped me to understand?*

After several minutes, Ron was startled back to reality by Gretchen's Jaguar passing loudly behind him. He glanced up, saw her taillights in the mirror and wondered further about the lifetime of choices he'd made that brought him to this moment. Heaving a sigh, he fastened his seatbelt, revved his engine and headed out once again into the bright lights of Hollywood.

The drive home that night was different. Ron heard nothing. No talk, no traffic, no radio. No inner voices.

Straight home to an empty apartment. No TV. No conversation. Dead silence. Just therapeutic, vacant, quiet space. He heated up a frozen pizza, choked it down with a Seven-up and went to bed.

*****

The Cameraman suddenly sat up in his bed, gasping for breath, covered in sweat. After a few moments, he glanced at the clock on the nightstand. It was 2:53 AM.

"Fuck." he said, breathing a heavy sigh, and slamming his forearm down across the bed. "Fuck." He turned over and tried to lose The Image and get a few more hours of desperately needed sleep, but he knew full well that his mind would replay this scene a hundred times for him over the next few months.

The Image.   His mind's photograph, from hours earlier.   The Image.

A female form, completely exposed to him in its most helpless and vulnerable state, her eyes meeting his for but a split second, an unspoken communication and ultimate attachment, forever burned into his mind.

The Image. Hovering. Suspended in flight. The unheard scream.

Replaying over and over incessantly, like a dreadful song stuck in his head. He stared at the shadows on the ceiling and struggled to catch his breath.

Of all the images that had passed through his eyes that day, this was the one he couldn't shake.

God knows it was not the one he would have chosen.

Chapter Three:

DISCOVERY

Monday, February 17th

Shelby was at the station early, sitting in a comfortable black swivel chair behind the thick glass door in the office of Leo Joseph, the long-time news director of Channel Six. Leo was a stocky man in his mid-fifties, with thinning, wavy brown hair, gray at the temples, the wrinkles on his broad face rutted deep by years of news-stress and alcohol. He was well respected in the industry, having worked his way up in a relatively short time, from news assistant and assignment editor in Salt Lake City to Managing Editor at the network affiliate in Denver. He was the obvious choice of station management to replace Frank Benz as news director about six years ago, when Benz finally decided to hang it up.

Leo had immediately taken the station into the 21st century. As soon as the budget allowed, he brought in an all-new infrastructure, as well as digital, high-definition cameras, fully computerized editing equipment, and of course, a new, futuristic-looking news set. The station's website was completely remade to become infinitely more user-friendly. His reputation as a visionary was proven out and, up until last year, the station's rating had never been higher.

Leo consistently showed that he was not afraid to take chances. He'd been known to enthusiastically approve going after stories, even occasionally those that did not pan out, wasting hundreds of dollars in the process.

Like the time a reporter and cameraman were flown all the way to Seattle on a phone tip about a Good Samaritan, who had supposedly saved a man from an armed robbery and ended up in the hospital. The caller sold it as a great story; Family man witnesses a crime, selflessly stops to help, and almost loses his life.

When they arrived in Seattle after a two-and-a-half hour flight, reporter Barbara Sterling visited the hospital and proceeded to interview the hero on camera. Though still bruised and beaten up, George Loomis was lucid enough to sit up in his hospital bed and tell his story in great detail. Loomis was, he claimed, walking to his car after work, when he overheard a struggle and saw a man with a knife robbing an older gentleman on the sidewalk outside a store. He ran over, jumped in and interrupted the robbery, only to be punched and kicked several times by the assailant, who ran away without taking any of the victim's money or valuables.

After the interview, Barbara and her cameraman shook hands with George, wished him well, and drove in their rented Chevy to the scene of the alleged robbery. The intersection described by Loomis was, it turned out, in the grimiest industrial port area of the city, populated by derelicts and homeless, and the "store" he described was actually Jacoby's, a 1940's era bar known over the years to the police for crime and unrest. It took very little investigation for Barbara to learn that the previous evening, Loomis had been at Jacoby's, and after a few beers, had mouthed off to a couple of strangers, whom he did not recognize as regulars, and had gotten his ass handed to him. Pretty simple bar-fight, cut and dried. No drama, no news story.

Barbara phoned Leo and told him that his tip had not panned out, and there was no story to be had there. Leo listened intently and ultimately agreed, and Sterling and her cameraman were on a plane back to Burbank that afternoon, sans world exclusive.

Upper Management could not have been happy with Leo's decision to fly a crew out of town 'on spec', but it was decisions like that one which earned him the reputation he enjoyed as the most creative and imaginative news director in the city.

Every few months, Leo would issue a memo, asking staff to submit their ideas and suggestions for 'sweeps' stories for the next ratings period. This led to some wonderful, creative stories, helping the stations ratings and winning them numerous awards.

He'd often brought in people who lacked experience in the business of television news, but were experts in other fields, and turned them in to 'specialists', reporters who knew volumes about what they were reporting - be it law enforcement, business, politics, fashion or a dozen other fields. Though lacking in on-camera skills, he believed that real people, who had experienced life from their own unique perspective, could often report on stories in a much more credible and understandable way than someone whose experience was limited to Journalism School. He was convinced that being on TV was the easiest thing a 'specialist' ever had to learn.

But times were changing in the news business. The days of the specialist were quickly coming to an end. Television journalists, now often simply referred to as "Content Providers", or "Multi-Media Journalists" were expected to perform every facet of the job. This had been the norm in smaller market cities and non-union stations for some time, but was beginning to creep into major markets like Los Angeles as well. Cameramen had, for a generation, already worked as one-man bands, performing all the tasks of the lighting technicians and soundmen who at one time accompanied them on assignment. Reporters were now often expected to write, produce, edit and shoot video for their stories. New hires, like Shelby, having learned all those skills in college, were slowly replacing the old-school reporters, and would eventually become the new standard. This allowed the stations to cut back on staff, saving precious dollars in a medium being challenged for viewership by all forms of entertainment and 'new media'. Rumors were already circulating that under orders from the network bosses, a significant number of layoffs were pending and a sense of dread had begun looming over the newsroom.

Shelby was to have been one of Leo's long-term projects. Although she was terribly inexperienced in TV news, and in life, he nevertheless saw something in her that he was willing to work with, something that in time he felt he could mold into an asset. He'd seen her resume video and knew that she had the technical and writing skills for the job and over time, he hoped that the "street-smarts" would come. But she had come into his office to let him know that this job was not for her, she missed her family and would be heading back to Delaware.

"I watched your live shot the other night, Shelby," said Leo. "I saw a lot of promise."

"What you didn't see," she replied, "was my knees shaking and the sweat running down my back. I just didn't want to be there."

"Look, that's completely normal on your first live shot. You did a lot better than some people." Leo reached for the stack of resumes on his desk. "I could show you some video of…"

"Reporting is just not in my blood," Shelby interrupted. "I don't belong out there. If it hadn't been for Ron, I would have crashed and burned the other day. I made stupid mistakes and was completely unprepared. I'm so sorry to disappoint you and Larry, and I do thank you for the opportunity, but I really think I should go."

Leo exhaled deeply, sat back in his chair, and shook his head, realizing that the battle was lost. They stood up and Leo opened the door. After they shook hands, Shelby walked out of the office, past the red Take a Number dispenser Leo had placed outside, and across the newsroom to her newly assigned desk. She picked up her bag, looked around the room for a few seconds, and left.

At around the same time, Ron had just arrived at the Los Angeles Zoo, on the eastern side of Griffith Park, just off the Golden State Freeway, about 15 minutes from the station. A press release had been sent out announcing a scheduled 10am news conference to introduce some newborn koalas, and he was thirty minutes early. Cute animal stories were always good for slow news days, when stations could use shots of cuddly baby monkeys or other furry creatures to fill the holes in their newscasts. Often though, the zoo animals became expendable when real news occurred and were the first stories to be cut from the newscast, much to the disappointment of the zoo personnel who looked at the stories as free advertising. They liked the chance to remind the public that Los Angeles still has a zoo and that attendance was needed to keep the residents and their keepers fed.

He pulled the van into the spacious, empty parking lot and called the contact number, which was still in his phone's memory, though he hadn't brought it up in several months.

"Los Angeles Zoo, Linda Haley speaking."

"Hey Linda, it's Ron… Ron Sharp. From Channel Six."

"Ron, how are you?"

"Good. I'm here for the baby koalas," he said. "Can you send out an escort?"

"Of course, I'll be right there."

Linda jumped up from her desk and adjusted her hair as she walked swiftly toward the administration office door, as if fearful that another employee would open the gate for him first.

Ron unpacked his gear and walked toward the locked admission gate, which would remain unmanned for another half hour until the Zoo's normal opening time. He could hear the electric cart making its way on the cobblestones from the zoo office to the gate and looked up to see Linda smiling broadly as she drove up the red concrete footpath.

"Nice to see you," she said, unlocking the steel fence and sliding the gate open, "How have you been?"

"Oh, you know, same stuff, different day."

"Well, climb aboard and let's go see some baby koalas."

Linda had been one of the docents at the zoo for the past four years, a familiar face to the camera crews whenever there was a media event. Her long, sandy blonde hair was usually tied back in a ponytail and her demeanor clearly conveyed a fun-loving, carefree tomboy who had the job she'd always wanted.

About a year earlier, Ron had repeatedly asked her to lunch, knowing that their schedules were both unpredictable and difficult. He was on the late night shift at the time, starting at three, and she worked nine to six every day. She turned him down a few times, but after seeing him repeatedly on shoots, and taking a few flirty phone calls, she finally relented and agreed to meet him for a quick bite before he went to work and during the short time she was able to actually get away from the compound for a bite.

They met at a little spot she liked in Toluca Lake and settled into a corner booth. Paty's had been there for years, well known to television and film people who worked at the studios in the Burbank area. Linda often spotted an actor, comedian, or TV star there, though she seldom knew their names, her interest in the media being minimal.

Fortunately, the wait for a table that day was only a few minutes, and for the next half hour, Linda and Ron shared stories of their childhoods and learned just how completely different their lives were.

He enjoyed hearing about how she had grown up in the San Gabriel Valley with lots of dogs and horses, even competing in some equestrian events as a teen, excelling in the steeplechase. She still carried a few photos of herself, taken years earlier with her Oldenberg, called Ditto.

"We won a roomful of ribbons and trophies that year," Linda said. "She was quite a horse."

"Wow," Ron said. "That's pretty amazing. I'm guessing that took years of practice."

"It did," Linda agreed. "And I'd still be riding if I hadn't taken a bad fall and fractured my ankle in three places. I couldn't compete for an entire season. Kind of put an end to the whole dream."

"Oh, I'm sorry. But I can see where you got your love for animals."

"Yeah," she said. "I'm generally much more comfortable around them than I am with people. Does that make sense?"

"Sure it does," said Ron. "Believe me, I see the bad side of people every day. I understand completely."

"The only time I watch the news," she said, "is when I know the Zoo has a story on one of the newscasts. Otherwise, it's just too depressing. I don't know how you can do it."

"Well, I try not to get too jaded, but sometimes it's hard. That's why I really enjoy doing stories with you. Gives me a break from reality."

"That's where you're wrong," said Linda. "My world is reality. Yours is brutality and ugliness."

"I envy you in some ways," he said, gazing into her light brown eyes. "Sometimes I wish that I didn't know what I know about the world. That I hadn't seen the things I have. But it's all part of life, you know? You can't shelter yourself forever."

"Well, I'm going to try. I have my three dogs at home and aside from my other family of wild creatures at work, they're all I need."

Ron paid the bill, and they walked together out to their cars, both certain that, although there was a strong attraction at work there, they were destined to remain no more than friends.

*****

Linda pulled the electric cart around and parked it next to the Animal Care Center, a short distance from the entrance, which was kept closed to the public. There, the veterinary medical staff took care of the newborn animals as well as those otherwise in need of special attention. Outside, there were two medium-sized pens, lined with sawdust and grass and bordered by a wooden fence. Horses and other larger animals could be attended to there, while the smaller creatures were kept in the main medical building, across the shaded walkway. The well-appointed facility was comprised of several separate rooms, with large picture windows that allowed guests to observe the veterinary staff and animal residents without actually entering the near-sterile environment.

Ron hopped out of the cart, grabbed his gear and began walking toward the building, while Linda answered a call on her crackly two-way radio.

"I'll be right back," she said. "Channel 8's crew is here."

"OK, I know the drill. I'll be right here."

By the time Linda returned with the other camera crew, Ron had already been shooting video through the window of the baby koalas being bottle-fed by the staff.

"How cute is that?" he said. "I can't get enough of this."

Just then, Ron's cell began to ring, the familiar theme from Police Squad breaking the morning silence.

"Microvan 21 at your service," answered Ron, giving Linda a wink.

"Ronnie," shouted Maggie, excitedly. "Forget the koalas. They found a body in Calabasas, off of Mulholland. They're pretty sure it's the Nealey woman. Head up there before the coroner pulls it out. It's just off of Cold Canyon. Do you want a map page?"

"No thanks," he replied. "I think I can find it."

"Sorry, but I've gotta go," said Ron, frowning. "Back to death and destruction. Can I get a lift back to the entrance?"

"Umm, of course," said Linda, crestfallen. "Are you sure you have enough footage? Too bad you're going to miss the news conference. It doesn't start for another twenty minutes."

"Yeah, I think I've got plenty," he said, climbing back into her cart. "I'm glad I started shooting before you got back."

Ron said a quick hello to Barry Long, the veteran Channel 3 photographer who was setting up as they drove past him down the hill.

"What's going on? Breaking news?" Linda asked as their cart neared the entrance gate.

"Yep. I don't know if you heard about that missing woman they've been looking for out in Calabasas, but it looks like they may have located her body."

"Oh," she gasped. "I hadn't heard about that. That's just terrible."

"Yeah, I'd much rather stay here and hang with you and the koalas, but that's how things go."

"Ugh. Well, be safe, Ron," she said, as he grabbed his gear from the seat behind him. "It was good seeing you."

"You too, girl. Take care."

✳✳✳✳✳

By 11, when Ron arrived on scene, several other camera crews were already set up on tree-lined Mulholland Highway, just east of the crime scene. Mulholland was closed and blocked by a patrol car, but the deputy moved his vehicle to open a lane for the news van. Ron pulled up parallel to the black and white and rolled down his window.

"Morning, sir," he said.

"Good morning," replied the deputy, motioning with his thumb over his left shoulder. "You need to stay to the right and park off the pavement near the other vans. The PIO just arrived."

"Got it. Have a good day, sir."

Ron parked the microvan several hundred yards down the road, behind the blue Channel 8 truck.

"Microvan 21 is on location," he announced into the mike.

"Roger that, Micro 21 on location."

He quickly carried his gear over to join the other camera crews in the area that had been set aside for them and roped off by deputies with yellow crime-scene tape. From there, they had a good vantage point of the detectives who, with assistance from the Los Angeles County Fire Department, were using heavy ropes and pulleys to lower themselves over the steep ledge of the canyon road. Within an hour, crews from every television and radio station in town had arrived.

The remains lying in the brush some 20 feet down from the road, out of view of the cameras, were that of a female in her late twenties or early thirties, partially decomposed. It appeared that a large hammer or some other heavy object had been used to cave in her skull.

Initially, homicide detectives will secure the scene and rope off any areas they feel may contain evidence. They gingerly measure and photograph the location and the remains. Only after the arrival of the coroner, however, can the body of the deceased actually be moved in any significant way. At that time, it is thoroughly inspected to help determine, if possible, the exact cause and time of death, as well as identification of the deceased. Often, depending on the condition of the remains, it is not until much later, after an autopsy and a raft of toxicology tests are completed, that some crucial questions can be answered. In some cases, even determining the gender or race of the victim is not possible in the field, but only after tests have been conducted downtown.

Fortunately, the body in the ravine had not been exposed to the elements long enough to completely decompose. It was clearly that of a partially clad female adult with sandy blonde hair.

Later in the day, after more detectives had arrived, Lead Homicide Detective Bill Braden walked slowly over to the media area, which by now was packed with cameras from every local TV station, as well as print photographers and radio reporters.

"We're being extremely careful and thorough with this investigation," said Braden. "But I can give you some preliminary information, if you like."

The cameramen and reporters turned on their wireless microphones and scrambled to arrange themselves so as to have a good shot of the detective.

"Everyone ready?" asked Braden. Then he began.

"Bill Braden, Los Angeles County Sheriff's Department Homicide. This morning, a tip was received that led us to discover some human remains in the canyon here. The remains are in a flat area, about 20 feet down the side of the road. The body is that of a female, and the clothing appears to match that in the description of our missing woman, Jennifer Nealey. We believe, based upon that tip, and the evidence at the scene, that this is, in fact Jennifer Nealey, however it will be up to the coroner to make the final identification. The cause of death seems, at this time, to be blunt force trauma to the head. We believe that she was killed at another location and her body taken here and dumped."

"This morning, Deputies arrested Peter Nealey at his home, and have charged him with the murder of his wife. We also have in custody a woman, a Debra Vaughn, of Agoura Hills, who we believe at this time to have been the actual killer. We believe that Mr. Nealey was in a relationship with Miss Vaughn at the time of the killing, and the two of them entered into a conspiracy to murder Ms. Nealey. We expect that they will be arraigned tomorrow or Thursday. That's all I have for you right now."

"Bill! Who called in the tip?"

"How long has she been there?"

Reporters were peppering Braden with questions as he walked away, prompting him to briefly turn back in their direction. "We'll have more information for you later this evening or tomorrow, but for now, that's all I've got."

While they waited, Ron checked in with Maggie at the assignment desk.

"They seem pretty certain that it's the Nealey woman," he said. "But this could go on for a few more hours before they bring her up."

"OK, well hang in there so we don't miss the body shot. Is the coroner there yet?"

"Nope, but they should be getting here any time now."

"Alright, I'm just hoping we can get something on the air by four." Maggie said. "I'll try to send you another crew to help out, but…"

"Lemme guess," interrupted Ron. "You're short cameramen again today."

"Pretty much, yeah," Maggie said, scrunching her nose.

"I'll call you as soon as I can get out of here and feed," he said.

"Alright, and we've got aerials and file for the early show. Just do the best you can."

"Sure will. Bye."

"Pathetic," Ron muttered to himself, placing the cell phone back in his pocket.

Next, Ron texted Steve to tell him that it looked like the missing woman's body had been found.

```
Ron: Looks lk they found
that missing woman In Calabasas-
Dead. Husband arrested. Toldja
fuckin nut-bags think they can
get away w/ this kind of shit
and Shelby and I were in the house w/ him
how insane is that?

                    Steve: Lets get a drink
                    tonight.  Take the edge
                    off a bit

Ron: Sounds grt. I cn use one.

                    Steve: Ill meet you
                    @ the Pony?


Ron: working some OT on this
```

The investigation stretched on for several more hours, with homicide detectives and crime scene technicians measuring everything several times and photographing the scene from every conceivable angle. Crime reports and evidence forms had been filled out in great detail until the investigators were confident that absolutely nothing had been overlooked, knowing full well that a good defense attorney would challenge every possible aspect of their evidence gathering in what was sure to be a high-profile case.

The news photographers had shot pretty much everything they could shoot when the Coroner's van arrived on scene and parked down past the patrol cars near the ledge. The coroner's technician spoke with detectives for a few minutes before, assisted by the Fire Department, climbing down to inspect the body.

Finally, the coroner's technicians pulled the gurney down into the ravine, signaling to the camera crews the impending 'money shot'. After about ten minutes of prepping and wrapping the body, and securing it firmly to the stretcher, they began to pull it up the steep hill and onto the road. There, as photographers shot video and snapped photos, they transferred the remains, wrapped in a dark blue body bag, from the litter to a wheeled gurney and loaded it into the rear of the white Coroner's van.

The cameramen and reporters packed up their gear and returned to their trucks, some to head back toward L.A. and others, the ones with Satellite transmission trucks, to set up for live shots.

"Channel Six Newsroom."

"Hey, it's Ron. Can I get Maggie, please?"

"Sure, hold on."

"Hey, Ronnie- What's up?"

"Got the body-shot. So I'm pretty much wrapped here."

"So is the body, I'm guessing."

"That's pretty funny, Maggie. You should do stand-up."

"That's more than she can do."

"OK, OK. So what do you want with this video?" he asked, trying to be serious.

"Alright," she said. "So you've got the whole package, wrapped up with a bow. So, get the video fed in. It's almost five and the producer's been waiting. They want it ASAP."

"Well, I can't feed it from here," answered Ron. "But I'll go find a spot where I can get a signal in."

For all the hours Ron had spent at the scene, there was relatively little video to be shipped in to the station. A few establishing shots of the scene, the sound bite with Braden, the detectives at work and the body being brought up and loaded into the van, and he was done. Everything, including the few shots of the baby koalas, was in house by 5:45 and Ron was headed back to L.A.

*****

Ron got back to the studio and took a minute to sit briefly with Jen Kuroda, the writer assigned to the story, filled her in with details and reminded her that he and Shelby had gotten an interview with Peter Nealey at his home a few days earlier.

"Yeah," said Jen. "You heard about Shelby, right?"

"What about Shelby?"

"Rumor is she quit. After one day."

"Really? Any idea why?"

"Just rumors," she said. "Nobody knows for sure."

"Hmm, interesting," Ron replied. "Thanks for that."

＊＊＊＊＊

Ron left the station at almost eight and drove about two miles up Cahuenga Blvd, to the Dog and Pony. He pulled into the crowded lot that the bar shared with a manicure salon, a tax service, and a Chipotle restaurant. It was perfect that Steve had suggested they get together, since the last thing Ron wanted was another night alone. Looking around the parking lot, he recognized Steve's black Ford pickup, and parked his mustang a few spaces away.

Walking into the noisy, crowded bar, Ron found Steve sitting in a group of other cops and cameramen, at what was clearly, a celebration. From the stacked-up plates of wings and near-empty pitchers on the table, it was clear that they had been there a while.

"What? Did you forget Phil's birthday?" shouted Paul Lewis, another photographer from Channel 8.

"Oh, I guess I did," answered Ron, looking apologetic as he walked over to the next table over to shake Phil's hand. "Happy birthday, Bro."

"Hey, sit down, have a beer." said Phil.

Phil Loudin had been a cameraman for Channel 8 for close to thirty years and was approaching retirement. He had informally invited friends and colleagues to celebrate his 63rd birthday, and at least a couple of dozen had shown up. Ron vaguely remembered responding to an email to RSVP a few weeks earlier, but was now embarrassed to have gotten busy and forgotten to at least bring a bottle of booze for his friend.

Ron pulled up a chair and placed it between Steve and his pal Greg Rodgers, an L.A. County Deputy Sheriff, also known as "Grog". His buddies had nicknamed him that because of his appetite for copious amounts of beer he enjoyed in his off time. He was an expert, really. Knew pretty much everything there was to know about the brewing process, what made beers taste different, what to look for in a foreign brand or micro-brew, everything. This knowledge made him extremely popular with his brothers in law enforcement, who often joined him for weekends on his boat at Lake Havasu, Lake Mead, or just nearby Castaic.

Also at the table sat Jessica Heller, longtime reporter for KFLC Radio, and Robin Russo, a female camera operator who worked with Gary at Channel 8. Upon spotting Robin, Ron rushed over to her side of the table and greeted her with a warm hug.

"How are you feeling, Girl?" he asked, still holding her tight.

"I'm OK," Robin replied in her deep, unmistakably sultry voice, "I've been back to work for almost a month. The Doctor says I'm completely clear, totally in remission."

"I just can't tell you how happy I am," he said, looking into her eyes, "I prayed for you more than I ever have for anything in my life."

"Well," she replied, smiling and kissing him on the cheek, "It must've worked. I'm back and I'm not going anywhere."

"See that you don't," he said, loosening his grip and returning to his chair, along the wall festooned with headshots of celebrities and broadcasters who frequented the place.

"Fuck cancer," she said.

There was an impressive turnout, with several other tables at the "Pony" also filled with Phil's friends and colleagues, but the loud music made it hard to include them in a conversation.

"I heard one of your reporters quit this week, Ron," said Jessica.

"Really," answered Ron, playing dumb. "And who would that be?"

"Some new gal, Shirley or something."

"Shelby?"

"Yeah, that's it. I heard she hated working with you," joked the slightly tipsy Robin.

"That must have been it," said Ron. "Where'd you hear all this?"

Robin pointed with her half empty beer across the room to where Teddy Beamon was waving his arms, sucking down a Corona and weaving tales of his helicopter heroics.

"Ah," said Ron, quickly looking down. "Don't believe everything you hear."

"Teddy said she was really green anyway. Says he can't understand how she got the job in the first place. Said it was probably her tits," said Jess, grinning devilishly.

"Well," said Ron, coming to Shelby's defense. "We've had much worse reporters in this town, and not just at our place either."

"I'll agree with that," slurred Phil, who probably should have quit drinking about four beers ago. "Remember that Lauren Brown chick at Channel 10? There was this one time I remember, when she was working the Morning News show, and there was a fatal wreck up on the 210 freeway. She was doing a live report, and joking around with the 'happy-talk' anchors about her wardrobe or some bullshit, and didn't even realize that they were wheeling a dead body to the van right behind her while she's laughing and shit, live on the air. I heard the station got tons of complaints on that one."

"How about that new Entertainment chick over at Channel 3, Misty something," added Robin. "She spotted Katie Holmes at a Red Carpet event

I was at a few weeks ago, and kept shouting 'Miss Perry! Miss Perry!' I about fell off the riser, I was laughing so hard. Where do they find these people?"

"Hey, that could happen to anybody," Ron said. "Like me. I'm a dope when it comes to stars' names."

"I suppose so," said Robin. "But you're not an entertainment reporter."

"Well," said Ron, leaning in and picking up his glass, "without a doubt the dumbest reporter I ever worked with was a guy named Carl Castle, who worked with us a few years ago.

"I remember one Sunday, a few days after Christmas," he began. The waitress interrupted, asking if anyone needed a refill. Robin and Steve held out their glasses. "Anyway," Ron continued, "there had been a fire in an apartment house, in a poor part of town, East L.A. or someplace. It was caused by faulty wiring of a Christmas tree, or candles, or something like that. A young child was killed in the fire and the family lost their home. Poor immigrant family, a real tragedy."

"So, we show up the next morning and I start shooting the outside of the place, and you can see where the apartment up on the second floor is just totally gutted," Ron said, motioning up to the ceiling. "What's left of the tree is still there, burned to a crisp, with the presents still wrapped underneath it, all burned up. The walls are charred through and the whole place has smoke and water damage."

"We look up, and the Dad is sweeping the place up, trying to find any trace of his belongings that he can salvage. He's a poor immigrant, dressed in whatever shabby clothes he has left, guy hardly speaks any English, but our boy Carl yells up to him 'Excuse me, sir! Can we talk to you? We're from Channel 6 News!'

"Well, the poor guy was still in shock, and probably had no idea that it would have been perfectly fine for him to tell us to fuck off and leave him the hell alone, but before you know it, Carl and I are in the guy's house, or what's left of it, and he's sitting on the edge of his dead kid's bed, answering questions from a dumb-ass reporter."

The waitress came over with a new plate of wings for the table and retrieved the empty ones, briefly interrupting Ron's story once again.

"Now, you'd think that if he had a shred of human decency," he continued, "that a reporter would try to sympathize with the man, ease his pain a bit. But no, not Carl. First thing he asks him? 'So, how did your daughter die, exactly?'"

"He didn't!" interrupted Robin.

"I swear it's true," said Ron, rolling his eyes and waving his glass in her direction, "But it gets better. The dad is beside himself with grief, understandably. He tells us, 'She was here in this bed, and they say she inhaled too much smoke.' So, then Carl asks him, 'So, besides your daughter, what else did you lose in the fire?' I swear I almost turned the camera off and ripped his throat out."

"What did the guy say?" asked Jessica, shaking her head.

"He was sobbing, and he said that they had lost everything. If I didn't know better, I'd have thought that Carl was being an asshole on purpose to get the guy to cry on camera, but I don't think he was smart enough to be that devious."

"So, anyway, I'm ready to end the interview, when Genius decides to ask one more question. Get this, he says to the guy, 'So, the kids you have left, how are they doing?' I swear to you, I almost threw him down the stairs. The guy was inconsolable, sobbing on the bed, unable to answer the question. I just turned off the camera and walked out of there.

"Later, in his live shot, I remember, he described the destruction as 'Mucho Damaaaaaj'. He was gone soon after that, thank God. I think he's working in Albuquerque or something now."

"Yeah, there have been some dumb ones, that's for sure," said Jessica, sipping her beer and running her fingers through her long, brown hair. "They seem to be everywhere. Not everyone knows how to deal with people."

"But you know what," interrupted Phil, half in the bag, leaning in on his elbows toward Steve, "I've run across some idiot cops, too. They need to know how to deal with people, too. *News* people."

"Well…" said Ron, trying quickly to think of something to say to keep the conversation from going sideways.

"I can't tell you," interrupted Phil, slurring his words and trying his hardest to keep his eyes open, "how many times I've been at a crime-scene, and people from the neighborhood are all walking around, up and down the fuckin' streets, but as soon as I pull up, the cops get all jittery, like their sphincters tighten up. 'You can't be here! You've got to move down to the next block!', shit like that. When did we become the fuckin' enemy, anyway? It's like they've never even read 409.5.

"I never used to argue with them, but now I don't give a shit anymore. I'll get right in the cop's face and tell him what a shame it is that I know the goddamn law better than he does. At my age, fuck it. Go ahead and arrest me. That'll make the news and embarrass you more than anything else I could do."

Steve and Grog had to admit that most officers had a different view of the media than they did.

"All I know," said Grog, "is that they never taught us much in the Academy about how to deal with you guys, except that you were pretty much there to get us on camera doing something wrong whenever you could. I still think the majority of you would embarrass a cop on the news in a New York minute if you had the chance."

"Oh, Man," said Phil, sounding more and more trashed. "That's such bullshit! If you guys respect us, we respect you back, for the most part."

Seated at the next table, amongst the other photogs and reporters, was Rich Baker, retired LAPD Sergeant and Channel 6's Police Specialist. He had been another of Leo's 'projects', but one who had worked out successfully. Rich had been a Public Information Officer for the Department, so, despite the fact he had no television reporting experience, the transition to reporting on crime and police matters on the news was natural one for him.

Fortuitously, he had started at the station just prior the L.A. Riots. The afternoon that the uprising broke out, right after the Rodney King verdicts were announced, KSIX management made the decision to cover the story wall to wall, the same as every other news outlet in Los Angeles. Canceling all Network programming, the station stayed on the air, and Rich reported nonstop from the helicopter throughout the first night and the following day. While the city burned, Channel Six had the advantage of a retired officer's trained eye above the mayhem.

At one point, late in the evening, while the chopper was hovering over an angry mob at Vermont and Manchester, Rich asked the anchor, Charles Hughes, if he could see, from their picture, the flashes of light in the crowd some 400 feet below the helicopter. Charles said that he could, but barely.

"Well," Rich said. "Those are not flashbulbs. They're gunshots. And if what you see looks like straight lines, what that means is that the shots are traveling parallel to the ground. If, however, you see flashing dots, then those are shots that are headed toward us."

Fortunately, only one of those shots actually hit the chopper, and had failed to cause any serious damage, although Rich and his cameraman were both sitting on bullet-proof vests the whole time.

The reaction from the public was gratifying to management. The demeanor and professionalism of their new reporter, along with his expertise, helped to eventually sweep the station to number one in the ratings.

Rich had retired from Law Enforcement after a severe back injury. He joked that he had hurt himself while on-duty, pulling a burning van full of nuns back from the edge of a cliff, but the truth was that it had happened moving a large piece of furniture at home. He took his twenty-year retirement from LAPD at age 42 and began his new career at Channel 6. Now in his late sixties, he had a seemingly never-ending supply of stories to tell, either about police work, or his life in news. That, and his nature as a practical joker made him one of Ron's favorite colleagues.

Rich had overheard the squabble between Phil and the cops at Ron's table, and came over to introduce himself. Steve and Grog both recognized him immediately from his years on the air and jumped up to greet him.

"Hey, brother," Grog said, "I love your work. It's nice to have someone on our side out there."

Ron stood up and shook his old friend's hand.

"How's it goin' Rich?" he asked. "We haven't worked together in a while…"

"Good, how are things with you?"

"Livin' the Dream, Baby," said Ron. "Livin' the fuckin' dream."

Rich immediately started regaling the deputies with tales from his long, storied history. Like the time he and his copper pals kidnapped Ralph, the German Shepherd mascot from the Sheriff's station in Lennox, and dyed his fur pink before returning him to the station.

Just then, an inebriated Teddy Beaman was saying his good nights and leaving the bar. From across the noisy, crowded room, they all heard him, loud and clear.

"Early call, tomorrow, everyone. Gotta go. See you from above! Don't do anything nasty, I can see in your windows!" He staggered over and shook hands with Phil, and wished him a happy birthday.

"See you out there, Buddy." Teddy then walked out with his arm draped over his girlfriend-du-jour, whom everyone hoped was old enough to be his designated driver.

Phil walked haltingly to the door with Teddy and the two man-hugged

"You be careful up there, Bud."

"Always, my man," replied Teddy. "There's no other way."

"What's the deal with that Beaman guy?" asked Grog.

"You mean 'the Demon'?" answered Ron, everyone at the table laughing. "How much time have you got? I could tell you stories all night about that guy. Dude's got a death wish. I won't fly with him anymore. Hardly anyone will. And I used to enjoy shooting aerials for the station, but ever since he had his license pulled for endangering firefighters, I refuse to go up."

"I heard about that," said Robin. "He was flying too low?"

"Yeah," replied Ron. "It was about two years ago. There was this huge fire, at a four-story hotel in Long Beach. We could see the smoke as soon as we passed over the Hollywood sign. It was roaring."

"So, we call in to the station, tell them we're en route, and they break into programming and put us on the air about ten minutes early, before the five o'clock show started. We're over this thing in a matter of minutes and I've got amazing flames, as high as you've ever seen. The building was probably eighty years old, at least, and all wood construction, filled with furniture and carpet, nothing but fuel."

"We're live over this thing for about a half-hour, with Teddy reporting and talking like he's an expert on fire-fighting. So then, he decides to get a closer look at how they're fighting the fire from inside the building. He drops down to an altitude of about 100 feet, just above the power lines, and the chopper is now fanning the flames. The Fire Captain inside told me later that they were never in fear for their lives until we dropped down like that. The noise from the chopper interfered with their communications, and the rotor wash spread the smoke throughout the building, making it impossible to see, so he and his crew had to run out of the building to escape."

"The Fire Department lodged a formal complaint against him, and Channel 6. The FAA took away his pilot's license. He appealed, apologized, and claimed temporary mental deficiency or something, and he got his license and his job back after a few months. I learned a lot from him, granted, but I still won't fly with the crazy bastard."

"That's a guy who is headed for jail someday," said Rich. "If he doesn't kill himself first. And I've got stories about his personal life that would curl your hair."

"Some other time," said Steve, getting up to use the restroom.

Rich Baker began telling them about how he covered the OJ Simpson case, from Day One- the homicide, the freeway chase, the trial. That was the trial that really put him on the map. Stationed at "Camp OJ", across the street from the Criminal Courts Building downtown, Rich was the live-shot reporter for many of the network affiliates across the country. This involved live reports as early as 5am in L.A. for the East coast stations, and throughout the day, into the afternoon for dozens of other affiliates newscasts. After the nine-month trial, most the population of the country likely had seen Rich's face on TV at least once. Rich was in the middle of a story about Johnnie Cochran, when Phil stumbled back to the table, fresh Budweiser in his hand, ready for a fight.

"So let me tell you about this asshole cop I ran into last week," he said, slurring his words. Rich, Steve, Ron, and Grog all looked at each other, as if to say "Here we go."

"We get this call," Phil continued, motioning furiously, "of a car over the side of the road, off of Beverly Glen. I'm on the West Side, I'm the closest camera, and so they send me. I'm listening to the scanner chatter all the way over there, driving as fast as I can down Mulholland. The paramedics have already hiked down the hill and gotten the trapped guy out of his car. They call for a Chopper to come in and hoist the guy up and fly him to UCLA."

"Now, I'm fighting traffic, hoping to get there before it's all over. I can see the chopper circling and hear him talking to the troops on the ground, so I know it's going to be a close call as far as getting there in time. I pull into the neighborhood, on to this residential street where I can see all the emergency vehicles."

"I hop out of my truck as fast as I can, grab my camera out of the back and start hoofing it up the street. This LAPD shit-head stops me. *You can't go in there,* he says to me. What are you talking about, I say. *It's a news story, and I'm the goddamn news!*"

"*My orders,*" he says, "*are to close the street and not let anyone in.*"

"So I look past him, and there are dozens of people from the neighborhood just walking around. *The street is open to the fuckin' public!*"

"I show him my Press Pass, and try one more time. This says that I can get in to the scene of an emergency. I say to him, *P.C. 409.5 says it's against the law for you to keep me out.*"

"So get this, he says to me, You can wait here til it's over, then you can go in. Can you fuckin' believe that?"

"I was just about to call him out for the prick he was, when I see the Rescue chopper lift up from behind the houses, about halfway down the block, and fly away. I missed the whole fucking hoist operation because this douchebag didn't know the law."

"He probably had a reason for keeping you out," said Grog. "They may have had too much foot traffic going on in there and needed room to work, or just concern for your safety. There are a million reasons for him to say that."

"Fuck him," shouted Phil, shaking his fist in disgust. "And fuck you, too. I'll worry about my own fuckin' safety. I don't need you to babysit me. That's not your goddamn job! Next time, I tell you, I'm just gonna walk right past him, or you, or you," Phil said, completely blitzed, sticking his finger into the off-duty cops' faces, "and dare you motherfuckers to arrest me. You're all just badge-happy pricks, and you can all kiss my ass."

Grog didn't flinch.

"I may be a prick," Grog replied, scratching his chin and preparing to throw the bomb. "But at least I know when to leave my gun at home."

Ron and the others cringed. They knew Grog's remark had crossed the line, and would strike a raw nerve with the already inebriated cameraman.

Phil had become the subject of folklore in L.A. some years earlier after being detained by the Secret Service when he showed up at LAX for the arrival of the President with a handgun in the glove compartment of his news van. Until that day, there had been no written policy about carrying a weapon for self-protection, and, although it was unloaded, Phil had absent-mindedly neglected to remove it before heading to the Airport. The Secret Service discovered the weapon during a routine K9 search of all personnel and equipment assigned to cover the President's landing. Officers had him wait in his vehicle, off to the side of the tarmac until the President and his entourage had left the grounds, at which time Phil was allowed to go on his way with just a warning.

The station fired him after learning that he had initially lied about the incident, telling them that he had missed the shot of Air Force One because of a camera problem. It was only after the Secret Service called and informed Leo that one of their dogs had found a weapon in the Channel 6 van, and that Phil had been temporarily detained that he came clean and admitted what had really happened. It took over a year for the Union to negotiate a return to work for Phil, and to this day, any mention of the incident, and his lack of judgment, understandably stirs up resentment and anger. But now, with the help of copious amounts of Budweiser, the short fuse was lit.

Phil started to lunge across the table at Grog, but was held back by Robin and Russ Nixon, from Channel 3. Ron also stepped between his friends, and helped usher Phil away from the table. It was clear that way too much alcohol had been consumed at this party for it to continue without trouble. Grog heard Phil yelling, from several tables away, that if the L.A. cops had been in charge of New York City on 9/11, the media would have been kept a mile away and would never have gotten any of the dramatic pictures the camera crews bravely captured that day. "They wouldn't have gotten shit if it was up to you!" Phil shouted.

Ron kept it to himself that he was largely in agreement with Phil about that. But things were changing, he thought, and he'd had just as many positive encounters with law enforcement recently, particularly since a couple of his close friends had been badly assaulted by Police Officers at the massive May Day rally in MacArthur Park a few years earlier.

Crews from several channels had been set up on the grounds of the park, next to the lake, reporting on the thousands of immigration activists gathering there for speeches after marching all day through the city. The reporters and photographers were just doing their jobs, and happened to be in the wrong place when the order came from LAPD to clear the park. The police skirmish line made its way rapidly through the park, along with the mounted patrols on horseback, and unfortunately, some poorly trained officers made no attempt to distinguish between the Working Press and the demonstrators. A number of the protesters, some of whom were cooperating and attempting to disperse, were beaten with batons or shot with rubber 'less-than-lethal' rounds, which cause significant discomfort, leaving a dark, painful contusion on the body.

At the same time, Press tents were overturned, equipment trampled, and journalists assaulted with police batons and pushed to the ground. A handful maintained injuries that kept them out of work for several months or longer, and one female photog, Pam Butler, a Channel 6 Camera Operator and close friend of Ron's, actually had to retire from her job after the severe beating she received from an over-zealous cop with a baton. Carolyn Sanchez, the KSIX reporter on the scene, had been pushed to the ground and manhandled by an overly aggressive officer. Her neck was badly wrenched, requiring surgery, and continued medical treatment. She was out of work for several months, and was left with permanent mobility problems.

The presence of dozens of cameras in the park was certainly an advantage that day, as the plethora of both professional and amateur photographers helped to document the behavior of the out-of-control riot cops, and pinpoint which ones had committed the assaults on the demonstrators and journalists. The incident in the park led to widespread changes in LAPD procedures regarding their dealings with the news media in L.A. It also cost the city millions in settlements.

Phil had moved on to another table, but it was obvious that he was still agitated as he spoke loudly to his friends, pointing and gesturing in the direction of Grog and his buddies. They knew that it was the beer talking and decided that the best course of action would be to call it an evening.

Ron said a quick round of goodbyes, and the three headed out to the lot. "It's barely 10:00," said Steve, over the sound of the patrol car racing Code 3 down Cahuenga toward Barham, "Where should we go?"

"I'm gonna pack it in, guys," said Ron, climbing into his car. "It's been a long day, and I've got an early call tomorrow."

"Me, too," Grog said, "And I think I've had enough abuse thrown at me for one night."

"See ya out there, guys," Ron said. "Be safe."

"Always," Steve answered. "You too."

Ron headed home to his apartment, to spend another fitful night with *her* hovering in midair above his bed.

Chapter Four:

CHANGES

Tuesday, March 10th

After almost four hours on the road, the Channel 6 News van reached the Mexicali border crossing. Producer Hank Resnik felt that all the Spring Break Madness stories he could find in Lake Havasu had been exhausted and decided to change things up a little this year by spending a few days in San Felipe with Ron and feature reporter Ben Reynolds.

The Federales at the border checkpoint flagged down the van, and Ron pulled over next to the dusty gray kiosk. They could hardly see through the filthy, cracked windows of the small building, but soon an officer emerged and instructed the men to step out. Several officers began climbing in and out of the van and rifling through all the equipment and personal belongings inside. Others examined the crew's paperwork, identification and hotel reservations, which were all in perfect order. After searching the duffle bags and pulling the camera gear out onto the pitted, oil-stained concrete apron, one of the officers began questioning Ron in broken English about the purpose of their trip.

"You come to Mexico, why?"

"We're a television news crew," Ron explained. "We're headed to San Felipe for Spring Break."

"How long you are here?"

"Three days, that's all," Hank answered, attempting to speed up the interrogation.

"You will film the Spring Break?" the officer asked, turning his gaze toward Hank.

"That's right, the kids, the parties, the…"

"The naked senoritas?" interrupted the officer, laughing.

"Whatever we see," said Hank, looking toward his partners and showing a bit of a grin.

"Ahh… Entiendo, entiendo," the officer replied, nodding and smiling for the first time, revealing an incomplete set of seriously infected teeth.

"We see now if you go through," said the officer, pointing to a large black metal box to the right of the gate arm, containing two traffic-signal lights, one red and one green. He stepped back into the kiosk with three other Federales. Everyone stared at the lights, the rules of the game being beyond obvious. A green light meant they could proceed, a red one would mean more red tape in their future, and likely a bribe.

After a few seconds, the green light illuminated, and the crew began to place their belongings once again in the rear of the van. Thanking the officers for their kindness and generosity, Ron drove slowly past the open gate and into Mexico. Once safely beyond the checkpoint, Hank began to laugh.

"What the fuck was that all about?"

The men continued down the highway, but agreed that they needed to stop for dinner before getting any further into Mexico. As dusk approached, Ron pulled the van into a little dive called El Pescador where they enjoyed flat iron steaks and Tecate beer before resuming the drive south toward San Felipe.

Traffic started backing up several miles from town. Vehicles packed with impatient, untethered young people lined Route 5. A parade of loud, smoky motorcycles snaked between the stopped cars. Suddenly, as they neared the city, the dusty streets became packed with pedestrians, mostly Americans and most already drunk.

Hotel rooms were at a premium, but reservations had been made weeks beforehand for three rooms at La Hacienda, a seedy, pink two-story hotel right on the beach. The crew got checked in, and Ron took the room on the first floor nearest the ocean. It was tiny but serviceable, the front room featuring a lumpy sofa, a small refrigerator and several sliding windows, which would presumably offer a nice ocean view once the sun rose over the Sea of Cortez. To the left were a cramped bedroom with a small closet, and a bathroom with rusty fixtures and a shower that dripped water around the clock. The front door opened out onto the beach, which gave the room a fishy, musty smell to go with the well-trod sand-filled carpets. But it was only for a couple of days, nothing he couldn't survive considering they wouldn't be spending much time in their rooms anyway.

It was well past ten by the time they had settled in, and the men agreed to meet in the lobby in the morning. Ben wanted to check out the town a bit and took a walk before retiring. Hank and Ron decided to stay in their rooms. Ron plugged in his ear-buds and listened to some jazz on his iPod until he dozed off, hoping that the unfamiliar surroundings would help put a damper on his recurring, plummeting nightmare. Perhaps the exotic locale would give him a few nights away from *her*.

Wednesday, March 11th

The crew had agreed to meet in the hotel restaurant at 10:00 for breakfast, but it was barely 8:30 and the sounds of blasting music and partying teenagers outside his door were already making sleep impossible. Ron climbed out of bed and parted the cheap, plastic blinds to see a small group of college kids getting an early start on their vacations; running, screaming and carrying on in the sand.

In the foggy morning daylight, he observed a number of things that had escaped his sight the previous night. How thin the walls were for one. The windows were filthy, and the locks on the windows and door were old, cheap, and probably not very secure. He suddenly became highly skeptical of the accommodations, but at this point, no other rooms were available in the town of San Felipe.

Ron showered quickly, dressed, and left the room to check out the beach for a few minutes before breakfast. He thought the prudent thing to do, considering the dubious security, was to keep his camera with him at all times. He attached a freshly charged battery and did his usual morning prep before leaving the room and locking the door behind him. Walking down the sand, the first thing he noticed was the filth being washed up on shore. Each foamy wave brought with it a collection of rotting fish, cigarette butts and other detritus that instantly made any thought of taking a dip in the Sea completely unappealing. On the bright side, he soon realized that Spring-breaking females, at least at this early hour, were much more prevalent than their male counterparts. He also quickly took note of the skimpiness of the young women's suits. Bikinis had given way to thongs, which, for all intents and purposes, didn't really qualify as clothing. *They're even smaller than last year*, he thought to himself.

There was a stage that had been built on a platform about a hundred yards down the beach, adjacent to the areas designated for volleyball, pickleball, and the bean-bag toss. A large, professionally printed sign hung on the back of the stage, facing the hotel with the words: "SPRING BREAK MADNESS!!!" in two-foot high white letters over a brightly colored image of a pristine beach with palm trees and golden sand, far from the reality of San Felipe, Mexico.

A smaller poster, mounted on the stage advertised the day's events:

WEDNESDAY:

Bikini Contest- 1:00

Wet T-shirts- 2:00

Beer Pong- 3:00

Drunk Jeopardy- 4:00

Behind him, several teams were already demonstrating their impressive imaginations by building x-rated sculptures for the Sand "Castle" competition that would be judged later in the afternoon. And the course was being constructed for "Dizzy flag", a game where contestants would chug a beer before being spun around several times and attempting to maneuver an obstacle course.

Feeling terribly old, Ron walked back up the beach, through the growing mass of young Spring Breakers. A couple of teens were making love on a blanket, completely unconcerned with the nearby crowd, or the cameraman walking past. A pair of cute coeds walking up the beach took note of the television equipment and smiled. One of them, a sexy brunette, pulled her bikini top to the side, giving him a wink, along with a good look at her left breast. He spun, walking backward for a few steps, and responded, "And good morning to you, too!" before blushing and spinning back around. He made his way to the café, pulled open the wood-framed screen door and saw Hank and Ben already seated in one of the dozen pale green naugahyde booths.

Hank was on his cell-phone and appeared troubled by his conversation. Ron slid in next to Ben, setting his camera on the floor beside him. Plastic menus sat unopened on the formica tabletop, which was losing its color in patches from being wiped clean several million times since being installed sometime in the 50's.

"What's going on?" Ron asked in a whisper, motioning toward Hank.

"I'm not sure," answered Ben. "But I'm glad we're not at the station today."

"Why? What happened?"

"It looks like the layoff notices have gone out."

"Oh, man, how bad is it?"

Ben just shrugged and motioned toward Hank, who would fill them in when he hung up the phone.

The waitress approached, and Ben and Ron gave her their orders. Hank ended his conversation and sat forward. He was visibly angry and simply ordered two eggs, toast, and black coffee. Ben and Ron began to interrogate their partner.

"Well?" said Ben.

"About a hundred layoffs in this round with more to come," answered Hank. "They've hit every department."

"How is that gonna work?" asked Ron, elbow on the table and chin resting in his palm.

"First to go are the free-lancers. Anyone not on staff is gone, starting Monday."

"Holy Crap," Ron said. "We don't have enough guys already."

"That's not the half of it." Hank added. "They're cutting writers, editors, hair and make-up people, everyone across-the-board. Basically if you don't have at least five years seniority, you're dust. And they also announced that they are not offering anyone buy-outs."

"That's just insane," said Ron, rubbing his beard and letting the news sink in for a moment. "So let me get this straight. All the young bucks, just out of school, who've learned all the new digital technologies and are gung-ho about working in news are out?"

"Yep,"

"And all the burned out old guys just waiting to retire? Those are who we're left with?"

"Pretty much."

"That's just fucking swell." Said Ben.

"It's company wide," added Hank. "Ratings are down everywhere, people aren't watching news on TV as much anymore. They've got other choices."

"Maybe so," said Ben. "But we still have to put out a good product."

"Somehow, that doesn't seem to be as much of a priority these days," Hank said, as the waitress brought their coffee.

"Let's concentrate on today," Hank said, pouring cream in his cup. "I was looking at some flyers and hand-outs in my room last night. There are all kinds of activities planned for this afternoon."

"We need to look for some of the more extreme games the kids are involved in," Hank added. "Drinking games, sex games, stuff that they can't get away with in Havasu. You remember all the arrests last year? The cops there are really cracking down. That's one reason I booked us here."

"Yeah, well there will be plenty of that stuff here." Said Ben. "I hear the San Felipe cops are only looking for hard drugs and violence. The rest of it, they turn a blind eye. They keep the arrests to a minimum so as not to tarnish the reputation of their city. Spring Break is huge business here. Brings in hundreds of thousands of dollars every year. The last thing they want is to scare off the kids. Or their parents."

Two young girls were finishing their breakfast in the next booth, noticed the camera by Ron's side, and struck up a conversation, asking what the guys were doing there. Ben didn't hesitate.

"We're from a TV station in Los Angeles," he said. "We're here to do a couple of stories about the goings-on during Spring Break. Where do you guys go to school?"

"We're from San Diego State," answered the brunette, her sheer top opening slightly with the breeze blowing gently in through the screen door.

"I'm Shannon and this is Amber," she said, introducing her friend. "I'm from Portland and she's from Waco, Texas."

"Very nice," said Ben. "Is this your first time in San Felipe?"

"I was here last year," answered Amber, whose red hair and freckles made her appear much younger than college age. "All year I was telling Shannon how much fun it was and how she had to come with me."

"So what's the most fun part about it?" Ben asked.

"Hanging out, dancing, drinking, you know… meeting guys."

"What will you be doing this morning?" asked Hank, hoping they would lead him in the direction of a story.

"Probably just lay out on the beach," said Shannon, as the two young women turned to leave. "You know, see what develops."

"OK, well maybe we'll run into you out there," said Hank.

"OK, Bye."

"Oh, here's my number," called out Ben, reaching over with a pair of business cards. "Call me if you see anything newsworthy." The girls glanced at the cards for a second, before giggling and slipping them into the bras of their swimsuits.

Amber and Shannon paid their bill and walked toward the door, Amber turning to smile and wave one more time, her torn Levi shorts and loose wife-beater t-shirt barely covering her tiny day-glo orange swimsuit.

"You're a married man, Hank," said Ben, waving his hand in front of the reporter's eyes. "Behave yourself."

"I love my wife, I love my wife, I love my wife," said Hank, drawing laughter from his partners. "But did you see the rack on her?"

*****

By the time they left the coffee shop, the sea was filling up with swimmers and jet-skiers, though Ron wondered what kind of yet-undiscovered maladies were being spread in the badly polluted water. On the shore, a stand was set up selling rides on "Banana Boats", inflatable crafts the shape and color of an oversized banana, which was attached and towed out behind a jet ski. Jewelry sellers and body painters patrolled the sand. A variety of entrepreneurs and vendors were already out in force, prepared to take advantage of the hundreds of young American kids in town for the week with ample funds and little if any self-control.

Around noon, the crew made their way out onto the sand and began interviewing kids on camera. A few were repeat Spring-breakers, who shared stories from previous years. But most had never been away from home for a week without an adult before.

Whenever Ron raised the camera to his shoulder and Ben turned on the wireless hand-mike, a crowd of screaming kids would gather behind the person being interviewed. Young people, especially inebriated ones, love to make fools of themselves around video cameras in any setting, and the teeming beach of San Felipe was certainly no exception. At first Hank let it go without comment, seeking to record the realism of the situation, obnoxious behavior and all. Uninhibited young men cheered, pulled up their shirts, made hand signs and waved their tongues at the camera, whatever came to mind as a way to shout "look at me!" Soon, they began encouraging the women to join in. Several took the cue, jumping up and down, screaming and flashing their breasts or mooning the camera, precipitating a roar from the boisterous crowd.

At that point, Hank and Ben had to step in, and ask for a little decorum and cooperation. They tried to explain that KSIX was a broadcast station with FCC standards and rules, blah, blah, blah...

Giving up on the decorum and cooperation, Ron shot some b-roll of volleyball and bean-bag toss, then a couple of generic stand-ups with Ben, though it was difficult to hear a word over the screaming kids who had gathered around. Ron was starting to shoot the hilariously designed but highly inappropriate sand castles, now near completion, when from far down the beach, he could hear from the stage the start of the Bikini Contest.

The host was Don Burr, a well-tanned man in his late forties who wore board shorts, sandals and a faded green Hawaiian print shirt, which only marginally covered his bulging waistline. He had the deep, gravelly voice of a Top 40 Disc Jockey or the host at a strip club. And his thinning sandy blonde hair, which he kept oiled and brushed straight back, gave him a look to match.

The Hip-hop music was deafening and the bass well past the point of distortion, pumping through the large, antiquated JBL loudspeakers mounted on stands at the sides of the stage. The thunderous beat telling the entire city of San Felipe that it was party time.

As the music faded, Burr began by introducing the eight bikini-clad contestants by name and college. He had them pose, one by one, for the cheering, intoxicated audience, and then strut back and forth across the stage, showing off their assets. Each one wore the skimpiest of suits and high-heels to accentuate their legs. After the eight had been introduced, a voice-vote was taken and the top three became finalists.

Burr named the three remaining contestants as if he were in Atlantic City, hosting Miss America.

"Our first finalist," he announced into the mike, "is Tracy, from U.C. Riverside!"

Tracy came bounding out to center stage to wild applause. She was a dazzling blonde who wore a bright blue suit the top of which barely covered the nipples of her artificially enhanced breasts. She had a deep, likely all-over tan and unrealistically white teeth. She basically looked like someone who competed in bikini contests as a career.

"Contestant number two," he continued, "is Becky, from San Diego State!"

Becky had a much more wholesome and natural look, although her bust line had clearly also been surgically modified. She wore a white bikini, which the young men in the audience all wished would somehow find a way to get wet. Her light brown hair was in a ponytail draped over her right shoulder. She smiled broadly for the audience and took her place next to Tracy on the stage.

They both waved their arms and wriggled their hips to rally their fans into frenzied cheers.

"And our third finalist," Burr announced, "is Jenny, from U.C. Irvine!"

Jenny, a beautiful Asian girl with perfect features and long brown hair, jumped up and down with excitement, almost coming out of her florescent pink suit, which was not a traditional bikini, but rather a one-piece affair, which barely covered her at all below the waist, came up her back and wrapped around her neck. Two two-inch straps came down, one from each shoulder to cover little more than her areolas, and met again at the bottom, where they wrapped around and tied in a knot at the waist.

Burr made a series of lame, off-color jokes which sent groans through the audience, and asked each contestant a few questions about their schools, ambitions, and what their ideal man would be like. Then it was time for the final judging. Each girl had one last chance to pose, strut and model her suit for the several hundred or so judges in the audience.

Finally, after conferring with his staff, Burr announced the winner,

"Drum roll, please… Ladies and gentlemen, the winner of this year's San Felipe Spring Break Bikini Competition is… Tracy from U.C. Riverside!"

Burr handed Tracy a cheap, plastic trophy as she posed at the front of the stage for the cameras, and the crowd once again went wild as all the contestants hugged and posed one last time.

The cheering subsided, and the crowd began to dissipate, some of them making their way up the beach following the news crew. Ron had begun shooting video of the Banana Boat riders, including one young woman named Lacy, who approached him on the sand, claiming to be a 'porn star', and asking to get on TV. After the ride, during which she stood up, threw her top in the water and waved repeatedly at the camera, she bounded off the Banana Boat and strutted ashore wearing only her bikini bottom. Swarms of intoxicated young men who had staggered over from the stage, surrounded the woman and began taking pictures. She enjoyed all the attention and appeared only mildly annoyed when a particularly drunk partier reached around and groped her breast while posing for a photo. She smacked him, playfully but hard enough to get his attention, turned away from the crowd and ran back into the water.

"Let's take a break, now," said Hank. "We don't need to shoot the wet t-shirts and I hate beer-pong."

"You mean hepatitis-pong," said Ron. "Can those balls be any less sanitary? Especially here."

"We need something unique," added Ben. "Something we haven't seen before."

They walked together along the bustling beachfront road, or Malecon, and stopped at the Backstreet Grill to grab a bite. Ron noticed a paper sign scotch taped on the glass insert of the old wooden door. It was a full-color ad for a 'Foam Party' happening that night at the Rockadile Club, just down the road.

"Hank," Ron said, pausing at the door, "Check this out."

Hank and Ben came over and looked at the poster. There were four small photos of near-naked partiers covered in soapsuds on a dance floor.

"I think we're gonna have to check out the Rockadile tonight, boys."

They were back on the beach in time for "Drunk Jeopardy", another game they hadn't seen in Lake Havasu. Ron set up off to the left of the stage as the contestants approached the stairs. Two teams of two girls each were brought on stage, each under 20 and each wearing tiny swimsuits. The audience of several hundred young men, many of whom had been standing stage-side all afternoon, were now in an alcohol and testosterone fueled fervor and began chanting almost immediately, "Take It Off! Take It Off!"

"There'll be plenty of time for that, Gentlemen!" shouted Don Burr, as the pounding music faded. "Let's get started with our game."

After introducing the contestants and cursorily explaining the rules of the game, Burr handed each contestant a red plastic cup of beer. His assistants would make sure that the cups remained filled throughout the game. Burr then read the first answer.

"This is the total number of United States Senators representing us in Washington DC," he said, "Now, audience, no helping the contestants, please. No help from the audience!"

The teams huddled and thought hard about their answers while the inebriated mob, unable to resist the temptation, shouted out an array of answers, most of them wildly and purposely incorrect.

"Remember," said Burr. "You answer must be in the form of a question!"

The team on stage left began jumping and waving, indicating that they had the answer.

"Cal State Fullerton, GO!"

"What is fifty?" yelled Becky, the short-haired contestant in the striped bikini, proudly representing her institution of higher learning. The crowd booed wildly, causing the girls to wince.

"*What is Fifty* is incorrect," said Burr. "Riverside, do you have the correct question?"

After a moment, Amy, the short blonde on stage right answered sheepishly, "What is a hundred?"

"That's correct!" said Burr, over the roar of the crowd. "The team from Riverside wins round one, and so the Fullerton team has to perform a task."

The girls from Fullerton stepped to the middle of the stage and Becky reached into a fishbowl, pulled out the slip of paper containing their "task", and handed it to Burr to read.

"Your task," he announced after unfolding the paper, "is to switch bikini tops."
The crowd was again in a frenzy, cheering wildly, "Take It Off! Take It Off!"

The girls moved to the rear corner of the stage, but hardly out of sight, and placed their beer cups at their feet. Then as the electronic music reached ear-piercing levels, they proceeded to execute their swap as quickly and demurely as they could, while laughing to the wild applause of the mob.

Ron shot the events, knowing that brief as it was, the editor would have to digitize the nudity.

"OK, well done! Very impressive!" said Burr, applauding and waiting a moment for the cheering to subside.

"And now our next answer. This NHL Team is the home of such players as Anze Kopitar and Jonathan Quick."

The girls from Fullerton both threw their arms into the air and yelled in unison, "I know! I know!" while the Riverside team was still mid-huddle.

"Fullerton, Go!" Burr shouted, pointing in their direction.

"Who are the Kings?" they shouted in unison.

"That's the correct answer!" Burr announced, to the yelps of the crowd. "It looks as if Riverside has a task to perform." He turned to face the losing team and motioned with his finger for them to come forward. "Girls…"

Dejected but laughing, the team from Fullerton chose another task slip and handed it to the emcee.

"Your task, girls, is to make out." Then after a pregnant pause, " With each other!" Burr announced, turning his leering grin toward the audience.

The cheers were deafening and the music pulsating as the girls laughed and looked at each other approvingly before locking lips together.

"YES!!!" Yelled Burr. "There you have it! That's what I'm talking about! What do you think, gentlemen?"

A roar of approval rose from the mob as the breathless girls finally released their embrace.

Neither team could correctly answer the next challenge, so a tiebreaker was devised.

"Alright," said Burr, "since neither team could tell me that the Capital of Vermont is Montpelier, we'll give both teams a challenge. Your task is to carry five balloons from one end of the stage to the other without using your hands," Burr announced. "You need to keep them from falling by pressing them between your bodies. There are two baskets here at the front of the stage. The first team to get five balloons in a basket wins!"

The crowd hooted.

While Burr had been explaining the rules, baskets were carried out onto each side of the stage, each filled to excess with fully inflated balloons. Burr led the girls to the rear of the stage.

"Are you ready, Girls?" he asked, while encouraging their consumption of beer from their cups. He had them finish their beers, and the assistants proceeded to tie their hands behind them with scarves.

"OK, Here's the first balloon," Burr announced, helping both teams of girls press them between their chests.

He counted down, "Five, four three, two, one, GO!"

Both teams waddled sideways, trying to keep the balloons from falling or breaking. The Fullerton team got one in their barrel fairly quickly, while the Riverside team struggled. Burr's bikini-clad assistants shadowed the contestants to keep score and quickly replace the balloons once they were successfully deposited in the baskets. They also started the teams over again at the rear of the stage when a balloon broke or was dropped prematurely.

Eventually, after several drops by the Fullerton team, the girls from Riverside pulled ahead, finally winning the competition five balloons to three. Their wrists untied, the girls threw their arms into the air and hugged while their fans cheered.

Both teams were now feeling the effects of the alcohol and, laughing uncontrollably, the brunette from Fullerton loosened her top and quickly flashed a breast victoriously to the audience. Not to be outdone, her partner flashed the electrified crowd momentarily, revealing both breasts, before pulling her top, formerly her friend's top, back on.

"Alright!" shouted Burr, "Time for the final round!"

"How are you feeling?" he asked the Fullerton team, the alcohol and blazing sun having a noticeable effect on the duo. Assured that they were prepared to continue, he turned to the Riverside team.

"You know what?" he announced, "You know what? It's hot up here and we're all thirsty. So just to make it fair…"

Burr handed each of the girls a fresh cup of cold beer.

"Drink It Down! Drink It Down!"

Each of them downed their beer, spilling generous amounts down the front of their bodies.

"OK, now for our Final Drunk Jeopardy answer. This author wrote such classics as 1984 and Animal Farm."

The busty young woman with the short black hair and a blue bikini on stage right quickly threw her hand into the air.

"I know this!" she yelled, slurring her words.

Burr walked quickly over to her side of the stage, holding out the mike.

"I read one of his books last semester!" she slurred. "It's George Orrr-well!"

The crowd roared, but was soon reminded by Burr that the answer needed to be in the form of a question, therefore disqualifying the team from Riverside.

Dejected, the girls learned their fate as Burr read their chosen task.

"You are each to drink a shot of tequila and switch bikini bottoms." He announced to another roar from the crowd.

The girls stood wide-eyed, mouths agape. They each looked down, laughing hysterically, then glanced at each other as if to ask, *"How on earth are we going to do this?"* They downed the shots and retreated to a corner of the stage to the lusty chants of "TAKE IT OFF!! TAKE IT OFF!!" As the booming music began to shake the stage again, the girls quickly turned their backs on the crowd. They swapped bottoms as quickly as humanly possible, then raised their arms in triumph and hugged each other as the deafening cheers persisted.

Burr brought all the contestants to the front of the stage for one last round of applause and thanked everyone for participating in Drunk Jeopardy.

Burr peered down at the thinning crowd as a shirtless young man at the foot of the stage wobbled, looking confused and uneasy. The group around him quickly cleared out to give him room as he staggered. Suddenly, he projectile vomited a stomach full of beer in the direction of the stage before falling face-first in the sand.

*****

Ron, Hank, and Ben arrived at the Rockadile Club at 7:30 pm to prepare for the Foam Party. They wanted to get a feel for the place while the lights were still on and before it filled up with rowdy Spring Breakers.

Jose Dominguez, the manager of the Rockadile club, met them at the door and gave them a quick tour. The dance floor was the size of a small skating rink and took up most of the downstairs area of the club. Upstairs, where the bar was located, a few tables and stools lined the wall, which overlooked the dance floor.

The DJ had his set-up just to the side of the dance floor, and the speakers were on the ceiling next to the strobe lights and mirrors.

About twenty feet above the center of the floor, attached securely to the ceiling at an angle were two foam machines, each about the size of a dishwasher, with long aluminum hoses attached. The hoses led down and off to the side of the floor. The dance floor itself was surrounded by a waist-high

Plexiglas wall, to contain the foam that the machines would be pumping out on the dancers.

Having gotten the lay of the land, Ron and his partners sat at the bar and waited for the club to open. At 8:00 sharp, the doors swung open and a long line of young people began to funnel inside. There was an age requirement of 18 years to enter the club, and two tables had been set up near the door to check IDs.

A line formed at the bar and it wasn't long before the floor was filled with barefoot Spring Breakers in swimsuits and shorts, holding red plastic cups full of beer and waiting impatiently for the party to begin.

Ron had gotten his gear and was standing near the entrance to the dance floor, just outside the Plexiglas wall. Suddenly, the lights were turned down, the music was turned up, and the foam began to flow from the machine suspended above. Ron's camera captured the first spurts of suds as they cascaded down upon the dancers.

With music blasting and lasers and strobe lights streaking across the club, foam began to fill up the enclosed dance floor. Soon, people were throwing foam in the air and covering themselves with suds from head to toe. Some couples disappeared under the thick, white bubbles, reappearing moments later. Others took things further, groping, stripping and taking full advantage of the fact that their parents were not within hundreds of miles and had absolutely no idea what they were up to.

After about a half hour, Ron told Hank that he had plenty of b-roll. They waded inside the foamy enclosure and tried to interview some of the foam-covered dancers.

"What a fucking blast!" one shouted, grabbing his date around the waist and disappearing into the clouds of flying foam.

"Woo Hoo! San Felipe Rocks!" yelled another, while the group behind him jumped in front, waving, screaming and throwing suds at the camera.

The slick, sudsy dance floor was full, and walking around in it became an adventure.

Soon, the pounding of the music and screaming revelers made any type of interviews impossible, but at the same time, Ron, Hank and Ben were having a great time, confident that they already had plenty of amazing video. None of them had seen anything remotely like a foam party before.

By 9:00, the crew was exhausted from a long, physically demanding day and started for the door. They stopped to thank Jose for his hospitality and told him to check the station's website in a few weeks to see the story featuring his club.

As they reached the door, a siren could be heard as an ambulance streaked down the crowded Malecon. Just north of the Rockadile was another bar, this one open to the street. Outside the door laid a young man who appeared to be bleeding from a stab wound to the stomach.

Ron fired up his camera, but as soon as he turned on the light, several bouncers from the club ran up and confronted him on the sidewalk, trailed by a small group of clubbers and the victim's friends.

"No! No! You turn that camera off now!" one yelled, waving his arms to block the camera's view of the injured man.

"Get the fuck outta here!" shouted an unseen, agitated voice coming from the back of the group.

Hank put his hand on Ron's shoulder and pulled him back.

"It's OK," he said. "We don't need this. Let's go."

A couple of the man's friends started to follow them, but were quickly stopped by the two huge bouncers.

The crew headed back south, passing the front of the Rockadile again on their way to the van. The sidewalk near the club's entrance was beginning to look as if there had been a snowstorm. A group of young men wearing only shorts emerged, covered in foam, laughing uncontrollably and shedding suds as they staggered into the street. The music was still blasting as more inebriated, soapy spring breakers trickled out of the club and back to their hotels.

"That was great," said Ben. "Leo's gonna love this story."

Hank speculated that he could possible make two full pieces out of the foam party alone.

It was close to 10:00 by the time they returned to La Hacienda. Ron parked the van and grabbed the camera. No way he was leaving it the vehicle overnight, padlock or no padlock. Hank and Ben grabbed their bags and began making their way up the stairs toward their rooms. Ron walked in the other direction, toward his room on the beach. "G'nite, guys," Ron said. "What, about ten in the restaurant again?"

"Sure, that's fine," Hank answered. Ben nodded in agreement. "G'nite."

The key turned a little too easily. The door to Room 112 had been left unlocked by the last person to leave. Ron knew instantly that something was wrong. He could not have left the room unlocked. Not a chance in hell. He had double-checked the lock just a few hours earlier.

He opened the door slowly and reached in to turn on the light switch. The front room was undisturbed, except for the small sliding glass window just to the right of the door, which had been pried open. The overhead light was on in the bedroom, and Ron could see that his duffle bag had been dumped out on the bed. About the only things not taken were his shaving kit and his reading material, a paperback copy of Hollywood Hills by Joseph Wambaugh and a few recent issues of Sports Illustrated. Every stitch of clothes was gone.

Ron stepped outside and dialed Hank's cell.

"Hey," Hank answered. "What's up?"

"Dude, you guys need to come down, I've been robbed."

"What? We'll be right there."

Hank appeared seemingly in seconds. Ben showed up a few minutes later, with the hotel manager in tow.

"You can see where they got in," Ron said, shaking his head and sliding the window easily over the now-broken latch. "They took everything, Man."

Ron walked them through and began to make a mental list of what was missing. A leather jacket, some of his favorite shirts, jeans, socks, underwear, his i-pod …

The manager assured him that he would have a locksmith out first thing in the morning.

"Are you kidding me?" Ron asked. "There's no fucking way I'm sleeping in this room tonight. You're gonna have to find me another room."

"I'm sorry Mr. Sharp, but we're booked up."

"Fuck it, then," Ron said. "I'll just have to bunk in with one of you guys tonight."

Ron picked up the reading material along with his cell phone charger, which was still plugged into the wall near the bed. He tossed them angrily into his bag. Hank picked up the charger with the spare camera batteries and carried it out of the room. After looking around once more to be sure he was retrieving everything that belonged to him, Ron threw his duffle over his shoulder, picked up the camera and tripod, and headed up the stairs.

*****

Thursday, March 12th

Ron awoke with the sun after only a few hours of fitful sleep. The sofa in Hank's room had a peculiar odor, perhaps seawater mixed with years of perspiration, alcohol, and sex. The pillow provided did little to support his head, worsening his already camera-sore shoulder. *She* was still there with him, but was now only adding layers to his more recent nightmares, not the least of which was what might have happened had returned to his room earlier and interrupted the burglars.

Rubbing the back of his neck, the cameraman swung his feet to the floor and reached for his phone to check the time. His body clock usually woke him at precisely 7:13, and today was no different. There was a text message that had been left for him at 6:04 AM. It was from Hank, who was now asleep just on the other side of the door. Ron brought it up and read the message:

```
Talked to Leo.
Had enough of Mex.
We're going home today.
```

Ron fell back on the sofa, trying to catch a little more rest before the long drive home. At nine, the bedroom door swung open and Hank appeared, in shorts and a worn t-shirt.

"Did you get my message?"

"Yeah, I saw it,"

"I told him that we've already shot enough for at least three sweeps pieces, and he said to pull the plug and come home. Are you OK with that?"

"Sure," Ron answered, still fuming from the previous night. "Why wouldn't I be?"

"Good, so we'll have breakfast and hit the road. Oh, and I've talked to the manager of the hotel. He swears that this has never happened before, but I think he's full of shit. Anyway, he's arranged for your room to be comped."

"That's fine, but the company is paying for it anyway, why do I give a shit?"

"You don't understand, Ronnie." said Hank, "They're gonna comp the room, but still give you a receipt for the full cost. That way you can turn it in and recoup some of the value of the stuff you lost."

"I can't do that," Ron said. "What if the station finds out?"

"How are they going to find out? I'm sure not gonna say anything. And besides, they had pre-approved the cost of the room anyway. No skin off their asses."

"I don't know. I'm not sure I'm comfortable with that."

"Tell you what," said Hank, shaking his head. "I'll give you the receipt, then you do whatever you want with it, OK?"

"Yeah ... sure, I guess."

Hank had been trying to reach Ben all morning, but figured he was in the shower and away from his phone. Hank was tired of waiting for a call back, so they decided to walk down the hall and knock on Ben's door. It took the better part of a minute for the disheveled reporter to answer, and, looking inside, it was quite obvious that he had not been alone in his room, or his bed.

"Umm ... what's going on, dude?" demanded Hank.

"Oh, sorry," Ben said, struggling with his shirt while standing before them in his boxers. He raked his hand through his hair and suggested, "Look, uh, I'll meet you in the restaurant, OK?"

"Did you get my message?" Hank asked, as he and Ron stepped into Ben's room, ignoring his request that they leave.

"I, I didn't see any messages," Ben answered, yawning. "I must have slept through it."

Just then, Amber from the café and San Diego State walked swiftly out of the bathroom and elbowed her way toward the hallway, wearing shorts and a bikini top, holding her other belongings in front of her.

"Excuse me," she said, mortified.

"No worries," said Hank, smiling. "Have a great day."

Ron clenched his front teeth and raised his eyebrows in silence, looking from side to side.

The door closed behind Amber. "She called me," Ben explained sheepishly. "She wanted to know if there was a way for her to get on TV. She came up, we chatted, and, y'know, one thing led ... "

Hank feigned anger at his reporter, but eventually he and Ron just laughed and shook their heads in amazement. Hank let Ben know that his fun was over, and they would be headed back to L.A. after breakfast.

"Alright," said Ben. "I'll meet you in about twenty."

"Oh, and have you got a clean shirt?" Ron asked. "I'm kind of out of clothes."

"Sure," Ben replied, grabbing a green short-sleeved shirt from his closet. "Do you need anything else?"

"Nah, I can just turn my underwear inside out."

*****

After breakfast, the crew got all their equipment together and checked out of the hotel. Hank had convinced Ron that he could possibly recover some of his loss by filing a Police Report and turning it in to the station, as well as his Homeowners Insurance Company.

They left the hotel and drove the short distance to the Headquarters building of the Policia de San Felipe.

The gray, stucco, single story structure rose from a dusty unpaved lot just off of Highway 5, the main road through town. A single patrol car, a black and white Ford from the mid-seventies, sat in the space closest to the entrance.

Several other vehicles of similar vintage were parked behind a chain-link fence to the side of the building. There were fortified, barred windows on all sides, so that no one could approach the building without first being seen and evaluated by heavily armed police inside. The officers must have had a good laugh at the sight of the three Americans strolling toward the door.

Ron scanned the lobby, seeing only stained, unpainted walls on three sides and a black stone counter beneath thick, opaque glass on the fourth. The floor, made of large, square sandstone tiles, was cold and gray.

"How'd you like to spend a few nights here?" Ben joked.

"*Can I help jou yentlemen?*" a heavily accented voice asked from behind the glass.

"Umm, yes… I need to fill out a theft report."

"*What did jou loose?*"

"No, I didn't LOSE anything," Ron replied. "My hotel room was burglarized."

"*Jou wait.*"

"Yes sir."

A door to their left creaked open and two officers emerged. One, an obese man with oily gray hair and a round pockmarked face, was clearly superior in rank. He stood, arms folded, scowling and silent. The other man was much younger, in his thirties, and slighter of build. He spoke acceptable English, as if he'd spent some time in the States.

"So, you want to report a theft?"

"Yes, sir. Last night, while we were out, someone broke into my room at the Hacienda and took all my things. I just need to fill out a crime report so that I can turn it in when we get back home."

"I see," said the officer, running his fingers through his short, thick black hair. "And where is home?"

119

"We're from Los Angeles. We were working on some stories for the news."

"I know," he replied. "I see your large truck outside. So you want us to try to find your belongings and catch the thief for you?"

"Not really," said Ron. "I'm sure that's not very likely. I just need a written crime report to take back home with me."

"Oh, well, you see," said the officer, looking up at his partner. "There are no 'crime reports' to fill out. We have no crime here."

"Really," Ron said, taken aback. "Well you had a crime last night, and I need to report it."

The officers frowned and looked at each other for a moment before the younger man held up one finger and moved toward the office door.

"Un momento," he said, briefly falling back into his native language.

"They have no crime here, didn't you know that?" laughed Hank.

After a minute, the officer returned, carrying a pen and a well-worn, black-covered Composition notebook. He opened it to the first unused page of lined, dog-eared, three-ring punched paper and handed it to Ron.

"Here, you write down what is missing from your room. Then you write, 'I hope that the Police recover these items for me'."

Leaning on the counter, Ron wrote his name, the date, the address of the hotel, and other pertinent information, then itemized the lost articles of clothing, the I-pod, and whatever else he could recall. At the bottom of the paper he wrote the awkwardly worded request, just as it had been dictated. He signed the bottom of the page and handed the notebook back to the officer.

The larger man tore the page out of the book and reached over to offer it to Ron.

"Aren't you going to sign it and make a copy, or something?"

"OK," said the smaller officer, who walked back inside the office, returning with a wood-handled rubber stamp. He pressed the stamp on the paper, leaving a dated red box, which he signed before handing the wrinkled paper back to the overly demanding and assertive American.

"There you go. We are done now. Goodbye," said the short officer, holding open the heavy steel-framed door for his guests.

"Umm... Thanks," said Ron. "Have a really nice day."

*****

"Man," said Hank. "I am looking forward to getting home. A little bit of Mexico goes a hell of a long way with me."

"No shit." added Ben. "Next year, can we do South Padre Island or something?"

"I don't know," Ron said, climbing into the van. "I hear they have crime there."

*****

Just after crossing the border into Calexico, Ron's cell phone began ringing with a call from the station's prefix. He didn't recognize the extension as that of the KSIX Maintenance Shop.

"Microvan 21."

"Hey, Ron? It's Danny Peralta, in the shop."

"Hey, what's up, dude?"

"Ron, did you hear what's going on?"

"What do you mean?"

"All the layoffs," said Danny.

"Oh, yeah," said Ron. "I heard about that. Did they get you?"

"I don't want to lose my job. Suzanne is expecting a baby and I can't afford to be out of work."

"What can I do to help you?" Ron asked.

"They said they're cutting way back on maintenance engineers," answered Danny, sounding nervous and frustrated. "And if I want to work here, I need to work out in the field. Look, Ron, I know how to build a camera from the bottom up. I can diagnose a problem and repair it with my eyes closed. But I've never shot five seconds of video in my life. Can you teach me?"

"Hey, whatever you need, man."

"I'm starting in the field on Monday. That's not a lot of time."

"It's plenty of time," Ron said, knowing it was a lie. "There's nothing to it. Listen, I'll be back at the station tonight, how late are you there?"

"I'm off at six."

"OK, that's perfect. So wait for me, I should be there before that. Here's what I want you to do. Pick up a camera and walk around with it on your shoulder. Get used to the weight, the feel, the balance. Turn it on and look through the viewfinder. Shoot stuff inside the room and out through the windows at the street. Just play with it. Zoom in, zoom out. Get used to the lens, which way to turn it to focus, how to open and close the iris. Oh, and turn off all the automatic settings. Don't be lazy. Just practice until the camera is like an extension of your arm and the lens is part of your eye. Think of some questions for me and I'll be there later tonight, OK?"

"OK, Ronnie. Thanks so much."

"No sweat. I'll see you in a while."

"Can you believe that?" Ron said, shaking his head. "The poor guy has to learn a whole new job if he wants to keep working."

"I've heard managers say that anyone can point a camera," said Hank. "Now they're out to prove it."

"Jesus," Ron added. "We work in Los Angeles, the number two market in the country. It's not a fucking school."

"They obviously don't care what our stuff looks like anymore," added Ben.

"It's such an insult," said Ron, exasperated.

"What do you mean?" asked Ben.

"I mean, think about it. We're all in the same union, right? The shooters, engineers, maintenance guys, writers, producers, all of us. So, do you think they'd take a guy out of maintenance and tell him to go write the newscast? Or produce the newscast? You're damn right they wouldn't. But shoot a camera? No problem," replied Ron.

"Don't get me wrong, nothing against Danny. He's a great guy, but they're telling someone who has never shot a camera and probably never wanted to, to go out, shoot video and put together a quality news story. 'It's so easy a trained monkey can do it.'" Ron continued.

"Yeah," said Ben. "But you can't take it personally. They're just hurting themselves."

"It's only a matter of time before the viewers notice," said Hank. "You can only cut corners and sacrifice quality for so long. It's like the Donut shop on the corner. They decide that they can water down their coffee and get an extra cup out of each pot to make a few extra bucks. The customers don't notice and everyone is happy. But then they get greedy, and water it down a little more, and then a little more. It doesn't take long before their daily customers start going across the street to Channel 3. I mean Joe's Donuts."

"That's exactly right," Ben said. "Economists call that 'the point of diminished returns.' These people have clearly never taken an econ class."

"You know," Ron added. "I remember not too long ago when they'd post a job opening on the newsroom bulletin board, it would always say 'Five Years of Major Market Experience Required'. You'd send in a tape and a resume to show your skills as a photog. Now, I guess the only question they ask is 'Can you lift a camera?' Man, this business is going to hell."

Chapter Five:

THE FUTURE

Monday, March 16th

Following another fitful night, Ron arrived at the station, large coffee in hand. He checked out his truck and camera equipment, and then called in, using the phone on the wall in the remote garage to ask for his first assignment of the morning.

"Before we do that," said Maggie, "I need you to come up to the newsroom. I've got something for you."

"Be right there." he said.

Ron threw his personal equipment bag into the van, then took the stairs to the building's Lobby level and walked down the hall into the newsroom. He navigated the maze of desks and approached the Assignment area.

"Congratulations," shouted Maggie with a hug. "You got an Emmy Nomination."

"Really?" asked Ron. "For which story?"

"Says here it's the one called 'Life-Altering Surgery' that you shot last year. Bobbi submitted it and you both got nominated."

"Wow, I'll have to call her."

Bobbi Steele was the field producer in charge of Medical and Scientific stories at the station. She had collected a roomful of Los Angeles Area Local Emmys and Golden Mikes over the years because of her talent for finding interesting stories with a medical angle and telling them in a visual and informative way. Bobbi did all the work of setting up the shoot, accompanying the crew in the field, conducting the interviews and sitting with the editor to put it all together, basically everything except shooting or appearing on-air. The voice track and an occasional standup were done by a reporter or anchor to make him or her a part of the piece, although they generally had very little to do with its production of the story.

This worked out well all the way around since the "talent" usually had very little time to go out in the field, even more so since the layoffs, but had the ultimate confidence in the stories she produced for them.

"Life-Altering Surgery" was a three-part medical feature story shot entirely by Ron Sharp over the period of several weeks.

Part one introduced the viewers to Lila Fowler, a divorcee in her forties, who suffered from a condition called "Essential Tremors", a neurological disorder that causes a rhythmic shaking, making simple tasks such as tying shoelaces or drinking a glass of water nearly impossible.

Ron and Bobbi drove out to Lila's place in Simi Valley and shot the first interview with her. Emotionally, she explained how the condition was affecting her daily life, making it difficult for her to drive, work, or even put on makeup or jewelry. They talked about her upcoming procedure, which promised to lessen the severity of her condition.

"Are you nervous about the surgery?" Bobbi asked.

"Not at all," replied Lila, "I've never been so excited in my life. The thought of being able to do all those things again, all the things everyone takes for granted..." Her voice cracked and trailed off tearfully.

After the interview, Ron shot B-roll of Lila, attempting to pour a glass of water at the kitchen sink, tie her shoes, and put in her earrings.

Bobbi put the story together for that evening's newscast, voiced over by Gretchen. They also promoted Part Two of the story, to air in about ten days, when the actual surgery was to take place. The station got hundreds of calls and e-mails from viewers taken by Lila's plight and the emotional way it had been presented.

Part Two was gripping. Ron and Bobbi arrived at the Outpatient Surgical Facility in Tarzana on the day of the surgery, and interviewed the surgeon, Dr. William Stone, who explained on camera how he was planning to implant an electrode deep in Lila's brain, and place a device similar to a pacemaker in Lila's shoulder, where she could turn it on and off to control the electric impulses. By sending just the right amount of electricity to a specific location in the brain, the Doctor explained, the tremors could be controlled, and hopefully minimized if not completely eliminated. He added that the only way to perform this procedure, called Deep Brain Stimulation, was to have the patient completely awake and conscious throughout.

Ron and Bobbi were given surgical scrubs and escorted into the operating room, where Lila was already on the table. She was in a semi-seated position, and her head was immobilized in a plastic cage-like device, so there would be no inadvertent movement once the surgery began. Three surgical assistants took their places around the patient, checking equipment, the patient's vital signs, and anesthetic levels. Ron set up his camera on the tripod, where he would be out of everyone's way, but still able to see every step of the procedure. There was a small camera placed above the chair, aimed straight down at Lila's head. Dr. Stone would be able to look up and observe the video on a high definition monitor that hung just above the patient's feet. Ron had a clear shot of the monitor as well.

Dr. Stone walked into the Operating Room, the wireless mike from their interview still attached to his collar. He sat next to Lila and began to explain to the camera what he was doing, each step of the way.

The most visual part of the procedure was when the Doctor actually drilled into Lila's skull. The camera picked up the dust flying from the drill, back-lit with surgical lights in a *fascinating and somehow beautiful shot, made even more intense by the sound of the drill motor and the knowledge that Lila was completely awake the whole time.*

Dr. Stone carefully inserted a narrow probe, about ten inches long with a small electrode attached, into Lila's brain. The positioning of the electrode was critical, as was the voltage which would pass through it. The disorder affected the electrical pathways from the brain through the central nervous system. Lila was kept awake so that at any point in the surgery, when instructed, she could attempt to perform certain tasks with her hand, such as holding a small cup of water, or writing words on a small white-board being held up to her right by a surgical assistant. When her hand was steady, the Doctor would know he had found just the right combination of location and intensity for the implant.

Lila tried several times to write her name on the white-board, with little success.

Ron used his talent to capture some incredibly emotional video; The surgeon's eyes, deep in concentration, his hands performing unimaginably delicate work, Lila's face, the monitors, pumps and gauges, the assistants watching intently. There was silence in the room, everyone doing the jobs they were trained, skilled and prepared to do.

Several times more, Lila was handed the marker, and asked to write her name, and each time she failed, but after what seemed like an hour, when Dr. Stone's probe finally arrived at that sweet, magical combination of location and intensity, she suddenly took the marker firmly in her hand and was able to write on the board in perfect block letters:

I   ♥   DR.   STONE

Everyone in the room was in awe. Some applauded. Some cried. Doctor Stone made certain to keep the probe in place exactly as he had noted, permanently locating the electrode in that precise spot in her brain. He then fed the thin wire through a tube in Lila's neck and into the small power supply box he had implanted earlier on her shoulder blade. With the controls within reach, she could turn off the device when she wanted, to go to sleep for instance, and to turn it on whenever she needed help to function throughout the day without shaking. Ron and Bobbi quietly left the room while Lila was being sewn up and the procedure completed.

Part Two of the story turned out much better than anyone expected: Breathtaking video, fascinating information, and an emotional conclusion. The input from the public was once again, terrific. Many viewers asked to see the results after a few weeks.

A month later, Ron and Bobbi returned to Lila's house for Part Three. They interviewed her again, and shot video of her functioning as a normal person would, performing the tasks that she had previously been unable to accomplish, like tying her shoes, putting in earrings, even driving her car. The third piece was a recap of the entire saga, featuring video from the first two segments, and again, they received rave reviews from the viewers.

It was only natural that Bobbi thought to submit the story for a local Emmy Award, under the category of Outstanding Medical Feature: Multi-Part, and no surprise at all that it received a nomination. Ron picked up a newsroom phone and called Bobbi upstairs at her desk to thank her for thinking of him and adding his name to the entry. Then it was time to get back to work.

He walked over and picked up the situationer that Maggie had printed for him:

Story Slug: DODGERS VISIT SICK KIDS

Reporter: None

Location: Children's Hospital of Los Angeles

Time: 12:00 Noon

Story: Current and Former members of the Los Angeles Dodgers will be handing out Caps, Shirts and other Dodgers gifts to bed-ridden children at Children's Hospital. Players TBA.

"Wow. My lucky day!" said Ron, smiling as he headed out of the newsroom and back down to the garage.

"Yeah," replied Maggie. "Just make sure you get a lunch break by 2:00."

On the drive to the hospital, Ron thought about how exciting it was to get an Emmy nomination, and how much he'd like to go out and celebrate after work. He picked up the cell phone and called Steve, who answered on the second ring.

"Hey, Dude. What's up?"

"Hey, you doing anything later?" asked Ron.

"Why? What's going on?"

"Well, I just got some great news, and I'm looking to celebrate."

"Oh, that's a bummer," Steve replied. "My brother and his wife are in town, and they want me to take them to Manhattan Beach to visit an old friend of hers from High School. Sorry, Man. What's the news?"

"Oh, nothing yet, really. We got nominated for an Emmy, but it'll be awhile before we find out if we win," said Ron. "You guys have fun. I'll talk to you later."

As he hit END CALL on the phone, Ron realized that aside from Steve he really had very few really close friends, hardly anyone with which to share moments like this. Suddenly it occurred to him to give Sandra a call. It had been a couple weeks since he saw her at the In-N-Out, so the timing was right. He never wanted to appear too anxious. He dug around his bag and found her business card. He grabbed the phone again, entered the number, and stared at it for just a moment, biting his lip before hitting SEND.

"Holliday and Weber," answered the operator.

"Sandra Thorne, please."

"Certainly, can I ask who's calling?"

"Ron Sharp from KSIX News."

"Hold, please."

It took only a few seconds for Sandra to pick up.

"Hello."

"Sandra, it's Ron Sharp. From Channel Six."

"Oh, Hi! How are you?"

"I'm good. Listen, I was just wondering, um, can I buy you a beer sometime?"

There was a slight pause. "Umm… yeah, I'd like that."

"How about tonight?" asked Ron, feeling a bit more confident.

"Uhh… sure," Sandra laughed. "I'm free. That'd be great."

"Great," said Ron, conjuring up a plan on the fly. "Have you been to Yamashiro?"

"That place in the hills above the Magic Castle? No, I haven't. But, I've always wanted to."

"Well, I work until 6:00 tonight, can I meet you there? We'll watch the sunset."

"That sounds great. 6:30-ish?"

"Perfect. See you then."

"OK, Bye." Sandra said, with a slight chuckle.

Ron hoped he hadn't sounded too dopey, or too rushed on the phone. It had, after all, been a few months since he had asked a woman on a date.

Ron pulled up in front of Children's Hospital and parked the van in the white Passenger Loading Zone on the street, behind the feeder vans from Channels 3 and 8, which had also just arrived on location. Together the photogs unpacked their camera gear and walked into the large, busy reception area on the ground floor where they checked in. The receptionist picked up the phone and called Pilar Gutierrez, the Media Relations Officer, to tell her that the new crews were beginning to arrive. In just a minute or so Pilar appeared, greeted the crews, signed them in and applied their paper, sticky-back nametags, which were required of all visitors. She then ushered the group down the long open hallway, past the infant's play area and the small, busy snack shop. These visits always inspired Ron to count his blessings, seeing the little faces of hairless children with their loving, desperate parents, hoping against hope for a miracle. Little ones with tubes in their noses and braces on their legs always got to him. They proceeded around the corner and into an elevator. Pilar pressed the button for the 3rd Floor, next to the little sign that read "Pediatric Cancer Ward".

The group exited the elevator and turned right, then a quick left. Down the hall, they could see a small crowd of nurses and hospital employees gathered around to get a glimpse of the visitors who had stopped by for the morning. In the midst of the group were Russell Martin, Clayton Kershaw and Justin Turner of the Dodgers, who had a day off from Spring Training in Arizona, and made a special trip in just to spend time with the kids. There was optimism on the team that this would finally be their year, since they came so very close to winning it all last year, despite so many key injuries.

The players had come to the hospital in uniform to meet and hopefully bring a little happiness to some of the kids who were undergoing cancer treatment at Children's. They went room to room, presenting Dodgers' caps and pennants, signing posters and posing for photos taken by an official Dodgers photographer, also in tow.

The television crews followed as Kershaw entered the room of eleven-year-old Yolanda Quintero, who had recently undergone surgery to remove a brain tumor. Her treatment had caused her to lose a great deal of weight, along with all of her hair, and though she was still in a lot of pain, she managed a broad smile upon seeing one of her heroes standing by her bedside. The all-star pitcher looked into her giant brown eyes and told her how beautiful she was. He then asked her if she was a Dodgers fan.

"I am," she said. "I just wish I could stay up and watch the games." He took a little extra time to stand at her side and hold her hand, then posed for a photo with her and told her he was looking forward to seeing her at the stadium as soon as she could make it. As they left the room, everyone, including Kershaw, seemed to have a bit of a tear.

The same thing happened with Martin and Turner. The camera crews followed them into the patients' rooms and recorded the children smiling and receiving gifts from the ball players. All the kids were smart, polite, adorable and thrilled to have the players come to see them. Ron stayed longer than the other cameramen just because he liked hanging with the ball players. He introduced himself and took photos with them in the hallway after the shoot.

Ron said his goodbyes and started heading toward the elevator with Pilar when he heard a man's voice calling his name. He turned to his right to see JayShawn Brown, whom he recognized immediately, exiting the men's room. He greeted him with the hug of a long-lost friend, found again by chance.

"Ron," he cried. "It's wonderful to see you again, how are you doing?"

"I'm good, JayShawn," he answered. "What are you doing here?" Right away, he realized there could be only one answer.

"It's KayDance, isn't it? Is she alright?"

"She's not doing well, Ron. Not well at all. "

"I'd love to see her," Ron said excitedly. "If that's OK."

"She's in the middle of some tests right now, so it's probably not allowed. I just stepped out to use the restroom when I saw you."

*****

Ron had first met JayShawn a few weeks earlier, when he and Bobbi had visited him, along with his three-year-old daughter KayDance at their Valencia home. JayShawn had written to the station, explaining how his little girl had been diagnosed with Acute Myeloid Leukemia soon after her first birthday. She had undergone aggressive treatment for the disease, including radiation and chemotherapy, which seemed initially to have been successful. Tests showed that KayDance was in complete remission until a few months later, when she suffered a severe relapse. At that time, they had taken to all manner of conventional and experimental procedures, but found that they were no match for the advancing leukemia.

KayDance's doctors informed them that the best hope for her survival was a bone marrow transplant. They searched the national database and found there were absolutely no matches to be found. Not a single person in the United States had registered with compatible bone marrow. That was when, out of desperation, JayShawn sat down and wrote to KSIX. Possibly, he thought, by raising awareness of the shortage of bone marrow donors, particularly within minority communities, other children could be saved, if not his own KayDance.

Bobbi and Ron both fell in love with KayDance at first sight. Her infectious smile lit up the house. The walls of her bedroom were covered with her colorful drawings, mostly of butterflies and angels, two things she loved. Everywhere there were photographs of her as a precious child, before and after losing her hair to the treatment. But even while suffering, she exuded love and happiness.

Once the camera crew arrived, JayShawn picked his daughter up from her bed and playfully held her high in the air, waving her in a circle, eliciting beautiful smile, sharing with her as much love and happiness as he could.

JayShawn carried his daughter down the stairs and placed her softly on a pillow, on the stone floor of the family room with a large pad of paper and a handful of colored markers. KayDance picked up the red marker, began drawing butterflies and trying to write her name.

JayShawn was miked and sat on the floor alongside his beautiful child. Ron got down on the floor as well and shot the girl's hands and face while she continued with her artwork. JayShawn spoke stoically about their situation and how he was hopeful that someone watching might come through as a donor.

He mentioned that he had recently asked KayDance if she knew why she was there, why God had sent her there.

"Daddy, I need to be here," she'd answered.

"Why do you need to be here," he asked, stifling a laugh.

"Because I have to write my name," she had told him.

There was silence in the room. They all knew that she was there so that her story could be told, and so that other children could benefit from it.

Ron kept shooting as KayDance stopped drawing on the paper and leaned back onto her father's chest. JayShawn explained how they had recently set up a system to provide KayDance with morphine as needed to ease her pain.

"It's not," she said.

"It's not easing the pain?" her father asked.

"No. I have pain in my leg," she said, starting to cry.

JayShawn politely got up and carried his little girl again up to her room, ending the shoot.

"I hope you have enough for your story," he said.

"We have plenty," answered Bobbi. "She's just wonderful."

Driving back to the station, Ron and Bobbi could talk of nothing but KayDance, and how lucky she was, despite her illness, to have been born into the family she was. It was clear that JayShawn would trade places with her in a nanosecond, to suffer her pain. It was also obvious that he was going to do everything humanly possible to help his daughter survive. They agreed that everyone should have someone in their life, just one person, who loves them as much as JayShawn loved KayDance.

✳✳✳✳✳

"It's not good," JayShawn said, "Nothing seems to be working. It looks like we're near the end."

"I'm so sorry," said Ron. "Promise me you'll keep me posted and let me know if there's anything I can do."

"I will. Thanks, Ron."

"God bless you, man," Ron added, with a tight hug. "Give her my love."

"I will. You take care."

With that, Ron packed up his gear, deep in thought, and drove away from the hospital. He headed back toward the station and called in.

"Was this thing any good?" Maggie asked.

"Yeah, not bad," he replied, "You've got athletes, kids, hugs, tears, all the elements."

"Great, the producer would like it for the early newscast. Can you get it shipped in and then..."

"I know," interrupted Ron, "Make sure I get my meal break by two. Priorities, I know."

"You got it."

"Wouldn't want the company to go broke paying me a meal penalty."

"Certainly not."

"Done. Oh, and by the way, I'm not available for any overtime tonight, Mag."

"Hmm... Do you want to tell me why?"

"Not really. Bye, Maggie."

*****

Ron finished his day at the station, shooting an interview in one of the now vacant offices on the second floor. The layoffs had been much more severe than anyone expected, and morale was lower than at any time Ron could remember. The newsroom was deadly quiet, unlike the recent past when it buzzed with activity seemingly around the clock. Many of the cubicles had been vacated, left with stacks of videotapes and old notepads containing stories planned long ago but never completed.

Most of the producers and writers who remained, seeing the writing on the wall, were sending out resumes and trying to catch on with one of the other stations in town, or getting out of news altogether.

Investigative Reporter Maria Lopez was working on a story about computer hacking and the fellow she was interviewing, an expert on the subject, droned on about fraud and cyber security or something. Ron paid little attention, beyond keeping the man in focus in the viewfinder, his mind on sweet little KayDance and the coming evening with Sandra.

He was glad that he always kept a change of clothes in his locker at the station, because jeans and sweaty work clothes were not going to cut it at Yamashiro and there was no time to go home and change. As soon as they wrapped with their interview, he handed Maria the video card and headed to his locker downstairs to change.

*****

By six, Ron was dressed in a new pale blue Polo shirt and a pressed pair of khakis he'd kept hanging in his locker. He climbed into his Mustang and headed up Hollywood Boulevard for Yamashiro. The restaurant was at the end of a steep, winding driveway that snaked around behind the landmark Magic Castle and curved up into the hills above Hollywood. Once there, he found himself in a line behind three other vehicles and nervously checked his watch, but by 6:20, he was at the front of the line, where he left his car with the valet and walked inside.

He had barely sat down in the waiting area and checked his phone for messages when, through the window, he could see Sandra sitting a few cars back in her silver Prelude, sunglasses glistening.

A well-dressed couple in a white Audi TT was just in front of her. The vehicle was brand new, so new that there was still no license plate on the front, or presumably the back. The driver motioned and pointed, seeming to give the valet special instructions to take special care of his new vehicle and not scratch it while maneuvering through the narrow, hilly streets. The attendant nodded, and the man reluctantly surrendered his keys.

Sandra pulled up in front of the door and stepped out of her car. The early evening sun, peeking through the tall trees, cast a golden glow on her face and hair. She looked cute but business-like, he thought, in a pinstriped navy suit jacket, with sharply pleated gray slacks, and heels. Her pale violet blouse was open just enough to reveal a silver chain around her neck, with a small starfish charm. Ron stood up and watched her as she handed her keys to the valet, took the ticket, glanced briefly at the glorious view of Los Angeles, and walked toward the door.

"Hey there," said Ron. "It's nice to see you again."

"What a pleasant surprise," she said, holding out her hand. "It was nice to hear from you."

The hostess led them in to a quiet area of the restaurant, and seated them at an intimate table for two, facing a long row of picture windows, through which they had a breathtaking view of Hollywood, West Hollywood, and, on this clear evening, the rest of Los Angeles, all the way to Catalina Island. The sun was about to disappear into the early evening clouds behind Century City and was painting the western sky a magnificent blend of pastel pinks, fuchsias, and oranges. They paused to watch the spectacle and listen to the soft piano music before entering into any meaningful conversation.

"Wow, this is amazing," said Sandra. "What a gorgeous view!"

"It really is spectacular," answered Ron. "I haven't been up here in years. I thought you'd like it."

"I love sunsets," she said.

"Really, you love sunsets?" he said mockingly. "And walks on the beach, and kittens, I'm guessing."

"Actually, I'm more of a 'puppy' girl."

"Wow, me too- I mean, umm… you know what I mean."

"Yes, I know."

A waitress passed by their table carrying a couple of entrees on a tray. The enticing aroma of a sizzling steak caught the attention of them both.

"What's your favorite food?" Ron asked, chin in his hand, looking at the sparkle in her eyes across the table.

"Let's see, how about big juicy cheeseburger from…"

"Wait, let me guess," Ron interrupted. "In-N-Out?"

"Absolutely," Sandra answered, cocking her head toward the waitress. "That or a thick steak, medium rare."

"Favorite Movie?"

"Umm, it's gotta be 'Dirty Dancing'", she replied. "You know, even after all these years, my girlfriends still all get together for viewing parties whenever it's on TV. You?"

"Me? I love baseball movies, you know, like 'Field of Dreams' or 'The Natural'."

"Oh, I love 'The Natural', that's the one with Robert Redford. Makes me cry every time, at the end when he's playing catch with his boy. Let me ask you something. Do you think that was supposed to be heaven, after he dies?"

"Gosh, I hadn't even thought of that. I suppose it could be. But just like everything else, it probably means whatever you want it to mean."

"I suppose so."

"What about Comedies?" he asked.

"Oh, let's see, there's Airplane, and some of the old Black and White Marx Brothers movies still crack me up. Oh, but Monty Python is the best," she said. "I grew up with two brothers, and they could recite 'The Holy Grail' word for word."

"I can do that," said Ron. "Bring out your dead!"

Sandra laughed loudly, grabbing her nose and replying, "I am Not a Witch, I am NOT a Witch!"

Ron couldn't tell if she was for real, or just saying what she thought he wanted to hear, but either way, this woman was just too good to be true.

The waitress approached to take their orders in the midst of their awful attempts at British accents. Slightly embarrassed, Ron ordered a Stella on draft, and Sandra asked for a glass of white wine.

"Wow, this is uncanny. Who's your favorite band?" he inquired.

"Oh, I like music from the eighties and nineties. And it depends on my mood. Sometimes, I like to put on some James Taylor or Sting, other times I can get into Van Halen, or Pearl Jam. You?"

"Those work for me," said Ron. "Or the Eagles or Thorogood. The reporters tease me. They say I don't listen to anything from this millennium. That's pretty accurate, I guess."

"Oh, and I absolutely love Elvis," Sandra added.

"Which one?" Ron asked.

"Costello, of course," she said, laughing. "Duh."

"Books?"

"Let's see," said Ron. "I don't have a lot of time, but the last book I read was 'Black List'."

"Oh, I absolutely love Brad Thor," Sandra interjected. "He really knows military stuff. I try to mix it up between fiction and non-fiction. The last book

I read was 'Unbroken' by Laura Hillenbrand. The story of Louis Zamperini, the Olympic athlete."

"I know it well, read it a couple years ago," said Ron. "I went out and bought it right after I met Louis. What an amazing guy."

"You met him?" she asked.

"I did," he replied. "A few months before he died. He was in town for an event promoting the Olympic trials."

"I'm so jealous. I want your job. I'm so glad you called me, I was hoping you would."

"Really? That's nice to hear," said Ron. "Sorry for the short notice. It's just that I got some great news today and I wanted to share it with you."

"Great news? What great news?" Sandra asked with anticipation.

"I received an Emmy nomination for a story I worked on last year, and it's actually pretty strong. I think we have a good chance to win."

"That's fantastic'" she said, grabbing his left arm, above the elbow. "What was the story about?"

"It was a medical story, a three-parter, about a woman who needed surgery so that she'd be able to stop shaking and just perform the tasks that you and I take for granted every day, like driving a car, and feeding herself. We shot her before, during and after the surgery to show how her life was changed. It was pretty emotional. I'll show it to you sometime. It's on the station's website, I can bring it up on my iPad."

"Oh, I'd love to see it," said Sandra excitedly.

The waitress brought their drinks. Sandra proposed a toast. "To acknowledgement of a job well done."

"Cheers," said Ron, before touching glasses and taking a long sip of his Stella.

"So, tell me about yourself," said Ron. "Where did you grow up?"

"OK, well I'm from Huntington Beach, born and raised. Went to school there, then to UCLA."

"How long have you been working in P.R.?" he asked.

"I started as a gopher at the firm about four years ago," she said. "But, I caught on pretty quickly, and soon I was dealing with clients, myself. Then, when they had an opening, they promoted me. "

"It seems like an interesting job," said Ron. "You get to meet different people all the time."

"Nothing like yours, though. You have just the most interesting job I can imagine."

"It has its moments," he acknowledged. "Like today, for example. When I called you, I was on my way over to Children's Hospital, where some of the Dodgers players were visiting kids with cancer."

He consciously left out any mention of KayDance or her father, thinking that such a sad story could wait.

"How cool!" she said. "I love the Dodgers. And that's so nice of them to do that for the children."

"You're a Dodgers fan, too?" Ron asked. "Because that's a requirement for me, you know."

"Absolutely I am. My Dad had season tickets for years," said Sandra. "And it's a requirement for me too. I learned that the hard way, when I married a Giants fan."

"Wait… Married?" asked Ron, taken aback.

"Yeah, I… I guess I should have told you," she said. "But we're going through a divorce right now. It'll be final in a few months."

Ron put his glass on the table, dead center on the cardboard coaster, somewhat deflated, and ran his finger pensively around the rim.

"Wow. I mean… I don't mean to pry, but what was the problem?"

"Well, I guess it's OK to talk about it, I've been keeping it inside for so long."

Sandra heaved a sigh and began her saga.

"His name is Jack. He's a cop. LAPD. We met in high school and he was just the greatest guy. You know, athletic, popular … We got married at 22, and a few years later, after trying all kinds of jobs, construction, sales, whatever, he decided he wanted to become a police officer. So he went through the Academy, and when he graduated, I was just so proud of him. It was the first time he had really accomplished anything meaningful in his life, you know?"

"So anyway, after the academy he started working patrol in Newton Division, you know, *Shootin' Newton* they call it, and after a few months things started to change." Her eyes left Ron's and sunk to her hands, fingers enmeshed on the table. "He'd come home late, sometimes drunk. And he could never learn to leave his problems at work. Every night I had to hear about how awful people are, man's inhumanity to man, and all that. He just became so angry and bitter."

Ron felt a nerve being touched when she brought up leaving his problems at work, recalling his own frequent nightmares.

"Did he ever mistreat you?" he asked.

"Not physically," Sandra replied, now staring at the glass in her hand and sucking on her lower lip. "But he became a totally different person than the man I married. Never saw the bright side of anything any more. Nothing was fun. So pissed off all the time, arguing with me endlessly about the stupidest little things. Just really depressing to be around, you know?" she added, rubbing her forehead and holding back a tear.

"I'm so sorry," said Ron, reaching to softly caress her hand. "You don't deserve that."

She bit her lip and stared out at the Hollywood skyline.

"So where does it stand now?"

"Well, he says he wants to work it out, but we tried that once before and, I don't know, life is just too short."

Her lower lip quivered.

"So, do you have contact with him?"

"Unfortunately, yes," she said. "He's always calling, trying to get me to go away with him, down to San Diego for the weekend or something. His problem now is that when he moved out, he had nowhere to go, so he moved in with his mother. He hates it there and wants to come back, but I keep telling him no."

Ron could see that his reticence to enter into a new relationship was well founded.

A crazy ex. Just what I need.

Tragic, he thought, that even someone as adorable and seemingly perfect as Sandra had such ample baggage that once opened, could find a way to spoil one's serene, contented life as an overworked, pathetic loner.

"What about you?" Sandra asked. "You've never been married?"

"Me?" he laughed. "No. I'm not sure that would be a good idea. So far, I've been a pretty lousy boyfriend."

"Really? How so?"

"Well, for one thing I have ridiculous hours. I'm never home. I work holidays, so there's that. My phone rings at all hours, whenever something big breaks. I have to have a bag packed and be ready to hop on a plane at a moment's notice."

"That's not so terrible," she said.

"It gets better. I can't have a pet because I'm never home to feed it. Hell, I can barely keep a houseplant alive. I had a pet rock, but it died."

Sandra chuckled and looked at him playfully.

"Oh, and on a date," he continued, "I'm just a barrel of laughs. No matter where we go, I can come up with a story of something awful that happened on that very corner." Ron gestured out the picture window at a random part of the city. "You see that street? Some guy was depressed after losing his job a few years ago and shot his whole family in that house right there. Oh, and last year a drunk driver took out a family of five at that intersection. I've got a million of them, all really cheery."

"I like your stories," she said. "I think they're interesting."

"Trust me," he said. "They get old fast."

*****

Ron and Sandra finished their drinks and walked outside the restaurant, through the patio, and into the plush garden overlooking the lights of Hollywood. A slight chill began in the clear spring air, as they stood, hand in hand, for a few minutes taking in the gorgeous view and the last few moments of twilight. He pointed out the lights of a large airliner in the distance, passing over downtown on approach to LAX to the south.

"Beautiful, isn't it," she said. "Sometime, I'd just like to climb on a plane like that and get away. Doesn't even matter where it's going. There are so many places I've never seen."

"There's plenty of time to live your dreams," Ron said. "Just don't let anyone get in your way. Not anyone."

"I hope that's true. I just want to be happy."

Ron sensed that she was about to cry, and put his arm around her. She pulled in close and returned the embrace. He wasn't certain if she was truly interested in him, or simply trying to keep warm, but it was nice either way.

"OK, here's a story for you," he said, pointing to the southwest. "Do you see that group of bright lights over there?"

"Sure," she answered.

"That's 'The Grove' Shopping Mall. The Farmer's Market is there, and CBS Television City, too."

"Yeah, I go there a lot. What about it?"

"So, I remember the first really big story I covered, after moving to L.A. It turns out that there's a huge pocket of methane gas under that part of Los Angeles. It's been there for centuries. Something related to the La Brea Tar Pits, I think. Anyway, nobody really paid any attention to it at all, until one day it exploded right under the Rick's Clothing Store there on 3rd Street. Blew the whole store apart. I remember it like it was yesterday. It was a Sunday afternoon and the place was loaded with shoppers. We got there pretty quickly because we heard it on the scanner. We actually got inside the store, where all the windows had been blown out and the ceiling was hanging down. The displays and mannequins were all knocked over, and there were injured people everywhere. Flames were actually coming out of cracks in the ground from the underground gas. Finally, the Fire Department made us get out of the building, but not until we had the most amazing video. I think about it every time I drive by."

"Or, when you see the lights from miles away," she added.

"Yeah," he laughed. "So you can see how twisted my mind is."

"I still think your stories are interesting."

"You're the one," he said, as they turned back toward the patio door.

"It was so nice seeing you again," Sandra said. "I'm glad we did this."

"I'm glad I called, I hope we can do it again. I really hope things work out for you."

He kissed her lightly on the forehead, and they walked together back to the parking valet to retrieve their vehicles. The sun had set into the Pacific and their evening was over.

Friday, March 20th

Ron finished out his week and was seated in a vacant cubical in the newsroom. He was working on completing his timesheet, when he felt a hand on his left shoulder.

"Shelby! What are you doing here?"

"Ya know," she replied with a laugh. "I'm wondering that myself. Larry kept calling me about once a week, to see how I was doing. He's a persistent guy, I'll say that about him."

"That's way true," said Ron.

"He said he'd really like me to come back and try it again. I kept telling him that I didn't want to be in the field, but he finally said they might be able to let me fill in doing weather or even sports. I told him I'd love that!"

"Perfect," Ron said. "You see that? Things have a way of working out."

"Yes, they do."

"Well, I'm really excited for you. Let me know if there's anything I can do for you."

"Of course," Shelby said with a wink. "As long as it doesn't require holding a bucket."

Ron dropped his chin sheepishly and smiled.

"I promise."

"Gotta go, Ronnie," she said. See ya around."

"See ya."

Shelby turned toward the door and almost ran full speed into Bobbi, who, at the same time, was walking over to speak to Ron.

"Ronnie, you got a second?" she said, sitting on the edge of the desk.

"Sure," he replied. "What's up?"

"Umm, I got a call this afternoon from JayShawn Brown, KayDance's father."

"Yeah?"

"She passed away at the house this morning," Bobbi said, fighting back tears.

"No!" Ron exclaimed, holding his forehead. "I ran into him at the hospital last week. He said she was not doing well, but I ... "

"They never found a donor, and she just couldn't fight it off anymore."

"I'm so sorry," he said, grasping her hand.

"I'm writing a follow-up story now for tonight." she said. "People will want to know what happened to her."

"Yeah. That's a good idea. When's the funeral?"

"He said they were still making plans, but he wanted you and me to know that we're welcome, if we want to come."

"Oh, I'll be there," said Ron. "I feel so bad for him. He's such a nice man. They didn't deserve this."

"No, they sure didn't."

Wednesday, April 15th

Richard Eliot Tatis was a family man who had been married to his high school sweetheart, Gabriella for five years, since they were both 22. A quiet man, slim in build and remarkably shy, he was the proud father of a four-year-old daughter, who worked full-time at what had been his late father's welding shop. He was also an accused killer. Richard was taken into custody after the star witness in the murder case against his brother had been gunned down on a dark street in Pacoima back in August.

Richard's older brother Roberto "Flaco" Tatis was well known to law enforcement as a long-time member of the Paxton Street Locos, a violent street gang in the northeastern San Fernando Valley. Flaco was in custody, charged in the shooting death of Pedro "Babyface" Cruz, a member of a rival Valley gang. His trial was to begin on August 27th.

The prosecution was prepared to call Yoli Navarro, a neighbor of Cruz, who had been at the party where the shooting took place. She was ready to testify that she had seen Flaco arguing with Babyface about a woman. Babyface had punched Flaco, who left the party, then returned a few minutes later and shot Babyface several times in the back before fleeing the scene.

The prosecution made a huge mistake by neglecting to protect their star witness. At 10:48 pm on Monday, August 26th, as Yoli stood outside her home on Lehigh Avenue talking to some friends, a vehicle described as a black Toyota Camry made the left turn from Louvre Street onto Lehigh. The driver parked the car two houses from the corner and quietly approached the group on foot. Without saying a word, he put two bullets into Yoli's head and walked quickly back to his car, which he had left running. The sedan made a u-turn and, headlights out, fled the scene.

The few witnesses willing to talk to detectives that night were confused about the shooter's description. One man said he was short, about 5'5" and

130 lbs. A woman described him as tall, about 5'10' and 160 lbs. Both say the man had short dark hair, a goatee and a mustache, but the sketch artist's drawings were largely dissimilar. Confusion by eyewitnesses at a crime scene is certainly not unusual. In fact, police say that circumstantial evidence is often much more reliable than eyewitness testimony in cases like this. And there was plenty of circumstantial evidence.

Richard, although not a member of any street gang, had ample motive to kill Dolores. His brother Roberto was much larger in stature than his younger brother, and had always protected him from the neighborhood bullies while they were growing up. Now that their father had passed away, if Roberto ended up in prison again, Richard would have no one to keep his young family safe.

Police also noted that Richard drove a dark green Nissan Maxima, a vehicle that could easily, on a dark street, be mistaken for a black Camry. The fact that he lived just four blocks away from Yoli also led detectives to believe he had sufficient opportunity to have committed the crime, and Richard was under suspicion by the morning after the killing. His arrest came several months later.

Richard protested from the beginning that he was totally innocent. His mother Lupe, fearful of losing both of her sons to prison, contacted Anthony Iglesias, a high-profile criminal attorney to defend her youngest son. After interviewing Richard and reviewing all the evidence, Iglesias was convinced that the charges against him were unfounded and that the District Attorney would have a difficult time bringing the case to trial, much less securing a conviction. He was so confident, in fact, that he placed a call to KSIX reporter Grant Butler, to ask if he'd be interested in covering a unique and fascinating case.

Grant Butler was well known to the Police and also among the huge street gang community in Southern California. For years, Leo had given him free rein to cover stories about the gang culture in Los Angeles, its perpetrators and its victims. He reported in depth about the root causes of the gang problem, from family structure to prohibition and the lucrative black markets it creates for drugs, guns and other contraband.

Butler had witnessed the corruption caused by the obscene amounts of money in black markets when he worked in Miami years earlier. Police officers, prosecutors, and even judges had often been unable to resist the temptation brought about by the incomprehensible amounts of cash within the illicit narcotics trade. He found that his knowledge of gangs' inner workings also served him well after moving to Los Angeles.

Over the years he'd gotten to know a good number of the players. He'd been escorted with camera crews inside prisons where he met the hard-core Mexican Mafia shot callers as well as the wanna-bes. He and his crews had done stories with innumerable families of gang members, some imprisoned and some deceased. He'd lost count of the number of mothers he'd seen weeping inconsolably on camera, bemoaning the loss of a child.

Predictably, despite their walls being coated with layers of spray-painted monikers and their offsprings' young bodies and faces covered with ink, most remained in denial, ignoring the signs until finding themselves faced with a cold, painful reality.

Butler had become so knowledgeable, in fact, that he had written a book about the inner workings of street gangs. **The Sub Rosa Network** chronicled the lives of those who controlled the gangs from inside prison walls and how they maintained their power while incarcerated. It also dealt with several reformed gang members who had turned away from the lifestyle and who, despite serving life sentences, were attempting to help vulnerable young men from getting trapped in the web of criminality that had ensnared them. His writings and news stories had won him numerous awards as well as a number of death threats. The station had even hired an off-duty officer for a time, to escort him from work to his Los Feliz home. Even so, he was highly respected by most everyone on both sides for his straightforward, honest reporting.

Anthony Iglesias, for one, had an enormous admiration for Butler as a journalist, and pitched him the story of an innocent young man, trying to provide for his wife and child, being accused of a crime he had not committed. He assured Butler that if he showed up in Van Nuys Court for the preliminary hearing, he would be astonished at the evidence he was ready to present that would prove his client's innocence. Or at least establish sufficient doubt, causing the judge to find the case too weak to pursue.

Ron and Grant interviewed Iglesias in his Downtown office the night before the hearing. Iglesias promised them a show the next morning in court.

Chapter Six

MORTALITY

Thursday, April 16th

Grant Butler had made sure that a Media Request Form was properly filled out the night before and faxed in to the Court Clerk in Department 104. He'd called in the morning to confirm that they had been approved by the Judge to cover the preliminary hearing.

He and Ron both knew from years of covering court cases that Judges can be very reticent to allow cameras into their courtrooms and those who did, often established arbitrary rules to make the job that much more difficult. Often the crew was made to set up in the very back of the audience, where a clean shot of the defendant's face was next to impossible. Other times, the crew was instructed to not show the Judge's face, or the defendant's face, or was allowed to shoot video only with no audio. No one could figure out where these random rules came from, but mostly the media went along with them quietly, thankful to be admitted into the courtroom at all.

Judge Mary Margaret Rosewood was different. She was young for a judge, probably in her early fifties, curly shoulder-length brown hair and striking features. A former prosecutor, Judge Rosewood was all business, knew all the games played by attorneys on both sides, and put up with none of it. She didn't often get requests for media since Van Nuys Prelim Court very seldom had a case interesting enough to put on the news.

While she'd never admit it, she did enjoy seeing herself on television, so she quickly approved the camera and allowed Ron to set up in the empty jury box to her right, just behind the court reporter. He was allowed to place a wireless mike on the witness stand and another on the Counsel's table. While he was setting up, Beth Collins, the Deputy District Attorney trying the case objected to the presence of a camera, but her dissent was ruled unfounded. Rosewood had the Bailiffs escort the defendant in and asked that the matter proceed once the mikes were in place.

Only rarely did Ron, or any other photographer, have a court case all to themselves. Trials in Los Angeles tended to create a herd mentality among the media, due to either the salaciousness of the story or the fame - or infamy- of the parties involved. It felt good to have an exclusive on a case and not have to "pool" the video to all the other stations in town and the tabloid shows, as is so often the case. Frequently the Judge will permit a single video camera and a single still camera in the courtroom, requiring the crews to make arrangements to duplicate the images for other journalists, most of whom waited outside. Because of Grant Butler's reputation and body of work, however, he was the only reporter contacted by Iglesias, and the only one with any knowledge of the case.

*****

Ron had been "pool camera" on some of the highest-profile cases in recent years. Rapper Lil' Toof, accused of beating his equally famous girlfriend, Mary Marie, brought throngs of media- broadcast, print and tabloid- to the Downtown Criminal Courthouse every time he had to appear for a probation hearing. When Jane Thayer, the elderly starlet from the '50s, was arrested for punching a Beverly Hills officer during a traffic stop, she became fodder for the media for several weeks. And when television actor Rob Barnes stood accused of shooting his wife in the head outside a North Hollywood restaurant, the media circus set up their trucks for weeks outside this same Van Nuys Courthouse. Ron drew the straw, putting him inside the Courtroom on at least some of the days of these trials, which he actually enjoyed more than sitting outside waiting for a break and chasing down the players afterward, hoping for a sound-bite. Barnes actually recognized Ron to the point that he approached him one morning outside the courthouse asking, in his tough-guy Brooklyn accent, "Have ya got any coffee?" as if expecting the cameraman to reach in his equipment bag and produce a cup of Starbucks on-the-spot.

Ron learned to take the responsibility of a pool cameraman seriously years earlier, when one day during Jane Thayer's trial in Beverly Hills, several stations had requested that the pool photog, Lou Waterbury of Channel 3, allow them to cable directly from the courtroom to a "mult-box" in the hallway, into which crews could plug in cameras or other recording devices, making the distribution of "dubs" that much quicker. Lou agreed, and a cable was strung from his camera, along the wall, under the door and into the mult-box. What Lou didn't realize, and should have been told, was that one of the cable-news stations, wanting to be first with the story, was airing the entire feed LIVE.

Lou was set up and preparing for testimony to begin for the day, when crews watching the monitor in the hallway saw him quickly zoom the camera in to the large calendar on the wall to grab a "white balance". Then, for no apparent reason, he zoomed in on a few members of the audience, in particular one of Miss Thayer's lovely grand-daughters, who had shown up in court wearing a mini-skirt and a tight, seriously low-cut blouse. Lou, always the joker, no doubt expected kudos from the other photogs after sending them pre-trial video of her ample cleavage and hiked up skirt with crossed legs, but soon the engineer from the network snuck quietly into the courtroom just as the Judge was taking the bench and whispered to Lou that his pictures were being transmitted live around the world, not just to the hallway. That day Ron learned the valuable lesson that any time the camera is turned on, there's a chance that someone will see the picture.

Prosecutor Beth Collins began with an opening statement, which explained the charges and the evidence that the prosecution intended to bring to trial against Richard Tatis. She established that while there was no evidence at all of gang involvement on Richard's part, the fact that his brother was a long time gangster on trial for murder provided plenty of motive for the crime. She stated that in the two years since his father's death, Richard had become closer to his brother and depended upon him for protection from the local street gangs. The thought of losing him to a life behind bars was just too much for Richard to accept. Then there was the car, the proximity to his home, and the description of the suspect, as provided by numerous witnesses.

Richard, dressed in a blue L.A. County Jail jumpsuit, sat nervously in his chair and whispered several words to his attorney. Ron primarily focused on the Prosecutor, but made sure to also get wide shots of the courtroom, a few cutaways of the Judge and tight shots of Richard's face reacting to the accusations against him.

By the time Collins had concluded her convincing opening statement, both Ron and Grant were forming doubts about Richard's proclaimed innocence. But it was time for Anthony Iglesias to tell his side of the story.

Iglesias began by presenting a short biography of Richard. He explained to the Judge that the Tatis family had moved to the Valley from Laredo, Texas about a decade and a half before the murder, when Roberto was in High School and his younger brother Richard was in seventh grade. Roberto immediately took up with the wrong crowd, skipping school and eventually dropping out to become "Flaco". Pedro Tatis was devastated and concerned that his younger son might follow the same path. He took care to spoil and pamper the boy he loved so much, guiding him through Boy Scouts and even the ROTC program at school.

When Richard, a kind and gentle boy, graduated from High School, he immediately went to work at his father's welding shop in Sun Valley, not far from home. He soon married his High School sweetheart and settled down. He used his money not for drugs, alcohol or guns, Iglesias pointed out, but to rent a house near his father, to buy a car, and to provide for his wife and young daughter Dolores. Occasionally, when business was good, he explained, Richard would save enough to take his family to the movies, or as a special treat, an infrequent Dodgers game.

At that point, Iglesias requested that the Bailiffs unfurl the rolled-up projection screen, which was kept on a stand in the corner next to the door to the Jury Room. Two Deputies stood it up, opened the screen to its full length, and then angled it so everyone, particularly the Judge, could see it without obstruction. After fiddling with his laptop and a small projector for a moment, Iglesias asked that the lights in the courtroom be brought down.

He approached the screen as the presentation began, showing video of a packed Dodger Stadium with a game in progress. Iglesias explained to the Judge that by incredible coincidence, an episode of the long-running comedy show, "Doubled Over" happened to be filming an episode at the stadium on the night of August 26th, the same night of Yoli Navarro's murder. And the scene they were watching just happened to take place with the show's star, David Benjamin, walking up an aisle in the Reserved section of the stadium, right behind home plate. The very same aisle where Richard had been seated with his young daughter.

The director had waited until sundown to begin filming, so the lighting would be consistent for each take. He shot the scene numerous times, from various angles and focal lengths, several of which, amazingly, offered a clear look at Richard and Dolores seated in Section 5, Row H, Seats 4 and 5. Richard's white Dodgers jersey made it easy for Iglesias to point him out on the screen. He also brought attention to the lower third of the frame, where the camera's "time-code" was superimposed on the video. The production used "time of day time-coding" while filming, which provided, among other things, technical help with editing, but also happened to supply an accurate and critically important piece of evidence in this case.

Iglesias was able to illustrate that from 8:22 pm to 9:56 pm, Richard and Dolores were in their seats. But filming done after 10:03 showed those two seats to be unoccupied. Richard claimed they had left their seats to get food and use the restroom, and did not actually leave the game until the ninth inning, a few minutes later.

The prosecution pointed out that the crime occurred at 10:48 pm and that Richard might have had time to drive to the Valley and commit the crime had he left the stadium at 10:00, which he likely would have done with a young child.

Iglesias countered with Richard's cell phone records, provided by his phone company, which he also projected on the screen. Records showed that Richard's phone was used at 10:14 pm, the signal hitting a cell tower on the hill behind Dodger Stadium. Iglesias argued that this proved he was still at the stadium at that time. Beth Collins insisted that all it really proved was that the *phone* was there. Richard could have easily handed it off to a friend in attendance at the stadium. She also speculated that had Richard received a call while in the parking lot, say from a co-conspirator, perhaps notifying him where Yoli Navarro was at that moment, 10:14 pm, he still could have sped from the stadium to Pacoima and arrived there in time to do the killing.

Iglesias laughed and mockingly asked her if she had ever attended a Dodgers game and tried to leave the parking lot in the late innings.

Judge Mary Margaret Rosewood slowly closed the file in front of her, dismissed everyone for lunch, and ordered them all back at 1:30 in the afternoon.

Grant and Ron had been fascinated by the arguments, and both of them remained torn. They tossed their theories back and forth over hot dogs at Cupid's, not far from the courthouse. Did Richard do it? Could he really be a killer? Was the defense accurate in their portrayal of Richard as a choirboy, or was he, as the D.A. insisted, just too close to the gang life to avoid getting caught up in it?

After the break, the Judge was quick to rule. She chastised the prosecution for wasting her time and attempting to bring such a weak case to trial. Without stronger evidence linking Richard to the crime, she said, they stood little if any chance of a conviction. She instructed them, as a teacher would a reprobate student, to do a better job preparing and presenting their case if they wanted to re-file in the future. Ron kept a tight shot of Judge Rosewood, but glanced away from his camera, scanning the courtroom for reactions.

"Case dismissed, Mr. Tatis, you are free to go."

Ron panned the camera quickly, just as Richard's head dropped to the table. He looked up at his family with a gigantic smile and tears flowing freely down his cheeks. In the audience, his wife and daughter cheered, cried and applauded as they jumped out of their seats, unaware that his release from custody would not come instantaneously, but several long hours later after being "processed" out of the jail.

Grant noticed Beth and the rest of the prosecution team swiftly packing up their briefcases and skulking toward the twin doors in the rear of Department104. He motioned to Ron and followed them into the hallway and around the corner to the gray marble foyer. James Wick, a young attorney on the team, pressed the DOWN button as they all waited for one of the six elevators to arrive on the fifth floor. Grant broke the awkward silence by asking Beth if she'd like to comment on camera about the case. She told him that she had no doubt of Richard's guilt and would not rest until they could prove it and bring him to justice. Judge Rosewood, she said, was inexperienced, rude and incompetent.

"She has no fucking idea what she's doing up there. And I can't believe you're going to put this bullshit story on the news."

Ron had broken down his equipment from the jury box as quickly as possible, grabbed his mikes and elbowed his way through the crowd that was exiting the courtroom. He reached the foyer just in time to hear Beth, entering the now open elevator car on her right, let out a stream of expletives that made him wonder what, if anything, Grant had said to her. The door closed, leaving Ron and Grant to wait with the crowd for the next car.

"What the hell was that?" Ron asked.

"I don't know," said Grant. "She's got a hair up her ass. I just asked her if she wanted to comment."

"I don't get it, you're normally so irresistible to women," Ron said as another elevator door opened and they stepped inside.

"I think you should call her at home tonight."

"Umm, I think I'll pass," Grant said. "But I don't know when I'll ever be able to call their office for help again."

*****

Gabriella and Dolores were ecstatic, and enthusiastically thanked Grant and Ron for their coverage of Richard's story. After long, tearful hugs, Gabriella assured Grant that they'd be watching the news that evening for his report, and then asked him for a photo and an autograph. He gladly complied. She also handed Ron a slip of paper and asked him for his signature. This had happened a few times before, mostly star-struck viewers who wanted the autograph of anyone who hung out with someone they'd seen on TV.

For the first time, though, instead of declining the request and insisting that his job was not that of a celebrity, he took the pen and wrote:

"Dolores, Stay in School, and Stay in Focus- Ron Sharp, KSIX Cameraman."

He handed it back to Gabriella and said, "This is for your daughter. Tell her we're praying for her." Gabriella wept and hugged him again.

Grant headed back to the station to work on the story, while Ron stayed through the afternoon, waiting on the sidewalk near the 'sally port' at the south side of the building with Richard's wife and daughter.

It was close to 5 o'clock when Richard exited through a nondescript door and onto the asphalt road that was used by the buses each morning to deliver inmates to the courthouse for trial. Wearing his street clothes and carrying a brown grocery bag containing his personal effects, he walked swiftly toward them. The hugs and tears of the reunion made a wonderful shot, Ron thought, certainly one worth waiting for. Ron asked each of them their feelings on camera.

"Relief," said Richard, holding his little girl and clutching his wife. "Pure relief."

"We just wanted him home with us," Gabriella said, "We know he did not do this and he belongs with us." The family once again thanked Ron for covering the story as they walked to the car, together for the first time in weeks.

Ron took the additional video to his truck and headed back to Hollywood.

$$*****$$

That evening, Ron got in bed and turned on the news, which he seldom did, but this night he was curious how his story would turn out. It was planned as a "set-piece" for Grant, meaning that rather than being a prepared "package", or a live-shot from a remote location, Grant would be live on the set to introduce his packaged story and then interact with the anchors briefly afterward.

About 15 minutes into the newscast, Ron sat up and stared hard at the screen. It was obvious that something was wrong. The beginning of the newscast showed both Charles Hughes and Gretchen Salvo sitting behind the anchor desk, just as they had since Gretchen's promotion to weeknight anchor a few months earlier. But after the first commercial break, Gretchen had begun introducing every story. There were no wide shots of the set, and Charles was nowhere to be seen. Gretchen was doing a good job of making things appear normal, but Ron knew her well enough to sense that she was under stress. She was doing so well, in fact, that the average viewer at home would most likely not have noticed anything out of place at all. But he could tell.

He grabbed the phone and texted Grant:

Is everything OK there?

Grant did not answer him immediately, because his piece was coming up in the next block. Gretchen introduced him right out of the commercial break. But again, no wide shot of the set, and no Charles.

Grant's piece looked good, the story of Richard Tatis, told in a way that allowed the viewer to make up his or her own mind about his guilt or innocence, while illustrating the emotional impact on his family and the absolute oddity of the Dodgers game footage.

After the piece, Grant threw it back to Gretchen and almost immediately grabbed his phone to text Ron:

Grant:It's Charles- ill in Anchor chair FD/EMS here now.

> **Ron: holy shit I knew it.**

Grant:thinking heart attack he doesn't look good -Idiot was smoking before show

> **Ron:is he Gonna b ok?**

Grant:dunno yet

> **Ron:can I help in   some way?**

Grant:Nope- ready 4 transport

> **Ron:Praying...**

Grant: We all are. Gnite Nice job today.

The Paramedics from LAFD Fire Station 82 had arrived at the studio very quickly after receiving the 911 call from Scott Castle, the nightside Assignment Editor. Instinctively, they entered the studio as quietly as possible and began resuscitation measures even as Charles lay on the concrete floor of the soundstage. Gretchen read the teleprompter flawlessly, never once glancing off to the right of the camera while CPR was being performed on her debilitated co-anchor. She threw to a package and checked anxiously with the EMS Supervisor.

"Is he going to make it?"

"We're doing all we can," he replied. "He needs to be in the hospital, so we're arranging transport."

Charles was placed onto a gurney and wheeled out of the studio, where he was loaded into the Rescue Ambulance. He arrived at Hollywood Presbyterian six minutes later.

Ron texted Grant again around 11:20, knowing the late newscast was over.

Ron: Any Updates?

> **Grant:I had to leave. Long effing day. Haven't heard anything.**

Ron: Thx. I'll call the Station

No one from the station had been able to get any information out of the hospital. Scott had called Charles' wife Linda and told her of his collapse, but had been unable to reach her since she left their home in Ventura County to meet him in the Emergency Room. Ron decided to try to get some sleep and get an update in the morning.

Friday, April 17th

Ron sat up anxiously in bed and turned on the KSIX morning newscast at 7:13, when his mental alarm clock proved reliable as always. They were in the middle of a story about the school board or something equally uninteresting.

When the piece ended, morning anchors Todd Mack and Roxi Peters appeared on camera. They were ashen, and as they had probably done numerous times throughout the morning, made the announcement to Southern California:

"Some sad news for those of us here at Channel Six this morning," reported Roxi, "Long-time evening news anchor Charles Hughes has passed away. He suffered a heart attack while on the air here at KSIX last night. He was rushed to a hospital but died early this morning with his wife by his side."

Ron hung his legs over the side of the bed and staring at the floor, shook his head in disbelief.

"All of us who knew Charles," added Todd, "feel an incredible sense of loss today. We pray for his family and we'll miss him deeply here at Channel Six. Funeral arrangements are pending."

Ron grabbed the remote, turned off the TV, and headed for the shower. Hell of a way to start the day.

*****

KSIX held a Memorial Service for Charles a few days later in the main studio. Ron had only a few minutes to attend before heading out on assignment. Leo fought back tears, saying that Charles had been a personal hero of his for many years. Rich, likewise, had wonderful things to say about his friend and colleague. Hundreds of letters of condolence had come in to the station from loyal viewers and decorated the walls of the set, along with enlarged black and white photos of Charles on the job and in the anchor chair.

Ron remembered how Charles had always talked of his love for his wife Linda, and seeing her there mourning his loss made him wonder if he would ever have someone so thoroughly devoted, with whom to share his life. They were blessed, he thought, to have the years together that they did.

Wednesday, April 22nd

Ron was up a bit early, stopped for coffee on his way in to work, and arrived at the station with plenty of time to gear-up. He headed up the stairs and into the newsroom to get his first assignment.

Walking into the newsroom, Ron noticed that Leo's office was empty, as it had been for several days, locked and dark. No one seemed to know exactly what was going on with him, whether he was ill, on an unexpected vacation, or gone for good.

Walking behind Maggie, who was seated at the assignment desk, he noticed the headline of an article she was reading on her computer, from the L.A. Times website:

LAPD OFFICER ARRESTED IN COLD CASE MURDER

Ron leaned in, over Maggie's left shoulder, to get a closer look. He knew that he had become acquainted with a good number of cops, from covering crime stories on the streets, but with some 10,000 sworn officers on the Department, the odds were pretty low that he would recognize the name. The first paragraph of the story, however, sent him reeling:

Veteran L.A.P.D. detective Rachel Larimore was arrested today at the Downtown Los Angeles Police Headquarters, in connection with a years-old murder case. The "cold-case" revolved around the death of Shannon Lee Russo, who was killed in her home in February of 2007, a few months after her marriage to Larimore's former boyfriend, James Russo.

"Oh, my God," said Ron, stepping back from the screen. "Are you kidding me?"

"What?"

"Rachel Larimore! I dated her."

"You what?" said Maggie, spinning in her chair.

"I went out with her, and around that time, when I first moved here. I can't fucking believe this."

He walked quickly over to a vacant cubicle, sat down, and brought up The Times website on the computer, where he began reading the entire article:

Cold-case detectives had recently reopened the case and begun to re-examine evidence and re-interview witnesses. They discovered, amongst the stored evidence, a sealed tube containing a swab with which detectives had recovered some saliva from Russo's forearm after a violent struggle in her San Fernando Valley apartment the morning she was shot and killed.

A DNA test performed on the swab showed conclusively that the saliva had come from a female, which brought a new twist to the case. Initially, it had been believed that a male suspect had killed Russo, likely after she had interrupted a burglary in progress. Now they had to look at the case again in its entirety.

Detectives Dave Jackson and Glenn Sarkis contacted the parents of the victim, along with others who had been part of the initial investigation. They were told that, in the days following the crime, homicide detectives were alerted to Officer Rachel Larimore, and told that she had been harassing Russo and her husband ever since they had started dating, and particularly since their wedding.

She and James had dated on and off since college, and Larimore was having a difficult time accepting the fact that it was over. For some reason, she was never interviewed in connection with the case, and detectives had never looked at the accusations against her seriously. Shannon's parents suggested that it had to do with the fact that she was a LAPD Officer, and the department wasn't interested in looking at one of their own.

Detectives Jackson and Sarkis, however, took the information and ran with it. They went right to the Chief of Police, Charlie Beck, and informed him that one of his veteran officers was being looked at in a murder case. The Chief arranged for the investigation to be conducted by a top-secret group of Internal Affairs detectives, and all information was to be shared only with the Chief himself. The fact that Detective Larimore's office was right down the hall from the Homicide Bureau made secrecy all the more critical, and much more difficult.

The female DNA was the key. They needed a sample of Larimore's bodily DNA to either confirm a match, or eliminate her as a suspect. It took several days of tailing her and watching her every move before she gave them what they were looking for. Last Thursday morning, Rachel and her young daughter made a trip to the Walmart store near their home, to pick up a few household items, and after checking out, decided to get something cold to drink at the small snack bar inside the store. As plain-clothes detectives watched from a distance, Rachel and her little girl sat down at a small table and enjoyed a few minutes together as mother and daughter, then got up from the table, tossed their cups in the trash, and left the store. The officers retrieved Rachel's cup from the trash next to the exit and sealed it in a plastic bag. They labeled the bag and transported it immediately to the downtown Crime Lab for DNA analysis. After a few days, they received their answer. The saliva on the straw contained DNA that was a positive match to the DNA recovered from murder victim Shannon Russo's arm, and they had their evidence linking Rachel Larimore to the killing.

Ron had met Rachel on a story in September of his first year in L.A. At the time, she was a beat-cop assigned to Van Nuys Division. He had just started working for KSIX a few months earlier and, being new to Los Angeles, took every opportunity to meet new people, particularly cute, interesting young women. Rachel was certainly that.

There was a call of a domestic dispute in an apartment on Lennox Avenue, which evolved into a barricaded suspect when shots were fired at responding officers. They pulled back, sealed off the area, and called for SWAT. Larimore was stationed at the corner of Sherman Way and Lennox, about a block north of the incident. Her job was to keep the intersection closed to pedestrians and traffic. When Ron pulled up in his news van, she directed him where to park, and where to set up his camera to get the best shots of the SWAT activity. The incident dragged on for hours, well past dark, and the two began talking. Ron learned, in that time, that Rachel had recently joined the department after graduating from Cal State Northridge, that she loved sports, particularly basketball, and that she did not like to date other officers.

The situation ended with SWAT firing tear-gas canisters through the first-floor window of the apartment occupied by the suspect, who surrendered to officers and was taken into custody. Ron got great video of the SWAT activity, and the suspect being handcuffed and transported to the Police Station. Before he packed up and left the scene, he and Rachel exchanged phone numbers. He promised to give her a call, and about a week later he called and asked her out on a date.

The relationship lasted well into the next year, when Ron met someone he really fell for, and broke it off with Rachel. But they remained good friends, and would occasionally run into each other at crime-scenes or police news conferences. She'd always greet him with a big hug and, particularly over the past several years, with updates on her life as a married woman and mother.

*****

The news that she was being accused of killing a romantic rival so many years ago was a gut-punch. Ron, as far as he could remember, had rarely, if ever, heard Rachel mention James' name, and when she had, her tone was one of describing a spurned ex- lover, certainly not someone still being pursued. He reached back in his memory to try to think of any signs that he could have missed. Or, was he oblivious the whole time, and not the trained observer he believed himself to be?

He tried to process the fact that DNA is overwhelming and irrefutable evidence, and he knew that it was just a matter of time before the name Ron Sharp was mentioned by somebody, perhaps Rachel herself, as a part of this case. Knowing that the detectives would surely be calling him eventually made him realize, regretfully, that he was destined to become something that he had always dreaded- part of a major news story.

Ron asked Maggie to keep it just between them, for now that he was involved in the Larimore Case, although they both agreed that it would have to come out eventually. When the case came to trial, Ron would need to recuse himself and not cover any aspect of the story, since he no-doubt would appear on the witness list, for one side or the other.

✳✳✳✳✳

"I've got a story for you, Ronnie," Maggie shouted, grabbing the situationer from the newsroom printer. "With Maria Lopez. Why don't you head up to her desk and she'll go over the details with you."

"Got it," said Ron, as he took the paper and prepared to hit the stairs up to Maria's office.

"Oh, and Ron," called Maggie. "I think this is as good a time as any to tell you."

"Tell me what?"

"I've given my notice. The Assignment Editor over at Channel 3 is leaving, and they offered me the job."

"Wow, that's great!" said Ron, suddenly realizing that the news was not so great for him or those left at the station. "So have they hired a replacement for you?"

"Ha ha, good one," Maggie said. "They're not hiring anybody at this point. They begged me, so I gave them a month, just to get people trained. The young guys are going to have to step up."

"Oh man, we are so screwed."

✳✳✳✳✳

Maria Lopez was smart, gorgeous, ballsy, and disarming, perfect for her position as the stations Investigative Reporter and Fraud-chaser. Ron always enjoyed working with her, just so he could spend the day with one of the hottest reporters in town, an energetic Latina with long brown hair, huge dark eyes, and an attitude. If not for the wedding ring, Ron could definitely have been interested.

Everyone called her the "Ball-buster", a nickname that was well earned. Her specialty was walking up on a crooked doctor, camera rolling, and asking him to explain how so many patients at his Clinic have become disfigured, or pressing an unscrupulous politician to explain where those compromising photos came from.

She was fearless. More than a few times, she and her camera crews had been followed or chased back to their truck, and on numerous occasions the station had found itself threatened with legal action following one of her reports. Only a long string of good luck had kept her from being involved in a violent confrontation with one of the knuckleheads she'd confronted.

Seated along with Maria in her office was Doug Benes, Maria's researcher and producer. They were discussing the story when Ron walked in.

"What we have here," said Maria, showing Ron a photo, "is a guy who's making millions of dollars renting out houses that he doesn't own."

"How does that work?" asked Ron.

"Well," she answered. "You know what a 'squatter' is, right?"

"Sure, they live in vacant houses until they get kicked out. We did a story a while back about all the bureaucratic hoops that a homeowner had to jump through to get a group of squatters evicted. It was insane."

"OK, well, this is a twist. We have video of this guy George Baker in court. He's accused of taking over foreclosed properties as soon as they're vacant, and renting them out to people. He's getting wealthy from collecting rent on houses he doesn't own."

"Pretty clever, huh?" added Doug, taking a sip of coffee.

"Yeah," continued Maria, spreading a stack of papers across her desk. "So, we've got all these court documents, explaining how he's doing this, and a couple of addresses of the houses, and some are pretty upscale. We're gonna go door-knock one, and see if the residents even know that they're squatting. They may think they're legitimate renters."

"I walked the neighborhood the other day, and talked to one of the occupants," said Doug. "He's an aspiring rapper who says he pays over three thousand a month in rent at this place. We don't know if he's aware of what Baker is doing, if he's involved in the scam or not."

"So is this Baker character in custody?" asked Ron.

"Nope, he's been arraigned, but he made the $250,000 bail. We have video of him in court and we'll be there for his next hearing in a few weeks."

"Sounds good," said Ron. "Let's go."

Ron followed Doug down the hall to the elevator, with Maria trailing the pack, after momentarily forgetting her cell phone and story file on her desk.

"So you heard about Maggie?" Maria asked them both, her voice in a whisper.

"Yeah, everyone with any sense is leaving," said Doug, also softly, as the three entered the elevator. "I heard that Les Champion is retiring, too."

"Seriously?" Ron said. "He's been our Managing Editor forever. He's the glue holding this whole newsroom together."

"Don't I know it," Doug answered. "He helped us set up this series. Nobody else could make a fuckin' decision. He's the only one with any balls. I mean, I don't care if you want us to change the story, go after a different angle, or kill it completely. Just make a goddamn decision. It seems like he's the only one capable of doing that and not sitting there with his thumb up his ass." The doors opened to the parking garage. Maria walked out first.

"He's gonna be tough to replace, that's for sure."

"And what's up with Leo?" asked Ron.

"Rumor has it he's been promoted," Maria answered, "which just means they want to move him out and someone else in."

"It makes no sense," said Ron. "I mean he took us from last to first place in the ratings. He's been a great boss. Why on earth would they make a change?"

"Office politics," Doug answered. "They probably wanted him to cut the budget more than he was willing to."

"We don't know if any of this is true," Maria said, shaking her head while opening the van's passenger door. "He could be just tending to a sick relative or some other family emergency."

"Yeah," said Ron, sarcastically, climbing into the driver's seat. "I'm sure that's it."

"You never know what goes on," said Doug, from the back seat. "It's probably best not to ask. Just keep your head down and do your job."

*****

Ron's history with Doug went back about ten years, to a sweeps series they were working on together about street-racing crews in Los Angeles County. Made up mostly of young males, the "crews" raced in the middle of the night on the public streets of cities like Bell and Commerce, areas filled with factories and industrial parks, whose roads would be bustling with delivery trucks and other traffic during the day but completely empty after dark. The wide, straight, vacant roads were appealing to street racers, particularly on weekends, so Ron and Doug's schedules were altered to allow them to work all night Friday and into Saturday morning.

They were given an address on Floral Drive in City Terrace, where they were to meet Paco Martinez, Doug's contact, who would introduce them around and put the racing crew at ease. At 11:30, they pulled into the lot of Tom's Burger #2, just as Paco had instructed them, and it was already teeming with street racers and low-rider show cars.

Ron parked the van on the street and the two of them walked into Tom's, past the brightly painted Ford Focuses, Toyota Celicas and Honda Civics, known as "Rice Burners".

A large fellow wearing boots, jeans and a black t-shirt covered with a well-worn denim vest was checking them out from across the room. He had spotted the pair right away and came over to introduce himself. Paco was a gruff, muscular Hispanic man, with the look of a former gang-banger. He was unshaven and covered with tattoos, sporting a long black mustache, but his broad smile and his prescription wire-rim glasses betrayed his age and the fact that, even though he still enjoyed the thrill of street racing, his real trouble-making days were mostly behind him.

Ron and Doug were introduced to a few members of the racing crew, who took up several tables in the crowded restaurant, eating burgers and drinking Budweiser or Tecate. Miguel was the crew's timekeeper, who kept track of record—setting times among the group. Julia dropped the flag to start the races. Frank stood at the end of the track with Miguel and judged the winners. His word was final. And Suzy kept track of the schedule, making sure the racers knew where they were in line.

The operation was very professional and well organized, though completely illegal. Every Friday evening, Miguel would head out to that week's designated street with a couple of cans of reflective white spray paint, and paint a broad stripe on the asphalt to serve as the starting point. Then, measuring by counting four telephone poles, he'd spray paint two white lines exactly a quarter mile down the road. The double-stripe, being much easier to see, served as the finish line.

With engines revving loudly in the parking lot, Doug interviewed Paco on camera, and he made a passionate case for opening a safe, legal track somewhere within Los Angeles County, that young people could use for racing. He said that he understood the danger to the public, and that that was the reason they used the empty streets of the industrial areas of the county, and not crowded, public thoroughfares. The interview had to be stopped several times, as the thump of loud music and cacophony of the engines echoed through the small, packed burger stand.

At midnight, after a number of the street-racers had been introduced to the TV crew, and assured that their identities would be protected, they were given the location of this weeks' racetrack, and started heading out, followed by dozens of other cars, filled with nearly a hundred observers and enthusiasts.

Ron and Doug were given an address in the City of Commerce, about a twenty-minute drive south through East Los Angeles.

The caravan made its way down Floral and entered the Long Beach Freeway southbound. The freeway was pretty much wide open at that hour, and a few of the racers could not resist maxing out their engines and redlining on the open road. As Ron and Doug continued down the 710, past the Pomona Freeway, traffic in front of them suddenly began to slow and swerve to the right. Ron grabbed the wheel and pulled the top-heavy news van into the next lane, and then over to the shoulder as quickly as possible, coming to a stop directly to the right of a serious collision. One of the racers at the front of the group had lost control on a curve and hit the center divider. His Honda had spun out and was struck by a van carrying six teens also headed to the secret destination. A total of five vehicles were involved, and while the Honda was now facing the wrong way in the center divider, the other cars were strewn, some disabled in the traffic lanes, with a wide-open freeway behind them.

Ron and Doug got out of the van. Doug ran, waving his arms furiously, to get the attention of the oncoming vehicles. Ron directed traffic around the wreck and helped guide everyone safely out of their damaged cars, off of the highway and onto the shoulder. Within a few minutes, all the cars were empty, and their occupants were standing safely alongside the freeway, with the exception of the Honda's driver, who was still behind the wheel, facing the wrong way, in the center median.

Over a dozen people now lined the side of the road, most using their cell phones, taking photos and waiting for help to arrive. Only the lane closest to the shoulder remained open, and in the light traffic, drivers moved over slowly to the right and crawled past the accident, craning their necks to observe the wreckage. Doug walked back over to see if anyone needed medical attention and was standing a few feet from Ron, when suddenly a tractor-trailer came upon the accident scene at high speed. The semi's driver hit the brakes hard and jerked the wheel to the right with as much strength as he could muster. For a moment, Doug stood frozen between the headlights that illuminated his body as the fully loaded 16-wheeler headed straight at him. Hearing the squeal of the brakes, Ron grabbed the back of Doug's collar with his right hand, and dived, throwing them both out of the way and onto the road's gritty shoulder. The truck driver yanked the wheel again, this time sharply to the left, and witnesses swear that the wheels on the left side of the semi actually left the ground momentarily before the speeding rig left the freeway and bounced, screeching to a stop against the retaining wall. At this point, Ron and Doug were both shaken and in a cold sweat, kneeling in the dirt and detritus alongside the highway.

Soon after, the Highway Patrol arrived and took control of the scene. The two officers held up traffic, called for ambulances, and helped the Honda driver over to the side of the freeway. The semi's driver had been able to climb down from his cab to check on Ron and Doug. He said that he'd seen them in front of him only for an instant and had done everything possible to stop his rig. He thanked Ron for getting the two of them out of danger. Then he took a seat by the side of the road.

There were no serious injuries that night, and thanks to Ron's quick actions, Doug was unhurt. The two had worked together dozens of times since then, and while never mentioning the incident again, each of them carried, indelibly, the memory of that night on the freeway.

The trio left the KSIX lot in the microvan. The GPS led them into the center of a pricey area in the Hollywood Hills, high above the Hollywood Bowl, to Outpost Drive, a narrow, winding street lined during the day mostly with older pickups and compacts belonging to cleaning people, gardeners and maintenance men.

"There it is, 7268," said Doug. "Looks like there's someone in the yard."

Ron found a stretch of curb just around the corner on Castilian Drive and parked the van there.

Doug climbed out first, holding his clipboard of notes, and waited for Maria to get her things together. Ron made his way around to the side of the van and removed the camera from its cradle, detached the hand-held microphone adorned with the KSIX logo, flipped the little switch at the base to turn it on, and handed it to Maria.

As they walked around the corner and approached the house, Ron joked to Doug, "You're not gonna get me killed this time, are you?"

They all laughed nervously. But in the back of their minds, they each knew that there was serious danger involved with stories like this one, even in such an upscale neighborhood.

Ron began shooting video, as Doug approached the dark brown, wrought-iron gate, over which they could see a woman tending to the property's lush garden. She was a young African American woman, probably under 30, wearing tight pink cotton shorts and a sweaty aqua-colored t-shirt. She had a pair of clippers in one hand, and a half-empty sport bottle of Arrowhead water in the other. Her long hair was tied back in a wild, frizzy ponytail, and she looked as if she'd been working in the yard for much of the morning.

Doug peered over the gate, as Ron and Maria stood a few paces behind. "Excuse me," he shouted. "Is this your house?"

"Yes it is," she answered, walking closer. "We just moved in last month."

"I'm Doug Benes with Channel Six. Do you mind if I ask you a few questions?"

"What's this about?" the woman asked, furrowing her brow as she neared the gate and saw the camera over Doug's shoulder. She took a long swig of water and leaned on the inside of the gate, relieved to take a break from the heat of a warm spring day.

"Do you know a George Baker?" asked Doug.

"Umm, I'm not sure. Who's he?"

"Do you write the rent checks every month for this house?"

"No, I don't. That would be my boyfriend, or maybe his business manager. What's this about?" she asked once again, reaching into her pocket to retrieve her cell-phone.

"Well," said Maria. "George Baker has been charged with fraud, for renting out houses that he doesn't own, that are in foreclosure. Unfortunately, the people who live in them, and pay him rent, are illegally occupying the homes, technically 'squatting' on the property."

"Just a minute," she said, stepping back into the yard and pressing keys on her cell. The crew could see that she was in an animated conversation with someone, but were unable to hear any of it, due to her distance from the gate, as well as the presence down the block of one of L.A.'s ubiquitous leaf-blowers.

She reappeared at the gate and informed them that they would need to talk with her boyfriend, who was on his way home.

"What's your name," asked Maria, hoping that a woman-on-woman conversation would prove fruitful.

"I'm Francesca," she answered. "And we've only lived here a few weeks. I don't know nothing about no squatters."

Just then a silver Jaguar with tinted windows came speeding up the hill and past the house to their right. Ron took note of the "DEAD END" sign on the side of the road, so he knew the car would be turning around at the end of the cul-de-sac up the curved road and returning in a matter of seconds. He aimed his camera up the street. Seconds later, just as he anticipated, the Jag raced up to the curb and screeched to a halt.

The doors flew open. Out of the driver's side jumped aspiring Rap star "D-Mayhem" and from the passenger's door exited his brother-in-law and putative bodyguard, the aptly named "Puffy Slim". Maria rushed toward the driver, and holding out the mike at arm's length, loudly asked Mayhem if he was paying the rent on the house. Mayhem instantly recognized Doug and charged around the front of the vehicle, past Maria and right at the producer, pointing fingers and fists, unleashing a tirade as crude and obscene as any of them could ever remember hearing.

"What the fuck you doin' here, Nigga?' You fuckin' think I'm a motherfuckin' squatter? Is that what you think, Nigga? You lied to me! You came here last week and lied to me, motherfucker!"

Puffy ran right toward the camera and with his hand out in front of his face, attempted to get between the lens and Mayhem.

"Turn off the fuckin' camera, Nigga," he screamed at Ron. "I said turn it off."

Ron remained cool, and shouted back. "I'm on a public street, man. I can do this all day."

The argument accelerated, Mayhem jumping up and down, and jabbing his finger in Doug's face.

"You lied to me, Nigga, you fuckin' said you was lookin' to rent a house in the nay-ba-hood, man. You ain't nothin' but a fuckin' liar, Nigga!"

At the same time, Doug loudly tried to explain,

"I never said that I was looking to rent! I never said that!"

The shouting grew more intense, both yelling over each other, and growing closer by the second to a physical confrontation.

Ron was moving like a boxer, using either Maria or Doug to screen out the bodyguard, and keep Mayhem in his shot.

"You turn that camera off, Nigga," shouted Puffy, again jumping to get between the camera and Mayhem. "Get it outta my face!"

"You don't want to touch me, Man!" said Ron indignantly. "You do not want to touch me!"

"I'll touch you, Nigga," shouted Puffy as he ran back to the car, threw open the passenger's door, and reached under the seat.

"Knife!" shouted Ron, and everyone froze. Puffy pointed an impressive looking sixteen-inch machete into the air.

"You niggas get the fuck outta here now, or *you* gonna be the fuckin' story on the news tonight."

"Shit, Man!" shouted Mayhem. "Put that away, Nigga. We don't need that kinda shit. Just put it away."

"I want these niggas outta here!" yelled Puffy, waving the machete wildly as he walked back to the car. He obeyed his boss and placed it back under the seat.

Mayhem continued shouting and finger pointing, as he walked back toward the Jag.

"You motherfuckers best be gone when I get back," he growled through his gritted, gold-plated teeth. He reached for the door, and stood with his right foot inside, still bellowing at the news crew, "Don't you be putting me on TV, you lyin-ass niggas, I'll sue your ass, fuckin' niggas."

He slammed the Jag's door, and floored it, almost taking out an old Toyota pickup belonging to the neighbor's gardener on his way down the hill. They could hear the tires squealing until the sports car reached all the way down to Franklin Avenue.

Francesca watched through the fence as the trio walked briskly toward the van, not saying a word. For safety's sake, Ron kept the camera rolling as he hit the unlock button on his key-fob, opening the side door. Looking over his shoulder, he placed the camera in its cradle and shut it off.

"That went well, I thought."

Chapter Seven:

MAGIC

Monday, May 4th

The Detectives received the call at about 9 a.m.

Gabi Hernandez, the manager of the century-old four-story apartment building near MacArthur Park had been up early doing some cleaning in the long-neglected basement ballroom. The building's new owners had told her of their intention to give the building a multi-million dollar makeover. Their extensive plan for the property was to turn the decrepit but classic U-shaped building into a modern 21st century condominium complex, complete with exercise room and banquet facilities as well as both indoor and outdoor entertainment and dining areas. Beginning early in the spring, the gardeners had treated the spacious front lawn with weed-killer and had recently re-seeded. An array of flowers had been planted. The overgrown bushes and trees in the large garden area leading up to the entrance were being replaced with more colorful and drought-resistant shrubs. They planned to update all the rooms, replace paint and carpets, install new appliances, pipes, and fixtures in all the units. Retro artworks would be hung in the newly painted halls and brand new elevators were to be installed within the next year as well. The plan was to give the complex a long-needed facelift, while striving to maintain the charm of the era in which the building was originally designed. Tenants would be offered the chance to purchase the unit they currently occupied or another if they preferred, but unfortunately most, being low income, could expect to be looking for new accommodations before the end of the year.

Gabi prayed nightly that she would be able to keep her job and not find herself being replaced by someone with no familiarity or attachment to the neighborhood and its rich history.

The musty, subterranean ballroom was dimly lit only by the morning sunlight which shone through the narrow basement windows running along the western wall just below the ceiling, sidewalk level to the building's drab, gray concrete exterior. The windows had, decades ago, been fitted with iron bars to prevent entry from the street in this once safe, but now increasingly dangerous neighborhood. The city was optimistic that the renovation of a number of nearby complexes and businesses, along with increased police patrols, would help revitalize the entire area.

Gabi ploddingly began the long-delayed task of cleaning out closets and sweeping the ancient hardwood floors downstairs. Looking over the faded, peeling wallpaper, lime green with raised red velvet fleur-de-lis designs, she began to imagine the type of festive events which must have taken place in the well-appointed ball room so many years before. She envisioned parties, dances and weddings; grand banquets with a piano or even a small orchestra, entertaining revelers who arrived in their large automobiles from nearby Hollywood to carouse on a special evening or a New Year's Eve so many decades ago. Almost hearing faint echoes of music, she feared that all those memories would be forever lost once the decorators arrived.

Suddenly something caught her eye, bringing her back to now. Right there, behind a stack of furniture in a corner storage room, sat three large brown leather trunks, undisturbed and covered with generations of dust. She felt somewhat ashamed that in the eight years she had managed the building, there remained such a sizeable area with which she was unfamiliar.

Curious and certain that after all this time the crates had no rightful owner, Gabi ran upstairs to her second-floor apartment to grab her small household toolkit, on the way running into her longtime friend and tenant Mary DiStefano. She quietly but excitedly told Mary of her find, and the two women hurried back down to the basement.

Together they dragged the trunks out into the light and pulled a pair of dusty banquet chairs over near the windows. Gabi then took a small screwdriver from her toolbox and one by one twisted the locks on the oversized crates. The first two she found completely empty, a surprise considering their weight, but she persisted. Hopeful of finding some sort of century-old treasure, the amateur antique-hunter tenaciously worked to pry open the lock on the third trunk.

The lock popped, and she raised the lid. Revealed was a trove of antiques and artifacts that Gabi initially saw as a gift from God, possibly items of great value she would be able to cash in, should she be forced to relocate by the new management.

"These things must be worth a fortune," she whispered, as the two women examined the contents closely.

First, Gabi held up what appeared to be a ticket stub. Putting on her glasses, she could see that it was, in fact, a souvenir stub from the 1932 Olympic Games Closing Ceremony at the Los Angeles Coliseum.

"Oh, my," she said, pressing her hands together as if in prayer.

Next, she held up a pristine crystal bowl, followed by a collection of classic, hardcover books, including a copy of "Peter Pan" signed by the author, James Matthew Barrie, and two black leather doctor's satchels.

She placed one of the satchels into her lap and handed Mary the other. Each contained a small bundle wrapped up in a few pages of the Los Angeles Times from the 1930s.

When the women unwrapped the bundles, they were stunned and horrified to find that each satchel held the mummified remains of a newborn baby.

Mary let out a short scream at first, but quickly muffled her voice as to not attract attention. Gabi made the sign of the cross on her chest and began to weep.

Gabi and Mary gently placed the bags back in the trunk and Gabi called 911 on her cell. Responding officers from LAPD's Rampart Station arrived within minutes. Gabi escorted them downstairs and showed them the satchels and the tiny corpses she had found. The officers immediately sealed off the room and called for detectives, who arrived about thirty minutes later.

Investigators quickly determined that the little bodies had likely been in the satchels, wrapped in newspaper for eight decades, and there was no need at this point to search for a suspect, if there had even been a crime committed at all.

The coroner would be called out to perform tests on the bodies and determine the manner of death, although one of them clearly appeared to have been born prematurely and may have been miscarried or aborted.

One thing the detectives hoped to learn was the name of the trunk's owner. They began examining the remaining items carefully and soon determined that the contents belonged to a woman named Jean Barrie. There were postcards addressed to her from Korea and South America and stacks of photos featuring a lovely young blonde-haired woman they surmised to be her. In one of the pictures, the woman was wearing a long, white wedding dress.

It struck investigators as curious, that Ms. Barrie had such a fascination with Peter Pan, quickly realizing that she had the same last name as the famed author, who passed away in the late 30's. They wondered if there was a family connection of some kind, or if she had been merely a dedicated fan, whose devotion was bolstered by a last name they shared.

News crews began arriving at around 10:30 and were kept outside the gate by officers securing the crime scene. Ron had been flagged down in the KSIX newsroom at the start of his shift and told to swing by the scene with Maria to see if it was, in fact, a newsworthy story.

"Just spray this. Don't spend a whole lot of time there," Freddie Blaine, the new daytime assignment editor instructed them, handing Ron the apartment building's address. "I've got another assignment for you for later that we can't miss."

"Whatever you say," said Ron, as they headed off to the garage.

"Just spray it!" Ron said sarcastically, as the elevator door closed and Maria hit the button for the parking garage. "I hate that expression."

"Yeah," she laughed. "Do they want the story told or not?"

"Clearly, these people have never been in the field," said Ron. "It's like asking us to go to a hockey game and just shoot the highlights."

They jumped in the van and headed south toward the location.

"I'm kind of hoping for an easy day," Ron said. "What do you think are the chances of that?"

"About the same as me getting laid tonight," Maria joked.

"I can't imagine that being a problem," Ron quipped.

"Charlie's out of town this week," she said. "So it's just me and the dog."

"OK, well call me if I can be of assistance."

"Oh, really? Do you dog sit?"

Ron pulled up on a side street, parked just behind the Channel 3 News van, and walked around the rear of the microvan. He flung open the side door and pointed out to Maria the abandoned mattress and the numerous bags of trash on the sidewalk, as well as the garbage in the gutter as he stepped over a half empty tequila bottle to retrieve his camera.

"Watch yourself," he said.

"Thanks," said Maria, as they headed up the sidewalk. "Look at all this. It's such a shame what's happened to this neighborhood."

"I know. I mean, look at these old buildings. The architecture is amazing."

The light changed as they crossed Grandview Street eastbound toward the old four-story gray building.

"This must have been a desirable area to live in, back in the day," Ron added. "Can't you just see the Model A's and Cadillacs rumbling down the street? I'll bet a lot of silent movie stars lived in this neighborhood."

Quickly, they met up with several other camera crews and reporters who had gathered outside the eight-foot tall wrought-iron fence spanning the gap between the two towers in front of the complex. Behind the ornate black barrier, a long concrete walk led to a staircase at the building's entrance. A modern touch was the electronic doorbell speaker system, which had been installed next to the knob on the heavy wrought-iron door.

Peering through the holes in the fence, the crews could see, from a distance, two detectives in plain clothes shaking hands with Gabi, whom the reporters correctly presumed to be the building's manager. The cops, holding large paper bags, moved slightly to clear the way as a third man, dressed in a blue jumpsuit, passed through the doorway. The patch on his chest, which read CORONER, became increasingly visible as he descended the staircase a few steps ahead of the detectives, with a small parcel wrapped in a white sheet cradled in his arms.

The photographers prepared to get the shot of the baby being placed in the Coroner's white Crown Victoria, while the reporters had their mikes turned on, hoping to get some comment from the investigators as they left the scene.

The gate swung open and a gray-haired detective, appearing to be in his fifties, held it for the Coroner's technician.

"Give him room, everybody," he said, as the crowd of journalists followed them down the sidewalk.

"Can we ask you a few questions?" shouted Carrie Lake, a reporter with KMA News Radio.

The detectives never broke stride, proceeding to their unmarked vehicles and placing the evidence bags inside.

"There's not much we can tell you right now," the younger detective answered, shutting the trunk. "We'll have to wait for forensics before we know anything."

The cameras turned to capture the Coroner's technician walking back through the gate and toward the building

"We just need runs, hits and errors," said Maria. "Whatever you know at this point. Who called it in, where they were found…"

"Really, we'd love to help you," the detective interrupted, "but there will be a news conference this afternoon at headquarters downtown. We'll have more information for you then."

They climbed in their vehicles and waited. After a few moments, the technician left the building once again, carrying the second body, this time followed by another detective, who had remained inside guarding the scene until all the evidence had been removed. He was pushing a handcart with several boxes on it. The boxes were placed along with the cart into the trunk of his car. Soon all the official vehicles were gone and the two tiny, lifeless beings had left their dark, lonely homes for the final time.

The crews from Channels 3 and 8 packed up and returned to their trucks to prepare for noon live shots, leaving only Ron, Maria, and Carrie outside the gate. Carrie pressed the buzzer. Gabi's voice came through the box, surprising them all.

"Yes, can I help you?"

"Umm… Yes Ma'am," Carrie said into the speaker. "We're with the news. Can we talk to you about this morning?"

"I'll be right out."

The three of them looked at each other in wide-eyed anticipation, also looking out for the other camera crew, which they hoped would not return.

After a couple of minutes Gabi appeared at the gate, introduced herself, and invited them to step inside. Ron set up his camera and tripod on the lawn just to the left of the concrete walkway.

"Tell us about your discovery," Maria asked, holding out the mike.

Gabi explained how she had found the large trunks and was examining their contents when she came across the babies' bodies. She described the condition they were in and talked about the way they were wrapped in newspaper.

"Here's a piece of the paper that I kept," she said, pulling a yellowed, folded page of The Times from her pocket. She held it up for them to see and Ron shot video. The date, July 12th, 1934, was still clearly visible on the well-preserved page.

"Wow!" said Maria. "Were you able to keep anything else, or did the police take it all?"

"I've got this!" Gabi answered, reaching into a pouch in her dress. She held up a thin, cardboard-covered pamphlet from the "Peter Pan Woodland Club", at one time an upscale resort near Big Bear, about two hours east of Los Angeles. Written in pencil on the back of the cover was a name.

"We think that the trunks belonged to this woman, Jean Barrie. She apparently lived here back in the thirties. There were photos inside with her name on the back. The police don't know if she's related to the guy who wrote Peter Pan or just a fan with the same last name."

"That's just plain weird," said Carrie. "What about the babies?"

"I guess they have to run all kinds of tests on them, bless their souls," Gabi said, crossing herself. "Then they have to try to find a relative of Miss Barrie somewhere and compare DNA."

"Can you show us where you found them?" asked Ron.

"Sure," said Gabi. "Follow me."

Again they shared a wide-eyed glance, as Gabi led them up the stairs toward the building's entrance.

Why didn't we ask her that to begin with?

Gabi escorted them through the dark but well-appointed lobby, still decorated with furnishings from the early 20th century, including a full-size black grand piano. The framed paintings and black and white photographs lining the crème-colored walls illustrated the owners' devotion to the period and their desire to maintain the feel of an era worlds away from that just outside the property's boundaries.

Maria and Carrie were taken by the décor, pausing to study the photos. Ron glanced outside and noticed the Channel 24 News van pulling up in front. Normally, he would have asked Gabi to wait and invite the other crew to come along, but he had already received a text from Freddie on the assignment desk reminding them to cut it short. And to be honest, the idea of an exclusive felt pretty good.

They walked to the left, past the lobby desk, upon which sat a single pink rose in a ceramic vase and a guest book, where visitors signed in upon entering the classic property. Gabi continued to the carpeted staircase at the end of the ebony wood floor and descended one short flight. There, she unlocked and opened a pair of large white doors, revealing the dark, musty ballroom where she had spent the previous several hours with the detectives. She cautiously entered and invited her guests to follow behind her until they reached the stacked chairs, which had been shoved randomly into the middle of the room.

"This is it," she said. "No further than this."

"OK, OK," Maria said, glad to have been invited on the premises at all. "Can you just point out where everything was? Where you found the trunks?"

"They were over there," Gabi answered, pointing toward the back of the unlit room. "There's a storage room behind that wall. That's where they were."

Gabi looked as if she was ready to cry as she made the sign of the cross once again and turned toward the door.

"We must leave now. I cannot be in here."

"We understand," said Carrie. "Completely."

Ron gave Maria a wink, indicating that he had enough video of the room. Along with the body shots from outside and the rest of his b-roll, this would be a great story.

As they exited the building, Ron, Maria, and Carrie thanked Gabi for allowing them to intrude on her privacy after such a traumatic morning. The Channel 24 crew was standing outside the gate, ringing the buzzer as they passed through on the way back to their vehicles. Ron half hoped that since they were from a Spanish language station, Gabi would invite them in also and share her adventure in her native language.

*****

"Wow," said Maria into the phone, as she climbed back into the van. "This is such a fabulous story. I'd like to follow up with the Police news conference later and make this our story for today."

"No?"

"Where?"

"Are you sure?"

"OK," she said, with a sigh. "We'll go take a break now and call you back."

"Unbelievable," she said, hanging up the phone. "They want us to take a lunch break and then head for Anaheim. They're holding tryouts for the new season of 'Dance Your Buns Off' at the Convention Center. It's a network show, so this is a must-do."

"Can't they get somebody else?" asked Ron.

"Apparently not. Frank is the only other cameraman who's credentialed for this and he's off today."

"OF COURSE he is."

*****

Maria had long been telling Ron about a great little Greek restaurant on Wilshire Boulevard, and this was the perfect time to try it. They were only a few minutes away and wanted to stay in the area in the event the producers came to their senses and decided to keep them on the dead baby story after all. Ron called in to tell the desk they were at lunch.

Suddenly, Dave Newman, another cameraman from Channel 6, appeared at their table.

"What's up?" Ron asked.

"They want me to take your video from the apartment building. I'll be working the story with Hank this afternoon."

"I'll be right back," Ron said to Maria, standing up and shaking his head. He swallowed a bite of his gyro as he accompanied Dave outside to swap memory cards and fill him in on the story.

"So, the manager of the building invited us in to see where she found the babies' bodies," he said. "She also showed us a piece of the newspaper they were wrapped in. And a book, having something to do with Peter Pan."

"Yeah, the whole Peter Pan thing is weird." interrupted Hank from the passenger's seat of Dave's van. "The cops are trying to figure out who this woman was. There's a news conference at three, so we're headed downtown to Police Headquarters."

"Thanks. Man," Dave shouted, hopping into the driver's seat. "Have fun in Anaheim."

"Yeah," scoffed Ron. "A million laughs."

"I've heard that dancing is your thing," said Hank.

"Only in the foam, my friend." Ron winked and gave him a middle finger as he walked back to the restaurant to finish his lunch.

"It's too bad we couldn't see that story through," Ron said. "I'll really be interested to find out what it's all about."

"Yeah," Maria concurred. "We'll just have to read about it tomorrow. That, or watch the show tonight."

"Not likely," he said. "That's past my bedtime."

Ron glanced at his watch, and seeing that they had less than ten minutes left of their lunch break, asked Maria what time they had to be in Anaheim.

"Tryouts start at three o'clock," Maria answered.

"It's already 2:15," he said, incredulous. "What are they thinking? They should have blown out our lunch breaks." They stood up, dumped their trash, and headed out the door.

"What? And pay you a meal penalty? That's why they didn't want us spending a lot of time on the other story. Just, you know…"

"Yeah, I know…*SPRAY IT!*"

Before they reached the van, the sound of police sirens suddenly became deafening. A Black and White LAPD cruiser flew past them eastbound on Wilshire, followed by two more closely behind.

"Let's check this out!" Ron said, hopping into the van.

"Umm, OK," Maria responded hesitantly.

Ron quickly locked in the frequency for LAPD's Olympic Division on his scanner and was listening intently as they left the parking lot.

"20A-49, I have a visual on one suspect through the front window of the jewelry store. Shots have been fired. There's a window blown out. I need additional units to close all entrances to the shopping center, Wilshire and Catalina."

"Holy shit!" said Ron, glancing toward Maria. "That's just a couple blocks up!"

*****

"A visual on one suspect through the front window."

Immediately, Ron recalled a robbery he had covered a few years before in Sacramento, another time he took gruesome visions to bed with him. He was working night side and as soon as he walked in to the station at 3pm, Maggie asked if he was prepared for an overnighter.

"There's a standoff with hostages at the Sam's Electronics Store in Sacramento," she explained. "They've got at least three gunmen inside the store and somewhere near thirty hostages. They're saying this could go on for a while."

Ron quickly packed up his gear, grabbed the bag out of his locker, and rushed to Burbank Airport with Jan Walters, a young reporter who happened to have worked in Sacramento for a couple of years prior to coming to KSIX. They took the hour-long flight, rented a car, and were on location on the city's south side by 6:15. The incident, to their surprise, was still ongoing.

News crews from all over California had descended upon the shopping center, where the police had roped off an area of the parking lot about 75 yards directly east of the front entrance of Sam's, giving the crews a perfect vantage point.

KSIX had been getting video of the incident from KJDS, the Sacramento affiliate, but soon Ron hooked up with their Satellite truck and began sending back live reports with Jan throughout the evening.

The hostages had been lined up, shoulder to shoulder, against the counter in the front of the store. They were sitting up, facing the front door, tied together with speaker wire, and about a dozen of them were clearly visible through the long lenses of the news cameras. The cameramen began giving some of them nicknames based upon their appearances. 'Cosby', a rather tall African-American man sat next to 'Gidget', a petite young woman whom they thought somewhat resembled Sally Field, the actress from Norma Rae, but cute, like she had been so many years before. To her left was 'Tim', a lanky, long-haired young man who could have been Tim Lincecum, the Giants' pitcher. Next to him sat 'Pedro', a doppelganger for the kid from Napoleon Dynamite.

Every so often, one of the robbers would pace back and forth past the window, carrying a 9mm. handgun in full view of the cameras, and presumably the cops. But having the hostages immobilized the way they were left the crooks feeling confident that no one would attempt to fire through the door for fear of harming one of the many innocent victims inside.

Negotiations with the gunmen, known members of a Vietnamese street gang, continued throughout the evening, until the police seemingly acquiesced to some of their demands, among which were $4 Million in unmarked cash, four bullet-proof vests, a helicopter and, strangely enough, a 1000-year-old ginger plant that could be made into tea.

At first, a Sergeant delivered one Kevlar vest in exchange for the release of a female hostage and two small children. Later, several more women and children were released and ran like hell through the door and across the parking lot to waiting officers.

But suddenly, around 9pm, the robbers grew impatient, and the situation took a violent turn. A male hostage was shot once in the leg and sent limping out the door to deliver a message to the news cameras that the robbers would watch on the bank of flat-panel televisions inside Sam's. Instead, the police cut the message short at the sound of another hostage being shot.

A short time later, an officer approached the store and dropped another bulletproof vest on the walk, to the right of the front door, just far enough out of reach that the gunman would need to exit the building, not just reach out to grab it. As the robber leaned out, a police sharpshooter took his shot. The door, however, had swung closed just enough that the sniper's bullet hit the aluminum frame, shattering the glass and the silence of the night.

As TV cameras rolled, one of the gunmen, sensing the end, ran down the line of hostages, shooting them one by one at close range.

At the same time, SWAT team members who had stealthily dropped in through the roof some time earlier, charged out of the rear storeroom and opened fire, killing three of the four gang members and rescuing all of the hostages alive, except 'Cosby' and 'Pedro', who turned out to be store employees, and an older man who had just stopped in that afternoon to buy his grandson a birthday gift. Ten others were transported to local hospitals with gunshot wounds but ultimately survived.

Jan and Ron had the lead story on the late newscast with dramatic and gruesome pictures of the shootout, and gave updates throughout the program. They stayed on scene until well past midnight and were back on the air by 5 am, recapping the story for the morning newscast, before heading back to L.A.

Coming home with Ron that day were the terrified faces of the hostages and the visions of their bloody executions, images that stayed with him for weeks. He collected thoughts that he didn't fully realize had taken up permanent residence in his memory and returned to his mind in technicolor at moments like these. Eventually, those memories would need to make room in his brain for other horrors, like the jumper, who would one day take up a place of prominence there.

∗∗∗∗∗

The news van came to a sudden stop at the intersection of Wilshire and Catalina as Ron spotted an officer, gun drawn, running in front of him across Wilshire Boulevard and taking cover behind a blue Rav 4 parked at the curb, facing south, just past the corner. Another officer was signaling him with hand gestures to watch the entrance of the jewelry store. They were too preoccupied at this point to worry about the news crew that was stopped, potentially in the line of fire. Ron heard more sirens and knew that within a minute or two, other officers would be arriving on scene, both as backup and to secure the perimeter. As he spotted a vacant parking spot and pulled to the curb, he grabbed the mike.

"Micro 21 to news desk."

"Go ahead Micro 21."

"We've got a robbery in progress here on Wilshire and Catalina with shots fired," Ron shouted breathlessly. "I've got cops running everywhere. We're getting out to shoot this. You're gonna want to get the chopper up!"

He had one foot out the door when the reply came from Freddie on the assignment desk.

"Negative, Microvan 21. We need you in Anaheim by three. We'll make a call on this other story."

Ron froze in his seat, incredulous and deflated.

"ARE YOU FU..." was all that was heard at the assignment desk, as he chucked the mike across the van's passenger's seat, almost striking Maria.

"...CKING KIDDING ME?! Make a call?! What the fuck do these people not get about breaking news?"

"Unbelievable," said Maria, witnessing the frantic police activity just outside her window.

Ron took a deep breath, shook his head and pulled the van back out onto Wilshire, tires squealing, then north on Vermont, toward the freeway. He'd never been so exasperated and pissed off. At Third Street, he saw a Channel 8 News van speeding south, no doubt toward the incident on Wilshire. Then, at Beverly Boulevard, as he was about to enter the 101 freeway, he spotted a bright blue van from Channel 3 exiting the freeway onto Vermont and racing south as well. On the scanner, he could hear that officers had set up a perimeter and were keeping all approaching vehicles several blocks away. He was furious at the lost, rare opportunity of being in the perfect place when a story was breaking, not getting there hours afterward.

"Can you believe how idiotic these people are?" he said angrily. "They're gonna 'make a call?' Who the hell are they gonna call?"

"I'm stunned," Maria replied. "We were right there. They just didn't care. They have no idea what it is to be a journalist, to be in the field and have to think on your feet. Where in the world do we find these people?"

"I don't know, but when I'm in charge, things are going to be different."

"Yeah," said Maria, smiling. "When you're in charge."

"Seriously," he added. "If I had anything to say about it, in order to work on the assignment desk, you'd have to spend at least one day a month out in the field, just to learn what it's like."

"Well, that's never gonna happen," said Maria. "They don't have enough people to spare as it is. I just hope we get a crew to this robbery before it's over."

"At this point I don't care," said Ron. "We deserve to miss this story."

"You know, ever since the layoffs, we've had nothing but incompetence," Maria said. "It's like we work with teenagers. And now Maggie's gonna be gone too. Oy."

"I know, nobody has any fucking sense anymore."

Ron glanced down and noticed that the mike he had thrown had become wedged between Maria's seat and the center console, and that the button on the side was keyed. Every word they said was being broadcast back to the assignment desk.

He reached down gingerly, pried it loose, and placed it back in the clip.

"Holy crap," he said, in a now unnecessary whisper. "Do you think they heard us?"

"I don't know," answered Maria. "Hopefully they're all in a meeting."

At 2:35, as they passed through downtown and prepared to transition to the Santa Ana Freeway toward Orange County, Ron heard Freddy's voice come over the two-way.

"Air Six, come in, please."

"This is Air Six, go ahead."

"Yeah, can you launch, please? And head for downtown. I'll have a location for you shortly."

"Gee, I wonder where *they're* going," Ron said sarcastically.

"News desk to Microvan 13, what's your location?"

"Unit 13, we're in Northridge."

"I need to send you downtown. It seems there's been a robbery, with a shooting homicide at a jewelry store on Wilshire Boulevard. Cross street is Catalina."

"Ten-Four. On our way."

"Air Six, Wilshire and Catalina for a robbery homicide. Police still on scene."

"Ten-four," said Teddy, at the controls. **"ETA twelve minutes."**

Ron and Maria just shook their heads, fuming silently, infuriated and embarrassed the rest of the way to Anaheim.

✳✳✳✳✳

The fatal robbery on Wilshire was the lead story on KMA News-radio all the way home from Anaheim. Carrie Lake was doing live reports every few minutes from the location, which was still active, crawling with officers and detectives. The LAPD had a PIO on scene, filling in the media about how a 58-year-old Jeweler had been assassinated in his shop in broad daylight. Police had made one arrest and were still looking for at least one suspect, possibly an Armenian or Russian hit man.

Ron and Maria both listened, continually shaking their heads and muttering to themselves, "Unbelievable," he said.

They sat silently, listening to updates from the scene, as Ron navigated the heavy afternoon traffic. Suddenly, Maria's curiosity got the best of her.

"Were you scared?" she asked him.

"When?"

"When the bullets were flying over our heads and the police were running all around us a few hours ago. Duh."

"Umm, no, I really wasn't. Hadn't really thought about it. I guess I should have been, right?"

The hot sun was setting as Ron pulled the news van in to the garage, having earned several hours of overtime sitting on the freeway from Orange County. Frustrated, exhausted and done for the day, he said goodnight to Maria and started packing up his gear to go home when his cell-phone began to ring. He saw that it was Scott Castle, the Evening Assignment Editor calling. He answered the call on the second ring.

"Microvan 21," said Ron.

"Hey, Ronnie," said Scott, "We've got an out-of-town assignment coming up later in the week, we're hoping you can do it."

"Yeah? What's the story?" Ron asked, without committing himself.

"It's just a two-day to Vegas for the Gadget Show. Jennie Martin is going with you. She'll be reporting live there, from the Convention Center on Wednesday night and Thursday morning."

"Sure," Ron replied. "Sign me up."

*****

Tuesday, May 5th

Tuesday afternoon, Ron made his way back to the station about an hour early, to prepare his equipment crates for the trip. He packed everything carefully in the station's well-worn padded crates, designed for air travel. He packed his battery charger, with two extra camera bricks in one case, along with video and audio cables and an IFB set-up. There was a long, black tube designed for his Sachtler tripod, and another large crate, which carried the Live-U backpack, which made it possible to do a live remote from inside or outside the Convention Center. Also in the crate were a video card reader and a laptop computer on which Ron would edit his package.

Ron left the crates stacked inside the equipment locker and headed home.

Early the next morning, he loaded everything into one of the station's Ford Explorers and, after meeting up with Jennie, headed off for Burbank Airport.

Ron paid extra for the additional baggage, then passed through the security line for the 9:15 flight on Southwest at Gate A5. As they sat in the waiting area, Ron noticed that they were sitting directly across from Penn Jillette and Teller, who were obviously headed back to Las Vegas to perform their stage show.

"Hey, I love you guys," said Ron. "Love your TV show, too!"

"Thanks a lot, man," said Penn, eyeing Ron's camera. "What are you shooting?"

"We're covering the Gadget Show, for Channel Six News."

"Cool. Good luck, man," said Jillette, in his friendly, but gravelly voice, "You should try to make it to our show at the Rio. We've worked up some new stuff you haven't seen before."

"I wish we could," said Ron. "But this is a quick trip. Maybe next time."

"Now Beginning the Boarding Process for Flight 242, Service to Las Vegas at Gate A-5."

Ron and Jennie were able to board early enough to sit side by side in row 14, Jennie taking the window seat. Ron placed the camera in the overhead bin, cushioned by his sweatshirt, which he knew would not otherwise be needed in Las Vegas. He thought back to the time, years earlier, when the station would actually buy a ticket for the camera, and he'd strap it in to the seat next to him. Jennie laughed when he told her about how they would purchase the ticket under the name "Mr. Cam Era".

"Those days are over," said Ron. "No way these people would spend an extra dime now."

"I know," agreed Jennie. "I haven't been out of town at all this year. I'm surprised they're sending us to Vegas."

"Obviously, someone else is paying for it," continued Ron. "One of the gadget companies or something. You know, some sponsor."

"Yeah, most likely." Jennie agreed. "So have you met the latest news director?"

"Yeah," Ron answered. "What's his name? Wellington James?"

"I know," she said. "Sounds like a little Prince, doesn't it?"

"I stuck my head in and said hello," Ron continued. "That's about it. What are you hearing about him?"

"That he's a heartless hit-man," she answered. "That New York sent him here specifically to cut the operation to the bone, and then cut it some more."

"How can they cut beyond what they've already done?"

"Just you watch. I heard that on his first day, he glanced out of his office into the newsroom and called our operation 'an embarrassment of riches'."

"You're kidding."

"No, I'm not."

The flight attendant interrupted with pretzels. Ron asked for tomato juice and Jennie for Coffee.

"Where did he work before?" asked Ron.

"Somewhere in Oklahoma, Tulsa I think. Small market. And, he brought his girlfriend along with him to be some kinda 'specialist', which should work out well, since he's married with a couple of kids."

"Crap, do the suits know about that? After all the 'Sex in the Workplace' seminars they make us sit through?"

"I'm sure they don't," she said. "But he's the 'Golden Boy' for now. He'll do what he's told and he can do whatever he wants beyond that. As long as he cuts the budget."

"So, who's the next to go?" Ron asked.

"Reporter wise? Whoever has a contract coming up, I guess. They'll have to take a pay cut or be replaced by someone who'll work for less. He did that for them in Enid, or wherever it was he came from."

"Well, this ain't Enid. He's gonna find that out when the next big earthquake hits, or the next plane crashes."

"Shhh... Don't say 'plane crash'," said Jennie. "I'm totally superstitious."

Flight 242 touched down at McCarran just after 10 and by 11 they had made it to the hotel. Ron got all of his gear unpacked and took everything he needed with him in the cab to the Convention Center. They spent the afternoon getting video of all the new electronic toys and devices that were on display but not yet for sale to the public; everything from Giant Flat Panel TVs that disappear into the ceiling, two wristwatches that double as credit/debit cards.

By 4:00, they were interviewing Roger Greene, a young sales rep from a new company called Digi-Ality. Greene told them all about the hit of the show, their new 3-D holographic projection system, with which you can see what appear to be live performances of your favorite bands, in three dimensions and six-channel audio, in your living room.

"With our new system of MSP, Multiple Synched Projection, there are no limits, beyond what you can imagine," Greene told Jennie. "Your favorite performers live in concert, night after night in your home. All you do is provide the popcorn."

Ron captured the demonstration of the projection system, knowing that even in HD, standard two-dimensional television would not do it justice. "And to think," said Ron. "Ten years from now, everybody will have one of these."

"I can remember," added Jennie, "when flip-phones were being introduced as a thing of the future. It really wasn't that long ago."

They walked around the Convention floor for a while longer, shooting a variety of displays that seemed particularly interesting or visual. The newest Gaming systems, cell phones with 30 mega-pixel camera, and other new toys. Ron was just about to try on a 3D Virtual Reality headset, when he heard a familiar voice from across the aisle.

"Ron! What are you guys doing here?"

"Hey, Sandra!" he answered excitedly, giving her a quick hug. "We're covering the show. There's so much cool new stuff here this year. How are you doing?"

Sandra was dressed to be a demo-model at the show, in a lightweight black-and-white checkered mini-dress, with a wide black belt. Her sandy hair was parted on the right and straight, except for a few curls, which fell in front of her ears.

She invited them both over to the Life-Tronics display, where she demonstrated some new household items.

"This," she explained, "is a mini solar power cell. You attach it to the window, say, of your office, with this suction cup, and this USB cable allows the sun to charge your phone, operate a small appliance, or whatever you need power for. How cool is that?"

"Very practical," said Jennie.

"And much less expensive than the Floating 4K TV over there," said Sandra.

"This little thing is neat," she continued. "This is a stapler that never runs out of staples, because it doesn't use them. It just pinches the corners your papers together really tightly and *Voila!*" she said, demonstrating.

"Have you ever gone diving, Ron?"

"Sure," he answered. "Love it!"

"Well, look at this. This is a scuba mask with no air-tank. These filters on the sides act as gills, actually separating the oxygen from the water, allowing you to breathe under water. How great is that?"

"That is cool," he agreed. "I'd like to try it. In a really shallow pool at first."

"Oh, and you'll like this one," she said. "It's called 'the Chipper'. What happens is you attach this tiny square-inch tile to your purse, your key-chain, your phone, whatever you want to keep track of. Then, if it's lost, you can use your phone to activate a tiny bluetooth unit inside it, and it will transmit a signal to help you locate it."

"Umm, what if someone secretly placed one in your purse or your car to keep track of you?" Ron asked, thinking of Jack.

"Well, I suppose that's always a possibility," Sandra replied. "But as with all new technologies, there are infinitely more positive uses than negative ones."

"If you say so," he added, unconvinced.

Ron asked Sandra to be a hand-model and demonstrate a few more items she had on display, as he picked up his camera and started shooting video. Before long, she got into it, mimicking the moves of a game-show "spokes-model", twisting at the waist and running her hands over the products in an exaggerated manner.

Jennie noticed the flirting and playful banter and decided to leave the two of them alone for a few minutes. She wandered a few booths away to check out some new apps for her phone.

"And this device," Sandra explained to the camera, "is a security camera where you can watch the inside of your house remotely. But this one is different. You can activate a little motorized arm that will throw your dog a treat. You can talk to Bowser through your computer or phone, tell him what time you'll be home- and reward him for protecting your house all day."

"Wait," said Ron. "Is there really a market for that?"

"You'd be surprised," answered Sandra. "People want to be super interactive these days- and safe, women especially. We also have this cell phone cover that doubles as a pepper spray container. If you need it, you just squeeze like this, and it shoots pepper spray at an attacker."

"Hey, be careful with that."

"So many women are uncomfortable with weapons," she added, "so this is a great alternative."

"Where are you staying," asked Ron in a half whisper, while continuing to shoot the display.

"We're at the MGM," Sandra answered.

"So are we! We have a live shot at 10, but we should be back there before 11. You want to meet up in the bar?"

"Sure," said Sandra, as they walked to catch up with Jennie. "See you there."

Ron and Jennie finished up with a little more b-roll and a couple more interviews, before heading to the pressroom to edit. The piece was cut and shipped back to the station by 6, so they grabbed a quick dinner, and had a little time to spend in the casino before going on the air.

Their live shot took place on the Strip, across the street from the Excalibur, with the traffic, crowds of tourists, and the giant flaming volcano in the background. Jennie intro'd her report at 10:26, threw to the video they had shipped in earlier, and wrapped up at 10:29 with her familiar sig-out: "Live in Las Vegas For K-SIX News, I'm Jennie Martin, throwing it back to you."

Ron called the assignment desk back in L.A. to make sure that they were clear from the show. The phone was picked up by the intern-du-jour.

"Channel Six News,"

"Can I get Scott, please?"

"Sorry, sir, but Scott has gone home for the day. Would you like to talk to Maggie?"

"Absolutely."

"Sure, and whom should I tell her is calling?"

"Tell her it's Ralph Kramden calling," Ron said, "She'll know what it's about."

"Certainly, Mr. Kramden, just a moment."

The theme music from the Channel Six News blasted from his phone while he waited on hold until Maggie was located in the newsroom and returned to the desk.

"Love that song, just love it," he whispered to Jennie, who was packing up her bag and hailing a cab.

"Hey, Ralphy-boy! Are you guys wrapped?" asked Maggie.

"Yeah, but I thought Friday was your last day."

"It was," she said. "But they asked me to stay for a few more days until Freddy gets back from vacation."

"Perfect," said Ron, "A damn embarrassment of riches, I tell ya. We're gonna head back to the hotel now and gear down. Should be off the clock at 11 or so."

"Sounds good, and remember you're live on the Morning Show in the 7 o'clock hour."

"Right," said Ron. "We'll call in around 6:30 and talk to the producer."

"Alrighty," she said. "Nice job there, have a good night."

"Thanks, g'night."

Ron got everything packed up and ready to go. He reminded Jennie about their morning live shot. "Oh, man," she said. "I'll be looking gorgeous at that hour, I can guarantee it." They jumped into a cab for the short ride back to the MGM. Ron stopped at the front desk to ask for a 6 am wake-up call for both of their rooms.

"Yes, of course," said the desk clerk. "6 am wake up. Thank you, Mr. Sharp."

Ron invited Jennie to join him and Sandra in the bar for a nightcap. "It'll help you sleep," he said.

"You know," she replied. "It's been a long day. Maybe just one. But I really don't think I'll have any trouble getting to sleep tonight."

"OK, meet you in the bar…" he said, entering the crowded elevator with his camera gear.

By the time he had washed his face and come back downstairs, he found Sandra sitting on the curved orange corduroy sofa in the lounge, listening to the pianist playing some old Billy Joel song. He sat down to her left as the waitress approached.

"A Seven and Seven for me, please."

"Another Screwdriver for me, thanks." said Sandra.

"So, how long are you in town?" he asked.

"Well, the show ends Friday," she answered. "But I may stay for another day or two. I haven't been to Vegas in a few years, and it's changed so much. I'd like to maybe see a show or two."

"Great plan," said Ron. "If you have the vacation time, you might as well use it. We're flying back tomorrow, after the morning show. We've got a live shot in the 7 am hour."

Just then Jennie sat down across the table, said hello, kicked off her shoes, and ordered a lemon-drop martini.

The waitress brought their drinks and Ron proposed a toast, to Las Vegas.

"So, what's the latest with you?" Ron asked.

"It's just been really busy. Never a dull moment."

"That's better than the alternative," he said. "Too bad you couldn't see our package tonight, I featured you prominently."

"Really?" said Sandra. "You did?"

"Yeah. I really like that doggie camera thing, or whatever it does."

"Hey, they make some really great products."

"Yeah, and they have a cute spokesmodel, too,"

"Are you sure this is your first drink?"

"I'm totally serious," he said. "You should be on TV all the time. You're adorable."

"Oh, stop it," she said.

Ron finished his drink in just a few gulps, and motioned the waitress for another.

"So, have you been on any exciting stories lately?" asked Sandra.

"Nothing out of the ordinary; just a couple of hundred-year-old fetuses. And dodging a few bullets. Nothing special. Oh, but I did get to cross one thing off my bucket-list last week. I went up in the Goodyear Blimp."

"You did?"

"I did. We do a feature called 'Find a Family' where we spotlight children from foster homes who want to be adopted, and we hang out with the kid and do fun stuff. This ten-year-old boy, Jeremy, wants to someday learn to fly, so we arranged for him to go up in the blimp and get a birds-eye view of L.A. I rode along with him and got to see his reaction to being up in the air for the first time. The blimp flew all the way from Carson to Downtown, then over Hollywood, then along the shore down to Long Beach. He was blown away. And I thought it was cool, too."

"That's so wild. One more thing that you've done that hardly anyone gets to do. I hope you appreciate just how lucky you are, Mr. Sharp."

"I'm sitting here with you," he said. "That's about as lucky as I expect to get in Las Vegas."

She scooted over closer to him. "Oh, you're so sweet."

"You two are so cute," said Jennie. "Did Ron ever tell you the story about how he was with me when I met my husband?"

"No," answered Sandra, raising her eyebrows and leaning in. "I'd love to hear it."

"Well, we were on a shoot," said Jennie, reaching her tired arm down below the table to massage her tired foot. "It was about this dating service called 'Just A Quickie', so we followed this couple who had been set up to meet for the first time for a lunch date. They had just an hour to spend together and decide if they wanted to see one another again. It's a great concept. No pressure."

"So, I put a mike on the guy," interjects Ron. "Then I shoot their introduction, and then their lunch date from all different angles, all corners of the restaurant."

"I could tell that he was trying really hard to impress this girl," said Jennie.

"Trying really hard to get laid, you mean," said Ron. "Talk about old, lame jokes."

"So anyway," continued Jennie, frowning at Ron. "Their date's over, they exchange numbers and they go their separate ways, back to work or whatever. I had to check back in a few weeks to see if it had resulted in a relationship, and…"

"And," interrupted Ron. "He got what he wanted and never called her again."

"Well, he never called *her* again, but he asked me for my number, and we're married now. Todd always laughs about that. He loves to tell the story about how Ron had him pegged from the very beginning."

"Trust me, it wasn't that hard," Ron replied. "I'm just glad he's not mad."

"Hey," added Jennie, finishing off her martini. "Guys know guys."

"I guess they do," laughed Sandra.

Jennie checked her watch and said, "That's gonna do it for me, kids. Don't stay up too late."

"OK, Mom," answered Ron as Jennie got up and left the table.

"G'nite. Nice to meet you, Sandra."

"Pleasure," Sandra replied, shaking the reporter's hand again.

"I like her," said Sandra. "She seems nice. And she seems to be very fond of you."

"Yeah," Ron answered. "She's a good reporter, too."

The pianist took a break at 11:45, and Ron reminded Sandra that he had to get up early for the morning show.

She leaned over to him, inviting a kiss, which he willingly returned.

"So," asked Ron, pulling back just a bit, and placing his chin in his nearly closed hand. "What's the latest with Jack?"

"Oh, screw him," she said, resting her head on his shoulder. "Or don't, as the case may be."

"Seriously, where do things stand?" Ron persisted, stroking her hair.

"I've told him that I can do what I want, and I want him to leave me alone."

"And…"

"And, I don't want to talk about him anymore."

Sandra had moved closer to Ron now, placing her left leg upon his knee.

Paying no attention to the foot traffic in the crowded casino lobby, she reached over and began to unbutton his shirt.

"You know," Ron said. "I'm really glad we ran into you here." She kissed him again, this time to stop the conversation.

"But," he whispered, barely pulling his lips from hers. "I'm not really sure that I'm looking for a relationship."

"Really?" she said, tilting her head and nibbling on his lower lip. "And just what *are* you looking for?"

"Well," he said with a sigh. "I really need a date for the EMMYS next month. Are you interested?"

"Of course I am," she answered, undoing another button on his shirt.

"So you want me to be your date. Do you know what *I* want?" He felt her warm breath, soft on his upper lip.

"No," he said, kissing her again gently, locked into her deep-green eyes. "What do you want?"

She pressed her lips next to his ear and whispered, "What I want is to maybe scratch a couple more things off your 'bucket list'." She then pulled her face back from his, and with her tongue slightly protruding from the corner of her mouth, locked eyes with him and awaited his reply.

"Whoa," he said, glancing at his watch. "It's getting late."

Their eyes met again.

Reading her signals, Ron threw back the last of the melting ice in his glass and asked, "Umm, would you like me to walk you up to your room?"

"No, I wouldn't," she answered breathlessly, her finger now resting on her eye tooth. "I'd like to see *your* room."

Ron's mouth was instantly dry as he stammered, "You know, it… it really looks like every other room in the hotel."

With barely a sound, Sandra stood and held out her hand for his.

As Ron reached for her, she whispered, "Show me!"

The elevators were full of tourists calling it a night, returning to their rooms after a show, or perhaps after leaving a month's pay in the casino. Ron and Sandra squeezed into the first available car, and wiggled their way into the back corner, attempting to stay out of sight.

A group of college kids and a family of four stepped off the elevator at the second floor, and then two couples got off on Three. By the time they reached the sixth floor, there was only one other couple in the car, an Asian man and woman, both in their late 50's or early 60's.

"Hi," said Sandra, unsure if they understood English. Her left arm was now into his unbuttoned shirt past the wrist.

"Shhh..." whispered Ron, and the two of them burst out laughing as the couple exited on Seven, never even glancing back.

Finally, the elevator reached the eighth floor, and they emerged, arms still wrapped around each other all the way down the hall to Room 815. Laughing, Ron grabbed the key card from his rear pocket and opened the door, struggling to move with Sandra clinging to him.

They stepped inside the darkened room and Ron flipped on the bathroom's light switch, then shut its door most of the way, allowing them just enough illumination to keep from tripping over the gear he had earlier left scattered on the floor. Every stitch of clothing was eagerly tossed, coming to rest on the carpet or on a random piece of television equipment.

Together they tumbled onto the bed, as if in slow motion. Sweaty, feral, and alone on the planet, they consumed one another in passion, fulfilling the desire they'd both felt building up in them for months. She felt the trust she had always craved, sliding herself into the embrace without reservation. They melted together, afterward falling asleep in each other's arms. And for the first time in months, *the jumper* did not spend the night in his bed.

Thursday, May 7th

The phone rang in Room 815 at precisely 6 am. Ron wriggled his arm free from under Sandra's head. Slowly rolling over, eventually answering the wake-up call by the third ring.

"Uhh…" he said, in a mumble. "It's morning already? I need to get…"

She placed a finger on his lips to shush him, mid-sentence, then rolled on top of him again. They made love once more, this time in haste, but with every bit as much purpose. Afterwards, they lay together for just a few minutes. The photographer's eyes studied her form in the sparse morning light, which was peeking through the slightly parted curtains behind her. He slowly ran his fingertips through her hair, around her ear, then softly across her shoulders. With his fingernails, he lightly traced his way down her spine and over her supple curves, softly illuminated by the diffused sunlight. She arched her back and purred in contentment.

"You are so beautiful," he said. "Do you even know that?"

"You make me feel that way," she replied.

Had time allowed, they would have stayed there in bed all day, but both were sadly aware that live TV doesn't wait.

"Damn job," Ron said.

Sandra hopped out of the bed, and naked, ran playfully into the bathroom ahead of him.

"But wait, I…" He heard her lock the door.

Sitting up on the bed, Ron stared at the clock, sighed, shook his head, and wondered how he was going to meet Jennie on time. Just then, there was a flush, and he heard the shower turning on. The door clicked, and he saw Sandra's foot kick it part way open.

He stood up, and walked into the bathroom, where Sandra was already behind the opaque glass hosing off.

"Mind if I join you, Ma'am," he asked, partially opening the glass door.

"Please do, sir,"

They briefly shared the warm, soapy water of the hotel shower, but Sandra swiftly rinsed off and made her escape, grabbing a towel from the rack.

"We'll have to do this again some time," she said, reaching in and patting him on the rear, before quickly dashing into the other room to gather her clothes.

Sandra was slipping her dress over her head when she heard the shower turn off. "Call me when you get back to L.A." she said from the other room.

"Oh, I will," Ron said, and opened the bathroom door as he toweled off.

"You look great," he said, although, hair tied back and sans makeup, she wore the black and white dress from the day before, now seriously wrinkled from a night strewn on a hotel room floor.

"So do you," she said, her eyes glancing down his wet, naked frame as she reached for the door handle to leave.

"It's only a model," he teased.

"Shhh…"

*****

Ron hastily threw on some clothes and stacked all the gear he needed for an outdoor live shot on his wheeled cart, and headed for the door. Glancing back around the hotel room to double-check, he realized that he hadn't taken the time to charge his cell phone overnight, but he grabbed it and took it with him nonetheless.

He met Jennie in the lobby about ten minutes late. She had already been on the phone to the station and assured the producer that they would make their slot, although she had her doubts. She spotted Ron rushing out of the elevator and waved him over. They quick-stepped it out the door, waved over a cab, and began to load it up with gear.

"Rough night?" she asked.

"Not too bad, actually," he answered.

"Yeah? You look like shit."

The smell of her coffee was killing him, but there was no time now. It was already 6:45 and their live hit was coming up at 7:18.

The taxi made it across town quickly in the light morning traffic. Jennie paid the driver while Ron hopped out and began to set up on the sidewalk outside the Convention Center. He aimed the camera so that his reporter would be facing the morning sun, and would have the large, draped Gadget Show sign in soft focus over her shoulder.

He connected and fired up the Live-U backpack, and used Jennie's phone to check in with news-control to be sure they were seeing his signal. He called up the IFB number, allowing Jennie to hear program audio and receive cues from the director in her earpiece. They were ready to go, with only a minute or two to spare.

Jennie was introduced, and said hello to the Todd Mack and Roxi Peters, the Morning Show anchors, who both expressed their envy at her Las Vegas assignment. The small talk continued for a few minutes until Jennie tossed to the piece they had cut the previous day. After the video, Todd asked Jennie how the weather was in the desert, and if they were staying for a few more days.

"Well," she answered. "It's not even June, and athough it's barely seven in the morning, you can already tell it's going to be a scorcher here again today.

And no, we're not staying. In fact, we'll be on a plane home in just a few hours."

"*Wow,*" Ron thought to himself, "*people actually watch this happy-talk stuff?*"

"Alright," said Roxi. "Have a safe flight, and we'll see you back here soon."

Chapter Eight:

DON'T YOU EVER JUST FEEL LIKE CRYING?

Monday, June 8th

The station had RSVP'd the invitation from the Hollywood Chamber of Commerce and made reservations days ahead for the ceremony. Bruce Roberts, star of dozens of films and television shows, was to be honored with a star on the Hollywood Walk of Fame. It was a well-planned publicity event. The timing was to coincide with the upcoming premiere of his latest film, The Unknown Prisoner, which would be opening on the 27th at the Egyptian Theatre, a Hollywood landmark half a block away. Television crews and still photographers began lining up for the Star ceremony at 9:30 for the 11:15 event, although they would be kept behind the red velvet rope until the podium and sound system could be set up and checked, the risers built, and the security in place, at a little past ten.

Ron pulled up in Micro 21 at about 9:45, and parking was already at a premium. He found a metered spot around the corner on Cherokee and grabbed it. He retrieved his gear and hiked up the uneven, trash-strewn sidewalk toward the theatre. The throngs of fans had begun to clog Hollywood Boulevard, some arriving as early as 6:00 AM. The steel barricades were in place along the curb, and he took his place in line for entry behind a handful of other cameramen.

Carol Parsons, the Public Relations manager for the Walk of Fame, made her way over to the growing line of journalists and began to sign them in, checking Press Passes against names and affiliations on her reservations list. One by one, they passed through the checkpoint and began setting up on the black, wooden risers. She recognized Ron from previous events, but checked his information anyway, just as a formality.

"Here it is, Ron Sharp, Channel Six," Carol said, and crossed his name off the list with a yellow highlighter.

Once approved, he grabbed his camera and tripod and slid past the Security Guards on his way to the riser. The narrow sidewalk kept all but the first three or four cameramen from having an ideal shot of the ceremony, the others being forced to level two or three on the riser, behind the first row, elevated only about a foot.

The risers were the same ones they've been using since there were only a handful of TV crews in town that would show up for these things, maybe half a dozen with the syndicated entertainment shows. Now, with dozens of blogs, websites and e-mags covering these events, space was more and more at a premium. This event was packed with media, more so than the usual Walk of Fame ceremony. Roberts was an international superstar, so there were photo and video crews from literally every continent, some using small cameras and Live-U backpacks to stream the event live, halfway across the globe. One young guy Ron didn't recognize had set up his tripod and had it rigged to hold his lap-top in front of him on a small desk-like contraption. He would be shooting and transmitting the ceremony live for his website, no-doubt seen by literally dozens of people around the globe. Ron admired the technology, but at the same time shook his head and ribbed the cameraman about taking up valuable space with all of his living room furniture.

Ron grabbed a spot on level two, and set up so that his camera's lens would be slightly above and between the cameras of Access Hollywood and TMZ, whose crews had been able to snap up the best spots on the lower level. Paparazzi were out in force, crouched down below and alongside the video crews, leaving not one inch of sidewalk uncovered.

By 11:00 the street was packed. Hundreds of fans of all ages, holding movie posters, glossy photos, cameras, and cell-phones, waited in the heat, pressed tightly against the barricades by the growing swarm. Young women and school-aged girls dressed for summer were there in abundance, mostly without their husbands or boyfriends, hoping to catch the superstar's eye.

Ron took advantage of the few minutes before the start of the event to pick up his cell phone and check in with Sandra.

"Hey," she said. "What's up?"

"Oh, nothing," he replied. "Except I'm down the street from you getting ready for Bruce Roberts to show up and get his star on the Walk of Fame, that's all."

"Yeah, I heard about that," she said. "I thought about walking over, but those things are always such a pig-screw."

"Yeah," he agreed. "And this one is worse than most. You'd have had to get here hours ago to see anything."

"I'll pass," she said. "But when am I going to see you again?"

"I'll call you,"

"You'd better."

"As soon as I can, I promise."

"OK, gotta go."

"Bye."

City maintenance crews had been out overnight with water trucks and hoses, doing their best to wash the grime off the streets and sweep away a ton of trash in an effort to present a positive image to television viewers, or visitors who might come for a glimpse at a real life Hollywood star. About a dozen pissed off homeless guys were forced to dismantle the tents that normally line the sidewalk and move around the corner and out of sight, with all their worldly possessions in tow. The smells of urine and trash are not exactly what you want your guests to remember, so at least for this day, the blemishes would be hidden and Hollywood would maintain a presentable face.

Dick Tuttle, the "Unofficial Mayor of Hollywood" stepped up to the mike at exactly 11:15 and began welcoming and introducing dignitaries. Friends and co-stars of Roberts gave testimonials and entertained the throng of cheering fans with stories of meeting and working with him on various projects throughout the years. Fellow actors, actresses, and directors all spoke, giving him praise for his impressive body of work.

First came Annie Butler, Bruce's co-star from his first film, Horrific Hideaway. She told the crowd what a pleasure it had been co-starring with the man of the hour, telling a story about how one morning on location, it was so miserable and rainy, that Bruce accidentally opened her trailer door and ran inside, not expecting to see her standing there completely naked, changing costumes. The crowd roared with laughter, and in the background, Bruce could be seen shrugging and nodding shyly, acknowledging his faux pas. Annie continued, reassuring the throng that after embarrassing her that way, he had been a complete gentleman, who apologized profusely, and stepped back out into the elements while covering both eyes. She congratulated him on receiving his star and handed the mike over to Hal Newman.

Newman had directed Roberts in several films, most recently The Killer's Game, a high-budget mystery that enjoyed a great deal of success at the box office. He related a story about the time he and Roberts were shooting in Paris for a few weeks. One night they were out on the town and Roberts was recognized and surrounded by a group of young French women. While neither of the men spoke the language, he said, that somehow was not a barrier. He kept the story PG for the audience, but there was no doubt what he was saying about Bruce's worldwide appeal.

At last Tuttle brought up the man of the hour, to the roar of the frenzied overflow crowd. Roberts stepped to the mike, dressed in a shiny gray Armani suit, a man much smaller than expected, but strikingly handsome, with thick, wavy salt-and-pepper hair. He waited for the applause to die down, and said a few words, thanking the fans and the Hollywood community for honoring him with such a gracious gift. Just then a red open-top double-deck Celebrity Tour Bus loaded with summertime tourists rolled down Hollywood Boulevard, and came to a stop alongside the ceremony, giving the out-of-towners aboard a little extra, unadvertised excitement to go along with their tour of the landmarks, gravesites and movie studios. The bus driver paused long enough for his passengers to cheer and take some snapshots from high above the crowd of fans in the street. Roberts waved and thanked everyone for their attendance and their continued support. Of course, he didn't miss the opportunity to mention The Unknown Prisoner and his hope that everyone in attendance would flock to see it, which they no doubt planned to do.

Roberts then stepped down from the podium and, using the gold ribbon, lifted the red wooden cover from atop the freshly embedded, shiny brass star embossed with his name. The celebrities posed together standing over the star, smiling for the cameras, following the directions being shouted out by the paparazzi, "This way, Bruce!" "Just one more in this direction, Bruce!"

Finally, his patience wore thin on this warm summer day, and he turned away from the cameras, briefly stepping into the adoring crowd to take a few photos and sign some autographs, before disappearing into the restaurant whence he had initially appeared.

The photogs began to break down and pack up their gear. A few fans started conversing with some of the cameramen on the other side of the barricades. There were the usual comments, like "Hey, how do I get your job?" or "Can we get on TV?" mostly from well meaning moms holding their babies, or students seriously wondering what a life in the media would be like. One man shouted out Ron's favorite question, "How much is that camera worth?" The question went ignored. *Not a chance in hell.*

But as Ron was working his way past the barricades toward his truck, he could make out a high-pitched voice shouting out in his direction, "Hey, Baby, you married?" He turned his head to see a short, stocky African American woman, perhaps 30, standing with a small group of friends, waving and flashing a cute smile at him. He smiled back, but did not answer. "You fool around?" He paused, bit his lower lip, shook his head and blushed as he turned the corner and headed up Cherokee to his vehicle.

"You're a popular guy," laughed Will Blanks, the photog covering the event for Channel 3, who happened to be walking just ahead of Ron, "I wish the women would throw themselves at *me* like that."

"You can be my wingman anytime, Will," laughed Ron. "I swear to God, I've got to get a shirt that says 'Come Up and Talk to Me Like You Know Me.'"

"Yeah," said Will. "Get me one, too. In Double X."

As they neared their vehicles on Cherokee, a filthy, disheveled street person sat propped against the door of a closed and shuttered printing shop. The man, who couldn't have been older than either of the photogs, was wearing what had once been someone's expensive dress slacks and long-sleeve pinstriped shirt, before they had been fished out of a dumpster and slept in a few hundred times on a filthy Hollywood street. His long gray hair was matted and his beard wild and unkempt. He smelled of wine, urine and a year's worth of body odor, and was clearly high.

"Hey gentlemen," the fellow said. "How about some change for an old vet?"

Ron answered first. "I can't, man. I'm working."

"I can see that, man, you've got money," he said, as he began, staggering, to follow the two shooters toward their trucks.

"Here, dude," said Will, reaching into his pocket and handing the guy a dollar. "Go buy some food."

"Oh thank you, sir," he said, offering a hit off his joint in exchange.

Will took a hit, holding the joint carefully, so as not to get any of the man's saliva on his mouth and handed it back to him, while Ron kept walking.

"Take it easy, dude," Will said.

"Likewise, sir. God bless you."

"Welcome to Hollywood," said Ron, stopping at his truck, Will having another half block to walk.

"No shit," replied Will. "That's the best way I know of to get them to leave you alone. See you at the next one."

"Later," said Ron, as he packed up his gear and called in to the assignment desk.

"Take a lunch break, and then I need you to pick up Carolyn Sanchez here at the station," said Freddy. "She's working on a story downtown."

"You got it."

Ron took his meal break at Arby's on Sunset, down the street from the station. He thought about checking in with Sandra again, but put it off. His fear of commitment was still alive and well, and with the Emmy's only about a week away, he knew he'd be talking to her soon enough.

*****

"Micro 21 is on the lot," Ron said, keying the mike on his two-way radio. **"You can send Carolyn out."**

"Ten-Four," replied Freddy. **"She's on her way. Oh, and I'll send Doug out to get your Hollywood Star video. That way you don't have to worry about shipping it in later."**

Carolyn Sanchez had been working for KSIX for almost 18 years. Prior to that she was a freelance reporter at a couple of the Spanish language stations in Los Angeles and before that in San Diego. There, she had been working as a Paramedic and Nurses Assistant for a time, to put herself through San Diego State, and had been married briefly to a local disc jockey before moving to Los Angeles to start a new life without him. She was born in Cuba, but escaped to America with her parents as a young child, and grew up with so many other Cuban refugees in the Miami area. Over the past 18 years, she'd become one of the premiere bilingual reporters in the city, talented, beautiful and knowledgeable enough to cover a wide variety of stories, and able to explain situations effortlessly to the audience, including the station's valuable and ever-expanding Spanish-speaking demographic.

"Hey, Big Guy!" Carolyn said, as she climbed into the Microvan, tossing her makeup bag behind the seat.

"Hey," said Ron. "So where are we going?"

"We have an interview with a member of the School Board," she answered, in her still detectable but fetching accent, "about that teacher who was arrested last week for molestation."

"Oh, yeah," said Ron. "What a piece of work that guy is. If I had a kid there, he'd have bigger problems than he's got now."

"I think a lot of parents feel that way."

"Microvan 21 is off the lot, for downtown," Ron said into the mike.

"Roger that."

Ron hadn't worked with Carolyn in several weeks, and always enjoyed hearing the latest stories about her husband, their girls and the horses they kept. She could no longer ride, since the May Day incident, but she still loved training and working with the animals, and Maddie and Mari, now in their teens, were becoming excellent riders.

She was telling him about a family they had met at the stables, a couple and their handicapped son, who had begun making tremendous progress in his therapy thanks to the horses, and was almost ready to ride unassisted. Carolyn worked with him on weekends while the girls were off riding the canyons near the stables. She found it infinitely more gratifying than the news business, which had left a sour taste in her mouth since the May Day melee.

The station had only half-heartedly fought for her in her lawsuit against the LAPD, and her settlement ended up being much less than she had expected. Jay Clark, the officer involved, had testified under oath that in his estimation, Carolyn appeared to have been reaching for his weapon, which justified his striking her several times with his baton. Numerous videos, from multiple locations in the park, provided ample evidence that such a claim was bogus, but simply by stating that he perceived such a thing to be true, the officer was ultimately cleared of any wrongdoing.

With Carolyn's ongoing medical expenses, the meager amount paid by the city, along with her medical insurance, still left a large sum owed to her doctors. It was no secret that she would have loved more than anything to leave the station and work full-time with the horses, if only money hadn't been such an issue.

But talking about her passions, her horses and her children always put a beaming smile on her face. Nothing else seemed to hold her interest the same way, particularly working the same stale stories every day. Covering the School Board was like marching in mud.

Carolyn's case had also caused hard feelings against KSIX, which she openly shared with anyone whom she considered a friend, and Ron was certainly one.

"Can you believe what's going on?" she asked.

"I'm hardly ever at the station," he answered, making sure this time that the two-way radio was turned off and the mike not inadvertently keyed, "What's the latest?"

"What a disaster," she replied. "We've lost our news director, our managing editor and our assignment editor all within a few weeks. Not to mention all the layoffs. I mean, how do you recover from that? There's nobody who has a clue anymore. It's like working with a bunch of children.

"Don't get me wrong," she continued. "Some of them are really sharp, completely on top of things, like Scott. But there are others who never wanted to work the assignment desk in the first place. They got into the business hoping to become reporters and got roped into working the desk. It's a tough job, and even tougher if you're not cut out for it."

"I know," said Ron. "Maggie was a huge loss."

"And the product we're putting on the air now is just embarrassing," Carolyn added. "I used to have pride in my work, I guess I still do, but it just seems so unappreciated."

"I know what you mean," Ron replied. "I just tell myself that I'm not doing this for management or anybody else. I'm not doing this for anyone but me. Don't laugh, but I try to make art. To take the best pictures I can take, and to tell a story that people find interesting. If just one person notices and thinks it was shot well, or learns something, I've done my job. I really don't care what management thinks."

"They sent me out to shoot with Danny the other day," Carolyn added. "He's a great guy, but he has no idea what he's doing with a camera. Half the video was blue. Everything was shaky, he didn't hold his shots, the package looked horrible."

"So, were they upset with you?" Ron asked.

"No, that's the thing," she replied, incredulous. "No one said a word about it. Nobody seems to care anymore. It's like they're not even watching."

"No, they're watching," Ron said. "They're watching their bottom line."

Microvan 21 approached downtown, and they were minutes away from their appointment with the Superintendent, when the display on his phone lit up, reading ASSIGN. DESK. Ron answered the call and put it on speaker.

"Micro-21," he said.

"Ronnie, I've been trying to reach you on the two-way," said Scott urgently. "Have you been listening to City Fire?"

"Umm… No, we haven't," replied the embarrassed cameraman, reaching to turn the two-way back on and adjust the volume on the scanner. "What are you hearing?" he asked, locking in City Fire's response channel.

"They've got a fire working at Third and Bonnie Brae. They just arrived on scene and asked for a couple more units. It sounds like it could be pretty good."

"We're real close to there," he said. "We'll check it out."

"Don't worry about your interview, we'll call and reschedule it."

"Thanks," said Caroline. "I'll call you in a few with an update."

Ron took the Alvarado Street exit and raced south to Third. By that time, the scanner was alive with chatter. Battalion 11 was asking for additional resources to stage on Bonnie Brae or Fourth Street. The Chief asked Metro Control to confirm all the units assigned to the fire. The list seemed endless, Ron counting eight Rescue Ambulances, five engines, and Four Task Forces before he lost count.

"Jesus," he said. "This must be a monster fire."

Looking to the east down Third Street from less than a mile away, they could easily see a thick column of dark gray smoke funneling straight up through the calm, cloudless sky. It was impossible to tell which building was burning, but one thing was certain- this was a densely populated residential area of Los Angeles, and this fire was quickly becoming a major emergency. Engines and Rescue Ambulances were coming in screaming from all directions, and still more were being dispatched.

"Micro 21 is on location, this looks like a good one," Ron shouted into the mike, as he grabbed a spot near the corner of Third and Burlington, half a block away, and leapt out of the van.

They ran in the direction of the fire trucks, camera rolling, and immediately encountered several firefighters, wearing masks and oxygen tanks, running from the three-story apartment building, frantically carrying and dragging injured victims out to the sidewalk. The acrid, toxic smells of burning carpet, building materials, and food was everywhere.

Carolyn called in to the station and gave them a size-up of the scene, suggesting that they launch the helicopter for aerials of what was likely to be the lead story of the night.

"Already done," said Scott.

The smoke was turning white and quickly beginning to dissipate, as the fire itself had been doused quickly after consuming several units on the second floor of the building. What remained, however, were dozens of residents who had been overcome by the noxious smoke, that had spread rapidly up the staircases and through open windows until it enveloped the entire structure. Someone, presumably a manager or maintenance worker, had bolted the steel fire-doors open, intending to allow for ventilation into the building and reducing the cost of air conditioning. But the purpose of the doors was to prevent situations precisely like this one, where smoke from a relatively small fire could spread to multiple apartments, and cause injury or death on a horrific scale.

Ron was the first camera on the scene, and quickly found himself in the midst of a chaotic flurry of rescuers and victims, darting past him in all directions, much too busy to be concerned about his presence. He watched as a firefighter climbed a wooden ladder to get to a family stranded on a third floor deck, their apartment filled with poisonous smoke. Women were tossing their babies from the upper floors, in hopes that someone in the gathering crowd would catch them, sparing them from death.

Suddenly, to his left, he caught sight of a large, obviously pregnant woman, limp and unconscious, her t-shirt covered with soot, being carried out through the glass front doors by a pair of firemen, and placed on the sidewalk, to be attended to by paramedics. They immediately began pumping her chest, her limbs and exposed belly bouncing and jerking wildly with each thrust.

There was a narrow, elevated patch of grass and dirt between the sidewalk and the building's fence, which was quickly being set up as a triage, although the growing number of victims soon filled the small lawn area to capacity. Ron did his best to stay out of the way of the rescue work being frantically performed all around him. He stepped up onto the deck of Engine 11, which was parked directly in front of the building, and climbed up onto the Fire truck's roof. This gave him a high-angle shot and allowed him to survey the scene and find where the most visual activity was taking place. From his perch, he saw several young children, limp and lifeless, being carried out and placed on the ground. The sounds of sirens, smoke blowers, and cries of desperate agony were deafening.

He climbed back down, and ran over to the triage, where a young father knelt over his ten-month-old baby boy who had stopped breathing and was black from smoke. The man, himself covered with soot and grime, screamed and wailed toward the heavens, begging for help from the overtaxed rescuers. Suddenly, a paramedic seemed to appear out of nowhere with an oxygen tank and a tiny mask. He jumped in next to Ron, began feeding the little boy oxygen and pumping his chest. Ron stood over him, and held his camera over the firefighter's shoulder, aimed straight down at the baby's face, now covered with the mask. The boy let out a plaintive cry. The excited firefighter announced loudly, "That's a good cry!" as he let off on the oxygen and the child began to stabilize.

By now, several lifeless bodies had been lined up on the concrete entryway and covered with white sheets. But there were many others still in need of attention. Ron looked up the street toward the ambulances, and could see that some of the gurneys were being loaded up with injured to be transported in Rescue Ambulances. He ran alongside one of them, bearing a young woman, being pushed by a pair of firemen toward RA 20. After she was loaded into the ambulance, Ron turned and saw an orange helmeted Fire Captain walking rapidly in his direction, toward Rescue 15, which was parked further up Bonnie Brae. The Captain was holding, in the crook of his left forearm, the limp and lifeless body of a young child, covered with black ash and soot, limbs dangling by her side. Ron back-pedaled, his camera capturing video of the infant's flopping body, then tilting up to capture the tears in the eyes of his rescuer, who himself was overcome by sheer horror and grief.

The residents of neighboring buildings had gathered in the street, many trying to help as police quickly set up yellow emergency tape to allow firefighters to work undisturbed. Ron had again joined up with Carolyn and she began interviewing residents of the burned building who had escaped the fire and now formed a stunned, weeping swarm on the lawn of the adjacent building. Rushing into the crowd, Carolyn asked questions in Spanish, and rapidly translated the answers for the camera. First to catch her eye was a young woman, crying and holding her infant daughter, both of them covered in soot, mixed with snot and drool.

"Yo gritaba y un muchacho me dijo que se la tirara a la niño, yo se la tire desde arriba…"

"SHE THREW HER CHILD OUT OF THE BALCONY!" Carolyn interpreted.

"What floor?"

"del segundo,"

"The Second Floor…"

Then, quickly turning to another woman, who was still in a state of panic and disbelief,

"Solo estaba gritando porque yo sentía que nos gibamos a morir ahi con los niños…" the woman wailed.

"I started screaming. I thought I was going to die, and my children were gonna die!"

Carolyn and Ron worked their way through the mob and past the dozens of pleading, traumatized faces. The looks of desperation brought a tear to Carolyn's eye, but she knew this was not the time to let her emotions get the better of her. This story was far from over.

Ron and Carolyn stood just outside the yellow tape that police had stretched down Bonnie Brae, marking off a section of ground for rescuers to work on the injured. They watched paramedics carry more victims onto the triage, still clearly overwhelmed by the sheer number of patients, filling it once again to capacity, as quickly as the earlier ones had been removed and transported.

Carolyn surprised Ron with a spontaneous outburst.

"I'm a trained paramedic," she shouted at the rescuers. "Do you need help?"

"Get in here!" bellowed an unseen voice in the crowd.

Carolyn told Ron emphatically not to shoot video of her providing assistance, as she did not want in any way to be the focus of the story. She handed Ron her microphone and stepped under the Crime Scene tape to begin working on a teenage girl who was lying unattended and motionless. She immediately began giving the girl CPR and mouth-to-mouth resuscitation. The girl vomited, but did not otherwise respond.

Ron could not hear his phone chirp through the cacophony, but felt it vibrating on his belt. Initially, he ignored it, instead shooting more of the pandemonium, which was continuing all around him.

His phone vibrated again, and annoyed, he quickly glanced at the text message, which had been sent by the news director himself:

GET HER OUT OF THERE- NOW! - W. J.

Ron walked briskly back to the yellow emergency tape, and yelled for Carolyn, who was now in the middle of the noisy triage, having moved on from the now dead girl to another young pregnant woman who needed her help. Ron yelled several times, "Carolyn!" before he finally got her attention. He held out his phone and motioned for her to come to him.

She stood up, angry, tearful and covered with soot, blood and vomit, walked over to the yellow line, where Ron showed her the text. They both looked skyward, knowing full well that it was through aerial video from a TV helicopter, not necessarily from Channel 6, that Wellington had seen her giving assistance on the ground. He was, no doubt, sitting comfortably in his office, on his ample backside, watching the bank of high-definition monitors on the wall. He had every channel, local and network, broadcast and cable available, so that he could watch every shot that KSIX or their competitors were broadcasting, whenever there was a breaking news story anywhere in the country. Assuming that they were still on camera, Carolyn looked upward at the assortment of helicopters, stuck her middle finger in the air, turned to Ron, and said, "Let him fucking fire me," before heading back in to rejoin the fray.

Other stations' crews were arriving on scene, but Ron knew that Channel 6 owned this story. He started moving in, becoming just a bit more noticeable, perhaps a touch more disruptive and conspicuous. He started stepping over hoses, and into the paths of some of the firefighters and police officers, hoping to draw some negative attention. Captain Steve Rhodes, the Fire Department PIO who had just arrived on scene, became aware of the presence of a large and growing contingent of media, and intervened. Yellow Crime Scene tape was strung across Bonnie Brae, about a half block south of the building, and the media was ordered to move behind the line, to give the fire crews more room to work. Ron immediately complied, and with a devious smile, set up behind the line, next to the other news crews. There, along with the other stations, he got some sound with the PIO, who could only provide preliminary numbers on the dead and injured.

"The fire was first reported at 3:47 pm, and the first units arrived on scene at 3:52. Upon arrival, they saw extensive fire on the second floor and immediately called for additional resources. A total of 52 Firefighters and Paramedics responded and had the fire knocked down in 17 minutes. Fire doors had been installed in the building, however they were propped open, perhaps to allow for ventilation. This allowed the smoke to spread throughout the complex, causing the tragic results that you see here tonight."

"At this point, we have twelve fatalities," Rhodes reported, "including five children and three pregnant women, but that number is preliminary. We have 22 transported to local hospitals with injuries ranging from cuts to smoke inhalation."

"I'll be back shortly with more up-to-date information for you when I have it."

With that, Rhodes walked back toward the command post and the news crews prepared to file their reports.

Soon, the last of the surviving victims was transported in serious condition to University of California Hospital, and Carolyn rejoined Ron outside the perimeter. Spent, she threw her arms around him and cried.

"It's OK," he told her, choking up and patting her gently on the shoulder. "You did everything you could."

"I know," she said. "It's just… all those babies…"

For a moment, they forgot about how much trouble they were going to be in when this was over.

Ron called the assignment desk as they walked around the block to the van.

"Channel Six News,"

"Hey Scott, it's us."

"Hey," he whispered, his voice clueing him in that there was trouble.

"How bad is it?" he asked.

"It's bad, Wellington wants me to transfer you to him as soon as you call in. He's not happy."

"Hey, you know what? She was saving lives," Ron insisted. "I have to go set up for a live shot now. I don't have time for this bullshit." Ron hung up the phone.

Ron's phone rang again, almost instantly.

"What?" He shouted.

"Ron, this is Wellington. Let me speak to Carolyn, please."

Ron handed the phone to his reporter and sent a signal with his eyes that she instantly understood.

"Hello,"

"Carolyn, I know you're busy, so I won't take a lot of your time. I need you and Ron to be in my office first thing tomorrow, 9 am sharp. Am I clear?"

"Yes, sir. We'll be there," she said softly, rolling her eyes toward her cameraman.

"Very good," said Wellington. "Have a good night."

"Good night."

Ron quickly raised the mast on the microvan and shipped in a few key shots of "tease video" and a sound bite from Chief Rhodes. It was almost five, and they were the lead story on the early newscast. Due to time constraints, Carolyn's report would have to rely heavily upon aerials. There was no time to worry about her appearance. She stuffed her IFB earpiece in her right ear and jumped in front of the camera.

Carolyn showed her experience and gave her live report on autopilot. No one watching could tell that she was covered with soot, mud, and vomit, and still emotionally overwhelmed by the events of the previous hour. She voiced-over the pictures and let the Chief provide the statistics. She did, however, have the presence of mind to tease the story that would be coming on the late newscast.

"We were the first camera crew on the scene here," she said. "And I can tell you, I've never seen anything like this in my life. The pictures we have for you on the Late News will touch you and make you want to hug your children extra tightly tonight. Now, back to you in the studio."

"Thanks, Carolyn," remarked anchorman Geoff Martin. "That was difficult to watch."

They sat together in the van for the next hour, reviewing the video and editing the package for the Late News. It was an emotional task.

"Every time I see that baby cry, it gets to me," she said, watching the video. "You did a wonderful job on this, Ron."

"Thanks," he replied. "So did you. It is hard to watch again, isn't it?"

The piece was cut, TRT 3:24, longer than they usually wanted for a story, but Linda Bodak, the show producer asked for a longer piece on this one. Carolyn still hadn't gotten her script approved, and it was getting late.

"Well," she said. "I guess I should call my writer."

"I suppose so," Ron replied.

"Channel Six News,"

"Scott, it's Carolyn," she said. "We've got our piece ready for the show. Do you have all the info you need on this?"

"Hey, are you guys OK? Wellington absolutely blew an O-ring in the newsroom earlier."

"We're fine. The story is the thing now. Can I talk to a writer?"

"Sure, Deb Chen's your writer on this, I'll transfer you."

"Hey, Carolyn," said Deb, "I've been working on your intro for you."

"Thanks," Carolyn replied. "You're the best, I've been a bit busy."

"So I've heard."

The fire video was teased throughout prime time, with Ron's dramatic pictures from the scene. It led the newscast, with an emotional intro by Gretchen, sitting in the anchor chair.

"Good Evening, I'm Gretchen Salvo. Thirteen dead, scores injured. Our Carolyn Sanchez was first on scene this afternoon as one of the deadliest blazes in Los Angeles history tore through an apartment building near downtown. Carolyn…"

"That's right, Gretchen. When we arrived on scene, there was pandemonium as firefighters rushed to rescue those who were trapped in the smoke-filled building here on Bonnie Brae Street. Many residents jumped from upper floors, or threw their children off of balconies to neighbors who had run over to help. Some of these images may be may be disturbing, but the heroics we witnessed this afternoon cannot be understated. Take a look…"

The station ran the package, and for the first time, Los Angeles actually got to see the intense drama of which they had been hearing all evening. Ron's breathtaking video painted an emotional picture of the scene, and elicited a strong reaction from viewers, who, in the following days, called and e-mailed the station to thank them for their coverage, and to offer financial aid to the victims and their families.

"There are no words to express what we witnessed here today," Carolyn said, coming back live. "The tragedy and the heroism were beyond anything my photographer or I had ever seen. We are praying for the families of everyone here at this devastating fire. Back to you in the studio."

The story was mentioned again several times throughout the newscast, reminding the audience of the catastrophe, and giving the number for Red Cross donations for those who wished to help.

The fire scene remained active throughout the night and into the morning. Overnight stringers were the only cameras still on location when the Coroner removed the bodies.

Before sunrise, crews from all the local stations were set up on the corner, reporting for the morning news shows, and TV helicopters circled the neighborhood to give a morning-after perspective. The story the following day on virtually every newscast would be the fire-doors, how their proper use could have confined the fire and smoke to several rooms and saved numerous lives.

Tuesday, June 9th

Ron and Carolyn were both in Wellington's office at nine as instructed, along with representatives from their unions.

The slam of the heavy glass door was loud enough to be heard in all corners of the newsroom; an announcement to all that something serious was going on.

"Sit down, please," said Wellington to the pair, as he maneuvered to sit on the corner of his desk, where he towered over his two employees. "I saw your story from last night. It was quite impressive. You should be very proud."

"Thank you, I am," said Carolyn. "Ron's pictures were amazing."

"Indeed they were," said the news director, peering down at the photographer and sucking his lower lip. "Congratulations."

"Thank you, sir," Ron replied unemotionally, looking straight ahead.

"I saw how hard you guys were working down there," he continued. "Those high-def cameras in the choppers these days are really something. You know, when there's a big story, I can sit right here at my desk, and watch what every station in town is putting on the air." He picked up a remote control and motioned to the bank of monitors on the wall behind them.

"I also saw you waving hello to me," he said, chuckling, playing back the video, which he'd saved on his DVR. Ron and Carolyn glanced quickly at each other, and then down into their laps. "That was very rude, what you did, Carolyn. Very rude."

"Yes sir it was, and I apologize."

"Now, you understand why I sent you that text, do you not?" Wellington asked Carolyn.

"Yes sir, I do. But at the time…"

"At the time," he interrupted emphatically, "was when it was important to follow my instructions, and do what I asked you to do. Not an hour later."

"Yes, sir," she said meekly.

"And you," he said, turning toward Ron. "How hard did you try to make her pay attention to my message and follow my instructions? Or was it all a big joke?"

"Um… no sir. It was not a joke," Ron replied. "Nothing that went on there was funny."

"My point is that you completely blew off my message. I even saw you laugh when she flipped me off."

"Umm, sir, we were swamped out there, you saw what was happening. I showed her the message. That's all I can do."

"So, you're willing to throw your partner under the bus here, is that it?"

"I'm not throwing anyone under the bus," Ron said. "It's… it's just that we had our hands full with…"

"What were you doing out there, exactly?" Wellington interrupted, turning back toward Carolyn.

"I was trying to help," she answered. "The firemen were overwhelmed."

"That's great," he said, leaning in. "And do you know the position you put this company in? Do you realize the risk of liability?"

"I'm a trained paramedic…"

"So you should realize that a good number of the people you try to help are going to die. Right?"

"Yes, sir."

"And there's a good chance that somebody is going to blame you for that, training or no training. Right?"

"But…"

"Sometimes we lose sight of our importance out there," Wellington said, walking around to sit behind his desk. "We are not 'first responders', we're not rescue workers. What we do is trivial. It's entertainment. We give the public pictures and tell them stories. They buy the soap we advertise. Do you guys get that?"

"Yes sir," they said in unison.

"Stories of life and death happen all around us, all day, every day," he continued, his gesticulations visible to everyone in the newsroom. "But we don't know about them because the media isn't always there. That's how unimportant we are. Do you know how many people died at that scene yesterday?" he asked Carolyn.

"I believe it was thirteen," she answered.

"That's exactly right," he said. "Thirteen. And, do you know how many would have died if we had not responded to the story at all and just drove right by?"

"Probably thirteen, sir."

"That's right, unlucky thirteen. So our presence there did absolutely nothing to help anyone, did it?"

"No, sir, but I…"

"You did *nothing* but put the company at risk," he interrupted sternly. "That's all you did. Do you get that, for Christ's sake?"

"Yes I do, but…"

"I have to know that you would handle this situation differently should it ever arise again," Wellington insisted. "I need to be confident of that. Can you assure me now, that you would not act the same way next time?"

"No I cannot, to be honest with you."

"What about you, Ron? Would you do anything differently?"

"No, sir. I would not."

"That makes me very unhappy," Wellington said, leaning back in his chair. "Very unhappy. I'll have a difficult time allowing you back on the street now, knowing that you're willing to make yourself part of the story like that."

"Look, sir," Ron said. "She specifically asked me not to shoot what she was doing, so she *wouldn't* be part of the story."

Wellington grabbed a copy of the Times from his desk and opened it to the Metro Section.

"Have you seen this?" he asked, throwing it down on the desk.

There was a large color photograph in the middle of Page one. It showed the triage area, filled with rescuers and patients. In the center of the photo, hunched over an unconscious victim, was Carolyn Sanchez.

"This story names you as one of the 'heroes' of the rescue effort. It says you worked on at least three patients, but that all of them passed away."

"That's accurate, but..."

"But what?" he interrupted, slamming the rolled up newspaper onto his left thigh and spinning in his chair. "What did they forget to mention? The phone number of the station's lawyers?"

Carolyn was running her hands across her scalp nervously as she tried to think of something to say that would set his mind at ease. She hoped that Lyle, the union rep would have something to say on her behalf. But nothing.

"You're off the street until we see how this shakes out," the news director announced to Carolyn.

"And you," he said to Ron, while glancing at Les, the rep from the photographer's union. "I'd suspend you if I could, but I'm going to settle for a warning. There will be a letter in your file, which I'll expect you to sign. A copy will be sent to the union, and one to Human Resources. You're expected to treat your job more seriously and respectfully in the future, Mr. Sharp. That, and you'll be ineligible for all out-of-town assignments for the foreseeable future. Am I understood?"

"Yes, yes you are," Ron answered, biting his lip.

"Oh, and by the way, Mr. Sharp," Wellington added. "I know all about that little prank you and your friend played on Shelby awhile back. I know about all your little jokes. And don't think that what you and Maria were saying about your colleagues in the truck the other day went unheard. I hear about everything."

With that, he opened the door and the two sheepishly left the meeting and returned to the deadly quiet newsroom. The union reps stayed behind.

Carolyn sat at her desk, and Ron walked slowly, fuming, to the assignment desk to get his assignment for the day.

Chapter Nine:

ACCELERATION

Friday, June 12th

"I'm Doreen and I'll be serving you tonight." The waitress at Firehouse 25 smiled and handed the couple their menus.

"Yes, thank you."

"I'd never even heard of this place," said Sandra, looking around in amazement.

"Yeah. I love it," Ron replied. "They were going to tear the building down after they stopped using it as a firehouse in the sixties, but then a few years later, some developer decided to turn it into a restaurant with office space upstairs."

"I think it's great that they didn't destroy it. And they left a lot of the original building intact."

"Right there behind you," said Ron, pointing over her shoulder, "is the old fire pole where they used to slide down and hop onto the horse-drawn vehicles that were parked right here, where we're sitting."

"So cool."

"And the floor is original and the heavy door in front is almost original."

Doreen asked if they needed another minute or two to decide.

"Wow. What should I get?" she asked, excitedly opening the menu.

"Oh, everything's good. I'm having the steak sandwich and the corn chowder. Oh, and an iced tea."

"That sounds great. I'd like a burger, medium rare with cheddar and a dinner salad with Honey mustard, please. And a coke."

"Sure thing," said Doreen. "I'll be right back."

"So, you're not very familiar with Downtown?" Ron asked.

"Certainly not as familiar as you," answered Sandra. "Most of the times I've been down here it was for a trade show or convention. I see they're really trying to revive the whole area."

"Absolutely," said Ron. "You should see what they've done with the old movie theatres on Broadway. Simply amazing. They want people to work here and stay here to spend their money, not just go home to the Valley at night. That's why there are so many apartments and condos being built right now."

Just then, Ron felt a hand on his shoulder.

"Hey, how ya doin' there, big guy?" boomed the voice of a well-groomed man in a ridiculously expensive suit.

"Hey Anthony, great to see you," Ron said, startled. "Sit down and join us!"

"Oh, I can't," he said, reaching out to shake Sandra's hand, which he held for just a second too long, "I'm Anthony. Anthony Iglesias."

"Sandra." she said, smiling and slowly pulling her hand back.

"I really can't stay, I've got a meeting. My office is upstairs. I saw you here and had to stop and say hello. Everything good?"

"Yeah, everything's great," Ron answered, neglecting to mention his semi-suspension. "You know, livin' the dream."

"It's always an adventure, isn't it?" Iglesias said, inching away.

"That it is."

"Nice to meet you," Sandra said.

"Alright, well, we'll see you in court," said Ron.

"You bet. Pleasure to meet you," he said, with a little wink to Sandra as he headed toward the door.

"That was Anthony Iglesias, one of the biggest defense attorneys in the country," Ron explained. "A real character. I didn't realize his office was in this building."

"I thought I recognized him, I guess I've seen him on TV," said Sandra. "You sure do know a lot of people."

"I've covered lots of trials where he was the defense attorney, usually some high-profile murder or celebrity case."

Ron turned in his seat to watch Anthony glad-handing his way out through the front door, looking every bit like a politician or movie star.

"He's always been great with the media. Win or lose, he'll stop and talk to us. I was just on a really interesting case with him last month. But I met him a couple of years ago while I was covering the Rudy Rodriguez murder trial. You know, the guy they called the 'Night Creeper'. Really bad guy. One day I was pool camera on the case, and the Judge made me set up in the rear of the courtroom instead of alongside the jury box. That always makes it more difficult, obviously, because you can't really get a good shot of the defendant's face, except maybe when he's walking in the door.

"So, I'm standing there, waiting for him to look to his right for whatever reason, or maybe to turn in his chair real quick, to see who's in the audience. I'm ready just in case, you know, so I can maybe get a clean shot of the guy. So the Judge calls a sidebar and the attorneys approach the bench for a little meeting. All of a sudden, Rodriguez spins around in his chair and glares at me. His look says, 'You know, I'd cut your heart out in about three seconds if I could.' I got the shot, and glared right back at him as if to say, 'I know you would, asshole, but you can't, so fuck you.'

"Anthony was walking back to the defense table and saw him, gave him a smack on the shoulder and told him to turn back around to face the Judge. After court that day, he actually came up to me and apologized. He's a stand up guy, even though his clients are usually scumbags."

"He wants to stay on the media's good side," Sandra said. "That's smart."

"I'll tell you what, if I ever get in trouble, call him, OK? Promise?" Ron said, as Doreen delivered their meals.

"Sure," laughed Sandra. "I promise."

"By the way," Sandra said, "I saw in the paper today that they completed the investigation into those mummified babies that were found a couple weeks ago. You remember that story?"

"Of course I do," Ron replied. "What are they saying?"

"They said that they appeared to be from an illegal abortion. But they couldn't connect either one to a mother, since they had no DNA to identify her. They closed the case. No charges filed."

"Yeah, that was the speculation at the time. They felt like this woman had maybe been an aspiring actress and a pregnancy would have ruined her career. Times were a lot different back then."

"That's for sure," said Sandra.

Sandra had thought of a dozen more things she wanted to learn about Ron, but wasn't quite sure how to bring them up.

"You have the best job in the world, don't you?"

"It really is," he said. "Except when it isn't.

"It's like, people always ask how they can get a job like mine. I used to give them a whole spiel, about 'stay in school, learn as much as you can, never turn down a day's work, blah, blah…' but now I just tell them that my job is not going to exist in another ten years, probably less. The only people being hired now are expected to write, report, shoot, edit, everything. They're hiring kids right out of school and paying them a third of what I make. The art of news photography is fading away, unappreciated. I'll just ride it out as long as I can."

"So, how did you know what it was you wanted to be?" Sandra asked, taking a sip of her coke.

"Oh, I guess I knew pretty early on," Ron answered. "As a teenager, I loved the action of cop shows, watched them all the time. But I had hearing issues that kept me from going into police work."

"That's too bad," said Sandra.

"But I was also fascinated with photography even as a small child."

He held up his fork as a prop.

"I can remember picking up a toy, a little plastic man maybe, and holding him up between the TV and me. I'd pretend he was on the screen, a character in the show. I'd change the focus from the TV screen to the little toy man using just one eye. When you think about it, little kids can teach themselves a lot of stuff when they're interested in learning. I learned about focus, depth of field, perspective, framing, all of those things, long before I went to college."

"Wow. Really?"

"And I always loved telling stories. I had this old video camera when I was a kid. I think my dad gave it to me. I used to make little home movies starring my dog, Jasper. We'd go spend the day in the park with my buddies and make movies. So I guess it was natural that I'd end up here. I'd go crazy if I had to work in an office all day."

Doreen returned to the table, checking on them and refilling Ron's iced tea.

"I guess you would," she said, taking a mouthful of salad. "So, what did you do at work today?"

Ron took just a small bite of his sandwich, trying not to be rude.

"Today was actually fairly boring. I started out this morning at 'crim courts' in department 30, downtown. That's arraignment court. We were waiting for a particular case, of course, that guy you probably heard about last month, who was setting all those fires all over town with his mother in the car."

"Allegedly", interrupted Sandra, sipping her coke.

"Right. Allegedly," Ron answered, taking another bite.

"Anyway, you learn a lot about people in arraignment court. It's pretty entertaining. You sit there waiting for your case, and you never know when it's going to be called. So you listen to all the other cases being brought up. Some defendants are in custody, normally the felonies, but a lot of them are just sitting next to you in the audience with their families. Lots of drug possessions, domestic violence, petty theft, that sort of thing. You can't predict what people are accused of by looking at them, you know? And of course, none of them are guilty. The jails are overflowing with innocent people," he said sarcastically.

"Do you think they're all guilty?" she asked.

"Probably the vast majority are. But they all have excuses, you know. Bad childhood, alcohol, sex addiction, blah, blah. Nobody wants to take responsibility."

"Don't you think it's always been that way, though?"

"I guess so, it just seems worse these days, somehow.

"You sure eat fast," Sandra noted. "You need to slow down."

"Oh, yeah. Sorry," he answered. "You can thank my job. See, you never know when you're going to get called off to run somewhere, so you've got to throw your food down when you can. Bad habit, I know."

"So anyway," Ron continued. "We're sitting there waiting until almost noon, when the bailiff finally walks over and tells us that our media request has been denied. The Judge doesn't want any cameras in the courtroom for fear of jeopardizing the prosecution by showing the guy's face all over town. I get that, but truth is, he could have told us that at nine o'clock and saved us all a lot of time."

"That's ridiculous," said Sandra.

"We're like Rodney Dangerfield. We get no respect. No respect at all."

"Wow, so did that ruin your whole day?"

"Not really. After lunch I met up with Bobbie Steele. We worked on a story about a new medical procedure that doctors have been performing. People are finding out that when they do extreme things to their bodies, you know like piercings and those huge, stretched out holes in their earlobes, that they can't find work as easily as they might otherwise."

"Umm... surprise!" Sandra said, raising one very cute eyebrow.

"Yeah, so a lot of them are deciding to have them removed. It's a whole new skill that these doctors need to learn. It's more than just removing something and stitching it up. Sometimes it takes a couple of visits over several months to get it right and prevent scarring. The same with tattoos."

"That's a lot of expense to remove something that probably cost a lot of money to have done in the first place," said Sandra.

"Yeah, well sometimes you need to learn things the hard way." Ron replied, sipping his tea. "A permanent reminder of a temporary feeling."

"I find that so often, many of a person's troubles are of their own making," Sandra said, no doubt thinking of Jack.

"Sometimes, but not always," said Ron. "I can't tell you how many innocent people I've seen get crippled or killed due to no fault of their own."

"I was thinking about that," Sandra said. "That must be so hard for you to cover those kinds of stories."

"You know," Ron said, working on his sandwich. "It gets easier over time. I remember the first fatal traffic accident I had to shoot. It was back in Phoenix. I pulled up to the scene and the two cars were smashed up in the street, about half a block apart. Police were talking to one of the drivers, giving him a sobriety test, you know, to see if he could walk a straight line or touch his nose. I walked down to the other vehicle and I could see the driver sitting behind the wheel. I don't want to get too graphic here over dinner, but let's just say that he was obviously dead."

"Yeah, umm… thanks for that," Sandra said, crinkling her nose.

"Well, you asked. Anyway, it affected me. All the way back to the station, all I could think about was how this poor schlub, probably with a family and a lifetime of memories and plans, was just done. Gone. In a flash." He snapped his fingers.

"Did you eventually find out his story?" she asked.

"No, you hardly ever do," he said, shrugging his shoulders. "I had a story all made up in my mind though, about how this guy was getting ready to watch a game on TV that night and ran out to the store to buy some snacks and maybe a six-pack. The store's only a couple blocks from his house, but like I said, wrong place, wrong time. Lights out forever."

"It bothered you, I can tell," said Sandra. "How did you deal with that?"

"Well," Ron answered, shrugging. "You know, by the next day, I was on to another story. And the next week, we had a triple homicide in Paradise Valley and I pretty much forgot about the first guy."

"Hmm…" she said, looking at her plate.

"You know, your mind does some really weird stuff. It's like it builds up scar tissue to protect you. I've talked to lots of other photogs about this, and most of them agree with me. I call it 'the Four Phases'. The first time you see something really sickening and gross like that accident, you start getting all philosophical, thinking about the meaning of life and death. You ask yourself if you really want to do this job, you know, if you can handle it."

Sandra squinted and stared at him with what could only be described as morbid curiosity.

"The second phase is, after a short while, you find yourself actually starting to crave it. It sounds sick, and it probably is, but when you hear that they're sending you to a fatal accident, you start hoping that it's a carload of people that were all thrown out onto the road in a bloody heap. Fortunately, phase two only lasts a short time."

"Hmm…" Sandra swirled a fry around in a little pool of ketchup she's made on her plate and held it up, nearly dripping on the table between them.

"French fry?" she asked, completely deadpan.

"Ahh, no thanks, I'm good."

"Anyway, phase three is when you get numb to it, when it's just another day at work. You can look at disgusting things all day long and not take them home with you."

"What's phase four?" she asked.

"Phase four," he said, stroking his chin, "is when you just don't care about anything or anyone anymore. You've just seen so much horrible stuff that nothing affects you at all. You burn out. I hope I never get to that stage."

"So you still care?"

"Of course I do. I really try not to get too jaded. I can't afford to get emotionally invested in stories, but sometimes it's hard to just walk away. I mean, I'm a human being. Sort of."

"So I'll bet the fire really affected you the other day," she said.

"You know, it really didn't," he answered. "I think what bothered me was that it didn't bother me. I mean, after it was over and the adrenaline was gone, I was sad that there were so many dead people, but while I was shooting it, it was like I wasn't even there. I was detached, looking at it through a little black and white viewfinder, trying to keep it all in focus. All I was thinking about was getting the best shot and not missing anything. Does that make me a bad guy?"

"No, Ron," she said, reaching for his hand. "It makes you a professional."

Monday, July 6th

"Channel Six News, can I help you?"

"Good morning ma'am, this is Assistant Chief Lonnie Woods of the Los Angeles City Fire Department. I'd like to speak with the news director, please."

"Yes sir. I'll see if he's available."

Sharon Boyd walked to the office next to hers and informed Wellington that there was a call he needed to take.

"This is Wellington James."

"Mr. James, this is Assistant Chief Lonnie Woods of the Los Angeles City Fire Department. How are you this morning?"

"Very good, sir. What can I do for you?"

"Well, first off, I wanted to let you know that we were extremely impressed by your station's coverage of the Bonnie Brae fire last month. That was some of the most dramatic video I've seen in a very long time."

"Thank you," said Wellington. "Yes it was."

"And the other thing," Woods continued, "was that viewers learned the importance of keeping their fire-doors shut, to prevent this type of incident from happening again."

"Yes, we're very proud."

"I'm sorry that it took me so long to call you, with the holiday and all, but I wanted you to know that the public response has been remarkable."

"It has been here, as well," said Wellington.

"Good," said Woods. "I'm glad to hear that. You know, Mr. James, there are certainly times that as an administrator, that I'm faced with difficult choices when it comes to disciplining a subordinate. Particularly someone who does something that he or she sincerely feels is the right thing to do at the time, in accordance with their training and the uniqueness of the situation."

"Go on..."

"Well, I want you to know that the Los Angeles City Fire Department has proposed presenting Carolyn Sanchez with a certificate to thank her for her heroic actions at the scene of the Bonnie Brae fire. She went far above and beyond the call of duty as a reporter, and acting as a concerned citizen, did not hesitate in the face of danger. She used her skill and training to help her fellow citizens. Our paramedics were clearly swamped and overtaxed there, and she was of great assistance to us until we could get additional assets on the scene."

"Chief Woods," said Wellington. "I think you know that…"

"My Department sees the actions of your reporter as a heroic act," the Chief interrupted. "And we believe that any effort to discipline either her, or her cameraman, would be a mistake and a terrible injustice."

"I understand your position, Chief," said Wellington. "And I expect you to understand mine. We cannot have our reporters jumping in and acting like first responders when they're on a story. The company is put in a terrible position in terms of liability."

"Yes it is," said the Chief. "But taken in its entirety, the situation was unique. Ms. Sanchez offered her assistance, and was invited by paramedics to enter the triage area. She took nothing upon herself. She gave CPR to a number of victims of smoke inhalation."

"She tried to save some individuals who subsequently died," said Wellington. "Our concern is that she, and KSIX could be held culpable for their deaths."

"And the Fire Department is prepared, through something known as the 'Good Sam Law', to support her with the full legal authority of the City of Los Angeles."

"I see."

"So, we want to make it clear to you that Carolyn is to be thought of as nothing but a heroine, a Good Samaritan. You can promote her actions as something positive for your station, with absolutely no hesitation."

"That's all good and fine, Chief," said Wellington, somewhat chastened. "But what about the fact that she committed insubordination?"

"Well, she's been off the air for several weeks now, I understand. Is that correct?"

"That's correct."

"That certainly seems like enough punishment, wouldn't you say?"

"I'll take your suggestion under advisement, Chief," said Wellington. "And when is she scheduled to receive this commendation?"

"Well," answered the Chief. "The wheels turn slowly at City Hall, as you know. But I certainly expect it to be before the end of summer."

"I see."

"So, are we on the same page?" asked Chief Woods.

"We are," said Wellington, irritated. "But I do plan to distribute a letter to our staff laying out our specific company policy regarding this type of behavior in the future."

"That's fine, you do have to make your policies and expectations clear."

"And we shall. Is that all?"

"Yes, Mr. James. That's it. Thank you for your time."

Wellington fumed as he hung up the phone.

*****

Ron, along with Rich Baker, had just left the station en route to their shoot at the Police Academy, when the phone in the news van began to ring.

"Micro 21," said Ron.

"Ronnie, it's Carolyn. Listen. Apparently Chief Woods from LAFD called Wellington and cut him a new one. He doesn't want us disciplined any further."

"That's great!" said Ron. "So you're back on the air?"

"And he said they want to give me some kind of award. I really don't care about that, but if it happens, I want you there with me."

"Done," said Ron. "That's great news."

"OK, I've gotta go," she said. "I'm back on the air tonight!"

"Perfect! Later, girl."

"Looks like the Fire Chief called and gave Wellington a piece of his mind," Ron told Rich. "Carolyn's off suspension and back on the air. I hope that means that I'm cool now, too."

"Yeah, let's hope so," said Rich. "Wellington totally over-reacted. I mean, I get the liability stuff, but Jeez, she had to help save lives."

"One would think so," said Ron. "But it's becoming clearer by the day that they don't pay me to think. They pay me to keep it in focus. Hopefully now I'll be allowed to travel again."

"That's good," said Rich. "Because I got a call from General McKellar, you remember my contact with the Defense Department?"

"Yeah, I think," Ron replied. "You mean the guy who got us on the Carrier?"

"The Nimitz, yeah." answered Rich. "Seems he's got another shoot coming up in a few weeks and he specifically asked for you."

"Really? What is it?"

"He couldn't say, but he tells me that it's of a 'CLASSIFIED' nature."

"Well, sign me up," said Ron.

*****

Rich had been invited to take a cameraman with him to spend a few days aboard a Naval Aircraft Carrier while at sea. He pitched the story to Leo, promising to deliver a series of interesting and visual pieces for sweeps and the news director approved. He then asked his buddy Ron if he was interested and, of course, he immediately jumped at the opportunity.

The two of them packed their bags and left the station in the middle of the night for the long drive to the San Diego Naval Base.

They arrived with just enough time to stop at Clayton's Coffee Shop on Coronado Island for a quick breakfast of eggs, bacon, coffee and toast before heading onto the base to meet Diane Pope, the Public Affairs Officer, at 9 o'clock sharp.

They sat and waited a few minutes at the gate while Rich got Diane on the phone. Soon her pale-blue Dodge pulled up alongside the news van. She waved and escorted them past the gate and through the maze of roads to an airstrip, six miles past the entrance and right on the water's edge.

On the tarmac sat a C-2 Greyhound, otherwise known as a Carrier Onboard Delivery Aircraft, or simply "COD". The COD was used to shuttle high-priority cargo, mail and passengers between shore bases and Carriers. This particular plane would be flying the news crew along with a load of provisions and replacement parts for the fighter jets which were in use aboard the USS Nimitz.

Ron was slightly disappointed that he would have to stow his camera in the cargo hold and not be able to shoot any video of their flight out to the Carrier, but he soon realized that the accommodations afforded them aboard the COD were less than luxurious; cramped to say the least.

"Get used to it," said a smiling Crew Chief Chris Mann, while helping them with their cranial helmets and seat harnesses, "You're gonna wish you were a lot shorter than you are for the next few days."

The seats faced the rear of the plane and were only sparsely padded. Khaki colored burlap straps came down over both shoulders. The latches at the bottom attached to another belt that was tightened over the waist and had a rudimentary buckle in the middle, designed for quick release in event of an emergency. Ron found it disconcerting that there were no windows, and once the plane's rear ramp was lifted, no visual of the ground, sky, or water. The only light at all came from the cockpit, which was behind them. The decades-old plane had the indelible smell of jet fuel mixed with musty fabric, sweat and rusted metal, and the noise, even through the cranials, was deafening.

After checking and double-checking the aircraft, the crew removed the triangular wooden chocks from the wheels and began to taxi to the southeast end of the runway. The four powerful props elevated the plane easily and the hour-long flight was actually quite smooth, considering.

The USS Nimitz was a couple of hundred miles off the coast of San Diego on routine patrol. As the plane approached, they could hear and feel the engines begin to slow. The COD banked sharply, and Ron turned his head and was able to catch a brief glimpse of the Nimitz through the cockpit windshield.

"Gorgeous," he thought to himself.

Mann stood up, keyed the mike and made an announcement:

"We are on approach to the USS Nimitz. We will be landing on the deck using the trap cable system, which will decrease our speed rapidly. We will hit the deck at just over 180 miles per hour and come to a stop in under two seconds. At this time, please fold your arms across your chest and lean your head forward as far as possible, until the plane has come to a complete stop."

Mann returned to his seat and strapped himself in as the plane slowed for approach, and all those aboard followed his instructions. Suddenly, the tailhook on the underside of the COD caught the third arresting wire on the deck of the Nimitz, and the aircraft instantly jolted to a halt.

As they unbuckled their harnesses, Ron and Rich shared a smile, knowing this was going to be anything but an ordinary day.

"Yikes," said Ron as he climbed down the plane's ramp to the Carrier's deck. "You haven't lived until you've done that at least once."

"Definitely an 'E' Ticket," Rich answered, wondering if any of the young crew members even knew what that meant.

For the next two days, the KSIX News crew was given access to all aspects of the Carrier, its operations and crew. Ron shot video of flight ops, navigation, food service, crew accommodations, and general operations of the ship.

Flight ops ran most of the night. The sound of F-14s and F-18's being catapulted off the deck and the bang of arresting cables reverberated and kept them awake well past midnight, despite their berthing compartment being six floors below the flight deck. That, and the fact that they were sleeping, or trying to sleep, in racks only large enough to accommodate an average adolescent. But eventually they were able to doze off for a few hours.

Immediately after sunrise, Rich and Ron followed the crew members on their ritual foreign object damage, or "FOD" walk, when flight operations are shut down and sailors walk the length of the flight deck, looking for rags, pieces of paper, tools, nuts, bolts, or any other loose objects that could potentially cause damage by coming into contact with an aircraft.

Ron paused for a moment to look around and appreciate his assignment. After a quick breakfast, he spent the rest of the morning out on the deck, enjoying every minute of the adventure, occasionally stopping to look up at the "Island" which held the ship's bridge, and admiring the large CVN-68 insignia painted broadly and proudly on the side.

The Nimitz crew had been thoroughly helpful in getting them everything they needed. The takeoffs and landings started up again before noon. Rich and Ron picked out several interesting pilots to profile. One, Lt. Dale Shrum, was of particular interest because he was a graduate of Notre Dame High School in Sherman Oaks, a suburb of Los Angeles. It was always an advantage to add a local element to any story. The other, Carrie Holliday, was one of the first women to graduate from Top Gun Training. The two flyers were interviewed in depth about their lives, and Ron was able to get shots of them taking off and landing on the Carrier. Carrie was in the middle of a story about her journey to flight training, when an F-18 dropped in for a landing with a sudden roar that shook the camera.

"Tell me that didn't make your dick hard," she said, smiling.

By the second afternoon, they had enough stories "in the can" to more than satisfy Leo and justify all of the overtime the two men were accruing. It was time to head back to shore.

With the pilot warming up the COD, Rich and Ron thanked the sailors, pilots, and officers for their help. Robert Dutch, the Captain of the Nimitz, presented each of them with a certificate officially confirming their visit, along with an 8x10 photo of the Carrier.

Chief Mann again welcomed them aboard the COD and they took their seats, strapping themselves in as though they had done it dozens of times. What they had not done yet, however was to be catapulted off the Carrier. A trap landing was one thing, a "cat-shot" was something else entirely.

Mann gave them instructions for how to prepare for takeoff. The COD, he said, would be propelled the same way as the fighter jets they'd been observing. An Aircraft Carrier, not being long enough to provide a normal runway, would need to assist all departing aircraft using the catapult system. The Nimitz had a runway of only about 300 ft., far short of the 2000 feet needed to launch a typical aircraft.

The pilot taxied the COD onto the center of the flight deck where a crewmember hooked the towbar on the plane's nose gear to a shuttle device that sat in a long groove in the middle of the runway. At the same time, the jet-blast deflector was raised behind the plane, to protect crew members from the heat and noise of the departing aircraft.

The COD began to throttle-up and, below deck, steam pressurized the heavy pistons, which provide the thrust for takeoff.

Ron held his breath. The revving of the engines told him that takeoff was just seconds away. Fists clenched and arms crossed over his chest, he heard the piston thrown and felt the inertia through his body, snapping his head forward and this time propelling him against the safety harness in his rear-facing seat.

The plane reached 165 MPH in just over two seconds, with a short, sudden drop in altitude as it left the flight deck.

"That was fun," he thought, unable to express himself over the din of the engines. "Terrifying, but fun."

*****

"Whatever McKellar's cooking up, he's being really secretive about it," said Rich. "But he needs your date of birth and Social Security number. I need to get it to him by the end of the month."

"Done," Ron replied. "I'll write it on my card for you."

"So, what's our story at the Academy?"

"Well," Rich replied. "The Department has called off the freeze and started hiring police officers again, so we're following the new class of recruits. I'm not sure what exactly they're doing today, but we'll find out when we get there."

"Cool, it's about time they hired some more cops. How long has it been?"

"The last graduating class was three years ago," answered Rich. "And with retirements and attrition, the Department is down several thousand coppers. It'll take them years to catch up."

*****

Ron took the Stadium Way exit from the 110, which led up to Academy Road, with Dodger Stadium to the south. He drove up the short, curved road past the packed Academy parking lot and up to the two tall gray-brick towers, between which hung the wrought-iron sign with shiny brass letters:

LOS ANGELES POLICE ACADEMY

"Can I help you?" asked the guard.

"We're from K-SIX," Rich answered from the passenger seat. "We're here to see Captain Black."

"Yes, sir. He's expecting you," the officer said as he pointed up the hill.

Ron continued up the steep, narrow asphalt driveway, passing the auditorium and the Revolver Club on the right. He pulled in through the first driveway on the left and parked alongside a chain link fence. To the west was a large open area made up of the athletic field and an outdoor stage, used for Academy graduations.

As they exited the van and Ron went to retrieve his gear from the back, Captain Tom Black walked up and greeted his old friend.

"Hey Rich," he said, extending a hand. "How long has it been?"

"My God, probably ten years," answered Rich. "You're still a slave to the system, I see. When are you going to hang it up and get a real job?"

"Like yours?" the Captain laughed. "No, thanks."

"Hey, what's wrong with my job? I get to see all the same things you do, and I don't get shot at nearly as much."

"Maybe," said the Captain. "But I don't have the pretty face for it like you do. Even when we were in the Academy, people said you were too good looking to be a cop."

"But I liked playing with guns," Rich replied. "By the way, this is my partner, Ron Sharp. He's a good guy."

"Tom Black," the Captain announced, as he reached out to shake the photog's hand.

The three continued their conversation as they crossed the road to the open lanai area between the Academy's kitchen and the shooting range.

"What would you like to see first?" Black asked.

"Whatever the recruits are up to," answered Rich. "What week are they in now?"

"You're in luck, Rich. This is the sixth week for the first class, so they'll be running, shooting and doing situational incident training, what we call 'scenarios'. But we also have a second class that just started last week. They'll be getting introduced to their firearms today. That's always interesting."

"Cool," said Rich. "And can we get some sound with you first, explaining the department's new surge in hiring?"

"No, let me get you someone who's a little more TV friendly," Black said, as they walked into the dining area. There, a number of training officers were taking a break and comparing notes on some of the cadets.

Black called over to Lieutenant Mitch Hill and asked him to come to meet the crew.

Mitch had the strong, chiseled features of a Marine, which is exactly what he had been before joining the Department. His three tours in Kuwait and Iraq had toughened the Indiana boy and prepared him for patrolling the gritty streets of the City of Angels. He kept his flat-top haircut, and his steel-blue eyes projected the authority needed in a training officer.

"Mitch, this is Rich Baker from Channel Six, and this is his cameraman, I'm sorry, what was your name again?"

"Ron... Ron Sharp," Ron said, shaking the Lieutenant's powerful hand.

Just then a class of about twenty recruits ran past them, up the brick walkway. They wore the standard blue sweats and gray sweatshirts emblazoned with their last names in large block letters front and back. They were completing a three-mile run, which began at the Academy, wound down Stadium Way and encircled Dodger Stadium before snaking back up Academy Road. They had earned a few minutes of rest and refreshment before beginning the afternoon's scheduled scenarios training.

Ron set up the camera on the tree-lined brick patio and Rich interviewed Lieutenant Hill about the progress the Department was making in growing their ranks. Hill said that he was encouraged by the size of the classes as well as the diversity and experience of the recruits. "These young men and women will have much to contribute to their fellow Angelinos," he said, as if reading a prepared script. "Their education and, in many cases, military backgrounds prepare them exceptionally well for the life they've chosen in the Los Angeles Police Department."

After the interview, Captain Black escorted the crew into the dining area. "Can I get you fellas anything?" he asked.

"Some water would be good," answered Ron.

"Yeah, some water, please," said Rich.

"I heard that you laid off the harder stuff a few years ago, Rich," said Black, grabbing a couple of plastic bottles out of the refrigerator. "How's that going?"

"Seventeen years and ten months sober."

"Wow! That's great. Good for you."

"Oh, believe me, I'd be dead if I hadn't quit. Way too many close calls."

"So I've heard. You're not alone."

Ron saw that they were standing among the group of training officers, now preparing to return to work for the rest of the afternoon with the recruit classes. He couldn't help but notice that one particularly tall and muscular officer had the name THORNE on his shirt. He observed him from afar, studying his mannerisms, but made no effort to introduce himself.

After a short break, Black escorted the crew a short distance down the hill, just past the shooting range, where the newest class was to be issued their weapons. Ron placed a wireless microphone on the training officer's shirt and stood back from the group, so as not to disturb the lesson.

Officer Lou Arkin began showing the recruits how to handle the weapon they will be issued by the Department.

"Ladies and gentlemen," Arkin announced. "This is a Glock 22. It's a .40 caliber handgun, and it is the weapon being issued to you by the Los Angeles Police Department. It's crucial that you know everything about it. You need to feel comfortable with it and master it, as you would a musical instrument. You may be called upon to use it with little or no warning, to save your own life or that of another human being."

One by one, Officer Arkin handed the gun to the new recruits to handle. It was obvious that some of them had had at least some experience firing handguns in the past. Others clearly were a bit spooked and had to be shown the workings of the weapon from the ground up.

"It's fine if it takes you a while to feel comfortable with the gun," Arkin said. "Better than rushing and trying to use it without being properly trained and prepared.

"The Glock is Austrian-made and offers numerous safety features. It is designed to not fire if it is dropped, which is always a good thing, and it has a safety switch built in to the trigger, right here," he said as he held it up for all to see and slowly spun it around to show everyone the safety.

"It's very lightweight, made of a strong nylon polymer. You'll appreciate that when you're carrying it on your hip for forty hours a week."

"Fuck the plastic gun," Rich whispered to Captain Black. "Give me a Beretta anytime."

Black smiled in quiet agreement.

"Are there any questions at this point?" asked Arkin.

None of the recruits asked a question, so Arkin continued showing them, one-by-one, how to load the weapon, how to inspect it and how to operate the safety. He had each of them open it, close it, and set and release the safety mechanism several times until they felt comfortable.

"Let me know when you have enough B-roll," Rich whispered to Ron. "We have other things to shoot."

"I think we're good," said Ron, as he retrieved the mike from Arkin and thanked the class for allowing them to intrude.

The more advanced class had begun live-fire training at the shooting range before the crew arrived. Captain Black interrupted long enough to introduce Ron and Rich, who put in their earplugs and set up in a corner, behind the recruits.

Ron shot video of them firing on command at the paper targets, which had been placed twenty feet away. After the guns had been emptied and lowered, the training officers brought the targets in to examine them and score the recruits for accuracy. Ron saw that Officer Thorne was teaching marksmanship to the class.

"Looks like he knows what he's talking about," Ron said to the Captain in a half-whisper.

"That's Jack Thorne," Black replied. "One of the most talented sharpshooters I've seen. He's got the medals to prove it. He still works patrol up in Foothill Division, but helps out here part time teaching the recruits marksmanship and gun safety."

After a few minutes, Ron told Rich that he had enough video of the shooting range, and was ready to move on.

"What's next?"

"Well, in a few minutes," Black answered, "this class will be down on what we call 'Main Street', practicing scenarios such as felony stops and bank robberies. They'll be using paint-ball guns instead of real ones, though."

"Cool," said Ron, always anxious to see something new. "Let's do it."

The recruits were given a fifteen-minute break, and told to report to Main Street, where they were given paint-ball weapons and safety gear. The first scenario, the training officer explained, involved a "felony stop" where they were to pull over a car ostensibly driven by a wanted felon. The 'officers' would shout commands to the driver, and follow the arrest procedures they had, up to this point, learned only in the classroom. They were told that some of the "suspects" would be co-operative, and some would not.

Ron set up his tripod on Main Street's sidewalk, out of the line of fire, but where he had a clear view of the training area.

The first pair of recruits pulled up behind the suspect vehicle and turned on the red lights on the roof of their patrol car.

The two officers stood behind the doors of the cruiser and one loudly called for the driver of the old, blue Pontiac to shut off his engine and toss the keys out the window of the car. The driver seemed to be cooperating and complying with their orders. He was then instructed to place his hands outside the window, open the door using the outside handle, and step out, keeping his hands in plain sight. He obeyed each command given to him. He stepped out of the car, turned his back to the officers, and walked backward toward the officer's voice, all the while with his hands raised high in the air.

He knelt on the pavement, crossed one ankle over the other, and interlaced his fingers atop his head. At this point the officers approached, keeping their eyes on the vehicle, and one handcuffed the 'suspect' using by-the-book procedures while the other held him at gunpoint. They had him remain kneeling in the street while they "cleared" the vehicle, to make sure there were no other occupants. First checking the trunk lid to be sure it was locked and that no one was ready to jump out at them. Then, guns drawn, checking the interior of the car before calling "Code four, Suspect in custody" into the hand-held radio, to the applause of the class and the training officers

The next scenario began identically, with another pair of recruits also performing a felony stop on a vehicle in the middle of Main Street. This time, however, the "suspect" was less than cooperative. He opened the door to the vehicle, but when instructed to turn off the engine, he did nothing. When told to toss out the keys, he did nothing. The recruits were forced to rely on their training to deal with this possibly armed and dangerous suspect.

"Driver! Let me see your hands! DO IT NOW!" shouted the recruit who had been driving the black and white, as he held his position behind the ballistic panel of the cruiser's door. They could see that the "suspect" was fidgeting in his seat, possibly reaching for something.

"Driver! Let me see your fucking hands! NOW!!"

Still refusing the commands, the driver stepped out of the car and faced the officers.

"I need to see your hands NOW!" shouted the young recruit once again.

The driver began walking slowly toward the Police car. The passenger/officer called for backup on the radio before reaching for the beanbag shotgun between the seats, believing that the use of "less-than-lethal force" was still called for, at least until they were in fear for their lives.

The driver kept coming, all the while keeping his hands behind his back.

"One more time, Mister! Let me see your hands! DO IT NOW!!!"

At that point the driver pulled a weapon from behind his back and began firing at the cadet, who returned fire from behind the driver's door.

The passenger officer instantly dropped the bean-bag shotgun and also returned fire.

The paintballs flew at close range. Each trainee emptied his weapon, while the suspect was able to get off three rounds, one hitting the driver/officer in the left clavicle area as he stood his ground and continued the gun battle. The suspect was hit numerous times.

The result: one dead "suspect", one seriously injured officer, another calling for assistance.

The T.O. began to review the procedures the recruits had followed and critique their performance. They were told that they had acted properly in ordering the suspect to comply, but should not have let the suspect get off any shots and reacted more quickly, at the first sign of a weapon. All in all, though, a passing grade for both recruits.

As the class was discussing the scenario they had just witnessed, Ron could faintly hear the theme from Dragnet coming from behind him. He turned and saw Rich reaching in his pocket for his cell phone.

"Baker…"

After listening for a moment, Rich motioned to Ron that they urgently needed to wrap up. He spoke several "Uh-huh"s into the phone and began walking swiftly up the hill toward the Revolver Club and Academy Office.

"OK, I'll find a TV and call you back," he said. "It shouldn't be more than a few minutes."

"Is everything alright?" the Captain asked, as the news crew suddenly vacated Main Street.

"There's a pursuit," answered Rich, without breaking stride. "Our chopper is overhead and we're on the air. They're coming up from Orange County, but the guy's really flying. We've broken into programming, and they want me to watch their live picture on TV and comment over the phone."

"No problem, follow me."

Inside the Academy café was a small bar area with an old Zenith 19 inch television set mounted behind it. Tom ran in, turned it on, and fumbled with the remote. After a few clicks, he saw a bright yellow Corvette being pursued on the freeway.

"There you go," he said. "That guy really is moving, isn't he?"

"Wait," said Rich. "That's Channel 8. I'm guessing every station in town is on this thing. I need *our* picture." With that, Rich grabbed the landline phone off the wall near the bar and called the K-SIX assignment desk.

"Oh, sorry," said Tom. "My bad." He grabbed the remote and started pressing buttons until finally landing the TV on Channel 6. "There you are."

"Hey, it's Rich, could you transfer me to the control room?"

Linda Bodek, who was producing the unscheduled news break, picked up the phone.

"Linda, it's Rich. I'm all set. I've got a TV in front of me and I'm watching your picture."

"Great," said Linda. "I'll let the anchors know. Stand by."

Rich watched the broadcast and made a quick analysis of the situation based upon his observations.

Gretchen and her co-anchor Geoff Martin had been on the air narrating the pursuit for about ten minutes, along with Teddy Beaman in the chopper. They had essentially no real information and were filling time speculating about the circumstances of the chase. Gretchen and Geoff were glad to have Police Specialist Rich Baker available to add an educated perspective to their coverage, since most of Beaman's commentary was nothing but the usual insipid bluster.

"Over the years, I've covered hundreds of these chases," Beaman boasted. " And invariably, the guy loves the attention we give him. I'll bet if we all just went away, he'd pull over and turn himself in. He's obviously…"

"We're joined now by our Police Specialist, Rich Baker," announced Martin, happily interrupting the insufferable pilot. "Rich, we've been over this chase for a while now. Is there anything that jumps out at you here?"

"Well," replied Rich. "There is really no way to tell what's going on in this person's mind. He clearly doesn't want to go to jail, so he's made the calculation that, even though his odds of getting away are very low, almost zero in fact, he's going to try to elude the police for as long as he can. As long as he's on the road instead of in a black and white in handcuffs, it's a good day for him."

The anchors sipped some water, and gladly let Rich carry the ball for a few minutes.

"As you can see, the suspect is in a Chevy Corvette, which, as you know, is an extremely high performance vehicle. Right now he's doing in excess of 95 miles per hour. He's on the 5 freeway, and at this time of the afternoon we'd expect him to start to run into traffic at some point soon."

Captain Black had been on the phone with the Highway Patrol and was passing information on to Rich by writing notes on an LAPD note pad he found behind the bar.

Rich took the notes and relayed the information to the audience without skipping a beat.

"My understanding is that this car was stolen out of San Juan Capistrano earlier this afternoon. Police spotted him in the Mission Viejo area and attempted a traffic stop. He entered the 5 Freeway at El Toro and proceeded north. The car has, at times, exceeded 110 miles an hour. I'm told the suspect is a believed to be two-strike felon who was just released from prison a week ago under California's "Realignment" program, Prop. 209. He's been on the phone to the cops and has told them that he will die before going back to jail again. This will probably not end well."

Ron sat at the bar with a bottle of water, writing notes for Rich regarding landmarks and upcoming streets, bridges, and exits. He was impressed at Rich's ability to turn the information around and broadcast it to the public flawlessly, never betraying the fact that he was being fed information by his colleagues.

"Where is he now, exactly?" asked Gretchen.

"Let's read the signs if we can," answered Rich, watching the live video on the small screen, which now had superimposed on the bottom: 'On The Phone: Rich Baker- KSIX Police Specialist'.

"He's still on the 5, northbound, passing Harbor Boulevard, so he's approaching Lincoln. For those of you at home, that's very close to Disneyland. But, at this speed, he'll be coming into Los Angeles County in just a few minutes. My advice to those watching is to stay off the roads in the vicinity of the Santa Ana Freeway until this situation is resolved. Whoa, that was close!" Rich yelled, as the suspect veered across all lanes of the freeway, narrowly missing several slower vehicles.

Beaman kept up with the car in the chopper, every few minutes updating the viewers with his speed and location on the freeway.

"He's doing about 85 mph now, passing Artesia Boulevard northbound, approaching the county line. He'll be coming up on the 605 pretty soon at this speed," announced Beaman. "Let's see which way he goes."

Within a few minutes, the Corvette had crossed into Los Angeles County and was continuing northbound on the 5 at extremely high speed. Encountering pockets of heavy afternoon traffic, the driver swerved onto the freeway's narrow right shoulder, kicking up dirt and debris behind the low-slung vehicle. Then, just as suddenly, he shot back across the freeway, sideswiping a green Mini Cooper, while narrowly missing several other vehicles.

"This guy just does not want to get caught," said Martin. "He's acting like a desperate man."

"He's now passing Rosecrans Avenue in the Norwalk area," Beaman stated. "He's swerving between vehicles now. As I widen out, you can see that he has at least six Highway Patrol cars on his tail at this point, along with a helicopter. They'll be approaching downtown Los Angeles very shortly."

Encountering surprisingly light afternoon traffic, the Corvette soon approached the East L.A. Interchange.

Ron's phone vibrated with a text message from the desk.

Pursuit headed North toward Downtown-Leave Rich there and try to catch up.

Ron packed up his gear and motioned to Rich that he was headed out the door. He pointing alternately to himself, the door, and the television. Rich got the message and gave him a nod as he continued narrating the pursuit, which was getting more interesting by the minute. By this point, about a dozen senior officers from the Academy had gathered around the small television to watch Rich at work, describing the spectacle.

The Corvette weaved through ever-increasing traffic as he passed through East L.A. The CHP had backed off, entering what they call a "tracking mode" hoping that the suspect would perhaps slow down, believing he was no longer being pursued. But with about a dozen helicopters overhead, there was no way this guy was going to think for even a minute that he had gotten away.

Ron pulled the van out of the Academy and headed down Stadium Way. He paused at the bottom of the hill, at the entrance to Elysian Park, and listened intently as Scott Castle, on the assignment desk, relayed the car's location to the units in the field. The driver had passed the East L.A. Interchange, from where he had opted to take the 101 Freeway toward

Downtown Los Angeles. He continued at a high rate of speed, swerving carelessly, sideswiping several more cars and again driving periodically on the freeway's shoulder.

Soon, the driver would have another choice to make.

"He's just entering the Downtown area from the east," Rich advised. "And in a minute or two we'll see what he does with the four-level interchange. He can continue on the 101 toward Hollywood, or he can get on the 110 Freeway, either north toward Pasadena, or south into Los Angeles."

Ron sat in the idling news van, trying to plan his own route to intercept the fleeing Corvette. Once the driver chose his route, Ron would know which freeway to aim for.

He called the desk on his cell.

He recognized Bobbie's voice. "Channel Six News."

"Bobbie? What are you doing on the desk?"

"They needed me up here, they don't have enough people. It's a madhouse right now."

"I can tell," said Ron. "Can you give me to Scott?"

"Sure, hold on a second."

"Scott, I need you to tell me the second he gets to the Four-level. He can go any number of ways. I need to know as soon as he chooses the route."

"You got it, Ronnie," said Scott. "I'm watching. He's in heavy traffic now, coming up on Alameda, in the number two lane. I'll talk to you on the two-way. Gotta go."

Ron waited anxiously, listening to the scanner and the two-way simultaneously, for the suspect to choose his route. Suddenly his phone began to ring, and he shook his head, wondering why Scott would use the telephone and not the two-way for information so urgent. He answered it on the second ring.

"Micro 21…"

"Ron, it's Sandra, I need your help."

He could tell she was completely distraught and could practically hear the tears streaming down her cheeks.

"What is it, Sweetie?"

"It's Jack," she sniffed. "He just called me and started ranting. He demands to know if I'm seeing someone."

"Listen," Ron said, with a sigh. "I, I really can't talk now. I promise I'll call you in a little while. We'll get together tonight and figure out what needs to be done. OK?"

"OK," Sandra replied, still sniffing. "I really need you."

"I'll call you as soon as I can," he said with a deep exhale.

"OK, bye."

"He's in the left lane, staying on the 101," Scott called calmly into the radio. **"He's heading toward Hollywood. Moving at a high rate of speed, but there's gonna be more heavy traffic in front of him."**

"Ten-four, thanks," answered Ron.

Ron started moving through Elysian Park a short distance down to Sunset Boulevard. He turned westbound and could see the helicopters overhead to his left, above the freeway. The Highway Patrol was primary in managing the pursuit, and now was joined by several LAPD units as well. Ron locked in LAPD's Air Unit and K-9 Frequency on his scanner.

"There's no explaining what a driver in this situation will do," said Rich, watching the Corvette's progress through Downtown, and into Echo Park and Silverlake. "He's pretty desperate, so we'll just have to wait and see how this plays out. We don't know how familiar he is with the L.A. area, or where he might be headed, if he even knows that himself."

"In my experience," Teddy Beaman interjected, "these guys usually head for an area they know well, where they have either some family, or friends, or homeboys."

"Often that's true," said Rich, somewhat annoyed at the pompous helicopter reporter. "But you really never know. That explains why the public is so fascinated whenever a police pursuit is televised. It's in some ways like a sporting event. It's totally unscripted, each one is different, and you don't know how it's going to end."

Ron's van was directly parallel to the chase for a short time. But afternoon traffic on Sunset was excruciating, and soon he could see the choppers getting further and further ahead of him, still to his left above the freeway. He turned left onto Echo Park Avenue south toward the Hollywood Freeway, but by the time he reached the on-ramp, Scott was on the two-way announcing that the Corvette was taking an exit.

"Everybody out there, he's getting off at Vermont! Off at Vermont! He fish-tailed at the top of the exit and turned right, heading north. He's still pushin' it."

"Ten-Four, thanks," Ron answered, trying to follow the chatter on the two-way radio as well as the police scanner, which blasted:

"All units on all frequencies continue to stand by, 2A-24 is now primary on the pursuit, northbound Vermont, approaching Melrose, at a high rate of speed."

Ron looked up and saw that the Vermont exit was still almost two miles ahead of him, and he knew that unless traffic eased between Silverlake and Hollywood, he was now at least five minutes behind the pursuit.

"He's gotten off the freeway," announced Beaman. "So now we'll see if in fact he's familiar with this area or not."

"This also changes the calculus and makes things infinitely more dangerous for the motoring public," Rich interjected. "What with cross traffic, pedestrians…"

"He's now made a right turn and is heading eastbound on Melrose from Vermont," said Scott.

Ron thanked his assignment editor again. His hopes, however, that the driver would continue eastbound toward him were short lived.

"This is a very narrow street," Geoff announced. "He'll have to slow down a bit here. And now he's making a quick left. This looks like much more of a residential street, perhaps his neighborhood."

Rich disagreed. "With the high speed he's going, and the fact that he's blowing through stop signs and red lights, he doesn't appear to be concerned at all about the citizens that he's putting in jeopardy here. It looks more like he's just trying to evade the police."

"All units on all frequencies, continue to stand by, 2A-24 is continuing in pursuit, now northbound on Virgil Avenue, approaching Santa Monica."

Ron was in heavy traffic on the Hollywood Freeway, listening to his radios, trying to keep track of the pursuit. He drummed his thumbs on the steering wheel in frustration, but realized that it did absolutely no good to stress about the vehicle's location, since the driver could easily decide to turn around and head back in his direction again at a moment's notice.

"He's flying down these streets," said Rich. "Let me tell you, I used to work patrol here and I hope this driver's aware that Virgil Avenue is not completely straight. It takes a little jog to the left up ahead at Fountain."

Ron saw the Vermont Avenue exit was still half a mile away, and quickly maneuvered ahead of a churning cement mixer and a Ralphs delivery truck to get in the right hand lane.

The Corvette zigzagged around a Honda and sped up as the light at Fountain Avenue turned red.

"Oh! Oh! Oh, my Lord," shouted Gretchen, Geoff, and Teddy simultaneously, as the Corvette bottomed out, missed the slight left turn that Rich had mentioned, hit the curb at high speed, and launched itself over the sidewalk and through the picture window of the Toro's Furniture store, which had been in operation on the corner of Fountain and Virgil since the early 1970s.

"Oh, my God!" yelled Gretchen. "It looks as if he never even hit the brakes."

"He may have tried to slow down at the last second," said Teddy. "But he certainly didn't have enough time, with the speed he was traveling."

"Police now have a very precarious situation to deal with," said Rich. "The suspect is somewhere in that building, presumably in the car, presumably armed, possibly injured, but none of that is confirmed. They will have to approach this scene extremely cautiously, mindful of their own safety as well as that of the suspect."

"Microvan 21, he's crashed into a building at Fountain and Virgil," Scott yelled into the two-way, **"What's your ETA?"**

"I'll be there in about three." Ron answered, pushing it up Vermont.

The Corvette ended up inside the rear of the store, hardly visible from the street and not at all from the air. Desks, tables, and other furnishings had been smashed and strewn throughout the store. Thankfully, there were no customers inside at the time of the crash, and the owners, Sirak and Houbi Abalian, who had been in the office, were able to escape through the front door and out into the street. Beaman pointed out that the Corvette had started to smoke, and the chopper's camera zoomed in to show the first wisps coming out through the front of the building. Officers immediately called for assistance from the Fire Department.

Of course, there was still the issue of a possibly armed suspect behind the wheel. Six officers entered the smoke-filled store, weapons drawn, even as fire was beginning to spread through the rear of the building. Cautiously approaching the Corvette, they could see that the driver was not moving, and appeared to be unconscious. Guns at the ready, they quickly surrounded the smoldering car. One officer opened the door and cut the seat belt, with which the driver was constrained inside. Soon four officers could be seen carrying the handcuffed suspect through the store, over shards of broken glass and wood, out to the street, to await the arrival of paramedics. The car was beginning to burn furiously, flames angrily feeding on the plastics and the stocks of treated wood products in the store. The Corvette's fuel tank had been ruptured, and the remaining gasoline burned as it flowed across the floor, consuming the old worn carpet and filling the small building with dark, acrid smoke.

Fire crews had just begun arriving on scene when Ron pulled up and parked on Virgil, half a block south of the pursuit's termination.

"Micro 21 is on location," he said into the two-way's mike.

"Ten-four, Micro 21."

The driver was semi-conscious and being treated for his injuries as Ron ran up on the scene, camera on his shoulder. He grabbed a quick shot of the suspect, now handcuffed, in the street. Ron then turned his attention to the raging fire, which had become the story.

"Battalion 11 is on location. We have a one story commercial building, well involved. I need one more task force, two additional engine companies, two RAs, and a hazardous materials squad. Also inform Building and Safety, we have a vehicle inside a structure and the building's integrity may have been compromised."

"We can see the suspect being wheeled to the ambulance," observed Geoff Martin. "When he recovers, he'll have a long list of charges awaiting him."

"This fire is growing now," added Gretchen. "The sign above the door indicates that this is a furniture store, so presumably it's full of all kinds of materials which could add fuel to this blaze."

Black smoke was now pouring out through the gaping hole in the front of the store, where the large picture window had once been. Firefighters were pulling hoses through the front door and toward the rear of the store and dousing the Corvette, which was now almost completely destroyed, as the flames worked their way throughout the store.

Additional fire units continued to arrive on scene and filled the intersection with equipment and hoses. Firefighters carried ladders and climbed up to the roof, where they used axes and chainsaws to try to vent the fire by opening up the attic. They blasted cool water downward in an attempt to stem the flames.

Ron noticed something inside the structure that he had rarely seen in his years of covering fires. He found the shape and pattern of the flames spreading across the ceiling to be quite mysterious, almost mesmerizing. The red and orange fire was forming what looked almost like glass balls, or small helium balloons, which were dancing across the ceiling, slowly toward the front window, where he stood, on the sidewalk just outside the building. The fire balloons were putting off only light smoke as they consumed the building materials of the structure's interior, which must have been coated with a dozen coats of decades-old paint. That, Ron reasoned, must be the explanation for the fire's odd coloration, shape and behavior.

Ron remained on the sidewalk facing the front of the building, trying to be inconspicuous and stay out of the way of the firefighters, who were rushing around him in every direction. He was barely able to see the skeleton of the Corvette through the smoke, but continued capturing, through the gaping hole in the front of the building, the dancing flames as the hypnotic fire-bubbles continued to advance, bouncing nimbly, almost beautifully toward him across the ceiling.

Suddenly, without warning, fire exploded through the store. The flames that had been tiptoeing so gracefully across the ceiling had all along been seeking precious oxygen. The only place they could find it was the window opening where Ron stood.

The blast instantly catapulted him backward through the air, his body crashing violently into Engine 82, which was parked behind him on the curb. His camera, torn from his grip, went flying; landing shattered a short distance away on the sidewalk.

Firefighters immediately recognized the explosion of flames and reported over the radio that there had been a backdraft, and that a civilian was injured and needed help.

"Whoa, did you see that?" yelled Geoff. "It appears that there's been some type of explosion. Can we circle the chopper around and zoom in on the front of the building, so we can get a better look at what's going on?"

"Yes we can," said Teddy. "As we look closer, it appears that there is a civilian being tended to by paramedics, on the sidewalk in front of the store. We can't tell at this time what happened, but it did look as if there had been an explosion that occurred inside the building."

"I'm guessing that was what they refer to as a 'backdraft'" interjected Geoff. "The fire burns and builds inside the closed structure until all the air is gone, and then, when it has no more, it leaps through the nearest opening to find a source of oxygen. As you can see by the person on the ground, a backdraft can be quite sudden and dangerous.

"We certainly hope that he's not too badly hurt." Said Gretchen.

"Wait, is that a video camera on the ground there? It appears to be. Oh, my gosh."

"I'm not completely sure," said Beaman, "but that could be a news cameraman."

Rich was not about to let on that he recognized his partner's clothing and knew that it was Ron on the ground. Not on live television. He quickly put the hard-line phone down on the bar, grabbed his cell, and called Bobbie at the assignment desk.

"Channel Six News."

"Bobbie, I think that's Ronnie on the ground. He left here and started chasing the pursuit."

"We know," she replied, "we're trying to get confirmation."

"OK. Gotta go."

Ron was dazed and bloody as paramedics rushed to his aid. They saw immediately that he'd been seriously burned on his right arm and hand, and had a contusion on the back of his head, which occurred when he was thrown back into the fire truck. He had a small cut just above his scalp-line from flying glass. Blood was spurting from his right eye-lid where the camera's viewfinder had impaled him prior to snapping off and flying across the sidewalk.

A paramedic rinsed Ron's arm with cool water and saline solution and wrapped it with a sterile bandage. Another applied pressure to his eye and scalp with gauze pads to slow the flow of blood, but it would require stitches to completely stop the heavy bleeding which had already ruined his shirt and jeans.

"What's your name?"

"Ron... Ron Sharp."

"Where does it hurt?"

"Pretty much everywhere," said Ron, still stunned, blinking rapidly trying to see through the blood. "What the fuck?"

"Let's load him up and get him to Holly Pres," he overheard the paramedic say. "He's gonna need some stitching up on this eye."

"My eye? Not my eye!" cried Ron through gritted teeth.

"You're gonna be OK," said the medic. "A few stitches and you'll be back to normal."

The medic continued applying pressure to Ron's right eye as he was placed on a gurney and loaded into the ambulance for transport.

"My camera. Somebody grab my camera!" Ron yelled, regaining his breath and his wits.

A firefighter ran over and picked up the camera from the sidewalk, then brought the broken and soaked piece of equipment over and placed it in the ambulance.

"You work for Channel Six?" asked the medic tending to his eye.

"Yes, I do," Ron answered.

"That must be interesting."

"It has its moments."

Chapter Ten:

THE PRIZE

It was a short drive to Hollywood Presbyterian Hospital, less than a mile away. The emergency room personnel were expecting them when they arrived, and based upon the information provided by paramedics, a specialist took over immediately.

Dr. Bernard Ambrose conversed with the ambulance crew for a short time privately and then turned his attention to his patient, who had taken to holding the compress on his right eye with his left hand, choosing not to move his heavily bandaged right arm at all. The paramedics lifted Ron from the gurney onto a bed, retrieved their gear, and departed.

A young orderly brought Ron's broken camera into the room and placed it on the floor next to the bed.

"Is this everything?" he asked.

"I think so," Ron responded glumly.

Dr. Ambrose introduced himself and took a cursory look at the eye as a nurse checked his vital signs. "Well," he said. "This isn't pretty. I bet it feels great."

"Yeah, I tore it up pretty good."

"You were shooting video of a fire, and it got out of hand?"

"Yeah," Ron replied. "Can't wait to take a look at *that* video."

"Can you see me OK?" asked Dr. Ambrose, removing the gauze for just a moment, "How many fingers am I holding up?"

"Six,"

"OK," chuckled the Doctor. "There's nothing wrong with your vision, but your eyelid has sustained a serious laceration. I can actually see your skull under there. We're going to get you stitched up as soon as we can. How about the rest of you? They've got your arm bandaged as well."

"I'm pretty achy to be honest with you. Feels like I was hit by a bus."

"I'll get you some pain relievers," said the Doctor. "Is there anyone you need to call?"

"Yeah," said Ron. "I need to call the station, and let them know what happened. Oh, and my... umm... my girlfriend. I have my phone right here."

"Alright, we'll leave you alone for a few minutes," Ambrose said. "But not for too long, make it quick, please."

With that the doctor withdrew into the bustling emergency room and closed the curtain around Ron's bed.

Ron called the assignment desk and once again Bobbie answered.

"Bobbie, it's Ron, I'm in the hospital."

"I heard," she said. "Are you OK? How are you feeling?"

"I've been better," he answered. "Can I get Scott?"

"Of course you can. He's talking to Wellington. It'll just be a second. I wanted to tell you though, that I've given my notice."

"You too? Why?"

"They told me that I wouldn't be doing medical stories anymore and I'd be writing or working the assignment desk. Today proved to me that I'm not cut out for that. Listen, we'll talk more about it later, I just wanted you to know."

"Thanks, I'm really sorry."

"OK, let me transfer you."

Ron notified Scott that he was in the hospital and the Assignment Editor made arrangements to pick up the truck from the fire scene. Another crew was already almost there anyway, having been dispatched the same time as Ron to follow the pursuit, but from the west side of town. They would also stop by the hospital to check on him, retrieve the camera, and hopefully be able to salvage the video of the incident.

"Don't worry about anything," Scott told him, "I'll log you out injured for as long as you need. Just call when you can and keep me posted. We'll deal with the Worker's Comp claim later."

"OK, thanks."

"Oh, and feel better." added Scott.

"Thanks, Dude. I'll talk to you soon."

His next call was to Sandra, who was still shaken about Jack, but less frantic than she had been an hour earlier.

"Hello,"

"Hi Sandra, It's me,"

"I thought you had forgotten to call me back," she said.

"Sorry, I've been a little, umm... occupied," Ron replied. "I'm in the hospital."

"Oh, my God! What happened?"

"I got caught up in the big car chase you probably heard about, and I had a building blow up in my face. Other than that, not much is going on."

"Where are you?" she demanded. "I'll be right there."

"You know what?" he replied, trying to dissuade her from making the trip. "I'll probably be released from here in a little while. They just have to stitch me up. Can I call you when I'm ready and you can come pick me up?"

"Of course," she said. "What hospital are you in?"

"Hollywood Pres, on Vermont."

"I'll be right there!"

Sandra's concern about Jack's call was now compounded by the prospect of her new beau being hurt. She was unsure just how much to believe Ron when he said he'd soon be released, and wondered if he might have been downplaying the extent of his injuries through denial or bravado, or just to ease her mind. The only way she'd know for sure how badly he was injured was to go there in person, even though as a non-relative, she'd surely be kept out of the loop and information would be difficult to obtain.

Sandra jumped in the car and sped down Olympic Boulevard, then north on La Brea. She'd taken this route almost daily to get to work in Hollywood, but it seemed like so much farther tonight.

She arrived at the hospital as Microvan 24 was pulling out of a parking space just under the red Emergency Room sign. She flagged the driver down in the small parking lot and introduced herself.

"Hi, I'm Sandra," she said. "I'm Ron's uh... I'm Ron's friend. Have you seen him?"

"Yes, we were just inside checking on him," said Carolyn Sanchez. "He's pretty beaten up, but he'll be alright."

"How beaten up?"

"Well," added Dave Newman, the cameraman driving the van, "check out his camera."

He motioned to the back of the van and unlocked the side door so Sandra could see the damaged piece of equipment for herself.

"Oh my God, what happened?"

"He was shooting a fire in a furniture store," Dave explained. "They think he got hammered by a backdraft and thrown against a fire truck. It's actually a good thing that truck was there behind him. He only flew three or four feet. He could have been thrown a lot further and really badly hurt."

"He's getting stitched up now," interrupted Carolyn, "and should be ready to leave in an hour or so."

"Thanks," she said. "I'm gonna wait for him and take him home."

"Listen," said Carolyn. "We've got to go, but it was very nice meeting you. You take care of him, OK? He's a good man."

"I know he is. Thanks."

Sandra slept off and on in the waiting area of the Emergency Room, despite the fact that there were twice as many patients as chairs, and at any given moment, there were probably half a dozen sick, screaming babies crawling on the floor, or being held and comforted by their mothers. One child in particular wrestled with his mom in the seat directly across from Sandra, crying in pain with a high fever and an obvious ear infection while waiting to be seen by one of only a handful of doctors on duty after 9 pm.

Just before 10, an attendant walked out into the waiting room and used a remote to change the channel on the television mounted in the corner. He was in the nightly habit of watching the Channel 6 News, but he was especially adamant about tuning in tonight, after word had spread throughout the Emergency Department about Ron and what had happened to him. Sandra watched in curiosity, to see for herself just how he was injured, although part of her did not want to see. She had a hard time hearing the television over the crying babies and murmurs of conversation, and that was fine with her. The pictures would tell her all she wanted to know.

It was the lead story. High-speed crash video in a box on the screen with the words "Pursuit Crash" super-ed underneath, as Geoff Martin told the tale from the beginning. The stolen Corvette, the chase through two counties, the crash, the explosion- and there it was, the video from Ron's camera. They showed it several times, twice in slow motion- flames leaping violently, straight toward the camera lens, too quickly for the cameraman to react. Sandra looked away, knowing the pain he must have endured. She hardly saw Carolyn's live shot at all, from in front of the burned-out furniture store, except to briefly recognize her as the woman who earlier in the evening had told her that Ron would be released from the hospital "in an hour or so".

"An hour or so" had stretched into the late night hours, and it was almost midnight when Ron was wheeled out the door to be released. A nurse tapped Sandra on the shoulder to let her know that it was time.

"I can't believe you waited," Ron said. "I really could have called a cab."

"Are you kidding? You need someone to take care of you for a few days. I'm not going anywhere."

His face was heavily bandaged, having received 36 micro-stitches on the inner layers of his right eyelid. His scalp had been partially shaved and bandaged. The contusion on the back of his head had been stitched as well, and his right arm and hand were completely wrapped.

The nurse quickly went over with Sandra the instructions of how to properly care for his wounds, change the bandages and dressings, etc. She handed her a bag with extra gauze wrap and antibiotic cream. There was also a prescription that would need to be filled the next morning.

Sandra pulled her car up to the white curb, the attendant assisted Ron in getting out of the chair and into the Honda's passenger's seat. She drove slowly out of the driveway and south onto Vermont Avenue, toward the freeway.

"Oh, my God," cried Sandra. "Are you OK?"

"I'll be fine," Ron replied. "I just need to get some rest."

"I saw the video on the news," she said. "That fire exploded right in front of you."

"I know. I've never seen that kind of thing before. I'm glad they were able to salvage the video. I hope my camera's not too badly damaged."

"Will you stop it?" she said angrily. "I can't believe you're even worried about that."

Sandra pulled into a space on the curb in front of Ron's apartment and shut off the motor. She walked around and helped him out of the car and up the steps to the building's lobby. He reached into his front pocket for his key and noticed how bloody his jeans were.

"Oh, man," he said, "Look at this. I'm a bloody mess."

"That's the last thing I care about right now," replied Sandra, holding the door for him as he limped to the elevator.

"You don't have to stay with me, you know," he said. "I'll be fine tonight."

"Are you kidding? I told you, I'm not going anywhere."

"I'm sorry I let you down, I mean about Jack calling," he said, opening his apartment door.

"You didn't let me down, you got hurt," she said. "It wasn't your fault."

Ron grabbed a banana from a bowl on kitchen counter and peeled it.

"But I want to be there for you, too," he said, leaning against the refrigerator while swallowing a bite of banana. "I'm going to try to sleep now. I promise we'll talk about it first thing in the morning."

"OK," said Sandra, kissing his bandaged head, "I'll be here on the sofa if you need anything during the night."

"Thanks, again," he said, walking slowly into the bedroom and kicking off his shoes.

He tossed the bloody jeans and shirt into a pile near the bedroom door and sat carefully on the edge of his bed. Massaging his forehead, he blinked his eyes a few times and lay back on the pillow.

The painkillers were taking effect, and Ron fell quickly into a deep sleep, completely oblivious to the uncontrolled sobbing in the next room.

Tuesday, July 7th

When Ron awoke, Sandra was sitting at the side of his bed, stroking his head.

"Good morning, Handsome," she said. "How do you feel?"

"Not very handsome," he answered.

"Here, take your meds."

She handed him a glass of water and two small pills.

"Thanks," he mumbled, sitting up just enough to swallow without spilling the water all over himself.

She saw him flinch when he raised the glass.

"Where does it hurt?" she asked.

"Here," he answered, pointing to his right forearm. "My arm hurts more than anything else right now."

"Let's get you up and change the bandages. The doctor said that we had to keep the dressing fresh."

"Can I get something to eat?" he asked.

"Sure you can. It's good that you're hungry. Would you like me to make you some eggs or something?"

"No thanks," he replied as Sandra walked into the kitchen. "I doubt there are any eggs in the fridge anyway. I'll just have some cornflakes if there's any milk."

"Yep, there's milk," she yelled. "And you're right about the eggs."

"Sorry about that," he said.

"That's OK," she replied. "I'll get a bagel or something while you're seeing the doctor. You have an appointment in an hour."

＊＊＊＊＊

The checkup lasted just a few minutes, and Dr. Ambrose was glad to learn that he was feeling better.

"Just take it easy and don't do any heavy lifting for a couple of weeks," he said. "That includes the TV camera."

"Got it."

"Come back in ten days and I'll most likely release you at that time to go back to work. In the meantime, take care of that young woman out there. She's a keeper."

Dr. Ambrose opened the door and led Ron back into the waiting room where Sandra sat, talking on her cell phone and typing on her iPad while finishing her bagel and coffee. Work, after all, wouldn't wait.

"I'm beginning to think so," Ron answered.

Saturday, July 11th

"And the Nominees for Best Medical, Cultural and Social News Story, Multi-Part are…"

Sandra held Ron's right hand tightly and felt the bulge of bandages under his suit jacket and the cold sweat of nerves in his palm. She glanced over to see his face. She'd never before known him to be nervous or anxious about anything. She gave his hand an extra squeeze for reassurance. Ron squeezed back and smiled.

They sat stage left in the darkened auditorium, about ten rows back, with the small contingent of Channel Six nominees. Programs in hand, they followed along as best they could as Kelly Turner, long time anchor at Channel 3, read the names of the five nominees. With each piece, a ten second clip was shown on the large screen above the stage. Ron's piece was the final nominee listed.

"'Life-Altering Surgery', KSIX News, Bobbie Steele, Producer, and Ron Sharp, Camera."

The KSIX section of the room, much smaller than in previous years, let out muffled cheers, the audience having been asked early in the presentation to 'Please hold your applause'.

"And the Emmy goes to… 'Life-Altering Surgery', KSIX News."

As the KSIX contingent erupted in hoots and applause, Ron leaned over and gave his date a kiss, then leapt to his feet, shuffled to his left toward the aisle and walked slowly up the steps to the stage. His slight limp, his stiff right arm and the bandage across his eyebrow shocked many in the audience, although a good number had by then heard at least briefly about his injury. Bobbie walked up the other aisle and they met with a hug behind the slender Plexiglas podium center stage. There, Kelly handed them each a golden statuette that they held up in celebration and triumph. Waiting for the applause to die down, Bobbie approached the mike.

"Thank you so much," she said. "This was a terrific story about a woman whose life was changed forever by a wonderful doctor, William Stone, and his caring staff. I'm so glad that we could tell her story, and I'm also proud that Ron Sharp helped me tell it. He's an amazing artist who never lets me down."

"This is also dedicated to all the wonderful, talented people who no longer work at our station. The writers, producers, editors, hair and makeup people, and the others. There are too many to name, but rest assured, we miss you all and you are not forgotten. We miss the pride, quality and professionalism that your work brought to our newscast, the likes of which we may never see again in this business. Thank you all."

Bobbie took a step back, as Ron approached the mike.

"Thanks, everyone," he said, raising his wrapped right hand to motion toward his bandaged eye. "As you can see, this is a brutal business." He waited for the brief laughter to subside.

"Bobbie Steele is the absolute best at what she does. She deserves the roomful of awards she's won and she'll no doubt continue her winning ways long after she leaves us at Channel Six. Her departure will be felt for a long, long time. If management were here, they'd tell you the same… never mind, they're not here. Screw it. Let's party!"

With that the audience once again cheered and applauded as Ron and Bobbie exited the stage.

Had they cared enough to attend, Wellington and the other managers from KSIX would surely have felt insulted by their remarks, but to no one's surprise, none of them were in attendance.

The statuette that is handed to a recipient onstage is an actual Emmy, but not the one the winner gets to keep. It's merely a prop, which is used over and over for each recipient. Ron and Bobbie congratulated one another backstage and were escorted outside the building to an area where the "real" Emmys were lined up on a large, circular table. There, each winner signs a paper stating that they received their award before posing for photos, statue in hand, to be uploaded on the Academy's website. They hugged and laughed before slowly making their way back toward the auditorium.

"Who's the babe?"

Ron turned to see a slightly inebriated Teddy Beamon standing near the crowded bar, cocktail in hand.

"Excuse me?"

"I saw you guys come in," said Beamon. "She's a real piece of work, I mean weapons-grade hot. Is she in the business?"

"No, she's not," Ron answered, shaking his head. "Behave yourself, alright?"

"Hey, no worries," he said, raising his hands chest-high. "I'm a trained observer, that's all."

Ron turned away and headed for the door.

"How are you feeling?" Teddy asked. "You look like crap."

"Thanks for that. I'm doing OK."

Ron quietly returned to his seat and handed Sandra his trophy, trying not to disturb the ceremony. He smiled and winked at some colleagues seated down the row.

"This is so cool," she whispered, caressing the golden statuette. "Do we have to stay in here? I'm getting thirsty."

"We'll go after the next award."

People were filtering out as the program neared its conclusion, loitering at the entrance to the auditorium. On the shaded patio just outside the doors, the Academy's photographers stood by a backdrop where Emmy winners lined up for photos with their spouses or dates. A few feet to the left was a bustling open bar, and down a short flight of concrete stairs was a large patio area with thirty round, numbered tables. Caterers were beginning to set up the buffet tables with an array of chicken, beef, salad and pasta.

The patio area was soon swarming with reporters, photographers and others from the news business in Los Angeles, only a few lucky enough to possess one of the coveted statuettes. Ron grasped his Emmy tightly as he and Sandra passed arm in arm through the large glass doors into the tree-lined courtyard, lit by large studio lights.

Heads turned as the couple approached the stairs. Ron, of course, was known to practically everyone, but few of his colleagues had ever seen him dressed in a tuxedo, not to mention the bandages and the limp. This night, however, belonged to his date.

Sandra was stunning in a tight, teal and cream, knee length dress. She was holding Ron's arm as they stepped down onto the patio, her heels tapping as they hit the gray stone steps. All eyes turned as if in slow motion as the golden sunset and streaming lights bounced off her glittering dress. With each step, each movement of her body, the swirls of rhinestones came to life. Her hair was up and off to one side, curls perfectly framing her face and accentuating her dazzling green eyes.

As Sandra turned to face Ron just for a moment, he noticed a brilliant streak of sunlight, which shone through her hair, creating an extraordinary halo effect, the kind that a photographer might work arduously to create. Yet she wore it so naturally, without an ounce of pretense or affectation. Ron looked into her eyes with pride and awe; a magical moment that ended abruptly with a firm slap on the shoulder that snapped him back to the present.

Ron received hugs and handshakes from friends and colleagues, not only from Channel Six, but reporters and photographers from all the local stations. He proudly introduced Sandra, who turned heads and made a thoroughly smashing impression.

Bobbi caught sight of them, walked over, and after giving Ron another congratulatory hug, introduced herself and her husband to Sandra.

"It's such a pleasure to meet you," she said. "Ron tells me such wonderful things about you."

"Likewise," said Sandra. "Ron is completely enamored with you. You're his favorite producer."

"Yeah," Bobbi quipped. "That's just 'cause I buy him lunch. He's a sucker for a meatball sandwich."

"Don't I know it? Toasted, with extra provolone." Sandra replied. "Are you at our table?"

"Actually, we're not," said Bobbi. "We've been invited to sit at the Channel Three table. I work there now, starting Monday anyway."

They continued through the courtyard where twinkling, multicolored lights provided illumination in the twilight as nominees and their dates mingled and started to fill their seats. Lines had also formed at the several open bars as well as the fully stocked, two-sided buffet stands.

$$*****$$

As Sandra reached her fork in to serve herself some spinach salad, it collided with one being thrust in from the other side of the buffet.

"Oh, excuse me. I'm so sorry," she said, still feeling a bit shy and out of place.

"No worries," the man replied, pulling his hand back. "Help yourself."

"Thank you."

"Not at all," he said. "I'm David Bing with Channel Three. Do you work in the industry?"

"Me?" Sandra replied. "No, I'm here with Ron Sharp from Channel Six. In fact, I see him now."

Ron had turned up a couple of chairs at table 14, and had begun the slow process of working his way through the crowd of friends and colleagues, all wanting to offer congratulations and ask about his injuries. He grabbed a plate and joined Sandra in line.

"Ah, so you're Bobbi's photog," said David. "Congratulations. That was a great piece."

"And you are…?"

"David Bing, News Director, Channel 3," he said. "It's a pleasure to meet you both." He turned, smiling again at Sandra, and walked away with his plate, now full of food.

Channel 3 was fast gaining a reputation as the station with the most attractive reporting staff in Los Angeles. Young women, mostly blonde, who also possessed street smarts and reporting savvy, a combination that was not easy to find. Many credited Bing for his ability to lure such desirable talent from other markets. But at the same time, cameramen secretly called him "David Bang" because of his reputation as one of the most lecherous news managers the city had seen in many years, and rumors had spread about his alleged dalliances with several women in his newsroom.

Ron did not leave Sandra's side for the rest of the evening.

Tuesday, August 4th

Ron had only been back to work for a few days when he got a call from Rich about the Defense Department shoot they had discussed a few weeks earlier. General McKellar had given Rich very little information in a cryptic e-mail describing their assignment. He had made arrangements for the pair to be flown to Beale Air Force Base in Sacramento on Wednesday night for a shoot that would involve a cross-country flight. Where they would end up, and when, he would not say.

Thursday, August 6th

Seven am came early, and Ron and Rich were barely on time for breakfast on the base. Lt. Randy Forte, The Public Information Officer, met them as promised at the base's café and fed them a little more information about their shoot, but not everything. They'd learn more on a need-to-know basis. For now, all they needed to know was that they'd be boarding a converted KC-135 and flying to an undisclosed location on the east coast.

At 8 am sharp, they climbed up the stairway into the huge gray Stratotanker, which sat with three others on the tarmac. They had handed their bags to an airman who placed them in the cargo hold beneath the aircraft, and Ron carried his camera and tripod aboard along with some spare batteries.

The planes had each been filled with over 180,000 lbs of jet fuel, which was a tremendous load even for a tanker to carry. With the added weight, the converted cargo planes would require nearly two miles of runway to reach sufficient speed for takeoff. The newsmen had been securely strapped into their seats, which rested against the wall forward of the right wing, facing the center of the fuselage. Acceleration was laborious and took what seemed like an hour to reach speed, but once airborne, Ron and Rich relaxed and felt once again confident that they were in the hands of professionals.

The passenger compartment was bare, with steel and canvas jump seats lining both sides and a thin metal floor. Overhead were pressure lines, tubes and cable conduits, all painted Military green, with black numbers stenciled seemingly on every possible part for identification. There were red and white warning stickers on tubes, walls, doors, wherever they would fit, and the smell of fuel was unmistakable. The cabin was completely enclosed, with one small port-hole window on each side, directly over the wing.

Once the plane reached cruising altitude, Randy told Ron and Rich that they could get out of their seats and begin "filming". News crews, of course, hadn't used film in decades, and Ron often found it somewhat annoying when people used that term. But in this case, he felt it best not to say anything and just go with the flow. They unbuckled, stood up and removed their helmets. The steady hum of the engines echoed through the fuselage.

"I'm not sure what it is I'm supposed to shoot," said Ron.

"Well," answered the escort. "Right now there's not a lot, except maybe interiors of the aircraft and the flight crew. There'll be a bit more to see in an hour or so."

"Alrighty then," Ron said, as he started shooting b-roll of the pilots, cut-aways of the cockpit gauges and instruments and whatever else caught his eye.

He shot for a few minutes, then he and Rich sat back in their seats, unsure just what to expect next.

Within a few minutes, Randy was standing in front of Rich and instructing the two of them to buckle their belts immediately and make sure the camera was turned off.

"We need you to remain seated and not film or look out the windows for the next few minutes," he said. "We'll be entering Tonopah airspace and the classified nature of the base requires that you remain in your seats."

"It's OK, really," joked Ron. "I won't shoot any of the UFOs."

"I'll let you know when you can begin filming again," Randy said, not amused.

Soon Randy was back, telling Ron that he could now get out of his seat and start filming out the windows. Ron glanced at Rich with a look that said, "Here we go," and unbuckled his belt. He stood up, grabbed his camera and headed for the porthole over the right-side wing.

"Holy crap!" he gasped. "Look at this."

Rich peeked out the porthole over Ron's shoulder. For a moment, the two of them were dumbstruck, staring open-mouthed at what was in front of them. Off each wing of the Stratotanker flew a brand new F-38A Stealth Fighter, which no one outside of the military designers had ever seen, except in mock-up concept drawings in magazines. Aircraft aficionados had speculated about the exact specs and design of the latest stealth fighter for several years, and now, thanks to Channel 6, the public will actually get a glimpse.

Some of the most recent versions of the stealth fighter had been plagued from the beginning with problems involving software systems that affected the planes' navigation and accuracy of their live-fire weapons. They also fell short in maneuverability and friend-or-foe identification. Those issues, plus the fact that hackers all over the world had likely accessed classified data relating to the aircraft, made the Defense Department swallow hard and eat a good portion of the billions they had allocated to the program and try to come up with a new design that was free of the vulnerabilities of the earlier models.

The Department of Defense also knew that the enemy in the Middle East was catching up in the sophistication of their weaponry, partially due to the captured American arms and aircraft. Through reverse engineering, they'd been able to learn many of their technological secrets and thus lessen their effectiveness. But now it was time to give the other side a peek at what would soon be coming their way, a totally re-engineered aircraft with completely new technology that, the Defense Department hoped would make the terrorists soil their tunics.

The F-38A was a flying miracle. It looked like a razor sharp, angular insect, smaller than one would imagine, silver-gray in color, with a small Plexiglas cockpit bubble. The wings were very short and the stabilizers almost nonexistent. Looking at it, Ron wondered how it flew at all.

Ron grabbed his camera and began shooting out the porthole window at the plane over the right wing. He had never used a tripod on an airplane before and wondered if the motion would make it counter-productive, but wanted to try it anyway, hoping for a steady shot of the fighter pilots' faces. He was surprised at how well it worked, and the shots of the plane were spectacular, despite occasional distortion caused by the warping of the double-pane porthole window. At one point, the fighters pulled away from the tanker to give the pilots a chance to test the maneuverability and acceleration. Ron moved up to the cockpit, where he was able to shoot them at a distance, along with two other Stratotankers ahead of them and their accompanying fighters. In one shot, he captured one of the planes about 100 yards ahead practicing breathtaking aerobatic maneuvers, while the sun threw a glint off its angular frame. He did a rack-focus to the tanker pilot in the foreground. It was one of those rare shots that could not have been set up more perfectly. Ron smiled, turned to Rich, and said, "Wow. I think I need a cigarette after that."

Refueling the fighters was done by maneuvering the plane to the underside of the tanker, where an operator controlled an umbilicus, a remote controlled aluminum and rubber hose contraption, which snap-locked into a hole just behind the fighter's cockpit. This operation requires precision on the part of everyone involved.

Ron was shown to a six-by-six foot curved Plexiglas floor in the rear of the tanker, where the refueling crew worked. He crouched on his knees and had a clear shot of the entire procedure from above. The view itself was breathtaking, seeing the Stealth from this angle and only a few yards away, and the beautiful green and brown earth below.

Each stealth fighter had a range of about 1,200 miles. That's where the Stratotanker came in. To reach the east coast, each F-38A would need to be refueled at least twice. Ron had all the video he needed, but took the time to get some interesting, artsy b-roll shots like the tanker's pilots' hands on the controls, and cockpit dials, gauges and lights. He went to the refueling station each time it was activated, and though the shots became repetitive, he never tired of the sight of the most futuristic aircraft on the planet in action. He watched for the little spritz of jet fuel that was emitted from the top of the fighter each time the umbilicus disengaged.

After the final refueling operation late in the afternoon, the crew finally learned of their destination. The fighters pulled off and headed southeast for Langley, Virginia, with the Stratotanker continuing on to upstate New York.

They landed at about 5:30 pm eastern time on an old airstrip at the former Plattsburgh Air Force Base, which had been officially decommissioned a few years earlier. The tankers taxied to a stop and a blue U.S. Air Force van pulled alongside. Ron and Rich climbed down the ramp, Rich already on the phone to the station. He filled Wellington in on where they were and they discussed what the plans were for the news that night.

Randy, along with Dieter, the local Air Force escort, provided them with a map of the area along with the phone number of the nearest taxi service. They promised to wait with them outside the gate until the cab arrived. Meanwhile, Wellington had Larry Garner on the phone with New England Satellite News, trying to hire them to arrange a meeting place.

It took forty-five minutes, but finally a car approached. It was a private cab, a dirty, subcompact Ford wagon that appeared to be listing to one side. The driver was a bony-thin sixty-ish fellow with a shock of dirty brown hair, wearing tan slacks and a stained white t-shirt. His yellow Members Only jacket looked as if he had worn it while changing the cab's oil.

"I'm Clem," he said, jumping out to meet his fares. "Where do ya need to get to?"

Rich was on a call with Larry and took the phone from his ear.

"How about Burlington?"

"Burlington is good, about a half hour's drive."

"Fine. Let's do that."

Rich and Ron thanked Randy for an extraordinary day, and their escorts drove off.

Larry had arranged for the satellite truck to meet them in Burlington at seven. That would hopefully give them enough time to get something to eat, and being three hours ahead of L.A., they'd have no problem getting on the air for the Late News.

The first challenge they encountered was getting all their gear in the tiny cab. Two big duffels of their clothes, a crate of lights, an edit-pack and a Live-

U backpack filled the trunk, such as it was. Rich climbed into the passenger's seat and Ron slid in the back with his camera and tripod.

The overloaded cab's worn out suspension bottomed out with every bump, so the driver took it nice and slow, all the way to Burlington. It was already close to seven. Just as the cab pulled into a gas station on the city's main drag, Ron spotted the large, white *New England Satellite News* truck driving by. Rich called the number Larry had given him and spoke to Brad Wilks, the truck operator, telling him to make a U-turn and return to the gas station to meet them.

Brad pulled the truck into a parking spot in the nearly empty lot and fired up the generator. After paying the cabbie, they hopped in, introduced themselves, and made a plan for the evening. Brad raised the dish on the roof and locked into a satellite. He booked two windows of transmission time while Rich began looking through the video and writing his story. He kept in touch with Deb Chen, his writer back at the station, who worked on finding file video of the fighting in the Middle East that Rich could use in his package.

By 9 pm local time, Ron had finished editing and their piece was in-house by about 9:15. This gave them time to grab some dinner, but they soon discovered that Burlington Vermont is not at all like Los Angeles. They stepped from the truck and saw virtually no lights on any of the stores for blocks in any direction. And very little traffic.

Brad was reluctant to drop the dish and drive them in the Sat truck to another part of town to find a restaurant, so he suggested they call a local pizza shop he knew that delivered until 11 pm. Having not eaten anything all day, they jumped at the chance to have food brought right to the truck, and by ten, they'd had their pizza and coke and both felt much better about things. They were fed, the story was done and shipped, and they still had a few hours to spare before the west coast newscast.

Ron called Sandra and began filling her in on the excitement of the day.

"Oh, Ron," Rich said, interrupting his conversation with Sandra. "I forgot to tell you, Scott wants you to call him at the desk. Says it's important. Sorry, I was working and forgot to tell you."

"Umm… OK then," Ron said. "Listen, Sweetie, I've got to go," he told Sandra. "But I'll call you in a while, OK?"

"Sure, Hon," she said. "I want to hear all about it."

*****

"Yeah, so there was a cop here at the station asking about you today," Scott said.

"Really? Any idea what it was about?"

"No. He was in Larry's office for a while. That's all I know."

"Hmm…" Ron said. "Thanks for the heads up."

"That's OK, I know you've been off the radar today, so to speak. I'm sure we'll find out more tomorrow."

There were only two possibilities Ron could come up with. Either Sandra's crazy ex, Jack, really was crazy. . . crazy enough to hassle him at work, or the Homicide guys working Rachel Larimore's case finally learned of his existence and tracked him down, months after her arrest. Neither option was pleasant. But for now, thousands of miles away, he wouldn't have to deal with it, at least for a while.

*****

The live shot had gone without a hitch and they were able to find a Quick-Inn on St. Paul Street that was perfect for one night. It was almost 2 am before they checked in, and morning came quickly. Up at sunrise, they ate a quick breakfast and took a cab to the Burlington Airport. Larry Garner had tried to book them on the first flight out of Burlington but had to settle for a puddle-jumper to Boston at 9:55.

Friday, August 7th

The return trip took a good portion of the day and by the time Ron and Rich dragged themselves into the newsroom, it was early evening. Larry noticed them walking through the newsroom door and hopped out of his chair to welcome them back.

"Great story last night, guys!" he shouted. "That plane is incredible."

"And," he added, turning to Ron, "beautifully shot."

Both the men thanked him as they continued on toward the assignment desk.

"Oh, Ron," he whispered, motioning to his office. "Can I see you for a minute?"

"Sure," Ron answered. "I'll be right there."

Larry shut the door and sat behind his desk. Ron took a seat.

"That really was incredible video, Ron. That must have been a thrill," Larry said.

"You know, boss. Stories like that are the reason you get into this business."

"Ronnie, an LAPD Detective was here yesterday asking about you," he said, reaching in his drawer for the cop's business card. "A Detective Silvera. Does that name mean anything to you?"

"No, no it doesn't," Ron answered, squinting to read the name on the detective's card.

"Well, he said it was important for him to speak with you. He asked for your cellphone number. I had to give it to him, but I told him you were out of town until tonight. I assured him that I'd give you his card and that you'd get in touch with him once you got back. He seemed like a reasonable enough guy, said he'd give you until Monday to call him."

"OK, then," Ron said, looking over both sides of the card. "*Detective Greg Silvera, LAPD Robbery Homicide Division*. Never heard of him. Look, I'll call him first thing Monday."

"Alright, but don't let it go. I gave him my word. He didn't seem like an overly patient man."

"You got it, Boss."

Chapter Eleven:

HONESTY

Ron was unsure how to broach the subject with Sandra. A detective was about to grill him about a former girlfriend and how much he knew about a murder she may have committed right under his nose years ago. How exactly does one bring that up in a conversation anyway? So, against his better judgment and his own personal policy of openness in relationships, he said nothing, instead hoping her first visit to The Dog and Pony with him would provide plenty of grist for conversation.

Saturday, August 8th

As the evening wore on, more and more news people began to arrive at the familiar watering hole. There was no birthday or retirement party, but being the end of the week, the usual coterie of reporters, writers and camera operators from all the stations in Los Angeles showed up to blow off steam and shoot the bull.

Sandra hit it off immediately with Robin Russo, Ron's photog friend from Channel 8. That was fine with him, since he loved Robin, even more so since her lengthy battle with ovarian cancer. The fact that two women he cared about were getting along so well left him feeling unusually gratified.

He also introduced her to James Foster, Jen Kuroda and Pam Butler. James and Pam were in the midst of a debate about whose station was being managed the worst.

"When I started at Channel 3," James said, "we had an entire planning department full of researchers who set up stories, contacted sources and made sure you had all the information you needed before you got your assignment. Now, they come in and read the paper and the blogs on line in the morning. That's it. If it ain't in the paper, it didn't happen."

"KSIX is just as bad," said Pam. "Except what happens is, nobody can make a decision, so the stories end up changing all day.

"One morning last week, they gave me an assignment when I came in at 9 am. They wanted me to shoot a news conference with the mayor of West Covina at ten. I'm like, 'I hope you don't need it very badly, because I'm not gonna be there in time.' So Freddy tells me to just get there when I can, since they don't have enough people."

"Shocking, isn't it?" Ron interjected sarcastically.

"So I bust my tail in morning traffic and at a few minutes to ten, he calls me to see if I'm getting close. I'm still about twenty minutes away according to my GPS, not counting the time it will take to set up, assuming there's still a spot available near the podium. I hate walking in after a presser has already started. You feel like such a loser, banging around with your gear and interrupting everything to set up a mike."

"So get this, he says, 'Turn around, we don't care about this story anymore. Can you head for Long Beach? You have a 10:30 shoot there.' I swear, they think we drive helicopters."

"No," said Ron. "They just have no clue what it's like to work in the field or how long it takes to get anywhere."

"One day last month," said James, "I get sent to an event at the fairgrounds in Pomona. David Beckham is going to be signing pictures and giving a soccer lesson to some underprivileged kids. Cool, right? It takes me two hours to get there since I'm coming from the Valley, so I'm late, of course. I figure it's gonna be packed, and every crew in the world is going to be there, but I pull into the lot and it's completely empty. The parking guy knows nothing about the event, so I call the station to get the contact's name. I finally get her on the phone and she tells me that it's the following week. Damn idiots wasted half my day. I swear to God, I see taillights in my sleep. Seriously."

"Happens all the time," said Pam. "They're so afraid of missing something."

"But then you find them a good story and they don't care," James added. "One night a couple months ago, I'm listening to the scanner and I hear City Fire call an 'Industrial accident with entrapment' on San Fernando Road. I'm in the Valley, just a few minutes away, so my ears perk up and I cruise over there. I'm just about on scene and I hear the size-up on the Valley frequency. Some guy at a meat-processing place has gotten his arm caught in a grinder. They've shut it off and unplugged it, but he's stuck in there up past his elbow and his hand is chewed up pretty good."

"So I get there and I'm standing on the sidewalk watching through the open gate as they wheel the guy out on a gurney with a huge part of the grinder right there in his lap, and his arm still stuck inside. They're gonna transport him with the grinder attached and dismantle it at the hospital."

"I had to time it just right, since I knew they'd kick me off the property, so I ran through the gate and right up to the RA and got a close shot of the guy getting loaded up for transport. The manager of the place was yelling at me the whole time to get back, but I'd already gotten what I needed. So then I follow the ambulance down the street where I get him being transferred to the Fire chopper and taken to UCLA."

"Now, maybe it was just adrenaline, but I'm thinking I've got terrific pictures of a great breaking story here. The station? They didn't care. They already had their late show all written and stacked. The last thing they wanted was for me to screw with their newscast by adding a story. But you know what? If they'd seen it on Channel 8, they'd have chewed me out for missing it. None of these dumb-asses have any idea what breaking news is. We bust our humps out there every day, and…"

"Oh," interrupted Ron, remembering the shooting on Wilshire. "Don't get me started."

Just then, Scott Castle walked up and poked his head into the conversation.

"Is someone feeling unappreciated over here? Can I buy you another beer?"

"No thanks," Ron answered. "I think we're good."

"So, did you ever find out what that cop wanted with you at the station?"

Ron flinched and glanced at Sandra, who perked up suddenly.

"What cop is that?" she asked.

"Thanks a lot, dude," said Ron.

"Oops," said Scott, raising his eyebrows and slinking away to the next table.

"Yeah, umm… can we talk about this later?" he asked Sandra. "It's personal."

Sensing that he was upset, she backed off.

"Just tell me this," she whispered. "Does it have anything to do with Jack?"

"No, no, nothing at all," he said. "I promise we'll talk later."

A few news managers had decided to show up to unwind at the Pony that night as well, but sensing the vibe from the resident malcontents, they grabbed a couple of tables out on the patio. Larry Garner, David Bing, Wellington James and a few others were half drunk and involved in a long, meandering conversation about ratings, lead-ins and talent. Through the bank of windows, Wellington noticed Maria Lopez walking to her table in the next room and soon the topic turned to evaluating the physical attributes of various female reporters in town and which ones they'd like to be with.

Bing recognized Sandra from the Emmys and remarked that she was certainly attractive enough to work for him. "I'd make her get her tits done, but she could be a weather girl for me next week. Cute face, great eyes."

Larry excused himself to use the restroom and walked through the bar, stopping at a few tables to say hello. Spotting Ron, he worked his way over to introduce himself to Sandra. Smelling of alcohol, he sang Ron's praises while inquiring about her, what she did, where she lived, how they met. Upon learning that she worked in public relations, he gave her a card and asked for one of hers.

"You never know when we can help each other out, you know, scratch one another's backs, right?"

"Sure," she said, giggling and rolling her eyes as he walked away.

"Dipshit," whispered Pam. "Managers are all the same. They kiss your ass until you need something, and then they act like they don't know who you are."

"Ain't it the truth?" Robin agreed. "When it hits the fan, you're on your own. They'll never back you up."

"Not if there's a chance it will cost them their job, or the company a few dollars." Pam said.

"Did I tell you what happened last week?" Robin asked. "You won't believe this.

"My reporter Molly Peel and I are on this story in Compton. A kid's been strangled and his mother is under investigation. They give us the address and it's this ratty apartment building on Poplar Street. We park out front and start shooting b-roll of the neighborhood. Molly asked a few neighbors if they'd heard anything. Nobody had, but they all point to the building where they'd seen all the police activity the previous day. Apartment 5, they said.

"So the front of the building is all fenced off and covered with plants and ivy, but there's a gate to the left that's propped open with a rock and a piece of wire. We follow the concrete walk inside to ask if some of the other residents had seen anything. Nobody's answering their doors at all, but when we get outside Apartment 5, we hear yelling inside. I motion to Molly to turn on the mike and I start rolling. She holds the mike up close to the kitchen window, as we're standing right outside the front door."

"These people are really goin' at it, I mean screaming at each other. I can hear them clear as day in my earpiece. So, the guy yells, 'You bitch, you're lucky it wasn't YOUR throat I had my hand around!'

"Molly and I just looked at each other and couldn't believe it. We got our asses out of there as quick as we could."

"Yikes," said Ron, looking at Sandra.

"So, we find a place to stop a few blocks away where I play back the video for Molly. She heard it too, plain as could be. We figure we've broken the damn case. The station's gonna want to let the police hear what we have, right?"

"Wrong. Molly calls our news director, who proceeds to chew us out for going on to private property. He never calls the police, says we can't air the video, and tells us never to do anything like that again."

"Meanwhile, a killer gets away, because our management has no balls. Unreal."

"Wow," said Pam. "That's just not right."

"I don't know where they get these management types," said Robin, leaning her head in the direction of the patio. "They're all the same. They get fired from one shop after running it into the ground, and then the station down the street hires them."

"You're so right," said Pam. "I really wish we had Leo back, but I guess he got tired of being a yes-man and the company moved him out. The last thing they want is someone who thinks for himself. They just want a company man, no matter how disgusting a person he is."

"Where did this new guy come from?" Robin asked.

"I think his last stop was in Oklahoma, but he's been in a dozen markets. He's a hatchet man- goes in, fires everyone, and moves on. The company loves him because he cuts personnel. Helps the bottom line, at least for a while. But he's a thoroughly horrible person."

"How so?" Sandra asked, now engrossed in the conversation.

"He comes into our place on his first day, he looks around the newsroom and says to Larry, 'You see all those people? Half of them won't be here in a month.' That's without knowing any of us, or what we do."

"Then," Pam continued, "after decimating the staff, cutting dozens of hard working, talented people, the bastard brings in his girlfriend. He creates a position for her and pays her 300 grand a year."

"Yeah," Ron added. "He's married, and he's carrying on an affair with his 'special consultant'. He puts her on the air to comment about our stories, and she's just awful. But he thinks she's terrific. This after they make us sit through those bullshit 'sex in the workplace' seminars."

"That's disgusting," said Robin. "We had a news director a few years ago who did coke in the lunch room every day. He'd been fired from every other station in the state, it seems like, but the geniuses that run our place thought he'd be great."

"What happened?" asked Sandra. "Did he get caught?"

"Eventually, but nobody wanted to say anything for fear of retaliation."

"What about the anchors?" asked Pam.

"Are you kidding me?" said Robin. "The main anchor was his supplier."

*****

On the way home, before they hit the freeway, Sandra asked Ron what the story was with the Police officer, and why he hadn't said anything earlier.

"Yeah, I'm sorry about that," he said. "It's something I should have told you about a while ago, but it's a bit embarrassing."

"You can tell me anything," she said, her interest piqued. "What is it?"

"Well, you may have heard, a few months back, there was a female LAPD officer arrested for a murder that happened a number of years ago."

"Rachel Larimore?" she interjected.

"Uhh… yeah, how did you remember her na…"

"Jack knew her. They worked together in the Valley before she made detective."

"OK, well, umm… I dated her."

There was an awkward pause.

"Jack said he knew she was crazy and wasn't surprised at all that she murdered someone," Sandra said, as if Ron's revelation had gone unheard.

"Well, he says that now, but I sure didn't get that vibe off her. Plus, she hasn't been convicted of anything yet."

"When did you date her?"

"I was with her a few months before the murder," he answered.

"I see."

"And a few months after."

"What?" Sandra paused, stunned. "And you had no clue?"

"None at all," he said. "I'm still freaked out about it. Kind of makes you look at yourself, you know, and question your ability to judge people."

"I guess it does," she said.

"But anyway, it looks like the detectives got my name somehow, as I figured they would, and they came to the station looking for me while I was out of town. They want me to contact them."

"So, you're going to call them?"

"Yeah, I'll call Monday."

✳✳✳✳✳

Sunday, August 9th

Ron slept in, past nine, knowing that he had the morning to relax on his day off. Not too many chores, just a quick trip to the grocery store, fill up the Mustang, and maybe get back to the gym. It had been a few months, and now that it looked like he might be in a serious relationship, it might be a good idea to get back in shape. He sat up in bed and Detective Silvera's card stared at him from his nightstand, as if calling out his name, not about to let him forget. But that call could wait until tomorrow.

The Channel 3 Morning News was on in the background as he showered and dressed. Nothing very interesting, mostly happy talk, recipes and stringer footage of last night's traffic accidents and house fires. He was rinsing off his breakfast dishes in the sink when suddenly there was a powerful knock on his apartment door. Three knocks, actually. Living in a security building, he wondered who the heck it could be. He knew the building manager's knock, and this wasn't it. The little woman from next door? Hardly. This was someone who meant business. There was some heft behind the knocks. Could it be that Detective Silvera had found his home address and had grown tired of waiting for the phone call?

Jeez. I was going to call you in a few minutes. Really,' he thought.

He squinted through the peephole just in time for the second set of knocks. There stood a large man, tall and muscular, in a dark suit, very official looking. The super wide-angle viewer distorted Jack's appearance, and Ron didn't recognize him until he opened the door a crack.

"Ron Sharp?"

"That's right. Can I help you?"

"My name is Jack Thorne. May I come inside?"

"Uhh... Sure," said Ron, scratching his forehead. "Come in. Can I, uhh, get you some water or something?"

"Yeah, that would be good."

Ron instantly thought of Rachel Larimore and how she supposedly murdered Shannon Russo. Had she knocked on the door, just as Jack did? Did she enter the apartment calmly? Did it all start as a relaxed, friendly conversation before becoming a brutal crime of passion?

Ron went to grab a couple of bottles of water from the refrigerator. Jack sat at the kitchen table, and the two men tried to get a read on one another. Jack saw Ron as just an average guy, not special in any way, good or bad, pretty harmless actually. Ron had observed Jack at work, the teacher, the authority figure, the marksman. But here inside his apartment sat a different person. He couldn't tell from his quiet demeanor if Jack was confused, sad, or irate. He waited patiently for him to break the silence.

"You know my wife, Sandy," he said with a cold stare.

"I do," said Ron, nodding slightly and sucking his upper lip.

"How well do you know her?" Jack asked, eyes locked.

"We're friends, she's... a great girl." Ron handed Jack a bottle and joined him at the table.

"How did you meet her?"

"I, umm, I work for Channel Six News and we met one day on a story," Ron answered, keeping his answers honest and brief.

"You took her out."

"I did," Ron said, nodding. "We met for a drink and that's when she told me she was married."

"But then she went with you to the Emmy awards," Jack insisted, frowning and motioning toward the shiny new statuette on the mantel.

Ron could feel the tension rising and tried to tamp down the heat, again remembering Shannon Russo and her fate.

"Look, she's a friend. I was nominated and had nobody to go with. I thought she'd enjoy the ceremony. Like I told you, I think she's a great girl."

"She *is* a great girl. And she's my wife."

"Well, you're a very lucky man," Ron said, taking a long drink of water.

"Did she mention that we're separated?" Jack asked, loudly cracking the cap off of the water bottle.

"She said you two had some issues you were working out, but it's really none of my business."

Jack took a long drink, stood up, and walked silently to the window at the rear of the apartment.

Ron scanned the apartment, looking for something, anything to use as a weapon, just in case.

"I think she's seeing someone, and I think it may be serious," Jack said, his voice quivering. He stared out at the street, placing the bottom of the bottle against the pane, fuming. "She's out a lot, and sometimes she doesn't come home at all."

"Really, Jack? You've been watching her house?"

This guy's nuts, Ron reasoned. You'd better be ready to crack his head open with a picture frame or something.

"You know, Ron," Jack said, forming a meaty, a muscular fist and choking back tears. "If I thought you were fucking my wife, I'd pick you up and throw you through this window."

Ron's throat tightened as his eyes quickly scanned the room.

I am NOT going to be on the news tomorrow covered with a sheet. How much damage can I do to this guy with an Emmy?

Jack stared at the floor and ran his fingers through his short, sandy hair. He said nothing as he walked over and sat down on the sofa, and took another drink. It instantly occurred to Ron that Jack was sitting in the exact spot where he and Sandra had worn each other out with marathon sex just a few nights before and prayed that there was no evidence left behind, no remainder of Sandra's arousing scent left on the cushions.

Ron stood up and walked to the middle of the room, placing him a bit closer to the blunt objects.

Jack rubbed his temples with his right hand as his eyes reddened.

"How can I get her back, Ron? Has she said anything to you?"

Breathe, breathe…

"Look, Jack," Ron said, thinking on his feet and swallowing hard. "All I know is that she needs to be respected. She needs someone who'll actually listen to what she has to say, someone who cares about her, cares about making her happy. She's a very smart woman, and very complex. She wants to be appreciated. Like most women I know, she just wants to feel important, to feel cared about. That's all I can tell you."

Jack sat silently, staring straight ahead.

"Does she miss me?"

"I'm sure she does, Jack. And she cares about you, very much. You just have to stop trying so hard. Whatever happens happens. Sometimes you have to let go and make it about her and not you. If you really love her, which I think you do, you'll be happy for her when and if she finds happiness, whether that's with you or not."

"But I need her," Jack said, his eyes welling up.

"And that's the last thing you should say to her. She needs support, encouragement and independence, not some needy guy who's just going to smother her."

Jack took a deep breath, pinched his nostrils, and nodded slowly.

"You're right," he said. "I'll give her some space, try to make her happier. She's my life, you know. We've been together forever."

"For now, you've got to let her be free. Give it time. And for heaven's sake stop stalking her, Jack. You know that's just not right."

Jack got up and headed for the door, shoulders slumped.

"Thanks, Ron," he said, with a sigh. "I hope I didn't freak you out too much."

"No problem, man. Anytime."

Yeah, right. Stop by any fuckin' time, dude. Jesus.

Dead. Bolt.

Ron had no idea where all the sage advice and words of wisdom had come from, but he was glad that he'd been able to bullshit his way out of a quick three-story drop onto Moorpark Avenue. Once Jack was gone, he grabbed his phone and texted Sandra.

Ron:Please be careful what you
say to Jack. He's not happy
with us.

Almost instantly, she replied.

                         Sandra: What???
                         Did he call you?

Ron:Something like that-
Just be careful.

                         Sandra:Oh- I'm
                           so   pissed.

Ron: Relax. It'll all work out.
You just need to play the game.
And please don't contact him.
It'll only make it worse.

It took a few minutes, but Sandra thought about it and responded.

                    Sandra: Was going to
                    call him, but ur right.
                    Letting it go for now.

Ron: That's wise. Talk 2U later.

Monday, August 10th

Ron only had a few minutes before he had to leave for work when he sat down to call Detective Silvera. He apologized for the delay and explained that he's been out of town on business.

"Mr. Sharp, my partner and I would like to ask you a few questions about your relationship with Rachel Larimore," the Detective said. "Is there a time when it's convenient to meet at a Police station near your home or work?"

"Well," Ron said. "I'm working evenings this week, so any day around noon works for me."

"We can do tomorrow. Are you far from North Hollywood station?"

"No, I'm not. Umm, not at all," Ron said, haltingly.

"Then noon it is. We'll see you then."

With that, Detective Silvera hung up, leaving Ron feeling as if he'd been slapped across the face with a cold, wet rag.

That didn't take long, he thought.

Tuesday, August 11th

Ron exited the North Hollywood Police Station at around two, giving him just enough time to grab a bite before heading to the station to work nightside. The midday heat took his breath away as he walked to the car, which had been parked in the sun since he pulled up around noon. The interview with the detectives had lasted longer than he expected, covering his relationship with Rachel in much greater detail than he had anticipated.

Of course the detectives wanted to know all about when and how they'd met, what attracted him to her and what their common interests may have been. Where had they gone on their first date? What kind of movies did she like? Was she a sports fan? Why did he stop seeing her? But they kept at it, picking his brain for any bit of information that might help make their case. If they had conclusive DNA evidence against her, as he'd read, why did they need to hound him about what kind of car she drove or what she liked to eat? Did she have any special skills of which he was aware?

Like what, exactly? Shooting a young woman and staging a burglary?

He hoped he was done, and they had gotten all the answers they were looking for. But, they assured him they'd be in touch and the District Attorney would be calling him if there were any follow-up questions. And he knew there was a good chance that his name would eventually appear on the prosecution's witness list. Seeing Rachel again, but on opposite sides of a courtroom, would be about the most bizarre thing he could imagine.

The sweltering afternoon air felt like a damp sandbag thrown over both shoulders. Ron opened the mustang's door and the heat leapt out at him from the black leather seats. This was the fifth straight day with temperatures in the 100s in the Valley and there was barely a cloud in the sky, except the huge white thunderheads over the high desert to the north and east. The warm breeze that gently rustled the trees along Burbank Boulevard provided no relief. There had been virtually no rain since February and none was likely before October or later. The barren front lawns and brown hills of Southern California thirsted for a drink that was nowhere in the forecast. Putting the convertible's top down was not an option. His personal rule was that he only dropped the top when it was between 68 and 80 degrees. The only solution today was to crank the a/c and wait.

Monday, August 17ᵗʰ

"Ron, you remember that interview we've been trying to get with Henry Brooks for the last few months?" asked Scott, sitting at the assignment desk.

"Yeah, the Councilman who's running for Mayor?"

"That's the one. We finally got him to agree to an interview. You're going to City Hall with Jerry Schram. He'll meet you in the garage."

Ron didn't mind working with Jerry. He was another of Leo Joseph's reclamation project, someone who was put on the payroll for his intellect, experience and writing skills, not necessarily his good looks. Jerry had been writing about politics and government for close to twenty years for the Times and other papers, and although he had no experience reporting on TV, Leo thought his expertise would help with the station's coverage of last year's Presidential campaign. Once the election was over, he was immediately put on the City Hall beat, where his knowledge and contacts were great resources, and before long another election, this time a local one, would be coming up.

His on-air performance was still a little stiff and uncomfortable, but improving. Everyone knew that with Leo's departure, his "projects" would soon be shown the door, in favor of younger, more attractive, less costly reporters, and Ron felt bad, knowing that the poor guy, while no beauty queen, was doing the best he could.

"So, we finally got this guy to agree to talk to us," said Ron, heading off the lot toward downtown. "I know you've been trying for a long time."

"Yeah, he's got to start doing some interviews soon if he plans to run for Mayor. We just happen to be his first."

"Great. How'd you manage that?" Ron asked.

"I have my ways."

"I know you do."

"There's just one thing, though," Jerry said.

"There always is."

"Brooks' wife is Manuela Estrada, the former State Senator. She's currently under investigation for failing to disclose over $300,000 in payments to the consulting firm Henry used to manage. That's a violation of the Political Reform Act."

"This thing has tentacles that could lead to both of them paying a stiff fine, if not spending time in jail."

"Wow," said Ron. "How does he expect to get elected Mayor with that hanging over his head?"

"The investigation is still kind of hush-hush," answered Jerry. "He's hoping they can settle, pay the fines, and have it all go away before the public knows anything about it."

"But you're not about to let that happen, are you?" Ron asked, with a knowing glance.

"Well, he gave us a list of subjects he's willing to take questions about today," Jerry said. "That way he thinks he can control the interview. He has no clue that we know about this. I'm going to break the story tonight about the investigation, so I've got to get his reaction to our story first."

"Alrighty then."

The 4 pm appointment was the earliest that Jerry could arrange, with Brooks having a full calendar of Council business. He and Ron cooled their heels in the foyer of his third-floor office and waited until almost 4:30. At last, they were escorted into his inner office to set up.

"Jerry! How nice to see you again," the Councilman bellowed, as he bolted in unannounced through the heavy mahogany door. "It's been a long time!"

"Well," said Jerry, holding out his hand. "You're a busy man."

"That I am."

Jerry introduced Ron, who proceeded to clip a wireless lavaliere mike to the lapel of Brooks' tan suit jacket.

Ron had seen Brooks dozens of times at Council meetings, and had interviewed him on a number of occasions, usually about some city measure or proclamation. His impression of the Councilman was that he was a sweaty, portly, overpaid, pampered politician with all the charm and cologne of a timeshare salesman.

Ron seated him behind the large wooden desk and angled his camera to avoid the window to the Councilman's left. He closed the shutters part way, allowing a small amount of natural light into the room from the afternoon sun. The shelf behind Brooks held awards, knick-knacks and assorted honors and gifts accumulated during his six-year tenure in city government. Ron framed the shot so that they showed up in soft focus over his left shoulder on screen.

Jerry sat camera right in the padded leather armchair, and when given the signal by his cameraman, officially began the interview.

"So, Councilman Brooks, we hear you've made a decision on your run for Mayor. Will you be making an official announcement?"

"My staff is working on that now," Brooks answered, in a deep, melodious, practiced voice.

"That's exciting," Jerry said. "Is there anything you can tell us now?"

"You know," he answered, maintaining eye contact. "I'd prefer to wait, except to say that this city is crying out for new leadership, a new hand on the wheel, someone who can do more than talk, who's been around City Hall long enough to know what it takes to get the wheels turning for the people of Los Angeles."

"Wow," said Jerry. "Sounds like you have your stump speech all ready."

"Yeah," he laughed. "I've had some time to work on it."

"This is like the worst kept secret in the history of the city, you know," said Jerry. "Everyone knows you're running."

"That's why we need a big rollout," Brooks replied with a chuckle. "If and when, I mean."

"So, let me ask you this," Jerry said, lighting the fuse. "This investigation of your wife, do you think that's going to affect your campaign?"

Brooks kept his chin in the palm of his right hand, with his elbow resting on his desk, his expression and demeanor changing slowly. His air of affability was gone, his toothy smile suddenly looking as if he had sucked a lemon. He leaned back in his chair and gently massaged his chin between his thumb and the knuckle on his index finger. Then, scratching the back of his neck, he squinted, as though he were in pain, while never making eye contact with either Jerry or Ron, who glanced at each other, not knowing what to expect.

"Shut off the camera!" he suddenly shouted, jumping out of his seat, pointing his finger angrily across the desk, his mouth now a spittle-flecked maw. "You agreed not to ask about that, Jerry! You knew what I was willing to talk about!"

Brooks ripped the lavaliere mike from his lapel and the transmitter from his pocket. He threw them in Ron's direction, but they landed on the floor in the rear corner of the office alongside the potted plastic fichus tree.

"But, I..." Jerry tried to reply, although his answer was weak and overpowered by the bluster and bravado of the hefty Councilman, who was now moving in his direction.

Ron kept shooting as Brooks stepped around the desk, still fuming. Jerry was out of his chair and backing away.

"I said to shut off the fucking camera!" he screamed, eyes wide, grabbing the lens and trying unsuccessfully to turn it away from himself. "This interview is over."

"Keep your hands off the camera!" Ron yelled, as Brooks again turned angrily toward Jerry.

"We had an agreement, and you broke it!"

"I did nothing of the kind!" Jerry shouted. "All I did was ask the question. You didn't have to answer it, and certainly not the way you did."

"This interview is over," Brooks sneered. "You've lost your chance. Now I need you to give me that video." He turned again toward Ron, holding out his hand.

"That's not happening," said Ron, visibly irritated. "That's not how this works."

Turning back swiftly and frantically to his left, Brooks pleaded, "Jerry, you're going to give me that video or there're going to be some real problems for you, my friend."

"No way in hell are you getting that video," Jerry asserted, opening the office door, in hopes that the thought of Brooks' staff hearing the commotion would temper his hostility and lower the emotional temperature in the room. Ron hustled to break down his gear and retrieve the mike from the floor. He threw it into his equipment bag and the two made their way toward the door and out of the office, Brooks still shouting obscenities and threats.

"I'm calling your boss and getting you both fired!"

"You do that, Councilman," said Jerry, as they made a hasty exit.

"Don't worry, there's nothing he can do," said Jerry as they left City Hall and approached the van, which Ron had parked along the curb in a MEDIA ONLY spot on Main Street. "You got all that, right?"

"What? Was I supposed to be rolling?"

"Very funny," said Jerry. "You do have it, right?"

"Of course, dude. And in focus, too. Don't forget who you're working with."

It didn't take long for Jerry's phone to ring. Wellington had already heard from Brooks, and the news director was calling him before they had even made it to the freeway. Ron answered the call and switched the phone to speaker.

"What happened there?" Wellington demanded.

"Just like we discussed in the meeting," Jerry answered. "I brought up the investigation of his wife's finances and he came unglued. You should have seen it. It was great television."

"He's demanding that we not use the footage," said Wellington.

"...And you said...?"

"I told him that I would look at it and make a determination."

"Really," said Jerry. "We didn't expect him to explode like that. All he had to do was decline to answer the question."

"He's obviously got something to hide," said Ron. "You don't act like that when you're innocent."

"OK, well, good job, guys. We'll see you back at the barn."

Wellington looked at the raw video and after consulting with the station's attorneys, as well as his 'special assistant' Renee, approved the story as Jerry had written it. They had planned to break the story about Brooks' wife that evening anyway, in a separate piece, and now there was material to give that story even more credibility.

✳✳✳✳✳

Ron was helping Sandra wash the dishes and clean up after another homemade meal. Cooking together was something they both had come to enjoy, much to Ron's surprise. Tonight had been stir-fry, Sandra's favorite. She even brought her wok to his apartment, knowing that the odds of him owning one were slim to none.

Ron was drying the cutting board when she broke the news.

"I talked to Jack today," she said.

"Yeah? How did that go?"

"He called to tell me that he had met someone and wasn't going to try to talk me out of the divorce anymore."

"That's great!" said Ron. "What else did he say?"

"He said he just wanted me to be happy. That's pretty much all. Oh, and to apologize for being a jerk."

"Wow. That's nice to hear."

"I wasn't going to, but I told him about us," she added.

"Umm… what exactly?"

"That you and I were a thing, and you know, since he said he wanted me to be happy, I told him that I was."

"And…"

"I couldn't tell if he was surprised," said Sandra. "But he said that you were a nice guy. Nice and smart, he said. I'm not sure how he knew that, but I guess he approves, not that it matters."

"It matters, Hon," said Ron, hugging her from behind. "It matters a lot."

Jerry's piece was teased throughout the evening, with a few seconds of video of a crazed City Councilman grabbing the camera airing in seemingly every prime-time commercial break.

"Council member goes berserk, threatens news crew!" Gretchen announced. "Tonight at ten!"

The story, of course, did not lead the newscast. The producer held it for the top of the B block, after the first break. They would tease it one more time, going into the commercial, along with an animal story and a Dodgers highlight, hoping to keep their audience for at least another quarter hour.

The show began with a weather piece, featuring Shelby live in Santa Monica where throngs had spent the day at the beach in an attempt to escape the unbearable heat. It had indeed been a scorcher, another day of record heat in the Valley.

It may have once been frowned upon to begin the newscast with a weather story, but producers now agree that it's best to open with whatever it is that people are talking about at work, at home, at the dinner table. Everyone in Los Angeles was talking about the heat, how long would it continue, and when there might finally be some relief.

"Where's your story?" Sandra asked, lying next to Ron on his sofa.

"The weather's the story this week, all this hype about 'fire season'. You know, the thing is, it's self-perpetuating. We haven't had any rain in months, so the news keeps talking about how dry the hillsides are and how they're ready to burn. Then, when we do get some rain, they talk about how the brush is going to grow and be an even bigger problem next year. Then, there's a fire and, of course, that just means the brush is gone, and we'll have mudslides next winter."

"Keeps you working," she said.

"Yep. Pays the bills."

The story of Councilman Brooks aired immediately after the first commercial break, with Jerry Schram on the set, a large monitor over his right shoulder, with a huge graphic of a stack of dollar bills and the words "Dirty Money?" in green block letters.

The story did just what Wellington had hoped it would do, both keep the audience for the first half hour of the newscast, and give KSIX a nice exclusive that would cause the other stations to scramble the next day and play catch up. No matter what happened with the investigation at this point, and whether or not Brooks entered in the Mayor's race, there was no way the story of a City Councilman and his wife being involved in a corruption probe could be ignored.

For now, the story belonged to KSIX. Surely by morning, all their competitors would be desperate to get sound with Brooks, staking out his house looking for his wife, and trying to figure out how it was they didn't know about this case while Jerry did.

Leo Joseph's intuition had proved correct once again. Jerry may not have been a hot young blonde reporter, but his instincts, skills and contacts made up for it and gave them an edge when it came to covering actual news, to the degree that they did that anymore. Wellington still didn't care for him, or his salary, but had to respect his work.

The intention was to break the story during the evening newscast, and run it again several times during the morning show, until most of Los Angeles had seen it, or at least heard the name Henry Brooks. KSIX wanted to saturate the city with their latest exclusive.

But as so often happens in the world of news, other events that evening would alter their plans entirely.

Chapter Twelve:

IN THE WIND

Tuesday, August 18th

A few minutes after midnight and the temperatures were still sweltering. Deputy Greg Rodgers took a long swig of the Big-Gulp lemonade he'd just purchased at the 24-hour mini-mart on Las Virgenes Canyon, climbed into his black-and-white radio car, and continued his evening patrol. He shook his head at the heat as the warm breeze wafted through the trees.

"All units, a 459 audible alarm at the Bank of Malibu, 17665 Pacific Coast Highway. Closest unit respond."

Rodgers turned south on Malibu Canyon toward the beach and grabbed the mike.

"223 Charlie 4, show me responding, ETA seven minutes."

"223 Charlie 4 is responding."

Ron's long-time pal, "Grog" was a decorated deputy, often called upon to work with new recruits. Nickname aside, once in uniform, he was all business. He had just celebrated 14 years on the Department, after signing up with the intent to be a pro-active deputy, not one of the corrupt, ineffectual ones so often heard about on the news, with the well-publicized scandals of recent years. The previous Fall, Grog had become a legend.

Deputy Rodgers was on patrol as a training deputy, with Chris McCall, who had completed his custody assignment at Men's Central Jail only a few weeks earlier. They were the only unit patrolling the Malibu area of western Los Angeles County that early October morning thanks to severe budget cutbacks.

Grog suddenly cut the headlights and pulled the cruiser over slowly to the side of the road. The two deputies sat in the dark on the shoulder of Trancas Canyon, just north of Pacific Coast Highway, facing the ocean.

McCall glanced over at him. "What's up?" he asked.

"Check out that car," said Grog, motioning ahead, through the chaparral. "Chevron station closes at midnight. Why are those four characters hanging out at the gas pumps? Can you read the plate?"

"I think so," McCall answered. "I'll run it."

The computer monitor in the cruiser quickly spat out the results.

"4SAJ566 is a 2005 Nissan Maxima, reported stolen at gunpoint in Oxnard on October 12th. Stake out if spotted, suspects are armed and dangerous."

"Damn," said Grog with a sigh. "Are you sure you ran the right plate?"

"I think so," answered McCall. "Hard to be 100% sure at this distance, though."

"Lemme see if I can get a little bit closer," Grog said, letting the black and white coast quietly forward a few feet over the gravel.

Suddenly, one of the four, a very young looking Hispanic male, spotted the deputies. In a panic, the group jumped into the Nissan.

With their wheels screeching out of the gas station, they headed north on Pacific Coast Highway.

"Shit, here we go," said Grog, lighting it up and grabbing the mike.

"223 Charlie 4 is in pursuit, northbound on PCH from Trancas. Vehicle is a 2005 Nissan Maxima, license 4SAJ566. Four male Hispanic suspects, all in jeans and t-shirts. Vehicle is traveling at a high rate of speed, still northbound on PCH. Request backup and an air unit."

From the radio, a soothing, unruffled female voice: **"All available units, 223 Charlie 4 is in pursuit, northbound PCH, north of Trancas. Any available units to back."**

The hopes of this being a run-of-the-mill traffic stop were quickly forgotten as speeds soon approached 100 miles per hour. Grog looked at his young partner and asked if he was OK.

"Yeah. Fine." McCall answered unconvincingly.

After a mile or so on the nearly empty road, with the Sheriffs on their tail, the Nissan blacked out.

"Oh, shit," Deputy McCall said, training his spotlight. "I can hardly see him."

"Imagine how he feels," said Grog. "How would you like to do 100 on this road without headlights?"

"No, thanks."

"223 Charlie 4 is still in pursuit, vehicle has blacked out and is doing in excess of 100 miles an hour."

"223 Charlie 4, your vehicle comes back carjacked out of Oxnard. Suspects considered armed and dangerous. Any units available to back..."

The closest backup units were responding from the Valley and as far away as downtown Los Angeles. The nearest car was 15 minutes behind them. But the chase was moving away from them, so as fast as they drove, they gained little ground. Air units were down due to fog and budget cuts. Grog and his partner were on their own.

"What was that?" shouted McCall, observing sudden flashes of light coming from the passenger's side of the Nissan. "Are they... throwing firecrackers?"

"That, or they're shooting at us."

The flashes and pops continued, as Grog slowed the black-and-white back to about 100 yards behind the now almost invisible Maxima.

"We're receiving gunfire from the suspect vehicle," he reported in a calm, steady voice, unwilling to betray the trepidation he felt. **"Still northbound PCH, now approaching Encinal Canyon."**

"223 Charlie 4 is approaching Encinal Canyon, receiving gunfire."

"Suspects are possibly headed toward Ventura County. Please advise Ventura that we're headed their way."

"10-4 Charlie 4. Possibly headed toward Ventura County."

The gunfire had ceased, at least for the moment, as they passed Mulholland Highway and crossed the border into Ventura County, still at 100 MPH, the Nissan still blacked out. The cruiser's siren blared unheeded in the desolate night. Backup was still close to ten minutes behind.

"What happens when they stop?" asked McCall.

"Hopefully they surrender," answered Grog. "But we know they're armed. Are you ready if we have to shoot it out with them?"

"Umm, yes sir."

The Nissan continued racing up the darkened Coast Highway, lucky to this point that the road remained fairly straight and clear of traffic. The patrol car kept pace with them, though at a safe distance. Barely visible, the Nissan passed Yerba Buena road, where PCH made a slight curve to the right.

Suddenly, the deputies lost sight of them and Grog began to slow down.

"The last thing we want to do is drive into an ambush," he said, as they approached the curve. Suddenly they saw the Maxima, smashed, smoking and resting sideways across two *lanes. Several cars parked along the right shoulder had heavy damage. The four gang-bangers were scrambling across the road toward the ocean, away from their wrecked vehicle.*

Grog and McCall scanned the area with their spotlights before exiting their patrol car.

"223 Charlie 4, the vehicle has TC'd, just north of Yerba Buena, all four occupants have fled on foot toward the houses beachside. We'll need multiple units for search and containment. Also, a K-9."

"10-4, Charlie 4. Vehicle has TC'd north of Yerba Buena. Units are en route. Be advised, Charlie 4, the air units are down."

"Swell. Just fucking swell."

Grog drew his weapon and slowly approached the disabled Nissan. Shining his flashlight, he spotted a Mac-10 Semi-automatic rifle on the back seat. He reached inside the open door, picked up the gun, and walked back to secure it in the trunk of the patrol car. The two deputies held down the fort until assisting units began arriving on scene sirens blaring about ten minutes later.

Two of the suspects were apprehended fairly quickly, one hiding under a raised patio and one in a large green trash container. It was several hours before the final pair were taken into custody; the last one only after the K-9 sniffed him out in the rafters of a house a few hundred yards up the beach. Grog had notched a small victory for the department against gang crime, and his giant steel balls made him an instant legend in the process.

✳✳✳✳✳

The wind buffeted the patrol car as Grog neared the bank. Dust, rocks and pieces of brush from the dry canyon whipped across the narrow canyon road, severely hampering the Deputy's visibility. With the parking lot ahead on the left, Grog could see that a large branch from a sycamore tree had broken off and blown into a power line, igniting a small fire and likely setting off the bank's alarm. He reached for the radio to request the County Fire Department, but before he could speak, a flaming branch flew through the smoke that now enveloped him and crashed across the cruiser's hood. He floored the accelerator in zero visibility, hoping there were no vehicles or downed trees in his way.

Hazy street lights were the only indication that PCH was ahead. Grog burst his car through the blowing smoke and turned quickly southbound and away from the fire. He called for backup and remained on scene to assist.

The swirling hurricane-force winds were rapidly spreading the flames across the road and up into the canyon, toward the homes and ranches nestled there, beneath the trees and hidden from view.

The first fire unit arrived on scene quickly and immediately called for assistance. Teams from Malibu, Agoura, Simi Valley, Santa Monica and the City of Los Angeles were mobilized. Crews ventured into the canyons to alert residents and a "reverse 911" system was put into effect, whereby the county phoned homeowners to alert them of the impending danger and urged them to evacuate.

The Santa Ana winds spread the fire rapidly and fiercely throughout the canyons. By morning, three dozen homes and businesses had been lost, including the Malibu Community Church, an inter-denominational place of worship, for years beloved by the widely diverse members of its congregation. Fortunately, all residents were seemingly accounted for and damage to this point was confined to property, except, sadly, for the loss of one horse and a couple of dogs. The cooler temperatures of the pre-dawn hours allowed firefighters to get a handle on the flames, but the warm winds were expected to kick up again before noon, rekindling a number of different fires, each begun by flying embers and now smoldering innocuously, soon to be awakened to wreak havoc all along the coast.

By mid-morning, numerous brush fires had been reported all across Southern California, some knocked down quickly, and others growing rapidly and requiring aid from neighboring agencies. Six of the 'brushers' were considered "major emergencies", one in Ventura, one in San Bernardino, two in Riverside and two in L.A. County. Inmates from Conservation Camp crews all over the area were en route to help at the various locations. All the available City and County airships were active, along with the CalFire helicopters, which had been called out early in the day. They dropped their loads of water and fire retardant chemicals in an unceasing ballet of attack. The ocean provided water for fighting the Malibu fire, and lakes and reservoirs, although drought depleted, would be used to fill the holds of the choppers working the inland brushers. The skies above Southern California were filled with a brown, choking haze, and any vehicle unfortunate enough to be parked outdoors was soon coated by a gritty snowfall of gray, ominous ash.

Newsrooms from all the local stations were scrambling to get each of the multiple brushfires covered. KSIX killed all other stories in the morning, assigning every available camera to the fires, their self-inflicted shortage of staff now causing them the long-predicted headaches, if not downright panic. The restrictions on overtime and meal-break penalties were partially lifted, and crews were told to expect long, hot, uncomfortable work, with little if any relief.

Cameramen made sure they had plenty of bottled water in their vans, along with the Nomex fire jackets the company had provided for them several years earlier. Most had also bought hard-hats, goggles, gloves and filtration masks on their own, knowing that the gear provided by the station would be of minimal protection, should they ever face a real emergency.

The fires in Riverside County, despite the frantic efforts of fire crews, had joined together, becoming the largest of the major blazes. It had blackened some 600 acres in a matter of hours, and was still growing. Homes in the Lake Elsinore area were endangered, and the flames were spreading quickly toward the Cleveland National Forest. Crews were lighting fire-breaks to try to cut off the expansion of the fire, but the winds swirled and changed direction with such unpredictability that as soon as one flank was knocked down, another hillside was ablaze.

TV Stations had live crews at work all day, reporting on the fires. Many of the photogs and reporters had never experienced an inferno as monstrous as they were now facing.

Experience and training tells you how to approach a brush fire. You've got to be prepared for a shift in the wind, which could come suddenly and push the flames in your direction. You always try to set up in areas that are protected, either by fire crews, wide streets, or areas that have already burned.

Plus, *always* park your vehicle in the direction of your escape route and keep the engine running.

Every newsroom in town was taxed to the limit, using all available resources to cover major blazes in multiple locations. In some cases, inexperienced shooters had to be teamed up with young reporters, both covering their first brushers together.

Such was the case with Danny Peralta, still relatively new to the field. Since being taken out of the KSIX maintenance shop a few months earlier, the assignment editors had tried to keep his assignments simple, such as covering a news conference, or a live shot fronting a story from the previous day. Today, though, he would be teamed with Jerry Schram, who was still not accustomed to spot news coverage and very shaky in live situations. They would truly be facing a baptism of fire.

*****

Ron was called in to work before sunrise to work the Malibu fire, the winds now having swept the blaze through Puerco, Corral, Solstice and Latigo Canyons. Pepperdine University was still in danger, but through the efforts of firefighters, looked safe for the time being and had suffered only minimal damage to the grounds and no lost structures. The spacious parking lots were being put to use as a Command Post for Fire and Law Enforcement, as well as a base for news crews.

Realizing it would be difficult to show the scope of the damage in an area the size of the Malibu fire, Ron let his instinct take over. First, go after active flame and firefighting activity. Then grab wide shots of the area, preferably from a ridge or high spot. After that, go back and shoot damage, which will be visual and smoldering for days.

Keeping his scanner radio on, he began on the western front of the fire, following the narrow, unpaved roads off of Kanan Dume through the Santa

Monica Mountains. The plumes of smoke were drifting high; visible from the Valley, blown by the ferocious winds west toward the ocean. He followed a Fire Crew and a Water Tanker up a fire road until he found a break in the smoke and jumped out to shoot.

The canyon was entirely overgrown with chaparral, milkweed, goldenrod and other plants native to the area, with just a few, widely scattered homes. The vegetation would have been a beautiful, multicolored blanket on the hillside under normal circumstances, but in this prolonged drought it was tinder-dry and kindling to even the smallest ember blown by the hot summer wind.

Ron knew he had to move fast. The wind could change direction on a dime, and any view he had of flame would be totally obscured by acrid, choking smoke.

He parked the news van on a narrow patch of dirt and cinched up the red bandana over his mouth. He opened the door and immediately the wind grabbed it, flinging it open past its limit, bending the steel behind the hinge. He hopped out, fighting the wind, and used all his strength to shut the door, with a metallic crunch that told him it had been forced out of alignment.

Ron ran to the other side of the van and slid the door open to grab the camera. Just ahead and to the right of the van was a small clearing where a wood-framed house was fully engulfed in flame. Dressed in his bright yellow Nomex pants and jacket, he walked down the gravel driveway and stood next to a County Firefighter who was doing his best to douse the fire with a line hooked up to a tanker truck filled with only about 1000 gallons of water, much less than would be required for a house this size. They could see that the fire had taken hold of the structure after embers had blown under the eaves and infiltrated the attic, then moved inexorably into the living quarters. Before the nearest fire crew could respond, a lifetime of memories and prized possessions had been lost. The family had grabbed what they could, thrown it into their pickup, and fled hours earlier.

Suddenly, there was a shift in the swirling wind. The fire was still burning fiercely, but no longer was there any visible flame. A wall of thick, dark smoke enveloped Ron and the fire crew, forcing Ron to retreat. His goggles proved ineffective against the hot ash and smoke. He fell to one knee, turning his back to the fire, and tried to catch a breath while wiping his eyes with a handkerchief. He pulled a bottle of water from his pocket and flushed his left eye. The water felt good streaming down his ash-streaked face as he felt the heat from the fire on his back.

Ron worked his way around to the rear of the structure, which sat on a ridge that had already burned. What had once been a magnificent view of the canyon was now an ash-covered vista of destruction. Smoldering trees and brush continued to spew smoke and embers up to the west, toward a line of homes, which would soon need to be saved if the wind did not change direction again quickly.

Walking through the backyard, onto the gray paving-stone walkway, Ron was careful not to tumble into the soot filled swimming pool. He slowly turned and looked behind him, through the skeleton of what once must have been a stunning structure nestled away from civilization. Through the smoldering beams, he could see the firefighters on the other side, working in vain to save any remaining portion of the building or its contents.

Glancing down he spotted, next to the pool, a small koi pond containing about a half dozen large orange and white fishes, now floating motionless, pale and bloated, having been boiled as the fire raced from the canyon toward the house. He stared for a moment and moved back toward the fence.

It was then that he heard the deep *thump-thump* of the County's Fire-hawk, the large, water-dropping helicopter that had been called in to assist with this leg of the fire. To his left, the huge, majestic craft approached slowly at just about his eye level. He trained his camera on the helicopter as it dipped into the canyon and dropped its load on a large hotspot just to his right, which had been crawling up the canyon wall toward the houses at the top.

Confident that he had enough strong video at this location, Ron moved on to see what else he could find.

*****

Danny and Jerry were approaching the Lake Elsinore fire from the north. The smoke had been visible from Los Angeles, but now that they were on the I-15, it was clear to them how monstrous this fire had become, whipped by the hurricane force winds and stoked by the ample dry fuel of the Cleveland National Forest. Jerry helped to navigate, giving Danny directions once he exited the freeway. Central Avenue became Riverside Drive, wound through town and past Marina Village, then became State Route 74, also called Ortega Highway, as it snaked up into the forest.

The crew was stopped by a Highway Patrol unit and told that the road was closed. The officer warned them of the fire ahead, then let the news van pass through the roadblock with a friendly but prescient, "Be careful up there."

"We will. sir. Thank you," Danny answered.

A few miles into the forest, the smoke became thick and dark. After several more hairpin turns, fire was visible off to the right, rapidly climbing up the canyon toward the road. Danny parked the truck on the opposite side of the highway, behind a green Department of Forestry crew truck. Danny set up his tripod on the shoulder and started shooting the crews using torches to set fire-breaks, sometimes referred to as 'back-fires', on the ridge to head off the approaching flames. Fire-breaks can be seductive to shoot, because they're real fire and burning close enough to feel the heat, but experienced photographers consider them somewhat deceptive since they aren't part of the actual brusher.

That didn't stop Danny. The bright flames drew him in and he stood shooting video of the crews lighting the brush on the shoulder, ignoring the big picture which was unfolding right across the road.

The Santa Anas had been violently whipping the flames through the canyon, closer to the highway, which firefighters had hoped would keep it confined to the area east of Long Canyon, where numerous homes had been built in recent years.

But without warning, a large, swirling tongue of bright orange flame leaped from the gorge and stretched fifty feet into the air, violently taking the hillside brush with it and causing a storm of smoke and dust.

Jerry saw it first. "Danny!" he screamed, grabbing his photog by the shoulder. "The truck!"

Danny spun around to see the wall of fire leaping across the road between them and the microvan. Flames were already eagerly consuming the trees on the opposite side of the highway and forming a front moving away from them and toward the truck. In a matter of seconds the news van would ignite.

"Throw me the keys!" Jerry yelled, and started running toward the vehicle, but it was far too hot to approach.

Danny, frightened and embarrassed, debated whether or not to shoot video of the microvan engulfed in flames. Perhaps, he thought, if he could show them back at the station just how quickly the van was engulfed, he could save his job. But he was ashamed that it was his decision to park in a narrow draw downwind of the fire that just cost KSIX a good amount of money.

The County Fire Department and Camp Crews would need to reposition themselves now that the front had jumped the road. After making certain that the news crew was uninjured, one of the captains immediately called for a series of water drops from the Department of Forestry. The first drop fell right alongside the burning van and drenched the surrounding area. Jerry and Danny stared as the charred vehicle sat steaming, obviously a total loss. Jerry took some photos with his phone, as they debated how they were going to break the news to Larry and Wellington.

"This is not going to go over well," Danny said.

"Not well at all," Jerry agreed.

*****

As it became afternoon, Ron had been out of cell-phone contact for over an hour, shooting fire video. He'd already gotten a row of homes going up in flames, along with a stable full of horses being rounded up in a panic by their owners and evacuated from a ranch in Corral Canyon. He asked the Battalion Chief if there were any other hot spots he should be aware of, areas with structures or animals endangered.

"Nope, I think it's dying down for now, at least on this front," the Chief said. "We've released the airships to assist in the Valley."

"Good work, Chief," said Ron. "I'm outta here."

Ron loaded his gear into the van and headed to high ground, where he'd be more likely to hit a cell. He kept hitting re-dial and on the third attempt, the assignment desk phone rang. He stopped the truck next to a blackened, smoldering oak tree, not wanting to move and risk losing the weak signal.

"K-SIX News," answered Freddy.

"Hey, it's Ron. Can I get Scott?"

"Hold on."

It took a minute, but finally Freddy came back on the line.

"Scott's tied up, what can I help you with?"

"I'm wrapped here for now," Ron said. "Wondering what you want me to do with this video."

"OK, so where are you at?"

"Excuse me?"

"Which fire are you on?" Freddy asked.

"Umm… Malibu. The one you sent me to this morning."

Lucky I didn't just get killed there. This crowd wouldn't have noticed I was missing for a week.

"OK, stand by."

The K-Six theme music played on hold and Ron rolled his eyes, exasperated.

"OK, Ron. We're super short right now with all the fires, and we lost a van today, so we're sending Pete Rackley your way. Where do you want to meet up?"

"Wait. We lost a van?"

"Yeah. Danny and Jerry were out in the I.E. and parked it too close to the fire line. Scott's on with them now."

"Oh, damn!" said Ron, grabbing his forehead. "Is everyone OK?"

"Yeah, they seem to be, but the van's a total loss. They're pretty freaked out. Wellington's pretty hot, too."

"Of course."

"So, where do you want me to send Pete?" Freddy asked again.

"Oh, how about the entrance to Pepperdine. Whichever one of us gets there first can get the latest update from the PIO at the Command Post. I'll hand off what I've got and help him edit if he needs it. You want me to stay with him to help out tonight?"

"No, just feed your video as soon as you can and hand it over to Pete," said Freddy. "We're about used up on overtime."

"Wait. Really? Even with three counties on fire?"

"Yeah, they want OT at a minimum. Oh, and did you get a lunch break?"

"What do you want my answer to be, Freddy?" Ron asked, with a sigh.

"It would be good for all of us if you had a break today."

"Fine. Wouldn't want to put the company out of business."

"Thanks."

"Oh, and you can tell the producer that I got some great stuff," Ron added.

"Yeah, OK. Bye."

*****

Shelby Falconer had been at the station to report the weather, but was pulled aside by Wellington and forced into service. She and Dave Newman in Microvan 22 had been headed out to the northern flank of the Riverside Fire, where the flames had jumped the entire 15 Freeway, destroying dozens of cars and semi-trucks and trapping hundreds of motorists. The flames were long gone, but they hoped to get sound with drivers who had escaped their burning vehicles, or at the very least were stuck in hellacious traffic on the way to Las Vegas. Teddy Beaman in Air 6 had captured some incredible video of cars and trucks going up in flames, as motorists ran to escape. Dave drove on the shoulder, but still ended up miles back from the damaged vehicles.

Scott re-routed them to help Danny and Jerry. They'd have to rely on aerials to tell this part of the story for now.

*****

Ron was driving southbound on Corral Canyon toward the coast, when he slowed to avoid a Toyota Four-runner parked half on the narrow asphalt road and half on the shoulder. Suddenly the driver hopped out of the vehicle and waved him over. A slim man, about forty, with straggly, thinning brown hair, stood in the road in cargo shorts, a well-worn short sleeved linen shirt and flip-flops. He certainly looked less than threatening.

Ron drove slowly past the truck and pulled the van over.

"Are you with the news?" the man asked.

"Umm, yeah," answered Ron, too exhausted for sarcasm.

"I'm George Bannister," he said, thrusting out his hand. "And I've got some great video from my drone." Retrieving the contraption from the road's dusty shoulder, he continued. "I was right here when this hillside went up, and I launched. I've got it rigged with a GoPro camera and with these here 'FPV Goggles' I can see exactly what the camera sees."

"That's pretty cool," said Ron. "What were you able to get?"

"I can show you if you like, I got some great flames and a couple of really cool water drops."

Just then, a Sheriff's cruiser pulled up behind them and the deputies approached.

"Hey, are you the guy with the drone?" asked one of the deputies.

"Yeah, that's me," said George.

"We need to talk to you."

"What about?" George asked.

"We got a complaint from the Fire chopper," the deputy answered. "He said the drone was interfering with him. He couldn't maintain the proper altitude to do water drops. Can you step back here with me, please?"

"That can't be possible," George muttered, retreating to the cruiser with the deputy.

The second deputy remained with Ron.

"He doesn't work with you, does he?"

"No," Ron answered. "He was just telling me about what he shot."

"Yeah, these guys are becoming a huge issue for the fire pilots. They fly those things right in the chopper's path. We've had a few near misses already."

"I can see how that could happen."

"Yeah," said the deputy. "They call them 'dridiots'. One of these days, we're gonna have a major problem."

Ron watched in his side mirror as George was cuffed and patted down.

"I've gotta be going," Ron said, putting the van in gear, disappointed not to have seen George's video.

"Take it easy," the deputy said, patting the door of the van as he walked back to join his partner.

Ron pulled into a space near the entrance to Pepperdine at about 4:30, giving him just enough time to ship in his afternoon video. He called in again and spoke to Linda Bodek, who was busy preparing for the early newscast.

"Hey, Linda," said Ron. "I guess Freddy told you that I got some pretty good stuff on this fire."

"No, I haven't talked to him."

"Why am I not surprised? Anyway, look at remote channel 45, I'm shipping it in now."

"OK, one sec."

Linda adjusted her monitor and began watching the feed.

"Wow, that's one heck of a water drop. Good stuff!"

"Just wanted you to know what I had, "Ron said. "There are also some huge flames and evacs from the Corral Canyon area."

"Cool," said Linda. "Thanks for letting me know."

"Any time, girl."

There was a knock on the side of the van. Ron slid the door open and there stood Pete Rackley. Rackley was a relatively new hire, though he'd worked as a reporter at a small station in Reno since graduating from Chapman University two years earlier. Wellington was under strict orders, that any new reporters hired would also be trained shooters and editors, ready to perform all the duties of a "Multi-Media Journalist" should the need arise.

The union contract had become badly weakened in regard to the jurisdiction of photographers. The ability of a reporter to shoot video for broadcast "in an emergency situation" was now so loosely interpreted as to be basically meaningless. An "emergency", the station argued, was too many photographers out sick, or a few on vacation simultaneously. So reporter Pete Rackley had been out in the field, shooting his own video for several months.

The crews knew that MMJs were the way of the future, and learned to roll with it, which would have been much easier had Pete not been such a prick. He was convinced that he knew everything there was to know about television news and Los Angeles, and reacted with offence if offered any advice at all.

Like most MMJs, Pete worked alone. The company issued him a small SUV, equipped with a set of gear, though a smaller version of the gear the staff photogs used. He had a camera, a tripod, a small set of lights, a laptop, and a Live-U backpack, everything he needed to shoot and edit his own one-person live shots.

Ron suggested he stay in the safe, well-lit parking lot area of Pepperdine for his evening live-shot. Some of the fire units would surely still be parked there for a good background.

"Yeah, I've got this Ron," Pete said, looking annoyed at the suggestion. "Thanks."

Ron took the hint, handed him his video card, climbed back into his smoky van and exited the parking lot for the station.

*****

It was almost 5:30 when Dave and Shelby pulled up behind the scorched microvan and parked on the shoulder of Ortega Highway. Jerry walked up to the driver's side as Dave lowered the window. Jerry shook his head and sighed.

"It just came up on us, with no warning," he said. "I don't know, the wind shifted, or something."

"It's OK," replied Shelby. "We're here. We'll get you back to the station."

"Do they still want us live at six?"

"I think they want us to show the van. Other stations are talking about how we lost a unit, so they need to show it."

"Oh, crap," Jerry said. "We'll look like fools."

"Not really," said Dave. "It could have happened to anyone."

Danny was still standing with his back against the hood of the burned-out news van, staring at his shoes.

He heard Shelby's door open and walked around the front of the van to face her.

"Hi," he mumbled.

"Hey, Danny, you OK?"

"Yeah, we're fine. Just feeling stupid. I never should have parked it here. The wind drove the fire right through the canyon and over the road."

Just then a CDF chopper passed low overhead, filled with water to make another drop on the fire, the front of which was now at least a mile up the road.

"Can we get out of here?" asked Danny.

"We have to wait for the tow truck to get here, and we're going to set up for a live shot," said Dave. "Do you have any video for me?"

Danny walked over to his camera, which rested on the road's sandy shoulder. He removed the memory card and handed it to Dave, who had begun extending the mast and setting up for the remote.

The four of them gathered around watching Danny' video on the monitor.

"There's not much here, Bro," said Dave. "Not a lot to work with."

"I... I know. We had just gotten here and started shooting when..."

"It's OK," Dave said. "Do me a favor and go shoot some pictures of the van."

"Oh, man, I really didn't want to do that."

"Sorry, Bro," Dave said. "We need it for the story."

The numerous wildfires, of course, led the newscast. First came an overview, with graphics showing the size and scope of the fires, then Gretchen introduced the numerous reporters out on location.

"We begin with our Shelby Falconer in Riverside County, where our crew was caught earlier today in a very dangerous situation."

"Well, that's right, Gretchen," began Shelby. "High winds whipped the blaze through this canyon with such force that one of our news vans was entirely consumed by fire."

With that cue, the station ran the video of the burned out van, and the aerials of the fire from earlier in the afternoon. Shelby voiced over the graphic showing the latest statistics of acres burned and structures lost.

"And now back out here live," Shelby continued, walking around the charred van. "You can see the skeleton of what was once one of our vans. I have with me reporter Jerry Shram, who was here, along with his cameraman Danny Peralta when the vehicle caught fire. Thankfully, they're both OK.

"What can you tell me, Jerry?"

Jerry's voice cracked.

"We were here covering the fire," he said, "when the flames just shot up through the canyon and before we could get the truck out..."

He was now biting his lower lip, flat out in tears, the emotion of the afternoon overtaking him.

"That's OK, Jerry," Shelby said, putting an arm around him. "It was obviously a terribly frightening situation out here. Thankfully everyone is safe. Now back to you in the studio."

Jerry walked over to Dave's microvan, where he and Danny sat silently until the tow-truck arrived to remove the burned-out husk of Micro 24. Dave had taken a number of photos, as Scott had requested. Once the tow-rig arrived, Jerry and Danny jumped in the cramped cab to be driven the 60 miles back to the station. Dave and Shelby were going to try once again to get through the bottleneck on the 15 and hopefully catch some disabled motorists still stranded there some three hours later.

*****

Ron had put in his 12 hours, and after a shower, had been able to enjoy a few relaxing hours at home. He took one last scoop of strawberry ice cream to put in his bowl, before putting the container back in the freezer. He took the two bowls over to the sofa and sat down next to Sandra just in time for the start of the late newscast.

The fires had died down a bit in the cool evening temperatures, but were still burning all over Southern California. Homes were still in danger and remained evacuated. On the screen, four boxes showed reporters prepared to report live, from locations in Riverside, Ventura and Los Angeles counties. The first report was from Maria Lopez, up in Sylmar, where the wind-whipped fire had ripped through Little Tujunga Canyon, destroying, within hours, over 400 Mobile Homes and leaving 1,000 residents homeless. The video was dramatic, flames spreading from one home to another, residents attempting to hold off disaster with little more than garden hoses, until realizing that they had no choice but leave everything behind except what could be carried and thrown in a car.

Maria had spent part of the day at Sylmar High School, one of the sites set up for evacuations, where she spoke with residents, many of whom were elderly and had lost everything they owned. Next, she had some sound with the Public Information Officer, who provided the latest figures on acreage burned and structures lost. He said they had called for search and rescue crews to look for bodies, although none had been found as of yet. They had, however, arrested three young men for looting.

Sandra sat wide-eyed.

"How devastating," she said, shaking her head. "Can you imagine being in your seventies or eighties, and all your life's memories go up in flames? That's just incredibly sad."

"Yep," said Ron. "There's just no explanation sometimes."

"Make sure you tell Maria that she did a wonderful job, when you see her."

"I will. She'll appreciate that."

The next report was to be from Pete Rackley in Malibu. His face appeared in a box covering the right half the screen, anchor Geoff Martin in the left-hand box. Ron could tell immediately that his advice had been rejected, and Pete had ventured away from Pepperdine, hoping to find some fire activity. Cell service was spotty, Ron had warned him, but it was not surprising that Pete was certain he knew better.

Pete had found a location down Solstice Canyon Road, where fire crews continued to battle hot spots and occasional flare-ups dotting the hillside. It gave him the background he was after, flashing lights and orange flames in the distance. The station had been having trouble communicating with him, because of his location in the canyon, but it seemed to have stabilized, and he assured the booth that he was ready to go.

Geoff was given the cue to throw to Pete, who had positioned himself in front of his camera, mike in hand, IFB dialed up and in his ear and the signal established with the Live-U.

Unfortunately, Pete had no partner, no one to let him know that he was on the air, but his phone line had once again dropped out.

"Fire continues to burn tonight in the hills of Malibu," Geoff announced. "Our Pete Rackley is there with this report. Pete?"

What viewers all over L.A. saw was Pete Rackley, staring into the camera, waiting to be given a cue that never came. He fiddled with the IFB box on his belt to no avail, finally announcing to the booth, in a frustrated tone, "I don't have it. It's going in and out, this fucking thi…"

The director, in a panic, threw it back to Geoff Martin, who was now having an awful time of it, trying to keep his composure. Ron and Sandra stared in disbelief.

"What the …" said Ron, sitting forward on the sofa.

"How does that even happen?" Sandra asked.

"I told him to keep it simple, to stay where there was a strong signal, but would he listen?"

"I know I'll never question your advice," Sandra said, snuggling close to Ron's chest.

"Man, is it ever gonna hit the fan tomorrow."

Chapter Thirteen

OUT OF THE BLUE

Thursday, August 20th

The sun was up and burning a brilliant, golden silhouette through the Oil Derricks of Bakersfield by 8 am, when Max Gilbert pulled his dilapidated Toyota pickup truck up the driveway and parked alongside the gas pumps. He walked inside the Chevron Mini-mart and waited in line to pay. In the four months since losing his job at the refinery, he'd learned to resist the temptation of all the snacks and lottery tickets on display at the register for folks like him, who needed no more than a quick tank of gas before heading back out on the road. "Pump four," he said, expressionless, as he slid the clerk a twenty and headed out the door.

It seemingly took just seconds to pump twenty dollars worth of gas, barely enough time to decipher the layers of graffiti etched and carved into the pump. Max could barely read the numbers as they raced by on the display. He stared in to see the counter stop at \$20.00 and shook his head in frustration while replacing the dripping nozzle on the pump. Just then, Darren Kerr approached the driver's side of the dirty gray truck.

"Fuck off, man," Max snapped, startled. "I haven't got any money."

"Hey, relax, dude" said Darren. "I'm just lookin' for a ride."

Max had just been thinking how tired he was of being alone, and out of work, and how it might not be the worst thing in the world to have some company.

"Where you goin'?"

"L.A.," answered Darren. "Or as close as I can get."

"Sure," said Max. "Hop in."

*****

The full moon had made sleep difficult, along with the bittersweet smell of ash that had permeated Ron's pores and caked inside his nostrils. Despite a late night shower, he knew from experience that it would take a few more days for the air to smell like sunny Southern California again.

All of the early morning newscasts were doing follow-up stories on the brush fires, using the "best" flames from the previous day, along with video shot before sunrise by the early morning photogs. The weathercasters all said the same thing. The winds had subsided a bit allowing firefighters to get the upper hand on the blazes, though full control was still days away.

Total acreage lost was in the thousands, along with property damage in the millions, and six souls. There was still fear that the intense heat and winds could return, imperiling even more structures and lives.

The previous day, the County Supervisors had agreed unanimously to request an early call-out of the "Super-Scoopers", a pair of unique fire-fighting aircraft that the county leases yearly from the Canadian Province of Quebec. Normally, they would arrive in September, in time for what is historically brush fire season. But this year, Supervisors agreed to bite the bullet and spend whatever the extra cost was to get the planes to L.A. a few weeks early.

As good fortune would have it, the Super-Scoopers were just wrapping up a call-out in Nevada, so they made the short flight to Van Nuys Airport at first light and would be ready to deploy by noon if needed.

*****

Darren told Max that he needed to get to L.A., Bell Gardens specifically. His uncle owned a metal plating company and had offered him some work if he could find a way there. Max said that he was giving up on Bakersfield; there was no future for him there. Unable to find work, he'd been living in his truck since moving out of his apartment on the first of the month and was moving to San Diego to live with his older brother, Russ. He neglected to mention the three arrests for assault, petty theft and drug possession that had contributed to him being unemployable. Darren offered him a hit off the tail end of a joint he had stashed in his breast pocket. Max hoped that he might have some gas money to contribute as well.

Interstate 5 was a long, torturous drive, particularly through the Grapevine. Max nursed the old Toyota up the steep grade, staying in the right lane, embarrassed that fully loaded semi trucks were passing him by. He pumped the gas pedal and pounded his fist on the sun-cracked dashboard, cursing the engine he depended upon. At the top of the grade, the road leveled out and he sped up. He heaved a sigh of relief and laughed as he and Darren shared another joint.

Aside from a few shimmies and coughs from the tired old engine, the drive from that point was uneventful. That is, until suddenly, the Toyota pickup died.

"Fuckin' piece of shit," yelled Max, pounding the steering wheel and coasting onto the shoulder next to a sign reading PYRAMID LAKE NEXT EXIT.

*****

Ron climbed into Microvan 21 and shook his head at the stench. Everything had been infused with smoke, the cloth seats, the floor mats, the dash. Chuck had given the vans a quick hosing down and wiped the thick layer of dust and ash from the edit shelf and rack, but the smell would be there for a while. He had tried to re-align the door-hinge, but it still made a loud cracking sound when opened or closed. He'd get to it in time, he promised, but the station couldn't afford to be down another unit, especially after losing one to the flames.

Ron's assignment this morning was to give the viewers a video tour of the Super-Scoopers, an inside look at the iconic yellow and red planes they'd all become accustomed to seeing in the sky since their first arrival in the 90s. He headed out to Van Nuys where flight crews were resting up in anticipation of another busy day.

*****

Max climbed out of his truck and walked around back. He moved some boxes of junk around and finally pulled out a large reflective sign, reading "HELP".

"Strange," Darren thought. *"This must happen a lot."*

Darren noticed several firearms in the back, but said nothing.

A man in a white Lexus pulled up after a few minutes, but had no tools or cables, so was unable to help. He continued on. Before long, the driver of a bright red KIA pulled over and turned on his flashers.

*****

Driving into the LAFD Air Support facility at Van Nuys Airport was always exciting, the huge choppers lined up and waiting, six in all. There were five available for either fire fighting or medical rescue and transport. The sixth was a smaller Bell 206B, used for observation. By the time Ron arrived, Fire 2 and Fire 4 were already out surveying the fires in the light of a new day.

He checked in with headquarters and had a cup of coffee with the flight crews, who were gearing up after a well-deserved night's rest. The crews from Canada were in their jumpsuits, standing by a large wall map and drawing on an erasable white board, discussing the game plan for the day. The L.A City Fire Battalion Chief pointed out the remaining hot spots where their assistance might be required later in the day.

When the conversation slowed, Ron introduced himself and asked for a brief interview and tour of one of the aircraft. Captain Jerry Stevens offered to give him the tour and they headed out through the glass doors to the tarmac.

Ron hung a wireless mike on Jerry's flight suit and picked up his camera. The captain showed him around the outside pointing out the features of one of the planes.

"This is a Canadair Bombardier CL-415 aircraft, otherwise known as a Super Scooper," the Captain said, ducking his head to avoid the bright yellow and red pontoon hanging under the wing. "It's called that because of its unique capabilities when it comes to fighting fires. This aircraft can fly up to 200 miles per hour and scoop up to 1,620 gallons of water from a lake or ocean in just 12 seconds."

Captain Stevens climbed through the door into the cockpit, and invited Ron to follow him aboard. The inside was cramped, certainly not designed for pleasure flying.

"A water tank with wings," remarked Ron.

"That's what it is," answered the Captain, nodding. "That's what it's designed for."

Ron completed the interview, then took a few minutes to shoot the cockpit, the controls and as much as he could of the confined interior. He took a nice shot of Quebec 2 through the cockpit window of Quebec 1, then thanked the Captain, retrieved his mike, and let him retreat to the air conditioned hangar with the rest of his crew.

With time to spare, Ron had shot ample video of the impressive aircraft from inside and out. His pictures would give the public a peek at these planes that they normally would never have. He made the rounds, thanked the firefighters, and said his goodbyes.

*****

Andrew Schmidt was on his way from Portland to Santa Clarita to visit his mother for her birthday. He'd enjoyed the complimentary breakfast at the Quality Inn in Gorman, filled up the car, and headed south. He was thinking to himself how peaceful and beautiful the wide-open road was when he spotted the Toyota in distress on the shoulder and decided to be a Good Samaritan. He carefully stepped out of his Kia and walked back to greet the two men with the disabled pickup. After a brief conversation, he pulled his car alongside and stretched out his jumper cables.

Several times, the Toyota's engine coughed and sputtered, but would not start.

"Sorry, man," Andrew said, removing the cables and placing them back in the trunk. "Best laid plans…"

"You're gonna have to tow this thing in and get it worked on, dude," Darren said.

"Yeah, fuck that," Max muttered.

Andrew had rolled up the jumper cables and thrown them back in his trunk. He had one hand on the trunk lid as Max suddenly appeared behind him with the 12-gauge shotgun and fired twice. Andrew fell forward, fatally wounded, onto the shoulder. Max walked back and grabbed a bag and a handgun from his disabled truck. He threw the bag and the guns in the trunk, slammed it shut, and climbed inside the Kia.

"Well... You coming?" he asked Darren.

"Uhh... No thanks, bro. I'm good."

*****

Ron once again drove his van past the Fire Department choppers, this time toward the exit. The sensor opened the gate automatically. He pulled off the airport grounds and called in to report that he was clear from his assignment.

"That didn't take long," said Scott. "Was it cool?"

"Yeah, I mean you don't realize just how huge those things are until you're next to one."

"Great. I'll tell you what, I think your next assignment is going to be in Hollywood this afternoon, so why don't you ship in your video, and kinda mosey in that direction and take a lunch break. Then check back with me and we'll see if anything has changed."

"Will do," said Ron, as he turned south on Balboa.

Lunch was at Beeps, a guilty pleasure he knew about on Sherman Way just off of Van Nuys Airport. News crews had been stopping there since the 80s for burgers, hot dogs, and pastrami, rationalizing that as long as it's not an every day thing, they can get away with a few greasy onion rings, and a strawberry milkshake from time to time. He found a parking spot, put up his mast, and soon the Super Scooper video was in house.

Service was actually quicker than he remembered, and the place a lot less crowded. Ron was convinced that was because people had begun eating less junk food, a practice that could extend the lives of customers, but drastically shorten the life of Beeps.

He ate a pastrami sandwich in the van and with half his lunch hour remaining, slowly made his way east on Sherman Way. At Van Nuys Boulevard, he turned south and found a shady parking spot on the curb just past Oxnard. He'd been carrying the latest Sports Illustrated and looked forward to cracking it open.

He checked in with the desk at 1:15.

✳✳✳✳✳

Traffic was light through Castaic and Santa Clarita. Max flew down the I-5 in the stolen Kia and was in the San Fernando Valley in short order. He realized that he'd made a huge mistake leaving a witness. Desperation, caused by the breakdown of his only means of escape from town, along with the dope, had caused him to lose his mind, to not think clearly.

What to do now, he worried. Even if Darren were in the wind, it still wouldn't be long before the mess he'd left behind would be discovered.

I should have taken his ID. Fuck.

He had plenty of gas, but knew the sooner he dumped the Kia, the better off he'd be.

He passed a CHP cruiser soon after making the merge onto the 405 and went into panic mode. He looked up and read the sign for the next exit:
Roscoe Blvd 1 Mile

Gotta ditch this thing.

✳✳✳✳✳

"Alright," Scott said. "We need you at Fire Station 27 in Hollywood at 4:00. The Chief is having a news conference talking about fire prevention."

"Sounds good," Ron answered, glad that he had a few minutes to finish the magazine before heading over the hill. Faintly, he heard the scanner.

"Control from Rescue 75."

"Go, 75."

"We just dropped off our patient at Hospital 5-4-Zero. We exited the emergency room and our rig is gone."

"RA 75, please repeat."

"Control from Rescue 75, our ambulance has been stolen. We dropped our patient at Hospital 5-4-Zero and when we came out it was gone."

"RA 75, are you requesting a supervisor?"

"Roger, Control. And PD for a report."

"Roger, RA 75. We'll inform LAPD."

By this time, Ron's ears had perked up, and he locked in on the scanner frequency. He reached for his ballpoint pen in the cup holder and grabbed the notepad from the center console.

RA 75 Stolen

Hospital #540

He knew from years of covering stories in the Valley that RA 75 was based in Mission Hills. He quickly Googled LAFD Hospital numbers to learned that Hospital #540 was Mission Community, on Roscoe near the 405 Freeway, about three miles behind him to the north.

He turned up the scanner, set the notepad on the seat next to him, and went back to his reading material. If there were any developments on the stolen RA, he'd want to hear them.

Ron was deep into a fascinating story about Mike Scioscia, the former Dodgers' catcher and long time manager of the Angels. He'd always been a fan, even before moving west. He was reading about Scioscia's relationship with Tommy Lasorda, the former Dodgers manager when something caught his eye. A set of flashing red lights approached in the side-view mirror. Nothing really unusual about that, and he just as easily could have missed it, except the fact that there was no accompanying siren. He knew that normally, an ambulance driving down the center of the road with the red lights on would be using their siren as well. But Max had not turned on the siren.

Ron had been so engrossed in his reading, he'd almost forgotten about the missing ambulance. That is until he saw the large 75 in white reflective paint above the rear door. There it was, big as life, passing him at about 40 mph. Jarred back to reality, Ron did a double take, momentarily at a loss for whom exactly to call. 911? CHP? LAPD? They wouldn't know what he was talking about. Instantly, he pulled the van out onto Van Nuys and played out the conversation in his head.

"911, what's your emergency?"

"Yeah, umm... I'm with Channel Six. The Fire Department had an ambulance stolen about a half hour ago, and I've found it."

"So, how do you know they had an ambulance stolen? And who is this again?"

Screw that, he thought, as he grabbed the mike.

"Micro 21 to news desk."

"Go Micro 21." Answered Scott.

"Yeah, listen. City Fire reported a stolen ambulance about a half hour ago and I'm right behind it."

"Stand by, Micro 21."

Stand by??? What the...

"News Base to Air Six."

"Air Six, go."

"Air Six, launch please. We'll have a location for you momentarily."

"10-4, News Base."

"OK, Micro 21. Give me your location please."

"We're southbound on Van Nuys, approaching Magnolia. It's RA 75."

"10-4, Micro 21, we'll call City Fire and LAPD."

The ambulance continued at a normal speed, avoiding traffic by remaining in the painted center divider. Ron tried to stay in the traffic lanes, but was falling too far behind, so he too moved over to the middle of the road, ever mindful of management's warning about tickets for moving violations. He'd learned the hard way more than once that you're pretty much on your own.

The light at Magnolia was red, and traffic was backed up about six cars deep. Max had no intention of stopping.

As luck would have it, an LAPD black and white was right there at the red light a few cars back on the opposite side of the street, in the northbound lanes. The officer behind the wheel, noticing the approaching ambulance, suddenly whipped his cruiser around the line of vehicles in front of him and pulled into the intersection. He turned on his red lights and stopped cross-traffic on Magnolia to clear the way for the RA. Ron followed a few car lengths behind, fully expecting the cruiser to give chase. He motioned and waved frantically at the cop, who remained oblivious.

Don't you listen to your radio? Don't you know a goddamn stolen ambulance when you see one?

But nothing. The tri-light soon turned green and the police car continued on its way, the cop inside completely unaware of what had just occurred.

Back to the station, end of shift, Ron guessed, shaking his head.

Max saw the Channel 6 van in his mirror.

"What the fuck?" he mumbled to himself, hitting the gas.

Ron kept up, until Max floored it and the RA passed through Riverside Drive, narrowly missing a green VW bug and a very lucky kid on a bicycle. Ron had to fall back. He watched as the RA took a sharp right and kicked up a cloud of dust, bottoming out on the 101 freeway on ramp.

"Micro 21 to News Base, he's gotten on the freeway. Westbound 101 at Van Nuys. I'll let you know where he goes from here."

"10-4, Micro 21. Air Six, are you up yet?"

"Air Six is warming up. We'll be up in a couple minutes."

Scott ran quickly into Wellington's office.

"City Fire's got a stolen ambulance and our unit is right behind it. I'm launching the chopper."

"The fires have already put us way over the max on helicopter hours this month. Can we wait?" Wellington asked.

"I don't think so, Boss," Scott replied, half out the door, headed back to the desk. "We found this thing. We own this story."

"OK, but I hope it doesn't last too long."

With that, Wellington burst out of his office, scanning the newsroom for any talent he could find.

"Shelby, get in the anchor chair. We're breaking into programming as soon as the chopper's up!"

"But I don't have any makeup on yet," she protested.

"You look fine, get in the chair and we'll fill you in on the story."

*****

Max was confused. He wasn't going to drive this thing all the way to San Diego. It was way more conspicuous than the Kia, and had already drawn the attention of the bastard behind him in the news van.

Maybe I can drive it back to the hospital and start over. Fuck, that's stupid.

He took the transition to the northbound 405. Ron told the desk that he was following and they were approaching Burbank Blvd. Max tore across several lanes to the left and sped up in the car-pool lane. Ron did his best to keep up, but the ambulance's engine put his to shame. Plus the fact that people were getting out of way of the ambulance with the flashing lights. The news van, not so much.

Ron worked his way over and crossed the double yellows into the car-pool lane. There were now a handful of cars between him and RA75, but he kept his eyes on it. There was no way to catch up staying in the same lane, he thought, so he pulled back into traffic lanes, weaving and driving at what he knew was an unsafe speed for the top-heavy news van. He'd long ago set a personal speed limit of 72, for the sake of safety. But that was pretty much out the window at this point. As he maneuvered between cars in light afternoon traffic, he could see that he was, indeed, gaining ground on the ambulance, and was now only a few car lengths behind it.

"Air Six is lifting off from Van Nuys," Beaman reported.

"10-4 Air Six. Our last known location was northbound 405 at Burbank."

Less than a minute later, the chopper was over the freeway.

"Did you say it was RA-75?"

"That's correct, Air Six."

"I've got him. He's northbound, approaching Roscoe. Still no CHP in sight, but it looks like one of our microvans is not far behind him."

"10-4, Air Six. That's Micro 21."

Within seconds they were on the air. A large, bright blue and yellow BREAKING NEWS banner covered the screen briefly, followed by an aerial view of the freeway.

"Good afternoon, I'm Shelby Falconer in the KSIX Newsroom. We have breaking news in the San Fernando Valley. A City Fire ambulance was stolen from outside a hospital emergency room a short time ago. It was spotted in Van Nuys by one of our news crews. The ambulance is now northbound on the 405 freeway, passing Roscoe Boulevard. At this point, there are still no police vehicles in sight, but we'll certainly keep an eye on him until they arrive on scene and can get him stopped."

Max stayed in the carpool lane and Ron in the traffic lanes, both doing about 75. Traffic got a bit heavier at Nordhoff Street, and Ron found himself pulling even with the ambulance. Max stared over at Ron angrily. He quickly lurched out of the HOV lane and was able to regain his speed. Ron was in the #2 lane, waiting to get behind the RA again when he noticed red lights approaching from a distance behind.

"It looks like there's a CHP unit approaching quickly from behind the RA," Teddy reported on air. "But, he's still got a ways to go to catch up. The ambulance is really stepping on it now."

"And they're still northbound on the 405 Freeway, is that correct?" asked Shelby.

"That's right, Shelby," Beaman said. "As you said, we picked up this stolen ambulance before the CHP arrived, and it was our assignment desk that initially informed the police and the Highway Patrol that we had located it in the San Fernando Valley. But now a black and white is getting closer and it looks like it will soon be a full-blown pursuit. We don't know anything at this point about the driver, or whether there is a patient in the back, but as you can see, he's moving at very high rate of speed, putting other motorists in danger. The Highway Patrol unit will be closing in behind him soon and no doubt others are on the way."

Max was now on Ron's tail and whipped the RA furiously around him to the left, returning to the HOV lane where he sped up once again. Ron remained close as the CHP unit was now only a few cars back. LAPD and CHP both had dispatched their airships, which were within a few minutes of the scene. Max was sweating profusely behind the wheel and beginning to panic.

They passed under the 118 Freeway transition at just under 80 MPH. Traffic was slowing again as it funneled toward the merge with the I-5. Ron pulled in behind the CHP cruiser as they passed through the tunnel and out again, continuing north. Once on the I-5, Max shot across three lanes of the freeway, the ambulance lurching and nearly missing a number of other vehicles. Within a minute, however, the CHP was on his tail again, with Ron not far behind.

Max had begun to recognize the scenery and realized that he was headed back where he had been earlier in the day, up the I-5, back toward the murder scene, back toward the dead end life in Bakersfield.

"Not going back there, ever," he said to himself.

Traffic had begun to slow, trapping Max once again in the HOV lane. Ron had been able to catch up and actually pass the ambulance once again as they quickly approached the Newhall Pass and the L.A. Aqueduct. Max made a last minute decision to change his route, and at the same time try to take out this pain-in-the-ass news guy who gave him up. He took aim between two small passenger cars, jerked the wheel and punched it, sideswiping a Dodge Charger and narrowly missing the rear end of a Ford Escape. He quickly caught up with the news van, and yanked the wheel violently, never giving Ron a chance to react. Purposely lurching the RA toward the news van, Max felt his vehicle shake. The van's front end was no match for the heavy-duty steel of the ambulance's rear bumper. Ron barely maintained control as his front bumper was sheared off and flew under his wheels. He jammed on his brakes, causing two vehicles and a motorcycle to swerve violently to avoid him.

"My God! Did you see that?" yelled Shelby. "He's bouncing off vehicles like a pinball!"

"This guy is putting lives in danger," Teddy added. "It's clear he's not going to stop willingly."

By this point, Wellington was out of his office and hovering over Scott at the assignment desk, screaming at him to pull Ron off the chase.

"I'll tell him, but I doubt he'll listen. If you haven't noticed, it's personal now."

Max swerved across all four lanes of the crowded freeway and made the transition onto the 210 toward Pasadena. Ron struggled to follow, drivers honking and swerving to avoid the damaged news van. He knew the right thing to do would have been to pull over and not leave the scene of a collision, but that was not about to happen.

"Whoa! He's driving like he really doesn't want to get caught," Beaman shouted. "He cut across the entire freeway. He's sideswiped several vehicles and made the transition to the 210 freeway."

"As you can see," added Shelby, "the CHP is having a hard time driving around the wrecked cars. Good thing they have a helicopter overhead. This guy has got to know that there's no way he can get away."

"That's right, Shelby. In fact at this point, there are several airships over this pursuit. We're not going away."

The ambulance was now on the lightly traveled Foothill Freeway and able to pick up some speed. The CHP cruiser was slow catching up through the traffic. A second unit had joined the chase at high speed, siren blaring and lights flashing, with Ron a short distance behind. Suddenly, the driver of a black Ford Explorer, noticing the red lights in his mirror, attempted to get over to the right, but miscalculated Max's speed and state of mind. RA-75 rear-ended the Explorer, spinning him out and sending him across the freeway in an explosion of shattered glass and smoke and further damaging the front end of the ambulance.

"Fucking asshole!" Max shouted, checking the freeway signs to try to figure out where on earth he was and where he was going. All he knew was that he'd never been in these parts before in his life and that this fucking vehicle was nothing but bad luck. The sign above said the next exit was Polk Ave.

"Fine," he said to himself, wiping his forehead and breathing deeply. *"Fine. Stay calm."*

He took the Polk exit and blew the red light at the bottom, this time pushing the ambulance between a Mercury van and a Honda Prelude waiting at the light. The Honda crumbled, being forced to the right, causing a chain reaction crash that blocked the off ramp. One CHP radio car had to drive up on the sidewalk to get around the collision. The other stayed behind to tend to the accident scene.

"Oh, my!" Shelby said. "This guy is knocking cars around like toys!"

"You know," answered Teddy. "We've covered lots of strange pursuits over the years. We've seen motor homes, buses, motorcycles, I even remember one involving a fully stocked soda truck being chased, but I've never seen a Fire Department ambulance having been commandeered and driven so recklessly before. This is really amazing to watch. And frightening."

Max continued at high speed westbound on Polk, weaving through the light afternoon traffic. The ambulance had begun to smoke, and he was having a hard time seeing through the windshield. He swung a left on Borden a little too wide and t-boned a pink Ice Cream truck, parked at the corner of Sylmar Park, surrounded by kids lined up to buy frozen Sundaes and Crunch bars. The ambulance came to a sudden stop, the crash shaking the Ice Cream truck violently. Miraculously, it remained upright as terrified, screaming children scrambled in all directions.

"OH NO!" yelled Shelby. "He's hit an Ice Cream truck!"

"That's right," responded Teddy. "We can't tell from here if anyone's hurt or not, but the ambulance isn't moving. It's smoking pretty badly, though. It will be interesting to see what this guy does now, assuming he's conscious."

"We've now learned that the ambulance was taken from outside an emergency room in Van Nuys," announced Geoff Martin, joining Shelby in the other anchor chair. "But who the suspect is, and whether he's from around here, or at all familiar with the Valley, we're not sure."

RA-75 was now putting out a plume of smoke from under the hood. With his ride disabled, Max grabbed his revolver and ran, desperately looking for another vehicle. Ahead he spotted Felipe Menendez opening the driver's side door of his red VW Jetta, which he'd just parked on the curb. Felipe and his six-year-old son, Hernando, had arrived early for soccer practice, and Felipe felt lucky to have grabbed an available parking space at the crowded park.

Suddenly, he found himself looking down the barrel of a large handgun.

"Gimme the fucking keys and get out!" Max yelled, grabbing Felipe by the left arm.

"No problem, mister," Felipe cried. "Get out, Mijo!" he shouted to Hernando.

Together, the father and son watched Max squeal off in their newly purchased vehicle, a shiny used VW with the unfortunate personalized license plate left by the previous owner: **CREWL F8.**

A crowd had begun to gather around the disabled ambulance that Max had left behind blocking two lanes on Borden. Dozens of park goers and residents, cell phones in hand, were laughing and posing for photos and selfies. A couple of teenagers actually climbed inside the ambulance and proceeded to carry out bandages, sheets and anything that wasn't nailed down, until an LAPD unit arrived to secure the scene.

LAPD had taken over the pursuit and was closing in on the VW as it approached Hubbard St. Max took a sharp right turn, narrowly missing a group of teens in the crosswalk. They each grabbed their cell phones and took video of the action. Max flew down Hubbard, and then took a left onto the wide-open Laurel Canyon. Frustrated and unable to shake the police, he took a right onto Van Nuys Blvd. and eyed the freeway again. But between him and the on ramp were two CHP cars, one facing in each direction.

"Goddamn it!" he shouted, turning a series of donuts in the middle of Van Nuys Blvd. LAPD now had three units following close behind while their suspect literally drove them in circles, which actually made them look quite silly.

Back in the newsroom, watching the video from Air Six, Scott spotted Ron in Micro 21, stopped about 50 yards back on Van Nuys, waiting to see what Max would decide to do. Wellington was standing over his shoulder, watching the chase intently. "Don't do anything stupid, Ron." he mumbled.

Max noticed the news van and aimed the Jetta for it, pulling up at Ron's door, a crazed look in his eyes. Seeing the large number of police units and thinking better of it, Max floored it and headed east once again away from the freeway. Ron waited for the procession of black and whites to pass before rejoining the chase.

Up ahead, he saw them one by one turning left on Laurel Canyon. He took Remick Avenue, a narrow, poorly paved residential street that paralleled Laurel Canyon, one block to the west, with stop signs and flood control dips at every intersection. He checked to his right at each corner and saw the parade of flashing lights flying by.

"He hit the strip," he heard an officer say over the scanner, meaning that the VW had driven over a spike strip and its tires would soon be flat.

"He's coasting to a stop at Laurel Canyon and Daventry. All units hold behind the vehicle. Suspect is armed."

Ron took a right and could see the disabled VW ahead. The chase was over. He took a left onto Laurel Canyon and spun a quick u-turn, parking and giving himself a nice position to get video of the arrest, but half a block to the north and safe from crossfire.

Several black and whites took position on both sides of Laurel Canyon to secure the perimeter, but the VW had two flat tires. Max was done.

Eight officers were now close behind the VW, standing outside their vehicles, guns drawn.

"You in the car," Ron heard one officer yell. "This is the LAPD! I need you to put your hands outside the window where I can see them! Do it now!" Ron recognized this exact scenario from the LAPD Academy training he had shot a few months earlier. But this was very real.

There was no response. Max, now totally disoriented, weighed his next move.

"Let me see your hands NOW!" an officer shouted.

Ron recalled other situations he'd covered like this in the past, some standoffs lasting hours, police eventually firing tear gas, bringing in SWAT in armored vehicles, or even deploying robots to finally apprehend the suspects.

After a few minutes, with choppers circling overhead and more police continuing to arrive on scene, Max was growing more and more desperate. *Did they know about the murder on the freeway, or just the stolen vehicles?* He could go away forever, he reasoned, and all because of that fucking newsman.

Suddenly, he noticed Ron's news van, across the street ahead on his left. He shifted the car into drive once again and inched forward.

Ron had set up his tripod behind the left rear corner of the microvan and was watching through the camera's viewfinder as the VW advanced ever closer. Once again he was detached, separated from the reality of the situation, instead concentrating on watching the scene play out through his camera lens, completely unaware of the three officers who had taken position behind him, directly over his shoulder, one of whom he would have instantly recognized.

"Straight through the brainstem," thought Jack Thorne, lining up his sight on the back of Ron's head and laughing to himself. *"One got away. Shit happens."*

Max got the car up to just a few miles per hour, driving on shredded tires, but he was now focused on the man standing with the camera, behind the news van, that fucker who brought all this trouble into his life. Slowly, the VW came closer, scraping bottom as it crossed Paxton, now literally a stone's throw from Micro 21. Police vehicles followed, as did officers on foot, shouting instruction for Max to halt. Ignoring their orders, he coasted across the painted center divider and placed himself within twenty feet of his target.

Once the VW had come to a stop, officers moved in and surrounded Max, leaving him no escape route. They positioned themselves to take him into custody, hopefully without incident, but remaining mindful of possible crossfire.

Ron's shot remained steady and tight. The zoom lens allowed him to finally get a good look at Max's face.

"Driver! Put your hands where I can see them!" an officer insisted. "Do it now!"

Then suddenly, without warning, Max raised the handgun from his lap, pointed it at Ron and shouted, "You sonofabitch…"

Rounds instantly flew from every direction. Some whizzed past Ron's left ear from behind, close enough for him to feel the heat. Before Max was able to fire his weapon, he'd been hit with three shots to the head and four to the chest. His arm and hand had been hit several times, sending the .38 flying out the window and on to the pavement, away from the Jetta, which itself had been peppered with over a dozen rounds, from five different officers.

"What the hell, man," yelled one officer standing just off of Ron's left shoulder. "We can't be responsible for you. You almost got yourself killed!"

Ron stood motionless, mouth open, ears ringing, in a cloud of gun smoke.

"For God's sake, what were you doing here, asshole?" Jack asked.

"I… I don't know," Ron answered incredulously, shaking his head to clear his mind. "I think it was me he was after."

✳✳✳✳✳

It took several hours to get the multiple crime scenes sorted out. LAPD and Highway Patrol officers had numerous streets and intersections blocked off, while Max's every move had to be mapped out, measured and documented. Detectives from Robbery Homicide Division were en route to the scene to interview Ron about his involvement. He'd been prohibited from leaving the scene, but the Sergeant allowed him to ship his video back to the station for use in the early newscast.

Afterwards, still waiting for the detectives, he sat behind the wheel of Micro 21, shaken. He thought about Sandra and how much he wanted to be with her, to hold her near. He tried her number, but there was no answer, so he shot her a text, to tell her he'd had a rough day, that he cared about her and he wanted nothing more than dinner at home with her tonight. Unsaid was how much he wanted to be the man she looked up to. He wanted nothing else in life but to be her hero.

But he had come so close to losing it all. He never should have made the decision to follow the ambulance, he thought.

That one decision changed him forever. He'd always gotten along with pretty much everyone. He could count on one hand the number of fistfights he'd been involved in as a kid. Never really had any enemies, and he liked it that way. Never felt seriously in danger. Oh, there had been a couple of crazies on news stories over the years, who had lashed out and become threatening, but for a moment this afternoon, it stopped being fun and games. He'd been caught between two seriously unstable individuals, each one armed, and each of whom he knew would have had no trouble at all taking his life.

Taking a deep breath and rubbing his eyes, he realized for the first time in a while that he indeed had much to live for; much that he cared deeply about. He prayed that, after all he'd witnessed and survived over the years, that he'd

380

never be in that place where nothing mattered to him, that his theoretical Stage 4 would forever remain theoretical.

✳✳✳✳✳

It was well after dark when he arrived home. Sandra had taken the time to make his favorite meal, glazed salmon over mixed greens and roasted potatoes. He hugged her at the door like there was no tomorrow. They spoke very little. He never wanted to tell her more than she needed to know, but just enough to explain his mood. She had heard about the chase, and he told her that it was he who spotted the stolen ambulance. She thought that part of the story was cool.

After dinner, they cleaned up the kitchen together and sat down to watch a movie on demand.

At ten, Sandra asked if she could put on the news.

"Whatever you want, Sweetie. I've already seen it."

Ron placed his head in Sandra's lap and she rubbed his tired shoulders. As expected, the chase the whole city was talking about was the lead story on Channel 6. They began with the aerials of the ambulance flying through traffic on the 405, with no law enforcement in sight. They showed the moment Max ripped the front end off of the microvan. Then, after the RA was disabled, Max was shown jacking the VW at gunpoint and throwing the driver out onto the road. Then came Ron's video of the VW, creeping ever closer to the camera on flattened tires. A perfectly framed shot of the driver aiming his weapon toward the viewer. At the last possible moment the video was frozen, but the audio continued. More gunshots than you could count, put an end to the chase. Antiseptically cleaned up and edited for a family audience.

"Oh, my God!" Sandra cried. "I had no idea you were so close. Are you OK?"

"I'm fine," Ron answered quietly, his head still in her lap. "I just kept thinking of you and how close I came to losing you." He grasped her hand and brought it to his lips.

Ron shed a tear. He couldn't remember the last time and made no attempt to hold it back.

"You know, I feel the same way. When you had your head injury, all I could think about was that I wished it had been me instead."

He turned toward Sandra and kissed her tenderly. He wanted it to be like this forever.

"I'm really beat," Ron said. "I think I want to go to sleep."

"OK, but there's something I needed to tell you," Sandra said.

"What's that?"

"David Bing called me today. You know, the news director from Channel 3."

"Yeah?"

"He remembered meeting us at the Emmys and wants to interview me for a job."

"Really, that's exciting," Ron said, pausing and leaning on one elbow. "What kind of a job?"

"He said he thought I'd make a good Multi-Media Journalist. He said I have the look and personality for it."

Ron's neck stiffened, but he did not sit up. She continued massaging his shoulders. He furrowed his brow and took a deep breath.

"Wh... what did you tell him?"

"I told him I was flattered, but I have no idea how to work a camera."

"So what did he say?"

"He said that's the easiest part of the job and somebody would teach me."

Ron sighed again, clenched his jaw, and closed his eyes as he lowered his head onto her lap, too exhausted to say another word.

EPILOGUE

It was well into the following year when the trial of Peter Nealey and Debra Vaughn began. The evidence showed that they had conspired to murder Peter's wife Jennifer with the idea using the money from Jennifer's newly acquired life insurance policy to buy a place for themselves in Washington. When confronted with the mountains of physical and circumstantial evidence against them, they turned on one another, placing blame for the actual murder on the other, seeking a lighter sentence after conviction.

It didn't work. Both were found guilty on all counts including conspiracy, lying in wait and murder with special circumstances. Both were sent off to prison for 25 years to life. Peter's sons were given to their maternal grandparents.

Ron had been out of town for a good portion of the trial, covering a large earthquake in Eureka, California, but had returned the Friday before the verdicts were read and was in court to hear the jury's decision.

A few months later, in the same downtown courtroom, Rachel Larimore's trial began. Ron had spoken to Wellington and recused himself from any pre-trial coverage for Channel Six since his name was on the prosecution's witness list. After meeting with prosecutors from the District Attorney's office, he was told to be prepared to testify in the murder trial of his former flame, a thoroughly awkward and uncomfortable notion. He freed up his schedule using a couple of weeks of vacation time and sat in the courthouse hallway for days on end, waiting to hear his name announced as a witness. He stayed occupied by reading the biography of Vin Scully, the Dodgers announcer, hoping that Vin's presence in the courthouse would serve to relax him, as his voice always had.

As the trial neared an end, prosecutor Brian Ashton approached Ron and told him that his testimony would not be necessary. The case had gone to the jury without either side calling him. His name had been brought up during the trial to the extent that Rachel had written about him in her journal, but neither side felt his testimony necessary.

The jury came back the following morning, finding Rachel Larimore guilty of the first-degree murder of Shannon Lee Russo.

As Rachel was escorted out of the courtroom, Shannon's parents, who had been in attendance for the duration of the trial, offered hugs to the prosecutors as well as to detectives Jackson and Sarkis. They were tears not of joy as much as closure.

Rachel was sentenced to 27 years to life in prison and Ron thankfully never had to lock eyes with her again.

Outside the courthouse, attorneys and family members were giving interviews to the media. Sandra, covering the verdict for Channel Three, had just gotten a soundbite with Brian Ashton when she spotted Ron exiting the building.

"Hey, Cowboy!" she yelled, turning toward him, camera on her shoulder. "Wanna be on the news?"

"Umm… no."

"Why not? You look so cute in a tie."

"Not today, Babe. See you later?"

"Of course, I'm off at six." She said.

"Cool. Have fun." Ron replied, heading up the stairs to the sidewalk.

Sandra was feeling more comfortable in the field after working solo for a few months. The quality of her work was improving rapidly thanks to the Ron's instruction and encouragement.

She had no regrets about leaving Holliday and Weber, certain that she had advanced as much as she ever would in the company. A new challenge would be fitting as she moved on without Jack in her life. Frank Holliday had assured her that her job would always be there should she decide to return. For now, only time would tell if her infatuation with newsgathering, and with Ron, would last.

DEDICATION

All my thanks go to my wife Stephanie and my wonderful children- Rod, Danielle, Alex and Adam, who dutifully waited for my return home from work at night, keeping dinner warm for me, often long after bedtime. When I did get home, they invariably wanted to know, "What happened at work today, Dad?" compelling them to endure my long-winded replies, which were boring as hell more often than not. It didn't go unnoticed that they also put up with me sitting in my office night after night, going through my journals while trying to assemble a novel that explained my crazy life. You guys are my anchors, and I love you beyond words.

I'd also like to thank some of my colleagues and mentors, who took this crazy ride along with me, witnessing the best and the worst of the last few decades. People like Steve Herren, Martin Burns, David Busse, Carl Stein, Martin Orozco, Gary Brainard, Shari Odell, Gerri Shaftel, Christina Gonzalez, Pat Lalama, Jane Wells, Rod Bernsen, Marla Fain, Dave Lopez, Les Rose, Mark Sudock, Kris Knudsen, Patti Ballaz, Chris Harris, Ed Laskos, Rick Lozano, Pete Garrow, Pete Noyes, Bob Tarlau, Dan Leighton, Dave Bush and dozens more.

Inspiration also came from a good number of friends who don't work in TV news, but had the patience to listen to my innumerable tales and offer advice on how to tell Ron's story. Thank you Sharon Johnson, Laura Dee, Katie Clark, Gail Kiejdian, KJ Aden and all the of others who nodded courteously when I mentioned that I was writing a book, without asking me if I knew anyone in Los Angeles who was currently *not* writing a book.

I can't write in a vacuum. I've got to have a little something in my headphones to keep my brain stimulated. Thanks to Joe Crummey, Dennis Miller and Brian Ibbott for your podcasts.

This was my first attempt at a novel. At some point I got the crazy notion that I could put words on a page just like my favorite authors, people I've been reading for decades. While it's clear, I'm no Richard Price, Pete Hamill or Brad Thor, and I'll never be an amazingly talented wordsmith like James Lileks, I like to think that I've absorbed just enough of their love for the written word to make my book enjoyable and fun. Thanks to them. Finally, I would like to express my sincere gratitude to my editor Brinka Lowe at Briton Publishing, without whose patience, wisdom and advice this project would have never succeeded.

You may ask why some of the story threads in the book are left incomplete. What became of Mayhem and his girlfriend, the alleged squatters? What about the jewelry store robbery? Did the robbers get caught?

Welcome to my world. Stories aren't always neatly wrapped up with a nice bow. As often happens, by tomorrow we've moved on to a new assignment in a new part of town, and the story that was important enough to lead the newscast last night is just another memory.

I hope you found this book entertaining and learned a little about the folks who bring you the news every night. We're human like you, and just like you, we're curious and sometimes bewildered by the unexplainable things we observe on a daily basis. The difference is, we see this stuff up close. Count your blessings that you don't.

ABOUT THE AUTHOR

Rodger Howard has had a thirty-year career as a television news photographer in Los Angeles, California. He covered major stories such as the Loma Prieta and Northridge Earthquakes, the Rodney King Police Abuse Trial and subsequent riots, both OJ Simpson trials, criminal and civil, and countless more. His work has earned him five Los Angeles Emmy Awards, three Golden Mike awards, an L.A. Press Club award, and a commendation from the Los Angeles City Council.

Rodger had the foresight to keep a hand-written journal, recording every assignment from day one, whether spectacular or mundane, the written record serving as an immeasurable aide when it came to keeping details of the stories reasonably true to fact.

His advice to aspiring photojournalists, looking to launch a career filled with adventure and a never-ending variety of unique and memorable experiences, is found in the title of this, his first novel:

Above All- Stay in Focus.

CPSIA information can be obtained
at www.ICGtesting.com
Printed in the USA
BVHW030831280621
610636BV00001B/17